Heir of the Elements

Cesar Gonzalez

For Nelida Valencia. Thanks for the memories, listening, and being so selfless. Your heart and soul are for keeps.

Of all the people. Of all the circles you could walk. Thank you for walking in mine.

PREFACE

On Planet Va'siel, there are a few beings that are born with the ability to wield certain elements. These gifted individuals are known as Element Wielders.

There are six basic elements and six advanced elements. Holding control of the advanced elements requires much more energy than a basic element. As such, wielders of advanced elements have become a rarity in Va'siel.

Basic Elements

Water: Water wielders control the element of water. Some advanced water wielders have been known to solidify water into ice.

Fire: Wielders who harness the very power of flames. The second stage of fire is blue fire. The third stage, which very few wielders have reached, is black fire.

Like water wielders, fire wielders are highly sought out for long missions. Their ability to create campfires in almost any environment has proven invaluable.

Void: Void wielders can wield all six basic elements; however, this power comes with limitations. Void wielders can only wield weak attacks.

No void wielder can wield blue or black fire, as those are advanced levels of fire. The only exception is Falcon Hyatt. For reasons unknown to him, he can wield basic elements and advanced elements.

Mind: Mind wielders can mold the minds of others. The extent of the control they have over people depends on the power of the mind wielder and the victim.

Some have been known to drive their enemies mad with false images of pain and suffering.

Mind wielders can also use their abilities to re-awaken thoughts that have been long forgotten. Most mind wielders are highly intellectual individuals.

Wind: Wind wielders can harness the power of wind, using that power in both defensive and offensive attacks.

Even though wind is a basic element, not many wind wielders can be found in Va'siel. The reason for this is unknown.

EARTH: These warriors are numerous in Va'siel. Their attacks are sturdy and strong. Their defensive abilities are some of the strongest a wielder can ever hope to create.

But their abilities go beyond the battlefield. Some earth wielders are able to mold and enrich soil with nutrients to create rich farmlands. The crops grown from capable earth wielders are some of the most delicious found in Va'siel.

The legendary warrior, Golden Wielder, was himself an earth wielder.

Advanced Elements

Space: The power of the cosmos is a mere plaything to space wielders. Not only can they summon the force of space to use against their enemies, but they can call forth universal anomalies like meteors, comets, and black holes.

Since there are so many mysteries in the great unknown that is the universe, the true extent to which gifted wielders can push their powers remains an enigma.

Poison: Poison wielders tend to be sick beings, both physically and mentally.

They possess the ability to create many attacks using venom and a variety of toxins.

In past times, poison wielders have proven useful during sieges, where they poison entire cities water or food supplies.

Darkness: Only the most cold-hearted and wicked beings can properly wield the powers of darkness. Wherever they go, pain and misery follows.

Dark wielders can control many of the forbidden wielding abilities that were banned long ago for their inhumane and unnatural power.

Chaos: Along with holy, chaos is the rarest of all the elements. In fact, in the past 10,000 years, Shal-Volcseck is the only known chaos wielder.

What exactly can a chaos wielder do? No one who has seen their power has been left alive to tell the tale.

Lightning: These wielders can summon the power of lightning. Most who practice this kind of wielding tend to be driven by offense. During battle, they rarely use their power for defense.

There are stories of exceptional wielders who have wielded red and green lightning, though most believe this to be just tales of legend.

Holy: Only the most pure and humble of beings can hope to control this power. As such, holy wielders are extremely rare. With each passing year, Va'siel has become more sinister and wicked, full of murder, deceit, and lies. It is for this reason that many believe that the power of holy will never return to such a cruel world. However, there are stories that indeed a holy wielder has been born in the small farming village of Asturia.

Chapter 1

The day was coming to a close as three wielders traveled the narrow path that cut through the sea of trees. Scattered rays of lights trickled through the few openings that the thick branches above provided. Droplets of water, from the rain that had now stopped, glistened as they coursed down the leaves.

Ahead of the group was Falcon, a dark-haired Rohad whose blue eyes missed nothing. He remained alert, looking for any sign of movement.

"What do you think, mate?" asked Chonsey. He pointed at the open space of dirt with two large boulders beside it. "Is this a good place?"

Falcon looked at his short friend and then into the forest and sighed. He had hoped to reach his hometown of Ladria before nightfall, but apparently that wasn't going to happen. "Let's move into the trees a bit. We don't want to set up camp directly on the road."

Faith, the emerald-eyed girl with the light skin, nodded. "Good idea. The last thing we want is to run into bandits, or worse."

Falcon stepped off the hard dirt path and onto the mossy forest grounds. The fresh aroma of wet dirt drifted into his nostrils. His short boots dug into the muck of the ground. It was times like these that he was thankful for his resistant clothing. The blue uniform and black jacket could withstand almost any terrain on Va'siel.

Chonsey followed closely behind him. "I wouldn't be too worried about bandits, mate. I mean, if it were just me, of course I would be on my toes. But not with you here, Falcon. You're a void wielder who is only supposed to wield the basic elements but has control of advanced elements." He grinned and turned to Faith who trudged behind him. She wore a pink jumpsuit with a white blouse underneath. "And you, Faith, you're the only holy wielder in ages. That's crazy." He took a breath. "I'd be more worried for the poor bandits that run into us. They wouldn't know what they'd be in for."

Falcon stared down at his gray emblem, recalling the many times the chaos power within him had caused him to lose control. At those moments, he couldn't distinguish friend from foe. "Having this isn't a solution to everything, Chonsey."

"Besides," Faith added. "The idea of staying off the road has nothing to do with whether we can beat bandits or not, and everything to do with the fact that they may be Suteckh scouts."

Falcon grimaced. He still couldn't believe the story

Chonsey had told him. It sounded like a nightmarish fairy tale. The capital city of Ladria was so powerful. How was it possible that the Suteckh Empire could have overtaken it in only a day? Surely his friend had exaggerated. Chonsey did have a tendency to stretch the truth a bit.

Falcon stopped and threw down his bag as they reached a small clearing. There were a few lingering bushes here and there, but nothing too troublesome. "This is a good place. Let's set up camp here."

Chonsey unrolled the light blanket he carried on his back and tossed it on the floor. "Good. I was getting tired, mate."

"Earth plateau," said Falcon as he bent down and touched the wet ground. In an instant two long plain stubs of dirt emerged. They stretched about two feet over the forest grounds. He felt ashamed as he stared at Faith. "I'm sorry you have to sleep in such a hard place again. I know back home you had a nice bed, and ever since you began traveling with me you've been living like a peasant."

Faith waved her hand dismissively. "You know I don't care about those things. Don't you worry about it."

Despite her words, he still felt a pang of guilt. He took a seat.

"What are you doing?" asked Faith, shocked.

Falcon looked at Chonsey then back at Faith, trying to figure out what he'd done wrong. "Errr…sitting down."

Faith took his hand and pulled him up. "Yes, I know. But you could at least wait until I set up a shield on your bed. That way you won't have to sleep on dirt. You don't want to get your leather jacket and hair dirty, do you?"

"Oh, no, sorry. I'll just go gather some wood while you do that."

Faith's white emblem that rested on the back of her glove intensified in brightness as she waved her hand. "Malawi Lesotho." An almost invisible blanket materialized and covered the earthy bed. It flapped as the wind drifted against it. "Now you try it."

Falcon stopped dead in his tracks. "Try what?" He was certain he knew what Faith was talking about. She had been drilling him on it every other night, but he simply couldn't get the handle of it. What was the use of making himself look like a fool again?

Faith took his hand and pulled him before the Earth plateau he had created. "C'mon, I know you can do it. Wave your hand around like this." She moved her hands from side to side. "Then think of a strong emotion, allow it flow from within. You did it once, I'm sure you can do it again."

He thought back to the battle against Lakirk. "That was under pressure. But when I'm in a calm environment, I can't do it."

"Sure you can. I know you can do it. Simply think of someone you love. Use their memory."

Her eyes met his, sending nervous jitters coursing through him. "Ummm…yes, someone I love. I'll just do that." He closed his eyes. Images of his two best friends, Aya and Faith, flashed before him. But instead of feeling peace, he felt turmoil. One second he'd be staring at Faith, only to be replaced by the image of Aya, her dark hair flowing behind her as she gazed at him with her almond shaped eyes. The words of Father Lucien came back to him. The heart cannot belong to more than two. Sooner or later you must make a choice. His eyes snapped open, his heart beating faster with each breath.

"Are you well?"

He stood up straighter, trying to convey a false sense of control. "Y…yeah. I'm fine."

She looked him over with an air of disbelief. "I'll do the cover. You go ahead and fetch some wood if you wish."

She didn't have to tell him twice. He immediately took off into the woods. Once he was far away from the camp, he settled next to a large rock and took a seat, cursing himself. Faith was patient, but how long was he going to continue failing like this? If he couldn't even make a cover, how was he expected to control holy barriers powerful enough to keep the chaos energy that raged within him in check? Unable to formulate the answers, he remained seated in place, staring at small patches of visible sky for what seemed an eternity.

Finally, once the heavy feeling in his stomach had dissipated, he got up, found a few scattered pieces of wood, and headed back.

"You were gone for a while," said Faith as Falcon marched back into the camp.

"Yes, branches were hard to find."

"Aha, I'm sure they were." The tone in her voice made it clear that he wasn't fooling her.

Falcon tossed the few branches he managed to find into a pile. He snapped his fingers as his gray emblem turned a deep red. Seconds later, a flame engulfed the few pieces of wood.

"It's nice having a fire wielder," said Faith, taking a seat next to the flames. She patted the spot next to her, signaling Falcon to join her.

He gulped nervously as he took a seat. It had been quite some time since he and Faith were alone like this. He turned over to invite Chonsey to join them, but his loud snores made it obvious he was already deep in sleep.

"Do you think Iris is doing well?" asked Faith in a low voice. "She was so sad when we left."

Falcon thought back to the peasant girl they had befriended back in K'vitch. He would be lying if he said he didn't miss her too. In the short time he'd spent with her, he grew quite fond of her. "I'm sure she's doing fine. She has Father Lucien looking after her, after all." His gaze dropped to the floor. "To tell you the truth, I'm more worried about Aya."

"Aya is strong. I'm certain she's fine."

"I'm sure you're right, but I'm more concerned about letting her down. I was tasked with warning Missea of the upcoming Suteckh invasion. Aya is smart. I have no doubt she succeeded in getting the city of Sugiko on our side. But me? I didn't even get to Missea, much less warn them. And now I'm headed back to Ladria, having accomplished nothing."

"You figured out who was kidnapping people from K'vitch, and you put a stop to it." Her eyebrows pulled down in concentration. "Do you think the people of K'vitch would say you accomplished nothing?"

Falcon grimaced. "I'm not too sure helping them was a good idea."

Faith gave him a hard stare. "Of course it was a good idea. Children were being taken from their parents. Their energy was being sucked out of them. Are you saying we should have let them die?"

"No. I'm simply stating that sometimes a few have to die, so that more can live."

"How is that different from letting them die?"

Falcon ran his hand through his hair, not sure how to express himself. Everything was such a jumble of confusion. "I don't know. All I know is that thanks to our interference, Shal-Volcseck finally got a hold of the last possible chaos emblem."

"He already had a chaos emblem," Faith said, her voice calm.

"You know what I mean, Faith. He had his chaos

emblem, but he couldn't destroy that one because that would kill him. Now he has one he can destroy."

Faith shook her head. "You're beating yourself up. Like always. Volcseck would have gotten that emblem whether we were there or not."

"But he got it on my watch!" said Falcon, raising his voice. "Demetrius died because of it."

"Calm down, Falcon."

Falcon's face grew warm. "It's wasn't enough that he killed my mom right in front of me when I was a kid, he had to wait until I grew up so he could take the emblem right in front of me, too!" He knew he should stop, but he couldn't. The chaos energy that raged within him beckoned him to give in to it. "And now he has eleven of the twelve element emblems. All he needs now is—" He stopped yelling as his eyesight landed on the pristine white holy emblem on Faith's glove. A small raindrop fell on the pearl. It trickled to the ground, darkening the dirt around it. A lump the size of a mountain formed in his throat when he noticed that it wasn't rain but tears. "F…Faith. I'm sorry. I didn't mean to remind you that that monster is coming after you."

"No, I'm the one who is sorry," Faith muttered in a shaky voice. "Volcseck came for me the day he killed your mother. It's my fault she's dead." She stood slowly. "Excuse me. I think I'll be going to sleep."

Falcon's chest tightened. First I remind her of the killer

who is hunting her. Then I re-kindle those feelings of guilt she's carried since childhood.

"Faith," he squeaked, staring at the shivering figure lying on the hard earth bed. "I don't blame you for anything. You know that. Please don't feel bad on my account."

"I'm fine, Falcon. Don't worry about me."

She didn't turn as she spoke, which only made him feel worse.

As he lay down on his makeshift bed, a sense of warmth engulfed him. He ran his hands through the near invisible cover. It was soft, much like he imagined a cloud might feel like. It also carried the scent of Faith. Peaches.

He took in the sweet aroma as he eyed the girl sobbing quietly. His fists clenched in anger. Even now, without being in his presence, Volcseck continued to make his life miserable. He wanted to comfort her. To promise her that everything would be fine, but he knew that as long as Volcseck was alive, he would never be able to make such a promise. And at that moment, as he took in the sight of his longtime friend, he felt something stir inside his chest he'd never felt before. He couldn't fully explain it, and he didn't try to. All he knew was that he would do anything for her.

And if that involved dueling the most powerful being in existence, so be it.

Chapter 2

"Hey, mate. It's time."

Falcon awoke to the sight of his small friend staring down at him. He had a look of concern plastered across his face. He grabbed his shoulder and shook him once more.

"I'm up," said Falcon, wiping his groggy eyes. Why did Chonsey have to wake him up? He was having such a nice dream for once. He had been training with his brother, Albert. Even though it was but a dream, it was the closest he'd been to his brother in years. Not since that fateful night.

"Were you having a nightmare?" Chonsey asked as he folded his blanket into a tight roll. He tied it together and put it on his back.

"No. Not really. Why?"

Chonsey looked as if he had suddenly lost the will to speak. "Um…no reason, mate."

"Why? Out with it."

"I don't know," said Chonsey apprehensively. "It was just that you were tossing and turning and saying 'Albert' over and over again. I thought you were reliving that night when he, well…you know."

"He killed the council of Ladria and disappeared."

"Disappeared?" Chonsey fidgeted his fingers. "I know your brother was crazy powerful and all, but he went up against the entire royal wielders battalion single handedly. And they used black fire on him. I don't think disappeared is the word for it, mate."

"He's not dead, if that's what you're trying to say." Falcon's anger rose. How could his friend not be on his side? "What are you trying to say? Do you also think my brother is a traitor? That he killed the council to take power for himself?"

Chonsey, who up until now had been normal in color, turned ghostly pale. "No, mate. I'm sure your brother was…"

"There you go again! Was! Don't speak in the past tense about him. He's not dead."

"What's going on?" asked a honeyed voice.

Falcon gazed over at Faith who had arrived with a bushel of green leaves. He collected himself. The last thing he needed was to make Faith sad again. "Nothing. We were just talking about some unimportant stuff."

She tossed the greens into a pot that rested atop an open flame. "If you say so, but it sure didn't seem like nothing." She took out a small bag and spread salt into the pot, followed by granules of pepper. With a large wooden stick, she stirred the broth in circles. "I hope you boys are hungry."

Falcon caught a whiff of the sour smell and immediately recognized it as Gladios plants. How many days are we going to eat the same old thing?

"Will we be having any meat with that?" asked

Chonsey, a second before Falcon could voice that same question.

"Meat?" asked Faith, in a voice that made it seem as if the concept of eating animal flesh was alien to her.

"Yes," added Falcon. "We know you're a vegetarian and all, but Chonsey and I would rather have meat with our soup. A nice squirrel or a lit, perhaps."

"Hmmm..." Chonsey licked his lips. "Lit legs are the best, especially with some larys syrup."

Falcon's stomach growled viciously at the thought.

Faith's face, on the other hand, was one of absolute repulsion. "There is no need for that. Plants have much more nutrition than any slab of meat can ever have. Don't tell me you haven't felt much more energized this past month?"

He had indeed felt much more alert than usual, but he honestly didn't care. He wanted meat. Nonetheless, he remained quiet.

Chonsey, apparently, had chosen to follow Falcon's example. He sat down and grudgingly forced down the thick liquid. When he finished his bowl, Chonsey smiled to himself, as if he had just won a great duel. His smile turned into a frown when Faith poured more soup into his bowl and insisted that he eat to keep his energy up.

"Well, I say we leave now," said Falcon as he finished his second bowl. He stood before Faith could offer another serving.

"Yes, that sounds like a plan, mate." Chonsey also stood.

Faith dumped the leftover liquid on the ground and handed Chonsey the pot. He tied it to his waist and they continued on their trek. The closer they got to Ladria, the quieter the surroundings became. The distant bird chirpings and soft squirrel footsteps gave way to an eerie silence.

"Why is it so quiet?" asked Faith.

"It always gets that way close to Ladria," Chonsey said. "A lot of the hunters hunt close to the city walls. Most animals have learned to stay clear. Those who don't, well…" He stopped and took a long sniff. "Were here. C'mon." He snuck under a long tree branch and beside a thick bush. He moved the dusty leaves to the side. "There."

Falcon's heart dropped to his stomach as he made out the charred corpses. They hung from above the city walls. Someone had nailed them to a log and erected them for the world to see. "So that's what that smell was."

"Oh. That's horrible. Why would they do such a thing?" Faith looked as if she was on the verge of tears.

"To send a message," said Falcon, speaking in a hushed whisper. "The Suteckh want the world to know what happens when they are opposed."

Chonsey pointed into the city gates. "That's not even the worst of it."

Faith whimpered softly. This time tears poured to the

ground as she mumbled something to herself.

Falcon's rage intensified as his eyes settled on the dozens of children who were tied on the ground with thick chains. All of them wore no shirt, exposing their bony ribs. It was one thing to attack adults. But children? This was a new level of evil.

"No, mate," cried Chonsey, holding Falcon back. "Stay back. You're going to give away our position."

"I don't care," fumed Falcon, his insides blazing. "I'm going to free those kids. They're on the brink of death."

"Don't you think people already tried that? For every rescue attempted, the Suteckh kill five children. No rescue has even come close to being successful, not with him here."

"Him? Who are you talking about?"

"The dual wielder, of course. The right hand of the Blood Empress—Draknorr."

Falcon settled back down. Draknorr. That is bad news. He recalled his previous encounter with the powerful wielder. Even in chaos state, Falcon had proved no match for him.

"How could this happen?" whimpered Faith. "I thought Grandmaster Zoen lived here in Ladria. My father always spoke highly of his ability. Surely he could put a stop to it."

"Zoen wasn't here at the time of the attack, and neither were most of the professors from Rohad and the Royal Academy. They were on the other side of Va'siel at the annual academies council."

"Do it!" thundered a voice from afar.

From behind the bush, Falcon recognized the large man who now stood at the foot of a child.

"Dad," muttered Chonsey, surprised. "I think he's doing it, he's going to save the—" Commander Meloth kicked a small girl, sending her rolling across the floor. The dangling chain echoed loudly as the girl clutched her stomach. Chonsey looked on with a slackened mouth. "D-Dad? What is he doing?"

Falcon was just as shocked as Chonsey. Commander Meloth had always been a tough man, but he'd never known him to be a traitor to his own city.

"Harder!" thundered the same voice from before. "If you don't follow directions, I'll kill her. Slowly." An armored figure emerged from the side of the commander. He had two long claws protruding from his right hand. His entire face was hidden behind a dark helmet. Only two red eyes glistened from under the visor.

"Yes, of course." Chonsey's father trudged over to the girl. He leaned down and picked her up by the neck. He pulled his fist back and slammed it into the girl's face. With a loud whimper, the girl fell hard to the stone ground. Blood and a number of teeth slipped out of her mouth.

Draknorr faced the commander. "Remember this next time you come begging for food for the children. Now be gone with you."

Commander Meloth bowed his head. "Yes, sir."

Falcon's balled fists turned a pale white. "Draknorr. I'll make him pay. I swear it. I'll make him pay."

"But how?" asked Faith, wiping away her tears.

"We need to free those children, but we also need to find the emperor," Falcon said. "He escaped. I'm sure wherever he is, he'll be glad to take in the little ones."

"But the emperor is gone, mate. No one knows where he is."

Falcon thought for a moment. Someone had to know something. How could the emperor simply disappear without anyone knowing his whereabouts? The longer he puzzled over the question, the more apparent it became that he was going to have to turn to him. His stomach cringed at the realization that he had no other choice. He swallowed his pride as he made up his mind.

He tapped his friend's shoulder. "Hey."

"What? What?" Chonsey's breathing was still shallow, no doubt because of what he had witnessed his father do.

"You snuck out of the city to find me. I need you to take me to the hidden entrance you used."

Chonsey's eyes stared off into the distance.

Falcon took a hold of him and turned him so that they were face to face. "Chonsey!"

His pupils returned to normal. "Em…yes, mate. The entrance. Y…yes. Follow me." He led them around the stone gate, which took most of the morning since the city was so large. It was midday when they arrived at the small cracked opening. Chonsey took a seat by a tree stump. "I'll wait here. I can't go in there after what I saw." He reached into his small bag and tossed two dirt-caked cloaks to Falcon. "You may need them."

Falcon patted his friend's back. He was actually glad Chonsey had volunteered to stay back. This mission might easily develop into a fight, and that was something that Chonsey, unfortunately, was useless in. "We'll be back before you know it."

Both wielders put on the brown cloaks and forced themselves through the small opening. The offensive smell of feces made his nose crinkle. Now he knew why no one had found this passage. It was in the sewer system.

Faith brought her hand over her nose. "Now what?"

Falcon took in the dark slushy water that travelled slowly down, deeper into the darkness. Moldy walls arched over them. A narrow slimy path was the only way out of this cursed place. "Now we go pay an old friend of mine a visit."

"Friend?"

He sighed. The memory was not one he liked to recount. "Yes. He was my friend years ago, back when my brother was still famous and loved by everyone. I was twelve at the time. We would always go down to the river to play. During the winters we would spend our days in the alleys of

25

Ladria, pretending to be the Golden Wielder."

"What happened?"

"When my brother killed the council, everyone turned on me, even him."

"Oh."

"It didn't stop there. One night, when I was living with K'ran, I snuck out to the city to spend time with him. I thought he'd be glad to see me, but instead he and his gang of friends ambushed me. I couldn't walk straight for a month after the beating they gave me."

Faith's face twisted in confusion. "So why are we going to go see him now?"

"Because he took over his father's pub. You'd be surprised how much information drunk people will reveal." He smirked. "If there's something you need to know, you can wager that he'll know something about it." Falcon cracked his knuckles. "We'll find him and force him to tell us what he knows."

"Or we could just ask nicely."

"No. Trust me, Faith. Violence is all this guy knows. A good beat down should get me the information I need. That's the plan, at least." He took a tentative step forward, careful not to lose control on the slimy surface. "Well, that and not falling in the river of gunk."

Faith cringed. "Yes, I would say that not falling is a sound plan."

Chapter 3

Falcon's eyes darted around Ladria as they crawled out of the sewers. From outside he had only a small view of the city, but now that he stood inside the gates, he saw how bad it really was. The small cottages that usually spread in even rows had all been burnt down, leaving only heaps of dark rubble. Suteckh soldiers, dressed in their usual black and silver leather uniforms, walked through the streets. Many of them held mugs in their hands, no doubt filled with wine. Countless Ladrian citizens sat huddled in corners, their terrified eyes following the passing soldiers. The few citizens who milled around the streets kept their eyes on the dirt-paved ground as they moved.

A husky Suteckh soldier caressed the skull emblem etched on his chest. He belched loudly as he tossed a half-eaten pichion drumstick to the ground. Immediately, a skinny woman with dark bags under her eyes crawled to it on all fours. She took the miserable scrap of meat and scurried back to the corner she had been settled in. Without bothering to clean it, she offered it to a young boy who sat by her side. The boy, who was no doubt her son, devoured it in seconds.

"Hey," said the fat soldier. "I wasn't finished with that." He stumbled over to the burnt wall, where the woman sat, clutching her son. "Do you think you can simply take a mighty

Suteckh soldier's food whenever you feel like it?" He scratched his behind as he spoke. "Well, do you?"

"N...no, of course not. You t-threw it on the ground—"

"And you got greedy." The man took out a whip that hung on his waist. He unrolled it, causing the woman to crawl deeper into the corner of the wall. The rest of the people watched in silence, their faces ashen.

The woman looked around, as if begging for help. Once she saw that no one was coming to her aid, she faced her attacker. "I only want to feed my son. I didn't mean any disrespect."

The soldier threw the whip into the air, causing it snap loudly. "So now you're saying that the dry grit we give you every week isn't good enough. Maybe after this beating I should also take your son to the gates to be tied like the rest of those dogs. Their parents got greedy too, and now their children are paying."

"No!" cried the woman. She hugged her sobbing son protectively. "Not my little Aaron."

"Enough!" He moved his hand and brought the whip forward with tremendous force.

Having heard enough, Falcon moved forward and took hold of the whip in mid-stride. There was a collection of gasps from the people.

The guard turned. The flabby skin hanging from under his chin dangled viciously. "Who dares? Remove that cloak and face me like a man."

"You like hitting defenseless women, do you now?" asked Falcon. He pulled the whip away from the man's hands and tossed it to the ground.

"Why, I'll teach you to raise your hand to a mighty Suteckh arghhh…."

The man crumpled to the floor as Falcon punched him in his oversized cranium. Falcon then grabbed the whip and used it to tie him by his legs.

"What are you doing?" asked Faith. "He's not going to be happy once he wakes up."

"That's fine," said Falcon, taking another look around. There were no other soldiers in sight. "This will be the least of his problems when he comes to." He pulled the man across the ground and into the sewers, which was harder than he had initially thought it was going to be. The man easily weighed over three hundred pounds. Once inside the dark tunnel, he untied his feet and kicked him into the feces-infested waters.

"What the?" The man eyes opened wide. "What's going on? Where am—" He closed his mouth as a stream of gunk slushed into his mouth. He spat the vile liquid as he flailed his arms in a fruitless attempt to swim against the current, which was now flowing much faster than before.

Falcon waved. "See you." Once the man had disappeared in the darkness, he made his way out onto the city streets.

"That was very reckless, Falcon," said Faith. "Nice but reckless."

Falcon shrugged. "Well, I had to do something. Let's see how tough he is when he comes out at the end of the sewage system in the center of the Jugtungla Jungle."

"Oh my god!" shrieked the woman. "You're Falcon Hyatt." She crawled to the rest of the people. "I knew the stories of you being a nefarious good for nothin' were not true."

"Let's hear it for Falcon," said Aaron in a small voice. "The hero of Ladria."

The crowd of people began to cheer his name. They started out low, but their voices grew with every second that passed.

Faith looked around nervously. "This isn't good. They're going to draw unwanted attention."

"Shh…" said Falcon, but he might as well have told them to get louder, because the cheers intensified.

"Falcon. Falcon. Falcon!"

"We have to go," said Falcon. He took Faith's hand and marched quickly down the road. Two soldiers, who had apparently heard the commotion, passed them as they headed toward the cheers.

"Where are we going?" asked Faith. "Is the pub close?"

"Somewhat. This is the poor district. Braden's pub is in the noble district. Let's just hope we don't run into any trouble along the way."

The way out to the noble part of town was littered with soldiers milling around. From time to time one of them would look over at Falcon and Faith, but none stopped to question them.

"We're getting close," said Falcon as they left the dirt roads behind and entered the stone-paved paths. Unlike those in the poor district, the homes in this area were still in one piece. Some had shattered glass or knocked down doors, but they were still standing.

"I wonder why they didn't burn down these houses?" asked Faith.

"They're using them for quarter," said Falcon. "It's a common tactic practiced during sieges. They will burn down everything, except what they plan to use." They turned the corner and entered the bazaar street. The usual shouting vendors and their stands that littered the streets were nowhere in sight. A group of soldiers were huddled at the side of the street, drinking and playing a game of stones.

"There aren't a lot of citizens in this area," said Faith as they quietly made their way down.

"You're right," said Falcon, noticing the same thing as well. "Maybe they were all killed."

Faith gasped silently. "I hope not."

"You wouldn't say that if you knew them," said Falcon, remembering how nobles had treated the peasant class.

"They were mostly a lot of cruel bigots."

"Don't say that. I'm sure many of them were lovely people."

"Aha," said Falcon sarcastically. "Very lovely."

"Is that it?" asked Faith. She pointed to a wooden building on the left side of the street. Dozens of barrels were stacked atop each other, covering most of the windows. Above the oak door hung a sign held by a dusty rope. The dangling sign had an etching of a snake with the words 'The Galloping Viper' above it.

"Yes," said Falcon. An empty pit in his stomach grew with every step he took. He hadn't seen Braden in years. Would he even recognize him? He held his breath as he pushed the creaky door open. The pub was filled with soldiers. Many sat at the front bar; a few others sat in tables with drinks in their hands. None of them bothered to look up at the newcomers.

"It's very dark in here," said Faith.

Falcon took a quick glance around, but to his dismay didn't see his old friend anywhere. He pointed at an empty table at the far right end of the small pub.

Taking his cue, Faith followed him and took a seat. A second later a tall young woman came to take their order.

"I'll just have some water," said Faith.

"Water for me too," said Falcon.

"You can't just get water, you know," said the waitress,

rolling her eyes.

Falcon sighed. "Fine then, give me a mug of ale." As the girl walked away, Falcon took hold of her apron. "Before you leave, miss." He lowered his voice. "I would also like to see the owner—Braden."

The waitresses' eyes widened. "Uh. There is no one by that name here." Without saying a word, she hastily took off through a set of swinging double doors behind the counter.

"I'll be back," said Falcon, standing up.

"Where are you going?" Faith asked.

"The waitress knows something, and I'm going to find out what it is." He walked slowly behind the counter; the last thing he wanted was to arouse any suspicion. Luckily, most of the soldiers were too busy drinking or talking to one another to pay him any attention. He opened the door and his stomach turned icy when he saw the long-nosed young man speaking to the waitress. Falcon reached for his hood and brought it down.

Braden smiled nervously. "My friend, Falcon Hyatt. I haven't seen you in a long time. How are you doing?"

Falcon glanced at the waitress. "Get out." The girl hunched her head and darted out of the back room. "You and I are going to have a little chat." He turned his attention back to Braden.

The pimple-faced man pointed at himself innocently. "Me? Whatever would you want with me? I'm a simple pub owner. What information would you want with someone so insignificant?"

Falcon took hold of Braden's collar and shoved him against a table, knocking down bottles of wine. They crashed loudly on the floor. With Braden still in his grip, he wielded a spear of ice in his middle finger. He willed the spear to grow, until the sharp point was pressing against his former friend's neck.

"Hey, hey, hey." Braden gulped as he brought his hands up. His breath reeked of alcohol. "No need for this violence."

"Where is the emperor? And don't say you don't know. You have your nose in everything that happens in Ladria. I know you know something"

"I want to tell you, I really do. But could you–"

Falcon pressed the ice tip an inch deeper. "Don't even try to talk your way out of this one. Spill the information, or I spill your miserable guts all over this floor." He held his breath, hoping that Braden would believe his bluff.

The double doors swung open, and Faith strode in. She took hold of Falcon's hand and pulled it back. "You're making such a ruckus that some soldiers are trying to come back here. The waitress is keeping them occupied."

"All the more reason I have to beat the information out of him," said Falcon, returning his gaze to Braden.

"Have you tried to simply ask nicely instead of

demanding answers?"

Falcon let out an exaggerated sigh. "Faith, I told you, asking doesn't work on guys like this."

"Yes, it would," said Braden in a squeaky voice as he pushed Falcon's hand away. He turned to Faith. "Ever since he got back here I've been trying to tell him, but every time I try, he threatens me."

Falcon felt a pang of guilt in his chest. He was so sure that Braden was the same person from their childhood that he never considered that he had changed.

Braden turned to Faith. His eyes were watery. "At least someone here isn't ready to kill me to get information from me. He thinks that because he's a Rohad, he can do whatever he wants"

"Please tell us what you know about the emperor's whereabouts," said Faith.

Braden wiped a tear. "Like I was trying to tell Falcon, I don't know where he is, but I do know who knows."

"Who?" asked Falcon.

"A few days ago I overheard a few soldiers saying that Draknorr believes Commander Meloth aided the emperor's escape."

"What about Hiromy? Is she alive?"

"I don't know, but last I heard, she was on the brink of death. It is possible she didn't make it."

Falcon felt the air leave him. His heart settled in his

stomach and stayed there as he recalled how Hiromy, despite her privileged upbringings, had always been kind to him. And despite such kindness, he never took a minute out of his time to thank her.

"Let us pass," said a deep voice from the pub. "What are you hiding back there?"

"It's the soldiers," said Braden. "Follow me." He pushed a crate to the side, revealing a bronze handle on the floor. He pulled it open. A set of stairs that led underground folded out. "This will take you to the entrance of the city. Hurry."

Falcon hesitated for a second. What if it was some kind of trap? But before he had time to think on it, Faith thanked Braden and jumped in. Seeing that he was out of options, he went down the stairs as well.

Braden reached for the handle. He wiped the tears from his eyes as he looked into Falcon's eyes. "They killed my dad and mom right in front of me. Then they kept me alive so I could provide them with drinks." He gritted his teeth. "Make them pay." With those last words Braden shut the door. A second later Falcon made out the scratching noise of a crate being pushed over the secret door.

Slowly, they made their way down the short stairs. They came out in a narrow tunnel, much like the one they had traveled in earlier. Except that, fortunately, this one smelled of wet dirt instead of excrement.

Falcon ran his hand through his hair as he took in a

deep breath. He felt like an idiot. How could he have invested so much hate in something that had happened so long ago?

"Our past defines us, but you shouldn't allow it to become your burden." Faith smiled at him and started down the dark path.

Falcon gazed at her golden brown hair that bounced evenly as she moved. All this time he had believed that Faith had a narrow view of the world, but now, for the first time, it occurred to him that he might be the one with a one-dimensional view of life.

Chapter 4

"What does it look like?" asked Faith as Falcon peeked out the small sliding door at the end of the path.

There was a large metal gate that extended to the skies. The giant double doors were opened wide, and dozens of children lay tied to the floor. He slowly closed the lid and turned to his companion.

"Well?" asked Faith. "Is it safe to come out?"

Falcon turned to her. "It looks like we're back at the entrance of the city. We can sneak out and try to rejoin Chonsey. I'm sure he can get us into his father's home."

"But we can't simply leave those poor children behind."

"My thoughts exactly," said Falcon. "Except that I don't know what to do. How are we going to take so many children out without being stopped? There has to be over two dozen soldiers out there, and every kid is tied down with chains. There is no way we'll be able to get every one of them free."

Faith grimaced as she rubbed her forehead; no doubt she was going over possible solutions in her head. Every once in a while she would sigh in frustration. Falcon leaned on the grainy wall. No matter how much he thought about it, he couldn't figure out a way to help, not without getting themselves captured in the process.

Slowly, he forced the words that had been forming in

his mind out of his mouth. "Maybe we should leave them behind. For now."

"What?" asked Faith, shock in her voice.

"We won't be much help if we're trapped too." He was trying to convince himself. "At least if we leave we'll be able to come back for them eventually."

"When? When they're dead and buried?"

Falcon lowered his gaze. He knew Faith was right, but he had a point too. What good could they be for the millions of other people on Va'siel if they got captured trying to help half a dozen?

"No," Faith continued. "We must get them free now, and I know exactly what we need. Space."

"Space? That would be great if we had the Ghost Knight or Sheridan with us, but they're not here, are they?"

Faith stared back at him expectantly. "They're not, but you are."

Falcon remained quiet, not sure how to tell Faith that he simply couldn't do it. Space was something he had very little experience with. Now he was supposed to simply teleport a dozen kids to safety? That was nigh impossible. To him, at least.

"You space wielded once before," said Faith, no doubt noticing his apprehension. "You can do it again."

"That was once, and besides that all I have is what I read in texts and the little I discussed with Sheridan." Inside he was kicking himself. He spoken to the Ghost Knight in private more than once, and never in those conversations did it occur to him to ask him for space wielding lessons.

"You can do it," encouraged Faith. "I've seen the way you pick up holy wielding. It's the same principle with space. Simply concentrate."

Falcon gulped. She was right. He had to give it a shot, for the kid's sake.

"Let's do it, then," he said, nervousness creeping into his body.

"I will try to give you as much time as you need."

Falcon pushed open the sliding door. Quickly, he hopped out of the secret passage. He blinked rapidly as the sudden brightness of the sun assaulted his senses. To his surprise, not a single soldier seemed to have noticed him. They all busied themselves talking, sitting playing card games, or walking from one place to the next.

Falcon tried to suppress his anger as his eyes darted to the chained children. He needed to concentrate if he was to help them, which meant keeping his emotions in check. He brought his hands together as he forced his mind to think of space wielding. He already knew how to create space force; all he needed to do was to elevate that to the next level.

He smiled inwardly as he sensed gravity increase around him. He was doing it! He opened his eyes and moved the invisible force over the children. In seconds he had it drifting over every single prisoner. Now all I have to is take it to the next—

"Hey, you there," called an unknown voice. "What do you think you're doing?"

Falcon felt his wielding weaken a bit as his gaze darted over to an incoming soldier. He was short, and his legs were so spread out that walking seemed to be a struggle. He didn't look like much of a threat, but Falcon was now looking beyond him at the dozen soldiers who had taken notice of him.

"I asked you a question, peasant!" demanded the guard as he unsheathed a sword. The rest of the soldiers did the same.

"Bubble charm," called Faith as she stood in front of him. She put both her hands over her head and spun them around, almost as if she were churning invisible butter.

"Get back, you wench," ordered the soldier. "Or I'll cut you down where you stand."

Oblivious, Faith continued churning.

"Die, then." The soldier brought his sword under his belt and ran forward.

Falcon looked from the kids to Faith. He had to make a choice quickly. He was seconds away from dissolving the force he had over the children when the soldier suddenly stopped moving. He bounced back and fell, his armor clinging loudly on the ground. The remaining soldiers met the same fate.

"What was that?" asked the stubby soldier furiously. Spit dripped from his mouth as he moved forward again, this time much more slowly. He suddenly stopped. Falcon suspected he had reached the same shield as before. He poked it with his sword. The weapon ricocheted. Another soldier tried to force himself into the obstruction, but he too bounced back onto the ground.

Faith had put up some type of shield! But it wasn't like any hard, firm shield Falcon had seen before. This one was barely visible, and it shape-shifted and molded itself like water.

"Everyone attack this bubble at once," said the short man. In an instant the soldiers slammed their swords repeatedly on the shield. A few of them even wielded balls of fire. Every attack bounced off harmlessly, sending loud ringing notes through the air.

"Falcon," moaned Faith, her voice strained. "Hurry up, please."

Falcon snapped into attention. Guilt gnawed at him. Faith had been putting all her effort into maintaining a shield up for him, and all he'd done was stand idly by admiring the shield. "Yes, of course." He concentrated on a vision. There was only one place he could think of that wasn't too far and where the kids would be safe. The vision of K'ran's home nestled between thick forest trees flashed in his mind. He could see it all vividly, the smoking chimney, the water-drenched wood, even the short, green grass.

The soldiers' yells became nothing more than useless echoes as he opened the force he had over the children. The kid's bodies stretched like dough as they whirled into the holes that had opened before them. A second later they had all disappeared.

Falcon felt a heavy weight leave him.

"Now get us out of here," said Faith breathing heavily. "I can't hold this bubble much longer."

"You're not going anywhere!" cried the soldier.

"Falcon!" called Faith once more, her voice pleading.

He tried to think quickly, but that only served to jumble his mind even more.

Faith brought one hand down, while the other continued churning.

"She's weakening," cried a soldier. "We got them now."

Her warm hand rested on his chest. Her familiar warmth spread from his stomach to the tip of his toes and to every last strand of his hair. Suddenly, his mind was clear. He pictured the opening in the gate where Chonsey was waiting for them. A hole materialized above him. His and Faith's body stretched into it. Like before, he felt no pain.

"Get back here!" he heard the men shout as he warped out of their grasps.

~~~

"He said what, mate?" asked Chonsey.

Falcon and Faith were now standing before Chonsey,

44

who still appeared shocked to have seen his friend materialize through a hole in space. The sun was close to descending.

"I already told you, Chonsey," Falcon repeated. "Braden said that if anyone has any information, it's your father. Which means that you need to get us into his home."

"What makes you think that I can get you in?" asked Chonsey, playing with his hair.

"Your father is the top commander of the Ladrian armies. I know all high-ranking commanders, council members, and generals have hidden passageways that lead out of their home. It's a security measure they have in case they are attacked."

Chonsey's gaze drifted from Falcon to the ground. "I'm guessing Aya told you."

"Yes."

"She must really trust you, mate."

A wave of anger and hurt spread through Falcon. He had known and been close friends with Chonsey since they were children. Was he saying that he was not to be trusted?

"I didn't mean anything by that, mate," said Chonsey, noticing the questioning look in Falcon's face. "It's simply that no one is supposed to know." He stalled. "I would have told you, but my dad would have killed me. You know how he is."

"It's no big deal," lied Falcon. "But you will take us to the hideout now, won't you? I'm sure your father would understand."

Chonsey nodded his head. "I don't want to see him. You saw how he kicked that little girl. He may have turned to the Suteckh. He always did crave power after all, just like Lao."

The unexpected mention of his former friend caused Falcon's stomach to twist. "Please, Chonsey. Lao chose his—" He took a breath, letting the thought of his dead friend fade to the back of his mind. "Lao and your father are not the same. Let's go speak to him."

"You go, mate. I'm staying right here."

Faith, who until now had remained silent, stood before Chonsey. "We need you. You're his son. He's more likely to give information to you than to two strangers."

In his face, Falcon could see Chonsey struggling to make a choice.

"Fine, mates," he said after a minute of silence. He slowly crouched and entered the opening in the wall.

"Where are you going?" asked Falcon, confused.

"The hideout is this way, mate. You actually probably passed it without knowing on the way into the city."

"If you say so." Falcon moved into the opening, followed closely by Faith.

"Your home city is so strange," said Faith once they had moved quite a ways deeper into the sewers. "Back in Asturia we have nothing like this."

"What do you mean?" asked Falcon, covering his face

with his sleeve as he spoke. The stench that assaulted his nose was now stronger than before. His eyes were close to watering.

"There are so many hidden paths and secrets here. It makes it hard to know who you can and can't trust."

"I suppose you're right," said Falcon. "But don't forget, I may have spent many years in Ladria, but Asturia is also my home."

Faith smiled. "Yes, of course."

"We're here," said Chonsey.

Falcon looked around but saw nothing out of the ordinary. There was the same slimy path, sludgy waters noisily moving down at his side, and grimy brick walls. "Where's the hidden entrance?"

"Actually there's something there," Faith exclaimed, pointing at a brick on the wall. "It's slightly less grimy than the bricks around it, which means that it's been touched more than the other bricks."

Chonsey's jaw dropped. "Wow. That's actually correct." He pressed the brick. It screeched loudly against the bricks that encased it as it moved in. The wall collapsed, revealing a torch-lit tunnel. "I'm sure glad you weren't hired to take out my family while we slept."

"Me?" asked Faith, pointing innocently at herself. "Take out someone? I think not."

Falcon tried to suppress a laugh at her reaction. "Let's

get this moving, shall we?"

The three wielders trudged quietly down the tunnel. The drips of water were the only sounds that broke the silence. They turned a few corners, their abnormally long shadows dancing on the walls as they moved up yet another set of stairs. Falcon wiped the sweat from his brow. The flames from the torches filled the tunnel with a musky heat.

"We're here," said Chonsey as they arrived at a dead end. The brick wall obstructing their path was much cleaner than the walls they had passed until now. Chonsey pressed in two left bricks then three bricks on the bottom, and finally he pressed a brick at the center of the wall.

Some type of code, thought Falcon as the wall opened straight through the middle. The young wielders moved sideways through the narrow slit.

Falcon's footsteps echoed as he stepped into a large kitchen. Rotten fruit and vegetables were stacked in neat piles atop a long table. Pans and pots of all kinds, colors, and sizes dangled above the many stoves aligned against the wall. There was a plate of moldy half-eaten food on the table, as well as a knocked-over mug of what appeared to be goat milk, though it smelled rancid.

"It doesn't look like anyone is here," said Faith.

Chonsey looked around sadly. "I suppose not. Most of my family must have escaped at the first sign of trouble, along with most of the butlers and maids. That just makes it more suspicious that my father is still here. Why didn't he escape with everyone else?"

"Let's go find out," said Falcon, eyeing the luxurious swinging double doors before him. Throwing caution to the wind, he walked out of the kitchen and into a narrow hallway.

"My father's study is this way," said Chonsey. He led them out of the hallway and into the grand hall. A crystal chandelier hung from the ceiling. Long windows let in rays of blue moonlight, illuminating Falcon's friend as he climbed the red-carpeted stairs. Once atop, Chonsey moved down another corridor filled with oil paintings of great battles and the occasional glass display filled with swords, maces, and daggers. That was when he saw it. At the very end there was a thick door that was slightly ajar. A bright light streamed out of it.

Falcon didn't need his timid friend to tell them that this room was his father's study. Chonsey's trembling face and slow gait were enough indicators. As his friend pushed the door open, the trembling intensified.

"Chonsey!" exclaimed the shocked commander in a thunderous voice. He was standing overlooking a large table. On the table lay an over-sized map of Ladria. There were scribbles of black, blue, and red ink over the map. "What are you doing here?"

"I could a-ask you t-the same thing, father."

The commander's eyes drifted from his son, to Falcon,

to Faith, and then back to his son. "I would have thought that was obvious. I'm overseeing the occupation we're under. The Suteckh are ruthless, I'm here to get the remaining citizens through this ordeal. Maybe, just maybe, some of us can make it as long as we follow orders."

"You mean as long as we submit like slaves," said Falcon angrily. He thought back to the dinner where the commander had made light of his warnings. "I told you this would happen. I told the emperor that the Suteckh were planning an attack on the capital cities, and you counseled him to not listen to me."

The commander stared down at his map. "I know. I know. We weren't ready, and when they attacked we were caught off guard. Which is why I feel the guilt of every single death that has occurred heavy on my conscience. It's up to me to save as many lives as possible."

"How are you going to do that?" asked Chonsey through gritted teeth. "By kicking children unconscious?"

Falcon stepped back, not believing what he was seeing. His friend was a timid boy, never one to raise his voice at anyone, especially his demanding father. What was happening?

The Commander stared at the floor. "I'm sorry you saw that." He gulped loudly. "But if I hadn't done that he would have killed her. At least this way she'll live."

"Yes, some life. Left starving and beaten half to death

by the man who is supposed to protect her."

"How dare you talk to me that way? I am your father. You will—"

"How dare I?" shouted Chonsey as his small frame shook. "How dare you? You're no father of mine. The father I knew would have died before he submitted to the enemy. He would have never turned into a groveling coward! What happened to all those stories I read about in those books about the great Commander Meloth?"

For once, the commander actually looked ashamed. He played with his finger as he slowly glanced at his son. Falcon found it awkward, to say the least, for such a large man to be scolded by such a small boy.

"Son," he whispered. "They have your mother, the love of my life. And they have your sisters. All I can do is play along and follow their orders. Maybe this way they'll live."

"Is that what Mom would want?"

An awkward silence filled the room. Falcon looked over at Faith, who looked just as uncomfortable as he did.

"You know Mom would want you to keep fighting, even if that meant her life. She would have never stood for this."

The commander crumpled on the wooden chair beside him, his face buried in his hands. "I was always the best. Always. On the battlefield I feared nothing. Whoever my foe was, I vanquished them with my power." He gulped. "But this kind of battle isn't one that requires brute power, and unfortunately brute power is all I know." Tears streamed down his face. He looked down, as if the sight of such a powerful man sobbing would shame his son.

Chonsey's hardened features softened. His hand travelled over to his father's hunched back, and he caressed it. "Then let me help you. You always overlooked me because I wasn't the fastest, the strongest, or the bravest. You completely ignored my affinity for tactics and strategy."

Falcon nodded. While it was true that, unlike Falcon, Chonsey had no raw power, Chonsey, along with Aya, had always been the best strategist and tactician at Rohad.

"With my brain and your strength, we can figure out a way to reclaim Ladria."

The commander gazed into his son's eyes. He looked determined. But more than that, he looked proud. "You're right, son." He stood. "First we will free your mother and sisters along with the rest of the prisoners. That way the Suteckh can't hold them over our head as threats. But it's going to be difficult."

"Not to worry," Chonsey exclaimed. "I already have a plan in mind. But first." He turned to Falcon. "My friends need some information."

"Anything," said the commander.

"We need to know the whereabouts of Emperor Romus. Do you know where he is?" asked Falcon. "And his daughter, Hyromi, how is she?"

The commander scratched his head. "I'm afraid I'm not privy to that information."

Falcon went cold. He had gone to so much trouble to get to the commander, only to discover that he knew nothing.

"But I do know who knows."

Falcon's attention peaked.

"My neighbor, Councilman Nakatomi."

Falcon gazed at the commander, not sure if the man was speaking truth. "Aya's father? How would he know?"

"He aided the emperor in his escape. I saw it myself."

Falcon's eyes widened. "The emperor was bound to have his own hidden routes from the palace. Why would he need Councilman Nakatomi's aid?"

"Perhaps you should go ask him, mate."

Falcon stared at his friend, realizing he was right. Standing around wasn't going to get him anywhere. "Good luck, Chonsey." He took his friend and shook his hand. "I wish I could stay and help, but—"

Chonsey held his hand up. "No need for explanations. You have your own duty to fulfill. Fortune be with you."

Letting go of Chonsey, Falcon turned and headed out the door. Faith followed close behind. As he headed down the stairs, through the grand hall, and out the front door, he couldn't help but smile for his friend. It had taken the sacking of their home, but Chonsey had finally become the capable man Falcon always knew he was.

Chapter 5

Falcon and Faith moved quietly through the yard. The moonlight drenched the grass, giving it a blue color.

"Are we going to jump the fence?" asked Faith, eyeing the large black metal fence that separated Chonsey's home from Aya's. Sharp black spikes rose from the top. "I don't think that's such a good idea."

"No," whispered Falcon, hoping to not alert the few remaining soldiers who patrolled the city streets. For once he was glad that his friends lived in mansions. Their yards were so large that they were a good nine hundred feet from the soldiers, which meant it was going to be that much harder for them to be spotted. "Aya's and Chonsey's parents are both top members of Ladrian nobility. They built a gate back here to connect their homes in the times they met." He frowned. "At least that's what Aya told me."

"Wait a minute. Are you telling me that you been Aya's friend for years, but have never seen her home?"

"Her parents never thought much of me."

"Why?"

"I don't know. I never asked, and she never spoke about it." Falcon stopped walking once he saw the bronze knob. "There it is." He opened the fence, which was made of the same black metal as the rest of the gate, and opened it slowly. He gritted his teeth as the fence squeaked softly. He turned toward the street, but the silhouettes of the soldiers remained oblivious as they moved up and down. Once through, they moved through the front yard, which was filled with statues of famous women, and over to a long window. Falcon peered inside. There was a large hall filled with furniture. There were a half dozen sofas, countless tables with hundreds of porcelain and glass decorations, and large candle sticks. It was strange seeing the place his friend had grown up for the first time.

"It looks like they're asleep," said Faith.

"Looks that way. Let's go in and have us a little midnight chat." Still crouching, he moved over to the doorknob, but when he was inches away from reaching it, the luxuriously patterned door opened. Falcon gulped as a short woman stared down at him. She wore the black blouse and skirt that were typical of a maid.

"My master has been expecting you," she said. "Please follow me."

Hesitantly, Falcon and Faith accepted the maid's invitation. His body warned them that something was amiss. How did Councilman Nakatomi know Falcon was planning to visit him?

As they moved through a series of doors, Faith stopped and stared, twinkle-eyed, at a vase of blue-streaked flowers that rested atop an oak-wood table.

The maid stopped, rolling her eyes at Faith. "Please keep up. My master does not have much time."

Faith nodded and continued on, though she gazed back at the flowers a few times.

Falcon's heartbeat intensified as he reached a black door. He suddenly realized that not only was this entire situation bizarre to say the least, but this was to be the first time he would meet Aya's father. What would he think of him?

"They are here, Master," said the maid as she knocked the door lightly. "Just as you said they would be."

"Good," came a voice from beyond the door. "See them in."

The door screeched open, and Falcon walked into the poorly lit office. There was a dying fire on the fireplace. Hundreds of books filled the walls. High, near the ceiling, there were dozens of paintings of past Nakatomis. A desk covered with scattered papers rested at the middle of the room. There was a long cushioned chair in front of the chimney, where a man sat with his back to them.

Falcon took in the aroma of firewood as he collected himself. "Hello, sir. I'm Falcon...Falcon Hyatt." He motioned to Faith. "And this is Faith Hemstath from Asturia."

Mr. Nakatomi turned, staring at Falcon as if he were an unwanted piece of trash. "I know who you are. Everyone knows who you are." His strongly chiseled face frowned as he stood and headed for the table. He grabbed a brown bottle of rum and offered it to Falcon. "Care for a drink?"

Falcon tried his best not to gag at the overwhelming smell of strong liquor emitting from the councilman's mouth. "No, I'm fine, sir."

"Very well, then. Something lighter perhaps?" He reached for a steel teapot that rested over the desk. He dug into his desk and pulled out three small mugs. With trembling hands, he poured green tea into them.

"Are you well, sir?" asked Faith.

"Why yes," answered Mr. Nakatomi. "Why wouldn't I be?" He offered them a mug. Not wishing to offend the man, Falcon took it in his hands. Faith did the same.

"You seem a little on edge," said Falcon tentatively.

Mr. Nakatomi's robes rustled softly as he turned the chair around and took a seat. The fire illuminated half his face; the other half remained obscured in darkness. "We're under a siege, how do you expect me to be? And to make matters worse, I now have a wanted criminal in my home." His gaze met Falcon's. "I knew after your little space display earlier you would come here. You aren't content with the dishonor you have brought upon my family, are you now?"

Falcon's expression turned to one of confusion.

"Don't pretend," continued the man. He pointed at the pictures that hung on the wall. "You see that? Those are all members of the great Nakatomi legacy: all men who held the family's honor above anything else. My daughter was to continue this great tradition." His teeth clenched. "But you…you ruined everything. By associating herself with you, she brought shame on this family."

Falcon felt a red fury take over him. "Me? I did nothing. Aya—"

"Don't talk back to me, boy! I'm the head councilman, and you're a simple Rohad. Or what? Are you going to turn into your brother and murder a councilman in cold blood too?"

"Don't talk about my brother," said Falcon, raising his voice for the first time. He wanted to pick the man up and slam him into the desk, to punch his smug face until he could no longer speak.

The man grinned. "Do it. Kill me. Prove that all I ever told my daughter about you was correct."

The mention of Aya caused him to stagger back. He balled his fists but remained unmoving. No matter what the man did or said, he couldn't lay a hand on him. He was Aya's father, after all.

"Please sir," said Faith in a low voice. "We are only here to find the location of the emperor, nothing else. As soon as you tell us where he is we'll be on our way."

The man burst into a fit of mock laughter. "The emperor? What do you think he's going to do? He's a coward who ran away as soon as this began. You'll get no aid from him."

"Just tell us where he is," demanded Falcon, his patience wearing thin. "We know you helped him escape."

"Yes, I did." He took a long sip out of the bottle before continuing. "As soon as I heard the attack was to take place I knew I had to act." He grinned widely. "And act I did. Now that so-called emperor is exactly where I want him."

Falcon and Faith turned to each other, their eyes wide.

"You knew of the attack?" asked Falcon.

"Of course I knew. I am the one who orchestrated it. I orchestrated everything."

"What are you saying?" said Falcon, still confused. Nothing the councilman was saying made any sense.

"Falcon," whispered Faith. "He's Suteckh."

The councilman clapped mockingly. "Bravo, young lady. You're not as thick-headed as this idiot."

Falcon staggered back, too shocked to even be angry. "B...but how. Y...you have served in the council for years."

"You mean I've been undercover in this wretched city for years. It was I who created a vacant spot for me to take on the council. Or what? Did you actually think Albert murdered the councilmen of his own accord? He did so because I made it so. And I've been gaining the trust of the idiots in this city for years."

Falcon remained silent. His head was spinning with a jumble of questions that he couldn't form into words.

Mr. Nakatomi burst into a fit of hysterical laughter. "I

can see you're quite confused." He stared daggers into Falcon. "You see, my family's legacy will live on because of my actions. Once the Suteckh take their rightful place as the rulers of Va'siel, no one will ever forget the name Nakatomi. My daughter will make sure of that."

"You're wrong," said Falcon, glad to see a fleeting moment of doubt in the councilman's eyes. "Aya will never go along with you. She won't continue your reckless path to destruction."

"Aya?" The councilman cackled. "Who said anything about Aya? No, Aya has been corrupted by the city and you. My legacy will instead live on through my true daughter, Selene, or as the world has come to know her, the Blood Empress."

Falcon eyes wandered aimlessly through the room. Aya had a sister. And she was the leader of the Suteckh? How?

"But Aya's sister was kidnapped when she was just a girl," added Faith quite suddenly. "She can't be the Blood Empress."

Faith's confession sent Falcon's stomach hurling to his throat. Faith knew!

Councilman Nakatomi smiled with satisfaction. "Like everything else, I staged that little kidnapping. I had Aya take Selene out to play and then arranged for Selene to be taken. Once back in Tenma, she was brainwashed and turned into the ruler she is today."

Faith looked at the man with a pained expression. "You put your two daughters through all that pain for power? Do you have any idea how much guilt Aya has carried with her all her life?"

Mr. Nakatomi stood. "I don't care! I was fortunate to have two daughters who were extremely powerful, much more powerful than anyone in our family line has ever hoped to be. It was this power that attracted the Suteckh nobles to them. Aya, naturally, was the first choice, but her older mind was much too sharp, too aware. So we opted for the much younger Selene." He gazed silently at the paintings above him. "We are simple pawns that will live and wither away in a few years, forgotten to history. But our legacy will remain for the ages."

Falcon stood with his mouth open. How could such a man have raised Aya? He'd always known the man was obsessed with his legacy, but he never thought it consumed him to this level.

He took a calming breath to gather his senses. He had so many questions but had no idea where to begin. So he went with the first one that came to mind.

"Why are you telling us all this? What do you have to gain? Blowing your cover doesn't seem like a smart thing to do."

With his face bathed in glowing red, the councilman appeared as an incarnation of a demon. "I like to see the face of my enemy as they realize they've been demolished."

"We haven't been demolished," countered Falcon. "Far from it. We will find the emperor and destroy the Suteckh."

"No, you won't." The councilman smirked. "The emperor is hiding in K'ran's former home. The fool will stay there, thinking he is safe, but soon enough they'll be on him." He turned to Falcon and Faith. "As for you two, Draknorr is on his way to take care of you."

Falcon's mouth went dry. How in the world was he going to get out of this one?

"How dare you, father?" asked a low voice.

Falcon turned to the sight of Aya standing in the open door, her face filled with a strange combination of sadness, disappointment, and anger.

Chapter 6

"Aya," said Mr.Nakatomi, obviously as shocked as Falcon to see her standing before them. "What are you doing here?" The air seemed thick, almost tangible.

"This is my home," said Aya, her expression hardened. "I heard of the attack and hurried to see how you and mother were. But I see you are quite well."

Falcon wanted to talk to Aya. To ask her how her mission went and how she'd been. But he composed himself. This wasn't the time.

"How much have you heard?" asked Mr. Nakatomi tentatively.

"Everything."

The councilman took a step toward his daughter. "This was not the way I had hoped you would find out about this but no matter. Now that you know the truth, I have no doubt you will choose right." He extended his hand. "Join me, daughter."

Aya stumbled back, her lips trembling. "You know I can't do that."

Her father slammed his fist on the desk. The teacup tumbled to its side, spilling its contents over stacks of papers. He didn't seem to care.

Falcon waved away the aroma of green tea as he stared at Aya, hoping there was something he could do or say to help her, but nothing seemed adequate.

"You are a Suteckh, Aya," insisted her father. "You were born in Tenma, where your mother and sister are waiting for you as we speak. Don't you want to join them? Don't you want to build a legacy with your family?"

Aya's chest rose and fell in shallow quick breaths. She faced the floor.

The councilman trudged over to his daughter and laid his hand on her shoulder. "Aya, I know you have a hard choice to make, but be quick about it. Draknorr will be here any minute, and when he arrives it's imperative that he see that we stand united."

Aya glared at her father with a determined look. "No. This decision is actually not difficult in the least."

"That's good to hear," said Mr. Nakatomi, a smile forming on his lips. "I knew you would see reason, my daughter."

Aya stood straight. "No. The choice I made is to free my sister from the prison you put her in. How dare you call yourself a father after stealing her life for your petty dreams? I…" Her voice staggered, and her eyes grew glossy. "I love my little sister. I will free her."

"I'm so sad to hear you say that," said a deep voice. "Now I have no choice but to kill you."

Falcon turned to the silhouette by the window. Oh no. Even through the darkness he made out the long double claws dangling from the right arm. Deep glowing crimson eyes stared back at him.

The councilman bowed slightly. "It is good to see you again, Master Draknorr." He turned his sights to his daughter. "As you suspected, she refuses to fight for our cause. Do as you wish with her. Kill her if you must. She mustn't interfere with my legacy."

"You have been a loyal servant of the Suteckh," declared Draknorr. "You shall be rewarded for your years of service. I will send you to our hometown of Tenma, to be with your family."

Falcon watched in horror as a skeletal hand, the size of a full-grown man, appeared out of seemingly nowhere. It took the grinning councilman in its clutches.

"Your mother will be pleased to hear of your death, daughter," said Councilman Nakatomi as the hand disappeared into nothingness.

Aya didn't show any sign of emotion at her father's words. Instead she remained still, her expression icy. She pointed at Draknorr. "You said you would kill me, did you not? Well, c'mon then. Let's see you try."

Falcon stared at Aya, mouth gaping. Her emotions were obviously getting the better of her. Did she really think she stood a chance against the dual wielder?

Aya gripped the small sticks around her waist, which immediately snapped to her usual blue batons. She took a defensive stance. "C'mon, Falcon. Between the three of us, we can take him."

Now Falcon understood. He unsheathed his katana. In the corner of his eye, he saw Faith summon her long, wooden staff. She held it before her.

"Let's even the odds," said the dark-clad knight as he pointed at Aya. A dark mist flew from his hands and into her nostrils as she staggered back.

Falcon looked back at her, worried. "Aya, are you okay?"

She batted his hand away, looking back at him with black-rimmed eyes. Her skin had darkened considerably, and her pupils were now a deep red.

"Aya, what's wrong with you?" asked Falcon. His heart was pumping now. He had to do something, anything to snap her back to him.

"She belongs to me now," bragged Draknorr, confirming Falcon's suspicions. "No one can escape a dark possession."

Falcon dashed toward Draknorr, vengeance driving him, his doubt now replaced by thoughts of vengeance. The dark knight stood calmly in place, not bothering to move an inch or offer any kind of resistance. Why isn't he moving? Inches away from reaching him, Falcon found out why Draknorr hadn't bothered to move. He looked down at his feet as they sunk into the ground. He tried to move, but the black tar that now engulfed his feet bubbled ever higher, making it impossible to take a step.

"I got you," cried Faith as she reached for him.

And that was when it happened. Falcon watched in disbelief as Aya slammed her body into Faith's unsuspecting back, sending her reeling into the desk. She slipped over the desk and landed on the other side of it with a loud bang. Without missing a beat, Aya jumped over and picked up the still dazed Faith by the waist. She drove Faith forward and through the glass window. Face first. Falcon made out Faith's low whimpers from outside.

"After her," ordered Draknorr. But before he had even ordered it, Aya was already diving out of the window, moving to finish her friend.

"Stop, Aya," cried Falcon. Harnessing all his strength, he willed himself forward, but all he managed to do for his efforts was sink even deeper. The warm tar was up to his knees now.

"Don't bother." Draknorr laughed. "She won't yield unless the person who cast the possession ability dies, and I have no intention of dying."

Falcon held his breath, painfully aware that there was nothing he could do to stop the dark knight before him.

~~~

Faith crawled on all fours. Small glass shards dug into her palms, causing her hands to spasm with pain. There was a crunching sound of feet stepping on glass. She turned to the

68

sight of Aya, staring down at her with a malicious look. She wore her usual white blouse with a lion insignia on her chest. A short black skirt moved, smoothing and wrinkling itself as Aya walked forward.

Faith stood. Ignoring the pain, she pulled out the glass shards, and they dropped to the hard brick ground. She appeared to be in the mansion's backyard. There were a series of servant cabins aligned in a neat row a few feet away from her. A number of trees dotted the large yard.

"Aya, stop," pleaded Faith, holding up her hands. "We're friends, remember?"

"You and I aren't friends," growled Aya. Her voice was unnaturally deep. "Ever since I met you I've hated you. You think you can just come and take what is rightfully mine?" She grinned widely as her emblem glowed a bright blue.

Faith took a few more steps back. "Aya, you're not thinking straight. Let me help you, please. I don't want to hurt you."

"You?" Aya pointed mockingly at Faith. "Hurt me?" She cackled maniacally. "I would like to see you try." With those words Aya dashed in. She brought her fist up in a high uppercut.

Faith had seen Aya fight before, and she knew that she wanted to be nowhere close to her fists. Aya was a master grappler; any hold could lead to a broken arm or leg, or worse.

A translucent shield appeared in front of Faith. A

second before making contact, Aya flipped over it. While still in midair, directly above Faith, Aya brought down a spear of water. Faith flicked her hand, and the shield moved to block the attack. Aya landed. She kicked. Again, the shield drove her back.

Faith inhaled. Forcing the shield to keep up with Aya was proving to be a handful.

The water wielder rubbed her hands together. A water hawk took hold over her left hand. A lion encased her right hand. The aqua gloves roared and screeched as Aya slammed her fists into the barrier. The first punch drove Faith back; the second punch cracked the shield in a thousand places. It fell to the floor, shattering like glass.

Before Faith could register what had occurred, Aya took hold of the holy wielder's legs and wrestled her to the ground.

Faith stomach tightened as she realized that she was in some serious trouble. There was no way she could stand against her on the ground.

Aya's elbow found Faith's forehead. She saw stars as her head bounced off the ground. Her opponent's strong arms wrapped around her right leg. Before Aya could lock in her grip, Faith drove her open palm into the middle of the hold, essentially nullifying the grip. Aya rolled over Faith and took hold of her hand.

Faith tried to pull her hand back into her chest, but Aya was much too strong. Faith gritted her teeth, suppressing the urge to scream as Aya pulled her arm back. She felt a tremendous warm pain on her wrist. She's going to break it. Think Faith. Think!

Aya was lying on Faith's other arm, but with the little mobility she had left she willed her staff forward. Her weapon flew out of the broken window and directly into Aya's cranium.

Aya let go, rubbing the red spot in her head where the staff had made contact. Her eyes closed and opened, as if she were having a hard time regaining her vision.

Without the threat of being snapped in half at a moment's notice, Faith's arms felt lighter. "Bubble Charm." In an instant the invisible shield covered her.

Aya's eyes were a furious red. "Shield, shield, shield! Is that all you do? Pathetic excuse for a wielder." She pressed ahead. "Ice." Blue water spiraled in front of her. In seconds, it hardened into a white slab. The ice emitted a clear smoke into the night air.

Faith watched in disbelief as the point of the ice pierced the shield as if it weren't even there. The bubble popped into a hundred smaller bubbles that took to the sky.

"Fine," said Faith, realizing that she had to stop holding back if she was to survive. "No more shields." She held her staff in front of her.

Aya grinned at the news. Both wielders met with a fierce clash.

The water wielder's gloves searched for an opening.

Faith spiraled her staff expertly, repeatedly driving Aya back.

"Kyaaa!" With a well placed kick, Aya snapped the staff in half.

Faith tightened her grip on both sides. She had repeatedly trained with double staffs. This was nothing new.

Aya went in with a low uppercut. Finally. An opening. Faith threw one half of the staff at her opponent, who deflected it with a punch. Blinded, she didn't see as Faith circled around her and drove the other half of the staff into Aya's ribs.

Oh, no. Too late Faith realized that Aya had done a double attack. Aya's kick headed straight for her face. It landed on her nose with a sickening crunch. Faith drove back, hard, into a tree. She tasted the blood that dripped from her nostrils.

On the other side was Aya, down on one knee. She took shallow breaths as she clutched her aching ribs. "Not bad, holy wielder. Not many people are fast enough to break through my defense."

Faith whisked her hands in front of her nose. Her holy aura flowed into the injury. Immediately, the bleeding ceased. The pain, too, became non-existent. That's it. I have to heal her too.

Aya cracked her fists as she stood up straight. "Healing, huh. I'm just going to have to beat you faster than you can recover, then."

"Well, here I am," responded Faith, sure Aya would take the bait. "Come and get me."

Aya gritted her teeth. "Gladly." With frightening speed the water wielder pounced. Faith remained still, allowing Aya to take hold of her in a bear hug. Aya tried to pick Faith up for a slam, but Faith ground her feet. Simultaneously, she closed her eyes and let the holy energy flow out of her.

"That's not going to work!" screamed Aya. They were face to face now, so close that Faith could smell the strawberry aroma from Aya's hair.

A sudden burst of pain rocked Faith. The darkness was fighting back. Dark tentacles wrapped around both wielders, threatening to overtake them.

Faith realized that with Aya fighting her, she wasn't going to be able to resist the darkness.

Faith opened her eyes. "Aya, I need your help." Crimson eyes full of hate stared back at her. "I need you to fight back with me, or this darkness will claim us both."

Aya's grip around her softened, and for a split second, Faith could have sworn she saw a hint of remorse in Aya's eyes.

"Aya," Faith insisted. As she spoke she released greater levels of holy, causing her body to glow a bright white. "Do it for your friends. Do it for Falcon."

Aya's red eyes changed to her usual black. A second later, they returned to a crimson and then back yet again to black.

"I...I'm t...trying," stuttered Aya, pain in her voice.

"Close your eyes and focus."

The girls closed their eyes. With her last ounce of strength, Faith fought off Draknorr's veil of darkness. She could feel Aya doing the same.

Then, quite suddenly, her body felt as light as air. She and Aya crashed to the floor, battered and exhausted. Above them a wicked coat of dark mist disintegrated into thin air, wailing loudly in the voice of a tortured woman.

Despite the loud screeches, Faith allowed herself a small breath, celebrating her small victory. But just as she relaxed, a scream permeated the air, chilling her to the core.

Falcon. He was in trouble.

Chapter 7

"Aya, stop." Falcon heard Faith plead from outside the shattered window, causing his desperation to intensify. He struggled to move again, but that only caused him to sink even more into the tar.

"It looks like one of your friends will be dead soon enough," mocked Draknorr. "Which one will be the one to survive, and which one will live? Now that's the golden question."

"Stop this!" ordered Falcon through gritted teeth. His friends were mere feet from him, and they needed him now more than ever. He willed the power that rested at his core forward. It warmed his body as it bubbled through him. His usual gray emblem turned a misty blue. Shooting stars moved through it at high velocity. A second later Falcon felt the familiar pull of the vortex. He disappeared inside the hole. When he appeared again he was standing in Aya's front yard. He breathed a sigh of relief as he trudged across the soft pasture. He had hoped to end up in the backyard where Aya and Faith were, but at least he was free.

He snapped his head around as the front doors unexpectedly flew off their hinges. With a loud burst, they crashed into the front gate, breaking into dozens of pieces.

Draknorr shook off a few pieces of scattered wood that

had landed on his fist. He took a slow step into the front yard. As he moved he growled softly. "No void wielder will ever be enough to defeat me, boy."

"Will a dual wielder suffice?"

No way. Falcon slowly craned his neck. Half a dozen guards who patrolled the streets lay on the floor, blood pooling from under them. High atop the fence stood the man who had made his life miserable for half a lifetime. His trademark dark robe hung from his skinny body. The ragged purple scarf was there as well. He wore a deep frown across his bony face, which was not unnatural in the least. Falcon had never seen the man display anything that resembled a smile.

Professor Kraimaster jumped down from the gate. His robes batted loudly on the air as he landed in front of Falcon with a thump.

"What are you doing here, professor?" asked Falcon.

"Zhut your mouth, Mizter Hyatt," ordered Kraimaster. He didn't bother to look back at Falcon; instead his eyes remained locked on the dark wielder before him. "You've cauzed enough trouble az it iz."

Me? What did I do? At least I haven't been hiding who-knows-where as the people of Va'siel suffered. At least that was what he wanted to say, but instead all he did was remain silent.

"I see you are a dual wielder like myself," said Draknorr, peering at Kraimaster. He brought his hands together and revealed his lightning and dark emblems. "Which means you have to be him. Drogan, the twin-headed serpent of Ladria."

Twin-headed serpent of Ladria? Falcon had never heard the professor be called by that moniker.

"Well, I suppose you're the one-headed serpent now. Your other half didn't survive my attack." He took a step forward. "Do you know how I killed her?"

If Kraimaster was fazed by his enemy's words, he didn't show it. His hardened face remained with its usual frown.

"I used the screeching banshee!" Draknorr cackled. "Oh, you should have heard her crying for her life, crying out your name for aid. It was pathetic!" His laughter grew loud and erratic. "Even as the Banshee tore her apart, she maintained the shield over the children. She could have saved herself had she not wasted the protection on them. That's why only fools care for others. It brings only destruction on oneself." He nodded his head. "And now look at you, Drogan. Ready to give your life for the same brat your wife died defending."

Falcon's mind received a burst of clear shock. He stood in place, but his mind was speeding through space. Were Draknorr's words really true? He had no recollection of such an event. It had to be a lie; it just had to be.

"Oh, so you don't know, boy," said Draknorr, noticing Falcon's confusion. His black armor plates clanked against each other as he took a few steps closer. The fauld jingled loudest of all. "I suspect a mind wielder's work. Grandmaster

Zoen, perhaps?"

Falcon ran to Kraimaster, his breaths heavy. "Is this true, professor?"

Kraimaster turned to Falcon with vengeful eyes, and for once he understood why the professor always hated him so. A lump formed in his throat as he struggled to apologize, but nothing came.

"Ztay out of my way, Mizter Hyatt." The professor's bony jaw trembled in anger. "I won't allow you to die and make my beloved'z zacrifice be in vain."

Slowly, Falcon moved back. He knew that no matter how much he wanted to get his hands on Draknorr, he could not. This was a one-on-one affair.

"I'll kill you both!" said Draknorr. He unsheathed the long double-edged sword that hung from his waist.

With a puff of smoke, an overly long scythe materialized in Kraimaster's hands. Its handle was pristine black. The long crescent blade at the end glistened as the moonlight bounced off it.

The weapons clashed.

Kraimaster twirled his scythe. The bladed part hooked his opponent's weapon. He brought it down. The sword hit the ground.

Falcon held his breath.

Draknorr pulled his sword free, but before he had a chance to mount an attack, Kraimaster came down on him with a flurry of scythe attacks.

The bladed weapons clanked as they smashed into each other time and time again.

Suddenly, a burst of red lightning burst from the sword's tip.

Kraimaster grunted as the lightning spread through his body. A second later, however, the lightning disappeared into his chest. He huffed and blew. Countless webs of red, blue, and green lighting flew from his mouth.

Falcon stood starry-eyed. He'd never seen anyone mix the elements like that.

As Draknorr stumbled back, trying to avoid the rippling attacks, a dark coffin took form behind him out of thin air. The dark wielder jumped back, unknowingly throwing himself into the trap. The black door shut, drowning away his angry yelps.

Falcon allowed himself a breath. Finally, that monster was going to die.

Kraimaster glanced at the ground under him. His eyes widened. "When did he have time to—" A giant scaly hand burst from the ground and took hold of the professor. Clear pus burst from the hand as its tightened its grip. With every passing second, the professor's face turned a deeper shade of red.

"Let me help you!" cried Falcon. He readied himself.

"No," said Kraimaster. He looked over at the coffin. "Liquid Decimation!"

Immediately the coffin turned into a thick liquid. Inside the moving mass of fluid Falcon made out a form struggling within. It kicked and punched wildly.

The coffin dissolved, and Draknorr crashed to the ground. Dark water dripped from every inch that covered his armor. Opposite of him, Kraimaster was also free. The hand that had encased him moments ago had now crumpled uselessly to the grass.

"Not bad, Drogan," said Draknorr. "A prolonged battle against you could lead to my demise." He held up his hands, as if baiting Kraimaster into attacking. "Unfortunately for you, I am not alone. The power of the Blood Empress is with me." He threw a small capsule that couldn't be bigger than a few inches into the grass. It burst instantly. A puff of smoke spread from it. At first it appeared as a shapeless mass of nothing, but slowly it took the form of a cloaked figure. The figure wore a feminine metal mask, dry blood gushing out of her eyes.

Blood Empress! mused Falcon. He had seen the leader of the Suteckh only once before. Of course back then he had no idea that it was Aya's sister who was behind the mask.

"Come to me," roared Draknorr. The ghostly image of the empress screeched a loud, unnatural sound as it drove into the dark knight's chest. His eyes glowed a blinding red. "Yes! The power of her highness has healed and powered me twofold. In your weakened state, you have no chance, Drogan."

Still frowning, the professor waved his hand. The scythe reappeared in his bony hands. "Not even the Blood Emprezz will be able to change your fate, Draknorr. You zhall perizh tonight."

Despite Kraimaster's brave front, Falcon was worried. The professor had obviously drained much of his energy. He no longer cared. He was going to help whether Kraimaster wanted his aid or not.

"Don't interfere!" ordered Draknorr. He brought both his hands together. Out of the balled fists a pale creature appeared. It resembled a malnourished woman mixed with a crow. Wrinkled skin sagged from her face. Hollowed pits resided where her eyes should have been. Instead of hands, she had long wings with dark plumage. "Get him, Screeching Banshee."

Screeching Banshee. It's the same creature that killed Kraimaster's wife. Before Falcon could form a strategy the woman took to the air, and then flew straight down at him, screeching loudly as it dove.

Every ounce of Falcon's body begged him to cover his ears. He had to drown out the sounds that rattled in his brain, threatening to drive him mad. Against his will, he forced his energy to drop in temperature. With a flick of his chilled fingers, icy spears shot forward. They clashed into the creature and dissolved harmlessly.

What in the world? His emblem changed into a deep

red. Fire spheres whizzed from his hands and into the woman's chest. Again, the attacks dissolved harmlessly.

Falcon braced himself, for the creature was now directly above him. It opened his screeching mouth even wider, exposing a set of evenly-aligned fangs. Falcon reached for his broadsword and drew it out. Without time to properly aim, he swung it wildly, barely missing the creature's head by inches.

The banshee flew back. Its saggy skin wobbled as it circled above. His nose wrinkled as the putrid stench of the banshee reached him. It smelled of dry blood mixed with rotten corpse.

The monster drew its sharp talons back and flew back in.

I got it this time. He brought up a fire net. The creature was coming down with such velocity that there was no way it could escape. But before he could bring his plans to fruition, the professor tackled him to the ground. He rolled through the grass violently, eating a mouthful of grass in the process.

Falcon stood up angrily, ready to demand an answer for the professor's actions. However, he grew silent as he noticed the blood dripping from Kraimaster's mouth and nose. He had six large holes in his robe, where the banshee had pierced him with its talons. The creature's torso lay on the ground as well. Its head had landed several feet away.

"This is priceless!" yelled Draknorr. "The first serpent

died saving this fool of a child and now the second serpent as well!"

Out of breath, Falcon threw himself by the dying professor. He looked down at the pale face that had tormented him for so many years. But, somehow, all the hate he had felt for the man was no longer present.

"Why did you do it?" demanded Falcon, his chest aching. "I had it in my grasp already. I had it."

Kraimaster opened and closed his eyes slowly. "You were going to die. Had to. Banzhee can only be harmed by dark attackz."

"You did this to save me?" asked Falcon. The hollow feeling deep in his stomach intensified.

"Farewell, Mizter Hyatt," whispered Kraimaster. His eyes closed. The frown remained.

Falcon's fury intensified. He craved nothing more now than to end the dark wielder, once and for all. With balled fists, he stood.

"Yes!" sneered Draknorr. "Now to take care of…" He paused. His head moved around as if he were searching for something. "Impossible, no one can escape my possession."

As if on cue, the door burst open. A shaky Aya stood by the entrance of her home. The dark rims around her eyes were no longer there, but she looked even angrier than before. Her gaze wandered over to the deceased Kraimaster and then back to Draknorr.

"I don't know how you escaped, girl, but you won't live to tell the tale."

Aya took off in a sprint. Draknorr fired balls of dark mass.

Falcon's heart turned into ice. He knew he was too far away to help Aya. The attacks were too close to her. There was no way she could dodge.

To his surprise she didn't try to dodge. Instead water engulfed her entire body as she sprinted. She grabbed the balls of mass with her aqua hands and crushed them as if they were nothing.

"Skeletal hand!"

A hand of dark bone burst from the ground. It took Aya in its grasp.

"Now die." Draknorr cackled. "Crush her."

Something was wrong. Falcon could see the hand squeezing, but Aya looked calm, almost bored even.

A second later, the sound of crackling bone echoed into the night.

Draknorr's eyes intensified again as his attack burst into hundreds of pieces. Out of the debris emerged Aya, still running, and still fully encased in water.

"Lightning wall." Red lightning crackled around Draknorr. "Let's see your water get me through aarghhh—"

"As you wish," said Aya.

A bubble of water surrounded the dark wielder's

armored face. His lightning dissolved as he flailed from side to side. Both his emblems glistened, ready to form an attack. Two large blocks of ice fell on his hands, crushing them to the floor. Even through the water, Falcon could hear a gargled scream.

Aya now stood directly in front of Draknorr. She touched the water on her prisoner's head with the tip of her finger and it turned into ice.

Before Falcon could assess what was going on, Aya uppercutted the block of ice. A thunderous blow echoed as the ice along with the helmet blew to the wind.

Falcon stood in shock. He had always thought Draknorr to be a human. But the red hollowed eyes, the four-pronged jaw that opened widely, revealing two sets of tongues, and the fur-covered face were definitely not human. He fell to his knees, his mangled arms dangling uselessly by his side as he looked up at the girl before him in awe, as if still in disbelief of what had just happened.

"This isn't over, girl," Draknorr finally said, his voice filled with wounded pride. "I took your sister, and I will take more and turn them before this ends."

"The dead can't take anyone," said Aya, as calmly as if she were describing the weather. Her hand drove back. A water lion appeared around it. A heart-stopping crunch emitted from Draknorr's neck as the punch landed under his chin, snapping his head back.

The hateful red in his eyes dimmed into dark coals as his head bounced off the ground and his breathing ceased.

Chapter 8

The three of them walked silently through the forest as they headed to Falcon's former home. Once Draknorr had been killed, Falcon had space wielded Kraimaster's lifeless body back to K'ran's home. Immediately after that, they hurried out of the city before the guards arrived in full force.

Falcon glimpsed over at Aya from time to time, trying to gauge what she was feeling. She walked with her head up, but Falcon could tell by her stern face that there was much going on inside her head. He had been far from her for months. He'd thought that seeing her again would be a cause for celebration, but instead it turned out to be a nightmare.

"Hear that?" asked Faith, a second before Falcon asked the same question.

"I think it came from the left," Aya added.

"Very good, Nakatomi," said a cheerful voice Falcon hadn't heard in quite some time. A tree before him twisted in circles until it became a mangled mess of dark brown. A second later Sheridan stepped out. He wore his usual trench coat that reached down to his knees. The tattoo over his right eye stood out from his pale skin. "I was hoping that I could sneak up on you, but I see that won't be happening."

Aya turned to him. "What are you doing here, Sheridan? I thought you were going to find Grandmaster

Zoen."

"I did." He scratched his head. "Well, he and Kraimaster found me to be precise." He scanned his surroundings with a confused look. "Speaking of that. Where is Hyromi? I thought she would be with you. And where is Kraimaster? Zoen sent him ahead to assess the situation in Ladria."

Falcon cleared his throat. "He's…" A pit formed in his throat. Days ago he wouldn't have thought Kraimster's death would affect him in any way. But now that it had actually passed, he found himself in disbelief.

"He's dead," whispered Faith. "Murdered by Draknorr. And Hyromi, well." Her eyes met those of Sheridan's. "We heard she was badly injured in a fight with the poison wielder, Dokua. We're hoping she's with her father."

"That's disheartening news," said a low voice. The air beside Sheridan twisted, and out of it emerged an ancient man with a large hump rising from his back. His dark robe flapped slowly as he scratched his wrinkle-marred face.

"Hello, Grandmaster Zoen," said Falcon, surprised that the ancient wielder had appeared out of a space rift. The grandmaster was powerful, yes, but he was a mind wielder, not a space wielder. That was until he noticed Sheridan's glowing emblem. Of course, Sheridan wielded him here.

The grandmaster looked around sadly. "Where is his body?"

"Back at my master's home," said Falcon. "We learned

that Emperor Romus is also there."

"And Hyromi, too, I'm sure of it," added Sheridan eagerly. He looked over at Zoen. "Master, you must head over to Ladria and avenge Professor Kraimaster's death. You're the only one capable."

Zoen's cane materialized in front of him. He moved forward at a snail's pace toward K'ran's cabin.

"You're going the opposite way," said Sheridan, pointing back toward Ladria. "Draknorr is that way."

"I think you'll find that the Suteckh general will no longer be a threat to the people of Va'siel," declared Zoen matter-of-factly. He didn't bother to stop, or even turn as he spoke.

Sheridan gazed over at Falcon, Aya, and Faith with an awed expression plastered across his face. "The three of you are amazing. You defeated one of the most powerful wielders of this era."

"Faith and I didn't do anything," said Falcon.

Now Sheridan craned his neck toward Aya. His jaw was so wide open that Falcon thought it might crash to the floor at a moment's notice.

"Don't say anything," said Aya. "I mean it." She still had the same bored expression on her face as she trudged behind the grandmaster.

Falcon looked on sadly at both girls. One was being hunted down by a mass murderer who had lived over ten thousand years and had defeated armies single-handedly.

The other had just found out her entire life was based on a lie, and to top it all off, her family was dead center in the Suteckh invasion.

Playing with his fingers nervously, he tried to find the right words to say to them, but no matter how deeply he searched, he couldn't shake the feeling that there was nothing he could say to help them.

Once again he was that child who stood defenseless as Volcseck murdered his mother before his eyes. Once again he was that boy who waited all night for his brother to return, the same brother who disappeared and abandoned him to fend for himself. Despite all the power he had gained throughout the years, he remained as powerless as ever.

He rubbed his stomach, taking in the warm feeling of anger stirring within. If he was to help them, he needed to rely on that unholy power, even if it meant his own demise.

~~~

The air smelled of medicine as they knocked on the door. Falcon felt weird doing so. With the death of K'ran, the old cabin belonged to him for all intents and purposes. Nonetheless, it felt wrong to simply barge in.

He staggered back as the door suddenly swung open with tremendous force. It snapped loudly as it bounced off the interior wall. A short, twitchy woman stood to greet them.

"Good to see some people using the door," said Doctor Solis. "Been having so many people appear out of strange ripples in the sky lately."

"Doctor Solis!" Aya exclaimed. For the first time in hours, Aya formed a smile as she hugged her medical mentor. "It's so good to finally see you."

The doctor tapped Aya's back awkwardly, almost as if she were trying to beat something out of her. "Very good to see you alive and well. Perhaps you can explain how people seem to be appearing everywhere."

"That's actually my fault," said Falcon. "I space wielded a group of children here and…"

"The dead man," finished the doctor.

"Yes," said Falcon, a bit irritated. It bothered him how she spoke of Kraimaster as if he weren't even human. But he remained quiet. He knew the doctor didn't mean it; it was just the way she was. Always rush, rush, rush.

"What are you doing here, doctor?" asked Aya.

"Emperor asked that I come here check on daughter. I come do that but then stay to keep on checking on her. Then kids come. Very malnourished. Nursing them back to health."

"Hyromi is fine. I knew it!" Sheridan rushed past the doctor so fast that he thought he might knock the small lady over. "Where is she? What do you mean by continuing to check on her? Is she in some kind of pain?"

"No. No pain whatsoever. However—"

Sheridan did a small dance which looked like some crazy mix of jumping jacks and spins.

Falcon didn't dance, but he did share in Sheridan's joy. He had been extremely worried, thinking that perhaps Hyromi could be seriously hurt, or worse. Now, he could finally breathe a sigh of relief.

The rest of the day was far less eventful. They went into the cabin and rested. Some of the kids came over to thank Falcon for what he'd done. But most of them kept their distance. Falcon couldn't blame them; he'd probably be acting the same if he'd gone through what they had gone through.

He had hoped to spend some time with Aya, but she had immediately locked herself in the guest room, along with Faith. He could hear their voices come through the thin wooden doors from time to time. He suspected they were speaking of what had occurred back in Ladria, which honestly saddened him a bit. Weren't they all supposed to be friends? Why were they ignoring him and leaving him out in the dark? He couldn't even count on the company of Sheridan. Upon hearing that Hyromi and her father had gone for a walk through the woods, he had taken off to search for them.

Falcon sighed as he looked out the window. From where he was standing, he could see Zoen sitting cross-legged over on a tree stump. He was chanting with his eyes closed, no doubt putting an enchantment over the area that would render the home invisible to any enemy that came near.

Restless and tired, he headed off to his room. He opened the long door and slowly stepped into his room. It smelled of musk and wood. He ran his fingers atop the grainy walls. Dust settled on his fingertips. Everything from the tidy bed to the painting of his hero, the Golden Wielder, that hung on the wall to the toy elemental glove on the floor took him back to those years he had spent with his master in the cabin: burning the stew, re-organizing the cabin, building a guest room from the ground up. How could he sleep with such memories of K'ran haunting him?

He closed the door and headed for the backyard. His stomach lurched as his eyes settled on the pile of rocks where his master lay. Next to it lay another pile of rocks, and above it was a piece of wood that read: 'Here lies Drogan Kraimaster'. Doctor Solis sure does work fast, he mused.

"Hello, Master K'ran," said Falcon as he walked in front of the grimy rocks. He swallowed the lump in his throat. He knew his master was gone and there was no chance he could hear him, but he needed to say something nonetheless. "Things haven't been going so well since you left us, master. The Suteckh have sacked Ladria. I've had some progress controlling the chaos inside me, but am still a long way from having full control." He sighed deeply. "I wish you were here to give me your guidance. But I have no guide. My father and mother are gone, my brother is gone, and now so are you." He reached out and felt the cold rocks. Soft green moss had overtaken some of them. "I'm afraid I'm going to need to give in entirely to the chaos. It is the only way I will be able to even stand a chance against Volcseck."

"I'm sure you'll find another way," said a voice. A hand landed on his shoulder and rubbed sympathetically.

Falcon breathed heavily. "I don't see how."

Grandmaster Zoen stood beside him. His eyes twinkled with sadness as he stared back at him, and for a split second he could have sworn that Zoen knew better than anyone else the power struggle he was going through. But that couldn't be true. No one in Va'siel knew what he was going through.

Zoen gave him a reassuring pat. "A good friend of mine told me that even in the darkest of nights, there is always moonlight to be found." He stared at the graves with great focus. "So you see, no matter how bleak our situations may be, there is always a light to guide us. It can come in many forms, be it a person, hope, love, or the desire to be the best one can be for the person who has left us behind."

"Yes," challenged Falcon. "But I doubt your friend had to face what I'm facing."

"You're right, he didn't go through exactly what you did." Zoen spoke softly, as if he were speaking to a child who didn't understand, which angered Falcon. He had enough people mocking him. He didn't need it from the grandmaster as well. "But, on the other hand, you also did not experience his tribulations."

"Whatever they were, I'm sure they were nothing special."

"You'd be surprised," said Zoen calmly. "The Golden Wielder faced many challenges in his life, as I'm sure you're aware of."

Falcon's mouth went dry. Indeed he was aware of just how unjust the legendary wielder's life had been. But despite these injustices, he had overcome. Could he do the same? Sometimes he thought he could. But every time he allowed himself to hope, something would bring him back down to bitter reality.

"Grandmaster?" asked Falcon, voicing a question he'd many times wondered. "How come you don't face Volcseck? The students at Rohad talk about your duel with the Golden Wielder. They say you fought him to a stand-still."

A wry smile came over Zoen. "I'm afraid those stories are greatly exaggerated. I was never a match for my good friend. If we ever tied, it was only because he was holding back."

"Oh," mumbled Falcon, feeling disappointed. "Then how come the Golden Wielder never even tried to put an end to Volcseck? Surely he had to know what Volcseck was doing."

"The Golden Wielder did attempt to find Volcseck." He took a long sip of his pipe, puffing out a trio of circles into the air. The air smelled of spiced cinnamon. "Volcseck knew this, so he hid himself from him. Even with the Golden Wielder's amazing energy-reading abilities, the chaos wielder's teleportation abilities allowed him to mask his signature very well."

Falcon scratched his head, blinking quickly. "He was scared of the Golden Wielder?"

"You could say that. This is all speculation, of course. But I'm not called the greatest mind wielder of my era for nothing. I'm certain that my deduction is correct." Zoen gazed at Falcon, his keen eyes full of knowledge. "I suspect Volcseck knew that fighting the Golden Wielder was too much of a gamble. He might have won, but then again, he could have lost. So he opted to simply forego the battle and wait until the Golden Wielder was no longer here."

Falcon smiled inwardly. All his life he'd heard nothing but how powerful Volcseck was. Many were the stories of his legendary feats: destroying armies, easily demolishing any wielder that got in his way, toppling entire kingdoms. To hear that the chaos wielder actually feared someone felt like a victory in itself. A small victory but better than nothing.

"But the Golden Wielder did not simply give up once it became clear he wasn't going to locate Volcseck," added Zoen. "He laid out a plan."

"A plan?" Falcon's curiosity peaked. This he had to know. "What kind of plan?"

"A story for another day, perhaps."

"But...but," said Falcon, looking around. "If there's a plan I think I should know it."

"Don't fret too much about it," said Zoen. "Ignore the

ramblings of an old man." Zoen tapped his shoulders reassuringly. "You're a good person. I'm certain that when the time comes, you'll do what is right and make these men proud." He motioned at the two piles of rocks before them.

"These?" asked Falcon, confused. "I could see K'ran being proud, but not Kraimaster."

"Why do you say that? Because he yelled at you? Didn't let you get away with anything? Demanded that you work harder than any other student? Gave you work study for any minor infraction?"

Falcon nodded. "Yes, that's pretty much it. He made my life miserable."

"Professor Kraimaster knew that you possessed a power unlike any other." Zoen retained his calm voice. It was so serene that Falcon was afraid the grandmaster would fall asleep in mid-sentence. "He made your life miserable, as you so adequately put it, to prepare you for the tribulations you were destined to face. He would have done you no favors by pampering you."

Falcon felt a cold lump of coal in his throat. How could it be?

Zoen turned and opened the door to head back into the house, but before he went in he stopped and took one last look at Falcon. "Things in this world are usually gray, not black or white as we would like them to be."

Still speechless, Falcon stared at the pile of rocks

before him, unsure of how to register this new information. "Th...thank you, professor." His breath came in quick bursts. He said his goodbye to K'ran and headed back into the home, still reeling from the news he had just gotten.

~~~

Falcon's ill mood lightened a bit once he opened the door and saw Hyromi staring back at him. Sure, he'd heard she was all right, but seeing her in the flesh made it all more real. She wore her usual tight-fitting blue jumpsuit. Her silky brown hair traveled down her back and ended at her thin waist.

"Nice to see you back," welcomed Falcon, taking a step toward her.

"No!" cried a chorus of voices around him. Falcon stared at the group of people standing in the living room, and that was when he noticed their worried faces. Everyone from Faith, Aya, Emperor Romus, Zoen, and even Doctor Solis wore a mask of sadness. The children he had saved cowered behind a sofa.

Falcon looked up and saw the thick, sharp icicles encrusted in Hyromi's fingers. She held them up, as if confused as to how they'd gotten there. She had blood across her waist, probably self-inflicted.

"Hyromi," said Aya tentatively. She walked slowly toward her. "I'm a water wielder too. Listen, you have to bring up the heat around your fingers. Or you could hurt yourself again."

Hyromi's eyes darted around in confusion. "Voices in my head! Telling me to...to...to—" She reached for her head, spike first. Aya raised her hand, and in an instant the icicles dissolved into mists of ice. Hyromi's hands landed on her head, unaware of how close she had come to impaling herself. She beat her fists on her skull. "Get out, get out, get out, get out..."

Emperor Romus came behind his daughter and grabbed her hands. Through tear-streaked eyes he begged her to stop, but she continued her relentless attack.

Faith marched up to Hyromi. She waved her hand, and a golden mist covered Hyromi's face. Faith snapped her fingers. Instantly, Hyromi's body went limp as she fell into a deep sleep.

Emperor Romus caught her before she fell. He hugged his daughter tightly, still sobbing.

Falcon stood in awe, scared for his friend and confused at what was going on.

Chapter 9

Hyromi sat in the corner of the living room. She muttered words under her breath as she held herself in a self-hug. "Where is he? He was there, there, there, there, there. I thought I saw him, him, him, him, him, him…"

A teary eyed Emperor Romus stood over her daughter, speaking softly to her. But he might as well have been invisible. She didn't pay him any mind.

"How could this have happened?" asked Falcon. His mind was racing, trying to register what he was seeing. Hyromi had always been a person full of life, bringing a smile to anyone she encountered. Now she seemed trapped inside herself, begging to get out.

"It be a poison wielder," said Doctor Solis. "Poison her mind, she did. Nothing my medicine can do to heal her."

Falcon gritted his teeth. He should have known. Chonsey had told him that Hyromi had dueled and killed the poison wielder, Dokua. But it looked as though the victory had come at a heavy price. Hyromi's mind had been twisted beyond any medicine on Va'siel. Wait. That's it! He faced Faith as hope energized him. "Faith, you can heal her, right?"

"Yes!" cried Emperor Romus. He took a hasty step toward Faith. "You're a holy wielder. Surely you can heal my precious daughter."

"I...I will try," said Faith. She glanced at the hunched figure in the corner. "But please don't get your hopes up. The damage done to her mind might be too great."

Emperor Romus grabbed Faith by her shoulders and shook her violently. "No! Don't say that. You must heal her!"

Fuming, Falcon took hold of the emperor and tossed him into the wall. "Don't touch her. This is all your fault!"

The emperor shook his head, as if unable to believe a simple commoner had dared put his hands on him. "My fault?" he asked, once he got over his shock.

"Aaaaaaarghhhh! Screams inside!" Hyromi beat her head with her fists. "Get out."

The emperor rushed to his daughter, but before he could reach her, Faith got in the way.

"Get back, please," she ordered.

"But—"

Zoen put his hand on the emperor's shoulder. "All this screaming is only aggravating your daughter's condition. I suggest you step back and let the young holy wielder try her method." The grandmaster faced Falcon. "You too, Mister Hyatt." Zoen's suggestion sounded more like an order, and both Falcon and the emperor stepped back and remained quiet, though Falcon still wanted nothing more than to put that pompous fool in his place.

"Do you think Hemstath can help her?" asked Sheridan as he stood beside Falcon. His usual wide smirk was absent, replaced by a mask of worry. "She can, right? She's a holy wielder, after all."

"I hope so," muttered Falcon. He felt a deep sorrow for his friend. Sheridan had been smitten with Hyromi for as long as he could remember. He was sure this was hurting him more than he let on.

Faith took a careful step toward the hunched figure in the corner. Her hand was held out, and a glittering mist flowed out of it and around Hyromi's head, surrounding her like her own personal solar system. This seemed to calm Hyromi, because she stopped yelling and hitting herself, and instead focused on touching the glow around her. The mist simply dissolved and rearranged itself as she ran her hands through it.

"Hyromi?" Faith crouched. "I'm Faith Hemstath. I want to help you."

The princess looked back at Faith with a look of confusion. "Voice tells me. Can't find him, can't find him..."

"Who are you trying to find?" asked Faith.

"Can't find him. Can't find him."

Faith closed her eyes and put her hand on Hyromi's forehead. To Falcon's surprise, the princess did not complain. Faith hummed quietly under her breath. After a few minutes, she turned to the emperor as Hyromi returned to playing with the mist.

Falcon felt his heart drop when she noticed Faith's

saddened expression.

"I'm sorry. She can't be fully healed."

The emperor, who up until now had looked hopeful, crashed to the floor, looking beyond defeated.

"I didn't say all hope was lost," said Faith, turning back to Hyromi. "I believe I can heal some of the damage that's been inflicted. However, we're going to need to go through sessions, at least two times a day for the moment. If she gets better, then we can lower the sessions to once a day."

"That mean she's going to have to come with us," said Falcon.

The emperor's eyes widened at this. "What do you mean by come with us?"

"I mean exactly what I said. Faith, Aya, and I are headed for Missea. You saw yourself what happened to Ladria. We need to warn them and get them on our side before the Suteckh sack them too."

"My daughter isn't going anywhere with you lot!" Emperor Romus moved toward Hyromi, but she backed away before he had a chance to get too close to her.

"It is the only way," said Zoen calmly. "Young Miss Hemstath must stay with Mr. Hyatt. He needs her to complete his holy training. And now…" He turned to the princess. "It looks as if your daughter needs her too."

"Then I will go with them," the emperor quickly added.

"I'm afraid that can't be done," said Zoen politely. "You

are needed here to rally your people. Draknorr may be gone, but the Suteckh army is still intact. We must use this moment of confusion to take Ladria back. The people of Ladria need you more than ever."

Emperor Romus looked from Zoen to Hyromi. Falcon could tell that he was trying to think of something, anything. Some clever ploy to refute Zoen's logic and prove that he needed to go with his daughter. But as the seconds trickled by, it became apparent that he had nothing to counter the grandmaster.

"Fine," he mumbled. Then he turned to Falcon, Aya, and Faith. "But you three better take—"

"Four?" Sheridan chimed in. "I'm going too. On my honor, I will make sure Hyromi is safe."

Falcon reeled back a bit. Never in his life had he ever seen Sheridan be so serious.

"You better." The emperor took another quick glance around the room and stormed out of the door, making sure to slam the door.

"Fool," mumbled Falcon under his breath.

"Don't say that," said Faith, looking offended. "He's failed his people, and now he thinks he might lose his daughter. It must not be easy being him."

"This wouldn't have happened if he had listened to me when I tried to warn him of the Suteckh threat."

"Yes, I know. But nobody is perfect. He made a

mistake. We all do, right?"

Falcon remained quiet. The anger in him wanted him to shout. To say that yes, not everyone was perfect, but what the emperor had done was beyond a mistake, it was pure idiocy. He cared more about parties and noble ranks than the safety of his own people. Staring into Faith's kind, emerald eyes made it impossible to voice his words though.

"So what now?" asked Sheridan.

Faith took Hyromi's hand and helped her up. "C'mon, sweetie. Come with me."

"Where are you taking her?" Aya asked.

"I'm going to begin the treatments now. The sooner the better." She opened the door, letting the sun sneak in in even rays of light. "But I'm going to need a few days to get her to a decent state. So no traveling for now at least."

Falcon nodded as Faith and Hyromi walked outdoors. Ideally he would leave at once, but Hyromi had been a good friend. How could he now deny her the help she needed?

During the following days, Falcon settled into the same routine. In the morning he would have breakfast and then head outside and train with Aya by the river. But it was much more than simple water wielding training. Aya had the most focused energy that Falcon had ever seen. Her ability to pinpoint power points was beyond human. If only he could learn to do the same, then perhaps he could retain some control over the elements, instead of relying on them to unlock at random moments.

Secretly, Falcon had hoped that he could use these training moments to speak with her, just as they used to do all those years ago. But, to his dismay, Aya acted much different. She was more silent and rarely spoke of anything that didn't have to do with the training. Obviously the news that she was a Suteckh had gotten to her.

On the third morning of their training, Aya showed up without her usual white blouse and black skirt. Instead, she wore a white martial arts gi and baggy brown pants. She steeped over the sharp rocks of the riverbank without flinching in the slightest.

Falcon cringed. "What happened to your clothes?"

"Those clothes have the emblem of the Nakatomi clan. A family entangled in lies. I won't be associated with that." Her face remained emotionless as she faced Falcon. "So, I was thinking today we could focus more on one particular element, instead of a group of them."

"Y…yes, let's do that," he muttered, deciding not to push the subject of her wardrobe.

"What elements do you think you have mastered?"

He scratched his head. "I think I have a good grasp of all the basic elements."

"Even mind?" asked Aya, with a look that told Falcon she didn't believe him.

"Well…not mind, but that's not really important. The

main ones that I need to control are holy and chaos. Chaos is the one that continues to threaten to overtake me, and holy is the element that I must master to control chaos. So I think I should focus on those."

Aya shook her head. "No. We're concentrating on mind."

"But I need—"

"No buts, Falcon. Mind wielding is the element that requires the most precision of all the elements. You can't simply go around throwing your immense pool of energy at anyone who gets in your way. That's what has been getting you into trouble up until now."

"Okay, then," said Falcon, mildly irritated. "Tell me what to do, then."

If Aya noticed his annoyance, she didn't show it. She pointed to the river, whose current was running slowly. "Pull up your pants to your knees and stand in the middle of the water. I will create spheres of ice by your feet. Without looking down, I want you to use your mind wielding to pinpoint these balls and gravitate them out of the river."

"Sounds easy enough." He hoped she couldn't hear the doubt in his voice. Of all the basic elements, he'd always hated mind the most.

He stood in the middle of the water and stared directly into the line of trees before him. A second later, he felt a small growth of icy energy floating beside his left foot. Without looking down, he focused his mind and called to it. The ball of ice glided out of the water and in front of his face.

"Good job," said Aya. "Now let's add a bit of movement."

The sound of an object rippling through the water surrounded him. No, not one object; he felt two, maybe three. He closed his eyes, trying to get some focus. That helped a bit but not nearly as much as he'd hoped. He still couldn't pinpoint the ice balls. One moment he would feel them circling by his right foot, the next second they were beside his left ankle.

Concentrate, Falcon. His hand reached out. "Come forth." Two ice spheres shot out of the water, smashing into each other and blowing frozen ice chunks into his face.

"I got it!" he cried.

Aya gave him a wry smile. "It was a bit…unrefined, but yes, you did get them." She waved her hand, and Falcon felt the icy energy under the water return. "Now let's see if you can do it without blowing them to oblivion?"

~~~

The lesson dragged on most of the morning, with Falcon finding mild success. He managed to get three spheres out of the water intact, but anything over three proved impossible.

Aya told him she was impressed with his performance, but Falcon was sure she only said that to make him feel better.

After the training, they headed back to the cabin. Faith and Hyromi were in the front yard. They were sitting face to face, holding hands. A light glow surrounded them.

"How is it going?" Aya whispered to Sheridan, who was sitting on a tree stump outside the white fence.

Sheridan smiled, looking much happier than Falcon had expected. "Hemstath is amazing. She actually got Hyromi to speak in full sentences for a bit."

"That's great," said Falcon, feeling more hopeful than he'd felt in a while. "What are they doing now?"

Sheridan shrugged. "Don't know. They have been like that for a long time now."

Both girls opened their eyes at the same moment and stood.

Faith took Hyromi's hand. "Let's head inside."

"Yes." Hyromi droned. She looked lost, as if her body was here, but her mind was somewhere else.

Falcon and Aya followed them inside, where a warm fire roasted on the chimney. Three cinnamon scented candles rested atop the kitchen table. Flanking it were a dozen plates of food.

"I didn't know you knew how to cook, Doctor Solis," Falcon said hungrily. He rubbed his growling stomach as he eyed the bowls of clam soup resting on the table.

"Before becoming doctor, cook I was." She poured

steaming milk into the empty mugs.

"Doctor Solis is the best cook I've ever met," said Aya, looking hungrier than Falcon. She took a seat on one of the empty chairs and reached for each of the food bowls at the center of the table. By the time she was done, her plate had a little bit of everything: drumsticks, bread rolls, clam soup, and dried berries.

Faith, being a vegetarian, only put berries on her plate.

Falcon winced, wondering how she could ever go without meat.

"Is there a place for me?" asked the emperor. Before anyone could answer, he took a seat on the large dark chair that rested at the end of the square table. It was the same chair that had once belonged to Master K'ran. Despite his annoyance at this, Falcon remained quiet. He focused on his food and let his anger at the man dissipate.

"So…" said the emperor. "How goes the healing session, holy wielder?"

"Very good," answered Sheridan. He seemed a bit happier than before. "She spoke a few words and even seemed to recognize her surroundings for a second."

He reached into a bowl and took a pichion drumstick, taking a large bite out of it. "I wasn't speaking to you, was I, boy?" His lips smacked loudly as he chewed with his mouth wide open.

Falcon took a deep breath. Obviously, the fact that

Zoen had returned to Ladria had put the emperor back in his talking mode.

"We are making very good progress." Faith gripped Hyromi's hand proudly. "I have managed to clear much of the mist obstructing her mind. I'm sure that she will soon be able to recognize people."

"That's it!" The short man stood as he slammed the table with his fist. The bowls of food bounced before settling back down. "All these days and that's all you have managed? To have her behave like a common chimp?"

Hyromi stood. Her body shook violently.

"Calm down, sir," Faith warned. "Can't you see you're scaring her?"

Emperor Romus pointed an accusing finger at Faith. His wrinkled face turned a deep shade of red. "This wouldn't be happening if you would only do your job properly. You're a holy wielder. Where are all those legendary healing abilities I read so much about?"

"Don't speak to her that way!" Falcon stood, sending the chair he'd been sitting on clattering to the floor. "She's been doing a great job with Hyromi." He stood face to face with the short man, fuming. "This is all your fault! This happened because of your insolence!"

"My head," shrieked Hyromi. The next series of events seemed to last hours, though they were mere seconds. The princess swept her hand over the table, sending bowls, mugs, meat, blueberries, and soup to the wooden floor. They crashed with a bang. The soup and milk intermingled in a pile of slimy mush as it raced across the uneven wooden floor. "So much noise. My head hurts!" She crouched down, banging her forehead on the hard table surface.

"Stop!" The emperor hugged his daughter.

She twisted his arm and, with a firm push, tossed her screaming father backward into the living room. He staggered back and fell over a wooden stand. The flower pot that had, until moments ago, rested atop the stand, shattered on the floor.

Blood ran down from Hyromi's forehead and down the side of her nose as she banged her head two more times.

Faith reached her hands around the princess and tried to pull her back, but even with Faith trying to hold her back, Hyromi still rammed her head into the table once more.

Falcon ran around the table, eager to get to his confused friend. Sheridan got there first.

Something strange happened. As soon as Sheridan's hand landed on Hyromi's shoulder she became as still as a rock. The entire cabin was ushered into a deep silence. Hyromi turned to Sheridan and took his hand as she stared into his eyes.

"I know you," she said. "I…I was thinking about you. Looking for you. Saw you in my dreams." Her hands reached around Sheridan as she took a step closer. Her head rested on his chest.

"Don't touch my daughter!" yelled the emperor, as he struggled to pick his large body up from the ground.

Hyromi's eyes widened. "Screams in my head. Screams in my head!"

Sheridan whispered something into her ear, and her eyes returned to normal, though she still retained a haunted look across her face.

Faith looked down at the red-faced emperor. Her finger came over her small lips. "Shhhhh. This is good." She spoke in a hushed whisper. "She finally recognized someone. She's making progress."

The emperor looked as if he wanted to continue screaming at the top of his lungs. His eyes travelled from Sheridan, to Hyromi, to Faith, and then to Falcon. Still shaking, he got on his feet and stormed out the door. Doctor Solis took ahold of the door handle before he could slam it again.

"I think you should leave, too," Faith suggested.

Falcon glanced around, trying to figure out who she was talking to. That was when he realized that she was looking straight at him. "Me?" He pointed at himself.

"Yes," mumbled Faith. "You and the emperor were the ones who caused this. Your presence right now will only aggravate Hyromi."

He lifted a finger, ready to protest, but a quick glance

around the cabin made him think twice. It was a mess, and whether he liked it or not, a lot of the blame fell on him.

"Fine," he said. Head hunched, he walked out the door, making sure to close it slowly as he stepped outdoors.

Why am I always screwing up? He leaned over the white fence and took in the woodsy smells. The stars had come out full force this night, illuminating the sky with their glow. Looking up at them reminded him of the space wielder, the Ghost Knight. He'd last seen him months ago, but his words remained with him: When I feel like I might lose myself, I think back to my most precious memories. You could try the same. Allow your dearest memories to become your barriers.

His brother had told him something similar when he told him to stop and listen without always being in a rush.

Albert? Where are you? Most people believed Albert to be dead, but Falcon refused to believe that. He was sure his brother lived. If he could find him and speak to him, then maybe some of the rancor he felt would go away. There were so many questions he had to ask. Questions that, left unanswered, only served to fuel his already substantial amount of anger. He had been so engrossed in his thoughts that he did not hear Sheridan approach from behind him.

"Hey, Hyatt."

Falcon turned, surprised to see him. "Shouldn't you be inside? Hyromi needs you."

"She fell asleep almost as soon as you walked out. I

laid her on the bed. Aya and Faith are going to look over her."

"That's good," said Falcon, feeling a bit relieved. "I was afraid I had screwed up things beyond repair. I'm good at that."

"Don't say that. You brought Hemstath. So in a way, you're also responsible for the progress Hyromi has had."

"That's really reaching, isn't it?"

Sheridan shrugged. "Perhaps. But like the Golden Wielder always said, 'If you can't find the light in the darkness, make your own.'"

"We're going to need more than wise words to help Hyromi." He thought back to that outgoing girl he'd known. His heart sank as he realized she was now lost forever. Never would she be able to smile the way she used to. Never again would she charm her way into getting what she wanted. Never would she be able to live a normal life. Instead she would always be a prisoner, trapped inside her own body, screaming to get out but never able to escape.

Sheridan stared directly into Falcon's eyes, which made him feel a bit uneasy.

"When I was ten years old, I was walking through the flea market," said Sheridan. "It is something I would do every morning. You know, head out and get the groceries for the meal of the night."

Falcon nodded, wondering what the point of this story was.

Sheridan took a seat on the old tree stump. "Most of that day is nothing but a blur, but there is one thing that I will never forget." His eyes turned dreamy. "That was the first time I saw her. She was the most beautiful girl I had ever seen."

"Yes," agreed Falcon, not wanting to say what he really thought. Hyromi was beautiful, but to him, Faith and Aya were on a class of their own. "She does have a beautiful smile."

Sheridan smirked. "Yes, she does. But that's not what I mean." He looked past Falcon and toward the stars. "My family has always been poor, but when I was a child, we hit an all-time bad. Both my father and mother had lost their jobs. They couldn't afford to feed my brothers and me. Being the oldest, I decided that I had to do something." His voice cracked ever so slightly. "I decided to kill myself."

"Kill yourself!" asked Falcon, shocked. He certainly hadn't expected such a revelation from his friend. "Isn't that a bit of an overreaction?"

"You had no idea how bad it was. We were literally on the brink of starvation. With me gone, there would be one less mouth to feed."

Falcon remained quiet, hanging on Sheridan's every word.

"Anyhow. I found the perfect place. Do you know that bridge that overlooks the garden sector of the city?"

"Yes," mumbled Falcon, thinking back to the red wooden bridge.

"Well, I was there, preparing for the jump. I had taken off my hat and shirt and thrown it on the floor. That's when I heard the bells of the royal horses. Sure enough, when I turned, the royal family was rounding the corner and coming straight at me. The emperor, the royal guards, the councilmen. They all passed by me without bothering to glance at me." His eyes lit up as he stared down at the grass. "In the rear of their group was Hyromi. And, without saying a word, she winked and tossed me a bag. At first, I was confused. Why would she give me this for no reason? But after a moment, it all became clear. She had seen the hat on the ground facing up, and taken me for a beggar."

"What was in the bag?"

Sheridan looked up. "Fifty pieces of gold."

"What?" asked Falcon, his head trying to register what he'd just heard. "Fifty? That's a fortune!"

His friend nodded. "Yes. It was that gold that got my family out of poverty. But it was much more than that. I was a nobody. Just another nameless kid from the streets. Yet, the princess of Ladria had reached out to me. Do you have any idea how wonderful that made me feel? She is physically beautiful, yes, but that's just a bonus. Her real beauty lies within. It is that beauty that I fell in love with all those years ago." Sheridan perched himself by the gate. "I don't mind in the slightest being there for her now, and for the rest of my life if need be."

As Sheridan finished speaking, Hyromi's scream rang out. "Where is he? Where is he? I saw him!"

Sheridan turned and rushed into the cabin.

Falcon pushed down the lump that had formed in his throat as he watched his friend disappear behind the door.

Chapter 10

Falcon wished that Faith and Aya hadn't woken him up so early. He'd gone to sleep late and was still tired. He didn't complain, though. They had already spent a week in the cabin. They needed to get on the road if they were going to reach Missea before a Suteckh attack.

Falcon knew the woods inside and out, so he led them through the narrow path that took them to the Nalia desert. Ideally, they would have travelled on horseback. Speed was essential; horses, however, were too loud and would be too easy to spot. Not to mention the fact that, in her current condition, Hiromy was in no shape to ride a horse.

"We're going the wrong way," said Hiromy for the third time in the last few minutes. "We're going East, but Missea is West."

Falcon was glad at just how quickly Hiromy's speech had improved. The sessions with Faith and being around Sheridan had obviously boosted her recovery. Nonetheless, he wished she wouldn't ask the same questions over and over again. They were becoming tedious.

"I told you," said Sheridan. "We need to go to the desert first."

"Oh, yes, right," Hiromy said as she nodded her head

eagerly. "I think I understand now." She took a few more steps before voicing another inquiry. "What are we going to the desert for?"

"We can't travel through the main roads to Missea because they are all being patrolled by the Suteckh," Faith explained calmly. "We also can't take any travel ships because those on the port are being inspected by the Suteckh. Which means we only have one option. Pirates."

"Pirates are scary," said Hiromy worriedly. She cringed and took Sheridan's hand. Her scared eyes darted around her, scanning the many trees and bushes that surrounded them.

I can't blame her, mused Falcon. He also cringed at the prospect of seeking help from a pirate. They were just a lot of conniving thieves in his eyes. They cared for nothing but riches, fame, and gold, which was why now the Rohads found themselves headed into the desert in search of oil rocks. The dark rocks could power up a ship for weeks, sometimes even months. They were dangerous to obtain, but if they could get their hands on one, then they could exchange it for safe passage to Missea.

Aya held her hand up, signaling everyone to stop.

"I hear voices," she said in a hushed whisper. "Sounds like a patrol." She pointed to a large green bush to their right. "Behind there, everyone."

The five wielders wasted no time. They ran and huddled behind the bush.

For a moment, Falcon was afraid that Hiromy might start talking and give away their position, but she remained silent.

Through the small gaps between the leaves and branches, he saw a group of a dozen men move at a steady pace. Two of them were mounted on horseback. They wore black uniforms with white helmets.

"They're no patrol group," whispered Falcon. "Those two are Suteckh commanders. No doubt they're going to reinforce their Suteckh forces at Ladria."

"I know," said Aya. "But there's nothing we can do about it. We'll just have to let Zoen and the others figure a way to stop them. We have our own mission."

Falcon cursed silently as the commanders and their escorts moved down the path and out of view. Letting the enemy simply walk away made him feel like a traitor.

Faith was the first to stand. "They're gone. Let's keep on moving."

Annoyed but ready to press on with his quest, Falcon stood and continued to lead the small group. It was mostly a silent quest. Once in a while Hiromy would say something random about a passing bird, or comment on the flowery scent the lilacs they passed emitted. But that was it. Everyone seemed too tired, sad, angry, or discouraged to speak.

When they finally reached the end of the forest, the two suns were about to descend.

"I think we can keep on going for a bit longer," Falcon suggested. "K'ran told me once that there is an oasis east of here. We should be able to reach it if we move at a steady pace."

The wielders nodded and trudged into the desert. It was barren, with only a random cactus plant dotting the red sand. Large rocks burst from the ground in uneven formations, making it hard to see beyond a few feet.

I hope I don't get us lost. Falcon didn't dare voice his worry out loud. The desert was large; any wrong turn could lead them in circles for hours, maybe even days. That was precious time they simply couldn't waste. And to make matters worse, the entire landscape looked like a crimson puzzle with no beginning or end.

"It's so beautiful!" Hiromy suddenly shrieked. She ran to a dry tumbleweed that had come to a stop by a prickly cactus. "It's like a maze in the shape of a circle." She moved around the tumbleweed, with mouth wide open. Her hand reached out to touch it, but at the last second she pulled back, as if the tumbleweed was much too precious to defile with human hands.

"It is beautiful." Sheridan took her hand. "But we have to keep moving."

She shook her head. For a moment it seemed to Falcon that she may burst out in one of her rants. But instead she waved goodbye to the tumbleweed and continued forward.

With each moment that passed, Falcon's nervousness grew. The stars and crescent moon had come out now, and he had yet to spot the oasis. Instead, all they did it seemed was move from one shapeless rock to another.

"I see a palm tree up ahead," said Faith. She pointed directly ahead, through an arched rock. "See it there?"

"Yes," Falcon answered, feeling rejuvenated. It wasn't the water from the oasis that made him glad. They had Aya for that. But the fact that they found the oasis meant that they were now only half a day away from the oil rock grounds. "Let's set up camp there."

Once they reached the small oasis, Falcon earth wielded a small shelter around the small pond and double palm trees. It was nothing special, just four simple earth walls that connected into a square. He left the top open so he could have a view of the night stars.

"Hey, Hyatt," said Sheridan. "How about you get a fire going for us? The night is chilly."

"Already on it." Falcon made a small circle of rocks and tossed a few dry twigs into the center. He waved his hand over them and a small flame burst out.

Sheridan lay down his blanket. "Put up a cover, will you, Hyatt?"

"I'll do that," offered Faith. "Falcon is still having a hard time with holy, and I think today he would much rather rest a bit."

"He's never going to learn if he doesn't try," said Aya as she laid down her blanket. "He needs to train if he's ever going to improve."

"Holy isn't like water wielding, Aya." Faith waved her hand. "Malawi Lesotho." A rainbow-colored, almost invisible sheet appeared over all the blankets. "There is a lot of feeling involved in it. Pushing when holy is still not wholeheartedly felt is a mistake."

"What is that supposed to mean?" asked Aya. There was a layer of annoyance in her voice.

"It means exactly what I said. Pushing through with training may be the method of choice for some basic elements, but it's not what works for holy." Faith took a seat and stared at Falcon. "What do you think, Falcon?"

Falcon looked from one girl to another. The fire suddenly felt hot. Very hot. Ever since they had met, they had been good friends. The two of them arguing, with himself caught in the middle, was not something he had anticipated.

"I...er...I..." He pulled down his collar, which felt as though it was chocking him.

"I'm going to have to take Hemstath's side on this one," said Sheridan.

Thank you, Sheridan. Falcon took a breath.

Sheridan sat next to Hiromy. "I know the books say that they are the same, but the Ghost Knight told me that pushing an advanced element too much can actually be a step back in training."

Aya narrowed her eyes. It almost looked as if she was going to punch Sheridan on the spot. But she suddenly took a seat and nodded. "I'll take your word for it, then. You two are the advanced wielders, after all. I just hope you're not making a big mistake, Faith."

"Thanks for your concern," said Faith. "But I think Falcon will be fine."

Falcon remained silent, hoping that Faith's trust wasn't misguided. He wasn't the only one. The entire camp fell eerily quiet, their heavy breaths the only sound that could be heard. Falcon fondly thought back to all those happy memories he had shared with his friends. Loud memories of jokes, banter, and conversations. He missed those innocent times. If only the Suteckh had never declared war. If only they had remained in their empire, then perhaps they would still be that way. But no matter how much he wished it, that would never be the case.

"I want to dance," Hiromy suddenly blurted out, breaking the awkward silence. She stood and pulled on Sheridan's hand. "Dance with me again."

"She remembers!" cried Sheridan. He held Hiromy close as he slipped his hand around her waist.

"I know how to sing a little," said Faith, shyly. "I usually don't sing, but if it will help Hiromy, I'll make an exception."

She cleared her throat and began to sing. "Little wielder boy resting under the spruce. What are you doing, my little wielder? You took your mother's love and ran away with it. Oh, my little wielder boy...."

As Faith sang, Falcon stared at Aya, who looked down at the ground quietly. Remembering how much she liked to dance and hoping to make her feel a little better, he got up and walked to her. He held his hand out, without muttering a single word. There was no need to; she knew what he was asking.

She looked up at him with sad eyes, taking his hand and allowing him to pull her up into his arms. He held her close as he swayed to the slow-moving song. The strawberry scent of her hair and the touch of her warm arms gave his skin goosebumps in a thousand places.

With Faith's soft voice in the background, he danced the night away in silence, hoping Aya wouldn't notice how nervous he was.

~~~

The following morning, they got up before the first ray of light made it into their earth camp.

"Why are we moving so early?" complained Sheridan. "My legs need a rest from last night."

"No whining," said Aya. "We're running late on our mission as it is."

Frowning, he got up and rolled his sleeping bag.

The rest of the morning they moved over the windy sands. The occasional weathered tree was the only thing that interrupted the usual scenery of tall cacti, large rocks, and dry tumbleweeds.

"I think I see it there," said Faith.

Falcon narrowed his eyes, trying to make out what Faith was pointing at. It didn't look like much, just a blob of black off in the distance.

"Are you sure?" he asked.

"Yes, I am." She frowned. "But I also sense something dark there."

Sheridan smirked happily. "That's good, isn't it, Hemstath? You sense something dark, and the black coals are dark. Makes sense."

"That's not what she means, Sheridan," said Aya, rubbing her temples. "I think she means something more like a being, or a creature."

Faith bobbed her head.

Falcon refrained from speaking. They were all tired, not to mention sleep deprived. The hot air blowing around wasn't making things any easier. He was certain that all these things were playing with Faith's head. It made no sense whatsoever that someone would make a home around the oil rocks. Miners were known to make seasonal camps around the oil grounds, but that was only during the frost, when mining was safer because of wild animals staying in caves to hibernate.

But right now they were in the middle of the scorch season. No one should be this deep in the desert. No one in their right mind, that is.

As they moved closer to the dark blob of matter, Falcon began to rethink his stance. The shapeless blob now became countless dark rocks that glittered brightly under the suns. From afar, it looked as if a sea of stars had fallen from the sky and condensed in that very spot. A large, dark wall of rock that went up over one hundred feet was directly beside the pile. No doubt, the wall had supplied all the oil rocks beside it.

"What in Va'siel is that?" asked Sheridan, referring to a large brown mound above the rocks. It moved up and down, almost as if it were breathing.

Tentatively, the young wielders took quiet steps forward. The closer they got, the louder the snoring became.

That was when Falcon realized the truth. That's no rock. It's a sandworm!

Chapter 11

Falcon analyzed the creature with utmost awe. He'd heard many stories of sandworms, though he'd never dreamt he would get to see one in real life. The Golden Wielder himself had been known to have tamed them in his time, though Falcon doubted he would be able to replicate such a feat. The creature before him was gigantic, easily over forty feet in length. It had a circular set of fangs around its mouth. Its skin looked hardened, as if it was made out of rock.

"What now?" whispered Faith.

Falcon shrugged, unsure of what to do to get past such a gargantuan creature.

"This is all wrong," said Sheridan. "I didn't pay much attention in animal class, but even I know that sandworms are native to Missea. What is one doing way out here on the outskirts of Ladria?"

"My guess is that it was left to protect the oil rocks," Aya said quietly. "I've heard stories of sandworms being trained from birth by large corporations. It was probably left here so that no one else could take the rocks during the scorch season."

"The reason doesn't matter," said Falcon. "We need to find a way to get the rocks without waking it up. Anyone have a plan?"

"I do." Aya took out a small leather bag from the pouch she'd been carrying. "I can be very light on my feet. I will tiptoe over there, get what we need, and come back."

Seeing that no one had any better plans, they all watched as Aya slowly made her way to the black rocks. Falcon cringed as Aya walked beside the sleeping worm. Every breath from its massive body made his heartbeat skip a beat. What if it woke?

Luckily, Aya seemed to know what she was doing. She crouched down, ever so carefully picked up a few rocks, and placed them in the bag. She moved at a steady pace, and in a matter of seconds the bag was filled to the top. She turned, gave them a thumbs up, and began walking back to them.

"It's a wormy!" Hiromy suddenly shrieked. "I want to go touch it." Before Falcon could figure out what was happening, Hiromy took off in a full sprint.

"Come back!" Sheridan half yelled and half whispered. But if the princess heard him, she didn't show it. She ran over the oil rocks at top speed with her hands held before her.

The worm sprang to life. It moved its head from side to side. It spotted Hiromy and roared at the top of its lungs. Even from afar, Falcon took in the rotten stench that emitted from the creature.

Hiromy seemed to have decided that petting the giant, man-eating worm probably wasn't the best idea. She moved back, muttering gibberish under her breath.

"Get away from her!" Sheridan dashed toward the worm. As he ran, he twirled both arms in a tornado-like fashion. From them, small meteors shot at the worm. The rocks bounced off the creature's thick skin with next to no effect.

That's never going to work, thought Falcon. He needs more power. Determined, he jumped into the fray, calling on his immense pool of energy. He threw himself in the air, feet first. He converged his energy in his stomach and then redirected it down to his legs. The air in front of his soles warmed as uneven lines of fire shot out. One missed the worm's face by mere inches, but the second attack hit it directly above its jawed mouth.

With staggering speed, the creature ignored the attack and jerked its body.

Falcon's eyes widened, as he noticed the large mass of hard flesh headed his way. Quickly, he jumped into the air, using wind to boost his jump to twenty feet in the air. He landed safely out of the worm's reach.

The creature growled angrily and slid toward Falcon.

Wind boost. Once again, Falcon called on the power of wind to take to the air. The creature, however, was smarter than Falcon had anticipated. It recoiled the top part of its body, almost as if it were forcing its head into itself. Then, with surprising agility, it jumped into the air with its mouth wide open.

Falcon's chest clenched as he noticed he was about to become lunch. Even if he wind wielded to the right or left, there was no way he was going to dodge in time.

Falcon was inches from becoming a meal when what appeared to be a translucent rainbow wall crashed into his face. A second later, the worm pummeled into the same wall. It screeched in agony as it crumpled to the floor, landing with a thunderous thump. The tall rocky wall beside them cracked, sending thousands of smaller rocks rolling down to join the oil rocks that had already fallen.

"Thanks for the shield, Faith," said Falcon, heaving with relief. "I thought it was over for me."

Faith nodded as she brought the shield down.

The worm shook its head, trying to regain its senses.

"We have to hit it together!" yelled Falcon. "Its body is too strong."

"No," countered Aya. She stood beside the other four wielders. "There's no use wasting our energy on this animal. Even if we beat it, there is no strategic advantage in it. We came for the rocks." She held the bag up. "And we got them."

"What do you suggest, Nakatomi?" Sheridan spoke in a hasty speech, as his eyes remained locked on the worm that was seconds away from continuing its attack.

"You and Falcon need to space wield us out of here. Send us to—"

"Watch out!" Faith's cry barely came in time. The four wielders scattered to the ground, dodging the worm's wild attack by inches. It quickly turned its head, drool dripping from its fangs as it brought its body down on the wielders.

"Aqua Trianja!" Without warning, a water trident half the size of the creature flew through the air and rammed into the back of the worm's head. It didn't pierce the hard skin, but it was enough to knock it out. The ground shook as the creature dropped face first into the rocks. It remained there, motionless.

"Great job, Aya," said Falcon, shocked. He'd seen Aya create water attacks before but never to such a scale.

Aya got to her feet. Her clothes were caked in black from the oil. "That wasn't me."

"Then who? Hiromy?" He looked around himself, and sure enough, she was standing behind them, huffing loudly.

"The monster almost squished Sheridan," she said between breaths. "Couldn't let it."

"Let's hurry and get out of here before it wakes up," Aya suggested.

Nobody argued with her as they all grouped up together.

Sheridan looked worried. "I don't think Hyatt and I are good enough to get us as far as Makeda. I've only been there once. It's going to be hard for me to picture the village."

"I've been there a few times," said Falcon. "Let me think of most of the images, you just provide the space energy."

Sheridan nodded and closed his eyes. Falcon did the same. Unlike other elements, space energy was more highly condensed in the eyes. He felt the power emit from there, until it travelled down to his chest and to the tip of his fingers.

The energy of the cosmos slowly surrounded them. Sheridan's energy was much more refined than his, but his had more raw power.

A large black hole opened and, without much of a whimper, the five wielders were pulled into it.

~~~

Their fall out of the black hole was less than graceful, to say the least. Falcon and Sheridan were the first to come out. They landed hard on their backs. Ignoring the pain, Falcon looked over at Sheridan, who was grunting under his breath.

Before he could ask where the girls were, three bodies rained from above, one of them landing on him.

"You were supposed to bring us out vertically," said Aya as she stood. Her clothes were now not only stained with oil but grass as well. Her silky hair, usually perfect, looked like a matted mess.

"Sorry," said Falcon. "I tried, but we don't coordinate all that well together." Memories of the Tiaozhan game he and Sheridan had lost to Laars flashed in his mind. He reached out to Hiromy, who had landed on him and wasn't moving, and tapped her shoulder. "Hey, are you okay?"

She lifted her head from his chest and smiled at him.

"Yes." Her eyes were full of wonder, like a child with a new toy. "I was listening to your heart. It beats at such a wonderful rate. I could listen to it all day."

"I'm sure my heart also beats at a wonderful rate," said Sheridan, hastily picking himself up. "If you ever want to listen to it!"

Hiromy stood, still smiling. "No, it's fine. I've had my fill for the day."

Sheridan frowned but refrained from saying anything else.

"So where are we?" asked Faith. Like Aya, her clothes were covered in grass stains. Her hair, too, was not as pristine as it usually was. He'd expected as much. After all they had crossed a forest, traversed a desert, and fought a sandworm in a matter of days.

"It looks like the riverbank that leads to Makeda." Aya turned toward the space wielders. "Good job, guys. You saved us a long walk."

Falcon took in their surroundings. Indeed, they were on a grassy prairie beside a raging river. Salmon jumped out of the water in perfect arcs, landing with soft splashes. No doubt they were on their annual migration. Off in the distance, a large jade mountain chain rose from the ground. A few scattered pine trees dotted the area around them but not too many. If this were any other time, Falcon thought, this would be the perfect place to have a picnic. Perhaps even fish for the day or go hunting. But it was not one of those times, and the way things were headed, he doubted it was ever going to be.

"Which way do we go from here, Nakatomi?"

Aya pointed south. "We follow the river. It will take us directly to the port village of Makeda. We'll find who we're looking for there. At least I hope we will."

The wielders took off, following the winding river. The scenery didn't change much. Once in a while they would see an elk in the distance, but they would all take off after they heard Hiromy's cheerful screams.

Falcon walked beside Aya. "You look tired."

"I am very tired."

"A lot has happened in the last few days. Do you want to talk about it?"

"No. I'm fine."

Falcon swallowed hard, trying not to show his uneasiness. He'd known Aya for years, and though she wasn't one to whine and complain about her problems, she never had a problem talking to him about what was going on with her. In a way he felt as though he was losing her. Or at least losing the friendship that he had counted on for so long.

Nonetheless, not wanting to impose, he left her alone.

A few steps ahead of him, Faith and Hiromy walked, deep in conversation. He couldn't hear everything they said, but he did make out a few words here and there coming from Faith.

"You shouldn't just run toward everything you see," she said. "It could be dangerous."

"But I just wanted to touch it." Hiromy glared at Faith, her smile turning into a frown. "I like animals."

"Me too. They are my favorite. But we must be careful. Some of them will attack you."

Hiromy looked confused. "Why? I just want to be their friend."

"They don't understand. So we must be careful."

The princess kicked small pebbles under her. "I don't understand. I...I..." Her body began to shake. She threw herself on the floor and sat cross-legged. The stone pebbles crunched loudly as she repeatedly beat them with her balled fists. "I don't understand, don't understand..."

Sheridan, always at the ready when it came to Hiromy, ran to her and placed his hand on her shoulder. This seemed to calm her a bit. She stopped hitting the ground, though she continued to nod and mumble under her breath.

"What happened?" asked Sheridan, his eyes glassy.

Faith answered without a moment's hesitation. "It's my fault. I was trying to help her." Her voice was full of guilt. "I didn't intend to trigger another outbreak."

"No," said Sheridan, helping Hiromy up to her feet. The princess rested her head on his shoulder. "You were just helping. She's tired, that's all. Once we get to Makeda she should nap for a few hours. I'm sure that will help."

Falcon, however, had his doubts. Hiromy had been showing progress in the last few days. Now, it looked as though she had reverted back to her old self. Who was to say that this wouldn't be a common occurrence? Taking two steps forward, just to later take three back.

"Hey, Hyatt!" yelled Sheridan. "Are you just going to stay back there?"

Sheridan's voice brought him back to the present. "No. On my way."

As they walked across the riverbank by the meadow, they spotted signs that they were getting closer to the village. Trees that had been cut down to the stump. Broken fishing rods that had been left atop large rocks. Stomped grass where picnic blankets had been set up. Shrubbery that had had all its blueberries picked clean off.

Sure enough, as they took a sharp turn to the right, off in the distance, veiled by a white mist, was a collection of buildings. From afar it appeared as nothing more than a blob of brown and gray, nestled between a large blue sea on one side and a mass of green on the other.

But as they got closer, the details took shape. Dozens of sea-faring ships bobbed serenely on the pier, being held by thick rope tied to their metal poles. The ground that led into the city was paved in yellow stones that had been carved evenly to create a flat walking ground. There was no wall around the village, which exposed row after row of tall buildings. In the streets, there were hundreds of people milling about. Many carried nets of freshly caught fish over their shoulders. Others sat atop horse-drawn wagons filled with everything from squid to seaweed, rice, salmon, carps, or mollusks.

"This place is almost as big as a capital city," Faith said.

Aya inclined her head, her attention fully on Makeda. "I suspect in a decade or so it will be a capital city. It's a hub for trade of all sorts." She held up the stained leather pouch of oil rocks. "Lucky for us, this also draws in pirates looking to sell the loot they've stolen. All we need to do is ask around a bit and I'm sure we can find information on one."

"You guys go on your search." Sheridan looked from Falcon to Faith. "I need to take Hiromy to rest."

"Agreed," said Aya. "Besides, the fewer people we have the better. We don't want to raise too much suspicion. The guards here are constantly on the lookout for pirates."

With that in mind, they moved into Makeda in search of an inn. It didn't take long. A few short steps into the village, and Falcon spotted a large wooden building with the words The Fisherman's Haven above the redwood door.

"These people sure love their fish," said Sheridan with a slight frown. "Even the village reeks of it."

Falcon couldn't argue with that. One of the first things he noticed when he neared Makeda was the fishy, almost salty aroma that hung in the air.

"They are a fishing town, after all," said Faith with a slight frown. "Kind of sad all those poor animals have to die, though."

"As long as they have some nice flowers to mask the stench inside the rooms, they can kill all the fish they want." Sheridan led Hiromy into the inn as he waved goodbye. "See you three in a bit. Come back with good news."

Falcon remained silent as he looked down at the ground. Finding a pirate was not going to be easy. Many of them would probably be out at sea, looking for their next big cargo to steal. And even if they did find one that took them in, who was to say they would not turn on them once they were at the middle of sea? Pirates were a deceitful, cowardly lot. More likely to kill their own mother for a gold coin than help someone in need.

"Let's go to the pub," said Aya, mirroring Falcon's own idea. "That's the best place to find some information." She pointed down the busy street. "If I recall correctly, it's down this way, toward the pier."

"After you," said Falcon, motioning Aya to lead the way.

The trio of wielders pushed through the crowd of people, which was hard to do, thanks to the puppet show that was going on. A man inside a cart, covered mostly by a red curtain with an opening at the middle, had set up a small play. Two puppets moved through the opening in some weird strange dance Falcon had never seen before. The kids seemed to like it. Their loud laughter and snickers drowned out all other noise.

"Excuse me," he said, as he squished between a chunky lady and her equally large son. "Many pardons. Let me just get through here." When Falcon and the girls finally came out through the other side, he felt as though he'd run a marathon. "That's something I never want to do again."

Unfortunately, the rest of the path wasn't much better. They had chosen the worst time of the day to arrive at Makeda. Most of the fishing ships were coming in, bringing in their morning catches, which meant that the streets were nearly impossible to navigate. Falcon lost count of how many times people stepped on his foot, or how many times he was slapped across the face by a careless fisherman swinging his net of carp, salmon, or mollusks.

"There it is," said Aya. She pointed at a medium-sized building. It had a dirt-stained window on its left side and a muddy straw and stick roof. It was strange seeing it, surrounded by buildings made of stone and brick. It was almost as if the pub had escaped from another time and forced itself into this era.

The pub fell silent as they pushed open the creaking door and trudged in. Dozens of men who sat in front of circular tables playing card and emblem games looked up at them. For a moment, Falcon thought they were going to throw them out, but after a long glance, they all returned to their drinking and games, seemingly uninterested in the newcomers.

They walked over to the only empty table, on the edge of the pub, and took a seat. Laughter and loud voices bounced off the walls. A short lady sat in a chair at the end of the pub, singing a lively tune as two men behind her played soothing melodies on their long flutes.

"Can I get you kids anything?" asked an older-looking lady. She wore a tattered dress and her face was grimy with dirt.

"Just some water would be fine," Aya responded.

The lady frowned. "You do realize that you're in a pub, right? We don't serve water. Either you get some of the strong stuff or get gone."

"Three mugs of berry wine will do, then," said Falcon. He lowered his voice. "And we would also like some information."

The woman raised an eyebrow.

"Where could we find a pirate?"

"I don't know nothing about no pirates." The lady swayed with uneasiness. "And I think it's best if you don't speak about that in here." She turned and hastily made her way behind the bar.

Falcon's questioning eyes moved between both his companions. "What's gotten her so riled?"

"Oh, don't mind Old Miss Rose," said a loud husky voice behind them. Falcon turned to see a large man sitting on the table next to them. He had a nasty scar running across his forehead, and long dreadlocked hair. "She simply doesn't like when people with no brains go around poking into things that aren't to be meddled with." He motioned at the small insignia attached to Falcon's jacket. "Especially when those asking are Rohads."

"What's wrong with Rohads?" asked Aya, caressing her own insignia of the double dragons.

"Let's just say that Rohads have a tendency to meddle with pirate affairs."

Aya nodded knowingly, and Falcon was certain she knew exactly what the man was talking about. She'd read every book there was on Rohad missions, after all. Many of them told stories of skirmishes and battles between pirates and Rohads who had been charged to bring them in to answer for their crimes.

"Today we're not here to take anyone in," she said. "In fact, it's the complete opposite. We want to work together with them."

The man clapped his large belly as he erupted in a fit of laughter. Once done, he took a large sip from his mug and slammed it back down, sending the little brown liquid that was left pouring down the sides and onto the table. "You hear that boys? These Rohads are in the business of working together with pirates." He said Rohads with spite, as if it were a worm he needed to squish under his heavy gray boots. "As if we're not all aware that it is them that have taken most of us to the law."

Falcon couldn't help but notice that the man had said, us. They were in the right place, after all, which didn't necessarily seem like a good thing. Most of the men were staring at them with bulging, murderous eyes.

"We want no problem with anyone," said Faith softly. "I don't know about any previous Rohads you've met, but these two are honorable. They speak the truth."

The man smirked and took another sip from his mug. "I suppose I'll just take the word of a nobody." He belched loudly toward them as ale dripped down his long, red mustache. His thick fingers ran over his chin and he hummed thoughtfully. "No. It would be much easier to simply kill you all." Many of the men stood, reaching for the curved swords hanging by their waists.

Once again, Faith smiled, seemingly worry free. "I don't think you want to do that."

"And why is that? I'm Captain Redclaw, master of the finest ship in the sea, The Crimson Maiden. I sail the seas, helping lowly folk who can't help themselves. I am the master of my own destiny!"

"What a cute name!" shrieked Faith. "Crimson Maiden. Why do you call it that? Is there a beautiful figurehead at the front of the ship?" Faith spoke dreamily, as if there weren't an entire pub full of pirates itching to run a sword through them.

"Or is it a mermaid?" She brought her finger up. "Yes, I'm sure it's a mermaid."

Some of the men laughed, and Redclaw stood with a stunned look on his face. His mouth hung open, and his eyes were wide. "Cute? It's not cute! We're cutthroat pirates, stealing from anyone who gets in our way!"

"Hurrah!" The men from the bar shouted at the top of their lungs.

"Oh." Faith looked disappointed. "I guess there's no mermaid, huh?"

"There is a mermaid, actually." He gulped loudly as he quickly added, "But it's definitely not cute."

"This girl is funny, sir," said one of the pirates.

"Yes," added another. "Let's take her with us."

"She can replace Rosalina."

Redclaw suddenly stood, drool dripping from his mouth in anger. "Who said that?" There was a stunned silence. "No one can ever replace Rosalina!"

Faith reached out to the man and caressed his humongous arms. "It's obvious you cared for this Rosalina greatly." Her voice was tender, as if she were speaking to a wounded animal. "You shouldn't worry about her being replaced. Wherever she is, she now lives in your heart and memories. No one can ever replace that."

Falcon's throat went dry. He half expected Redclaw to pick Faith up by the neck and toss her into the wall. But instead, the man looked at her with droopy eyes.

"You do remind me of her a great deal," said the captain. "You have the same innocent soul. And if it was only you that needed passage in my ship, I would gladly grant it." He turned toward Aya and Falcon. An intense fire lit up in his eyes. "But I refuse to have Rohads anywhere near my ship!"

Falcon secretly wondered why the captain hated Rohads so much. Curiosity would have to wait, though. He needed to get the man to agree to give them passage, and with the man showing a liking to Faith, this was his chance.

"We can pay," he said.

"We want nothing from Rohads."

"Not even valuable oil rocks?" countered Falcon. "And not those cheap imitations. We have a full leather pouch of the real deal. Straight from the source. How long do you think that could power up your ship for? Five months? Maybe six?"

Redclaw's bushy eyebrow rose a few inches.

"We are in need of oil rocks, sir," said a skinny man with a blue patch over his right eye.

"Quiet!" thundered Redclaw. The man cowered back to his seat where he had come from. "I'm fully aware of our needs." The man looked down at Falcon with a wild look on his face. "All you Rohads are the same, a pompous bunch."

"I'm not like—"

"I wasn't done speaking!" Redclaw stomped over to the table beside him and picked up a board with two dozen miniature emblems resting on it. Grinning, he brought it over to his table and set it down. He looked directly at Falcon. "Beat me in a game of emblems and I'll give you passage."

"And if you win?" asked Falcon.

"Then you give me the oil rocks and walk away."

Feeling confident, Falcon took a seat in front of the captain. A crowd gathered around them, eager to see the outcome.

Redclaw set up twelve emblems on his side of the board, while Falcon set up his twelve, one for each element.

"I should probably mention that I have never lost an emblem match in my life," said the captain with a smug look on his face. "And I don't plan to start now."

Falcon didn't offer a word. He drew in his breath, staring down at the board that seemed more terrifying all of a sudden. The black and gray squares that before had looked so bland now seemed like an impossible puzzle to solve.

"Relax, Falcon," said Aya behind him. She rubbed his shoulders, which only made him more nervous. "You're the best emblem player at the academy. You can do it."

The captain made the first move. He reached for the void emblem and moved it from its starting point, a gray square, to the black square directly in front of it.

What to do? thought Falcon as he reluctantly reached down to his own void emblem on the board. There were twelve straight lines, and the purpose was to take out the opposing player's dozen emblems. Should he move forward as the captain had done, or should he settle for the less-played and riskier horizontal move? If he moved horizontally, that meant his void emblem would be stuck with horizontal moves the rest of the game. Could he take that gamble?

Both men sat in silence, regarding each other without uttering a word. Falcon felt the weight of the entire mission hanging on his shoulders as he slipped his fingers over the polished game piece. He moved it horizontally over to a gray square.

Without much thought, Redclaw moved his fire emblem two spaces down.

Falcon smirked, seeing the opening the captain had created. He slid his water emblem in a zigzag motion around his own earth and lightning emblems and over Redclaw's fire emblem.

"First capture," he said, taking his opponent's fire emblem and setting it on his side of the table.

He had expected the captain to appear worried, or at least a bit flustered. But instead, the man looked extremely pleased with himself.

"You've left yourself open."

Too late Falcon noticed his fatal mistake. He cursed as he realized he'd fallen for a simple ruse. The captain had left his basic emblem wide open for an attack, essentially sacrificing a basic element for an advanced one. His gut wrenched as Redclaw moved his dark emblem over Falcon's chaos emblem and took over it.

The pirates cheered, and Aya and Faith moaned sadly.

Okay, I can still do this, he thought as he looked down at the board.

Things only got worse from there, though. In two moves he had lost his best piece. The mobility of the chaos emblem was instrumental to his strategy. And to worsen matters, his opponent's dark emblem was in his side of the board.

I'm going to have to fall back to a basic element defense.

The players continued to add on moves as the minutes trickled on. By the time the midday bell was rung, Falcon only had his void emblem remaining on the board. He had put up a valiant battle, especially after the atrocious beginning, but now it looked like the end. With every move Redclaw made, his defeat became more apparent. The three advanced elements (chaos, space, and poison) closed in on his single piece, trapping it in a triangle.

He moved his emblem forward one more time; he was now only one space away from reaching the captain's beginning panel. If he could only reach it, he would be able to bring back one of his emblems into the board.

"Obviate!" yelled Redclaw, a satisfied grin spread on his face. "A valiant try, kid. But victory belongs to me."

Falcon leaned back in his chair, sighing deeply as he

stared at the cobwebs hanging on the ceiling.

The pub erupted into a choir of hurrahs.

"I'll be having those oil rocks now." Redclaw extended his burly hand expectantly.

"Our friend has them back at the inn. We'll just go get them."

Redclaw stood, his frame shaking. "Do you believe I actually trust you to simply walk away from here? No, I need to make sure that you stay." He motioned to his men to stand. "Get the girls as collateral."

Falcon stood, but his interference quickly proved unnecessary.

Three pirates moved against Aya. With a sweeping kick, she floored two of them. The third one punched, only to have his potential victim sidestep. Aya took hold of his arm and twisted the screaming man over her shoulder. With a sharp crack, he landed on a table. Mugs of ale flew through the air, clattering on the wooden floor.

Five other men tried to get to Faith, but with a simple swipe of her hand, she sent them toppling over their fallen companions.

The pirates, who had been roaring with commotion seconds ago, fell silent. The dripping of a leaking faucet behind the counter was the only sound that pierced silence.

Finally, Faith spoke. "Please don't fight anymore." She turned to the captain then to Falcon. "I will stay back while my friends get the rocks."

"No way!" Falcon reached for his katana. He was not about to leave Faith alone with a group of drunkards who hadn't been with a woman in months, maybe even years.

"Please," said a mellow voice from the corner of the pub. "There is no need for this violence." Everyone turned to the source of the voice. A hooded figure stood from a chair, where he sat alone. "There is a simple solution to all of this."

"What is that?" asked Redclaw.

The stranger walked with a bouncy gait. Even the wooden boards that usually creaked under a person's weight remained silent. "I will accompany the Rohads and fetch the stones myself."

Redclaw stroked his long beard, deep in thought.

"You know full well you can't be seen out in the open," continued the stranger. "The guards will be on you in no time. But me? I can easily disguise myself and come and go."

"What are you after, Captain Armeen?" said Redclaw. "I have it on good authority that you have plenty of oil rocks for a year, perhaps even two. I have no intention of sharing the bag with you."

So he's also a captain, mused Falcon. That means he has his own ship.

Armeen removed his hood, and behind it was a face that Falcon had not expected, at least not from a pirate. The pirates he'd met so far had black teeth, leathery skin, and wild hair. But Armeen was the complete opposite. He had silky hair that fell over his eyes. His smile revealed a perfect row of white teeth, and his skin was a light tan.

The captain walked over to Aya and took her hand, his eyes never leaving hers. "The only reward I require is the honor of such a lovely lady travelling on my ship."

Falcon almost threw up in his mouth as Armeen leaned in and kissed Aya's hand softly. His anger increased tenfold, when he noticed the slight blush in Aya's cheeks. He had expected her to punch him across the jaw, maybe grapple him to the floor in one of her famous arm-breaking locks. But blush? That was the last thing he had anticipated.

Before the pirate had even let go of Aya's hand, Falcon had already made up his mind. He definitely hated Captain Armeen.

Chapter 12

When Falcon opened the door to the Inn, he found Sheridan sleeping in one bed while Hiromy slept soundly in the other.

Sheridan opened his groggy eyes and stared up, his face clearly begging for more rest. He didn't seem surprised in the slightest by the fact that a hooded man accompanied Falcon. "Where are Nakatomi and Hemstath?" He threw his head back down and buried it under the white pillow.

"Get up. We found a ship to take us across. Aya and Faith are waiting with the pirates."

"That was fast. I was hoping it would take you at least a day. I need my rest."

"Where is this bag of oil rocks you spoke so fondly off?" asked Armeen, his blue eyes darting around the room.

"Where is the bag?" asked Falcon, ignoring Armeen's question. He needed to get back to the girls as soon as possible. Aya might have trusted Armeen, but Falcon had his doubts. A pirate was never to be trusted.

Finally, Sheridan stood. He slipped his shoes on and opened the drawer the rested between both beds. He grabbed the bag and tossed it to Falcon. "There." Then he looked over at Armeen, as if having just realized he was there. "And who the blazes are you?"

"This is Armeen," said Falcon, lazily motioning toward his companion. "The man who owns the ship we'll be riding across."

"Captain Armeen," corrected the man. "Commander of the finest ship to have ever sailed the fourteen seas. The Gold Chaser."

"What an original name," said Falcon, rolling his eyes. "Way to mask your intentions."

"What's your last name, captain?" asked Sheridan.

"Daku," answered Armeen absentmindedly. His eyes were settled on the bag of oil rocks. "Those are the real things all right. They must have been hard to come by."

"Don't you worry about that." Falcon held the leather pouch a bit closer. The oily smell drifted before him as he turned to Sheridan. "Wake Hiromy up so we can leave."

"She barely had time to rest," said Sheridan. "It was hard enough getting her to sleep by herself. She wanted me to lay beside her." He tapped her shoulder lightly.

"Why didn't you?" asked Falcon.

He shrugged. "Not sure. It seems wrong somehow. We were alone. I thought—"

Armeen laughed loudly. "A girl wants to snuggle with you and you run away scared?"

"Shhhh!" Sheridan brought his finger to his lips, but it was too late.

Hiromy sat up yelling at the top of her lungs. "A voice in

my head. Get away!" Icicles formed in her fingers. She swung, cutting Sheridan across his arm. She turned her attention at Falcon and Armeen, tossing the sharp ice at them.

Falcon fire wielded the air in front of him, turning the deadly attack into a simple splash of water. Armeen rocked his head back. The icicles missed his head by inches as they encrusted themselves on the wall.

Falcon blinked, surprised at the captain's quick reflexes. The near death experience didn't seem to have scared him in the slightest. He was still grinning, apparently satisfied at what he'd caused.

"Calm down," cried Sheridan. "It's just us." He held his hands up pleadingly.

"Sh...Sheridan." The girl's gaze travelled over to the injury she caused. It did look rather gruesome. A small flap of skin was hanging off, and blood was travelling down his arm, dripping loudly on the floor. "I did this. I hurt you." Her voice was soft.

"No." Sheridan took a small rag and sloppily wrapped it around his injury. "It's nothing. I just fell. That's all."

"You're lying." Hiromy pouted her lips, her voice pained. There was no questioning whether she was crying or not now. Her small frame shook as tears trickled down her cheeks and onto the cushion. "I hurt you. I'm a danger. I did it with the worm, and now I did it again."

"No...no..." Sheridan ran over to the sobbing princess

and embraced her in a hug. Even he looked as though he might break out in tears, which was strange. He was usually so happy and carefree. Their foreheads met as he looked into her eyes. "It's only a small cut. Hemstath will heal it, no problem." Despite his words, Hiromy didn't look convinced.

"Sheesh," said Armeen. "A lot of drama going on here." He raised an eyebrow as his eyes travelled up and down Hiromy's tight fitting suit. "Can't complain with the lassies, though. Very beautiful."

Falcon took a heavy breath. The more he listened to the captain speak, the more he wanted to sock him in the jaw. The fact that he always seemed to have that suave aura hanging around him only made things worse. Despite his feelings, he stayed quiet. They needed a captain. And for better or worse, Armeen was all they had.

~~~

It took much longer to leave than Falcon had expected. Hiromy kept on stopping to point at the, in her words, "beautiful clouds that flew across the blue sea in the sky." It took even longer to find Armeen's ship.

"I can't simply leave it docked in the Makeda pier, can I?" complained Armeen when Falcon voiced, for the third time, how annoying it was that they had to traverse deep into the woods to find his ship. "The guards would confiscate her in a hurry."

"Her?" Falcon lifted an eyebrow.

"Yes. The Gold Chaser is the most powerful vessel you will ever see, and she's the fastest as well."

As if on cue, the ship's mast came into view. And though he didn't want to, Falcon found that he had to agree with Armeen's description of the ship. It certainly looked imposing enough. The mast towered over even the highest trees surrounding the lake. Plain black sails were attached to the mast, giving the ship a grandiose look. The rigging and the long red hull looked brand new, as if they had been barely built (or barely stolen).

"How in Va'siel did you manage to get such a large ship onto this lake unnoticed?" asked Sheridan. He looked as impressed as Falcon.

Armeen didn't answer immediately. He remained quiet, looking slightly offended. Finally he spoke. "The sea clears out into a short but wide river miles behind Makeda. The river, in turn, feeds into this lake. If the authorities in Makeda paid more attention to what surrounds them, I have no doubt they would find the ship in no time. Lucky for us, they don't." He pointed at the ship as Aya, Faith, Captain Redclaw and dozens of pirates came into view. They were all standing at the edge of the lake, not doing much. "But if you want to know how that ship got in here, then you'll have to ask Captain Redclaw. You see, that is his ship."

"His ship?" Falcon strained his eyes, searching. "I don't see any more masts from this distance. Where's your ship?"

"You'll see it once we get a little closer," Armeen said, meeting his eyes. "Trust me when I say, you won't be disappointed."

He did indeed see the ship once they got closer to the edge of the lake. His heart sank as he noticed the old, scratched hull that looked as if it might shatter if you looked at it the wrong way. Unlike Redclaw's ship, the Gold Chaser had three masts, though they were much shorter. Each mast had four long flags, giving the entire ship a total of twelve. Unlike the dark flags on the large ship, this one had white flags. At least Falcon thought they were once white. They were now so stained with yellow and black blotches that it was hard to tell.

Falcon swore under his breath, as he came to grips with the fact that their entire mission rested on a slab of old wood that didn't look as if it could get them out of this lake, let alone across the sea. Maybe it wasn't too late to switch to Redclaw's ship. He was sure he could work out some type of compromise. But Aya shattered whatever hopes he had of jumping ships.

"What do you think?" she said once they were face to face. She motioned over at the Gold Chaser. "The Chaser sure looks fast enough, doesn't she? The mast layout is a bit archaic, but the sleek design is sure to cut through the sea in no time."

Armeen grinned and took a step closer to Aya. "You're a lassie after my heart. You sure know your ships. You must, no doubt, travel a lot."

"Only a little. Most of it I learned from books."

Ignoring the scene before him, Falcon marched over to Redclaw. "A deal is a deal. Here." He set the bag in Redclaw's waiting, gigantic hands.

Clearly satisfied, Redclaw brought the bag to his nose and sniffed. "Yes, that's the real stuff." He tossed the bag to a short man behind him. "Mr. Nathal. Put those in the coal engine. With some favorable winds and the power of the coal, I have no doubt we can sail into Illusionary Island by nightfall. I intend to put my time to proper use and get drunk tonight."

The men cheered. "Hurrah!"

"If you really wanted to help people and put your ship to good use, you would raid the Suteckh." Falcon met gazes with the bearded captain. "Not just get drunk."

"Say that again!" Redclaw's face turned as red as his beard.

"Surely. You say that you steal to help the common folk, but if that was true you would raid the Suteckh, not just Imperial ships. The Suteckh are the ones that are trying to take over Va'siel, after all."

Redclaw reached for his broadsword. The men behind him did the same. Falcon reached for his dual swords as well, but before he had a chance to bring them out, Faith stepped between him and the captain.

"Please put away your weapons," she said.

160

Falcon was surprised to see that the large man obeyed, signaling for his men to follow suit.

"What Falcon says is true. The Suteckh are a menace to Va'siel. Having the aid of you and your ship would surely be of great value." Redclaw brought up his hand to retort, but Faith continued before he could say a word. "However, you're free to do as you wish. If you'd rather not cross the Suteckh, then we respect that and won't judge you because of it." She unexpectedly moved toward the captain and gave him a hug, which seemed to have caught everyone by surprise, including Redclaw. He staggered back, his mouth quiet for once. "All your help was much appreciated, sir."

Redclaw patted her back, his arms so large that Faith seemed to have gotten lost somewhere between them. "You truly do remind me so much of my daughter, Rosalina." He stepped back. For a split second, Falcon thought he saw a tear wanting to form in the captain's eye. "I will ponder on your words, young miss. But don't expect much. I have no desire to cross blades with the Suteckh."

And just like that, he was gone. He boarded the Crimson Maiden without bothering to say goodbye to anyone but Faith, grabbed the ship's wheel and piloted his ship out of the lake.

Falcon offered him an energyless grunt. He watched, with spirits draining, as the majestic ship moved down the river, toward the sea. The large mermaid figurehead at the front seemed to mock him. He swore he could almost hear the laughter echoing in the rippling water. His eyes travelled over to the ship that was left over.

One by one, they boarded the ship. The crew was much smaller than Falcon had anticipated. Including Armeen, there were a dozen pirates. Most of them wore raggedy shirts and dirt-stained loose pants. Short broadswords hung by their waists.

"Are you coming or not?" asked Armeen, standing atop his ship. That was when Falcon realized that he was the only one who had yet to board the ship.

He stepped on the ramp, his footsteps echoing noisily. He looked over at Armeen and motioned toward the words that had been sloppily scratched on the side of the ship. They read: The Gold Chaser. They were deep and uneven, as if someone had taken a knife to it.

Armeen beamed, as if the words were written in majestic gold. "It may not look like much, but the Gold Chaser can run circles around any ship out there. That includes any Suteckh ship and the Crimson Maiden." And, quite suddenly, he took the hands of all three girls and kissed them softly. He took an annoyingly long time holding Aya's hand. "It is my great honor to welcome you three lassies to my pride and joy. Allow me to give you a tour of the deck and the bottom of ship."

Falcon and Sheridan were left standing alone as they

watched the girls disappear below deck with the captain.

"It's going to be a long trip," said Sheridan. His face was twisted somewhere between anger and shock. The fact that Hiromy had left his side so willingly had obviously gotten to him.

"I couldn't agree more."

Chapter 13

Falcon did not sleep much that night. The boat shook and rocked so much that he found it difficult to keep his eyes closed for more than a few minutes at a time. The fact that he was in a room with a half dozen snoring, sweaty, and smelly men did not help. For what seemed like the hundredth time, the rope hammock he was sleeping on slammed against the wall beside him.

When daylight finally trickled though the small holes in the deck above, he couldn't wait to leave the dark, depressing room and go up to the deck. Careful not to wake Sheridan, who slept on the hammock beside him, or any of the other men, Falcon moved slowly. He cringed when his foot landed on the floor, causing the panels to creak. No one seemed to notice.

He opened the door and walked out into the narrow hallway. To his surprise, the door directly left of the one he had emerged from also opened. Faith and Hiromy were coming out. Unlike Falcon, they appeared well rested. There were no tired bags under their eyes, nor was the white around their pupils webbed in red.

Faith brought her hand to her mouth, as if to suppress a scream.

"Falcon!" she muttered after a moment of silence. "Are

you well? You look as if you got no sleep."

"I didn't. It was impossible in those hammocks."

"Hammocks?" Faith appeared genuinely confused.

Falcon looked past the girls and into the room they had slept in and immediately understood. The room they used had actual beds. Sure, the white mattresses didn't look all that comfortable, but he was sure it was ten times better than the old rope he was forced to endure all night.

He pointed over to the room he shared with the pirates. "I had to sleep in one of those."

"Hey!" cried Hiromy, spotting Sheridan as he rocked back and forth in his net. She waved her hand. "Hi. Sheridan. Hurry up and join us up top soon, okay? I missed you last night!" The fact that he was obviously in a deep sleep and therefore couldn't hear her did not seem to bother her in the slightest.

"So? Where were you sneaking off so quietly?" asked Faith.

His nerves heightened a bit. "I just needed to get some fresh air and some quiet before everyone woke." He decided to leave out the part where he was planning to search the ship, looking for anything incriminating. He didn't care what the girls thought. He still didn't trust Armeen.

"We were going up to train," said Hiromy cheerily. "Isn't that right, Faith?" The princess took off down the hallway and up the stairs.

"I better go after her," said Faith, hurrying behind the princess.

When Falcon got up to the deck, he had expected it to be mostly empty, but he quickly saw that that was not the case. Many of the pirates were already up. Two of them were up high in the overlook. A few more of them were climbing up the ropes.

"Prepare the riggings, Mr. Gertie!" yelled a suave voice.

Falcon turned over to the sight of Captain Armeen. He was steering a giant half-broken wheel that looked as if it might fall off and roll across the deck at any moment.

"Yes, sir!" yelled Gertie, a short, wrinkled man who wore a black and white striped shirt that could barely contain his massive belly. He grabbed the rope and began to climb toward the riggings.

"Don't look so scared, Mr. Falcon," said Armeen, patting his back.

Mister? thought Falcon. That certainly sounded strange coming from Armeen, considering that they looked to be about the same age.

Armeen continued. "Mr. Gertie has been climbing and descending those ropes since before you were born." The captain was now wearing a long velvet coat. He also wore a long tricorne hat that covered most of his hair, except for the long ponytail dangling behind him. A golden oval earring, depicting a coin, dangled from his ear.

"All ready!" came the scream from above. Gertie had now opened all the sails and had joined the duo of pirates standing at the top overlook podium.

The sails opened, and quite suddenly the ship gained speed, bopping and bouncing over the waves.

Falcon felt his stomach turn. He darted over to the side of the ship, fully expecting to throw up the little food he'd eaten. But besides gagging noises, nothing came.

A strong pat landed on his back yet again, making his stomach whirl viciously. "Don't worry. You'll get used to it in no time. It takes most landlubbers a few weeks to get used to the movement of a ship, especially one as fast as the Gold Chaser."

Weeks? The sound of that made him wish he were back on land facing murderous Suteckh. In a battle he was at home. But here? Stuck in the middle of the sea in a rickety ship that was sure to sink at any moment, he was but a lost soul.

To add salt to the wound, Faith and Hiromy walked over to Armeen. Neither of them looked the least bit affected by the ship's uneven movements.

"Excuse me, Captain," said Faith. "My friend and I were hoping to meditate. But it occurs to me that you may need some help around the ship first. Is there anything we can do?"

"Oh no!" Armeen looked genuinely shocked. "No guests of mine will lift a finger on the Gold Chaser." He pointed toward the back of the ship. "The stern is an excellent place for that. Feel free to use it as you wish."

"Thank you," said Faith. She turned to Falcon. "You don't look so well. Want me to use some holy wielding to heal you a bit?"

Armeen snickered. "We have some herbs down in the hold that can help. However, it's usually saved for women and children." He eyed Falcon from top to bottom. "Not fully grown men."

Feeling like an idiot, Falcon tried to stand upright and display confidence. His wobbly legs sure weren't helping. "No. It'll just take me a little while to get used to it. That's all."

"Okay, then," mumbled Faith, looking unsure. She and Hiromy headed to the backside of the ship and sat cross-legged. All along the captain watched them go, nodding to himself and mumbling under his breath.

"You better not get any ideas about Faith," warned Falcon. "She's a good girl."

"Oh, her?" Armeen shrugged indifferently. "While that pretty lassie is certainly easy on the eyes, I have no interest in her."

Falcon breathed a sigh of relief.

"I'm much more interested in the feisty one. What's her name again? Oh, yes, Aya. And whatever I put my eyes on, I acquire."

"You best get used to disappointment. Aya wouldn't

waste a breath on you." Falcon wasn't sure if he himself believed those words. He'd seen Aya around the captain, and she certainly seemed different when he was around.

"I wouldn't be too sure about that. We spent the night alone in my quarters drinking wine, and she certainly seemed to welcome my company. Now please go wake your friend, Sheridan. I require your assistance manning the ship."

Falcon was left at a loss for words. Certainly Armeen had to be bluffing. He'd gone to sleep at the same time Aya had. There was no way she had spent any time with the captain.

The captain eyed him. "Are you simply going to stand there all day? Light is being wasted. Come to me when your friend is with you." Before Falcon could say anything, Armeen moved to the rear of the ship and disappeared behind the door to his quarters.

Still a bit perturbed, he went downstairs to wake Sheridan. On his way there he ran into Aya, who was just walking out of the room.

"Oh, good morning, Falcon," she said. The oil lamp that hung above them barely emitted enough light to illuminate her face. But even through the darkness, he could make out a slight smile. The first smile she'd given him in ages. "Where are you headed?"

"Just going to wake Sheridan. Armeen said he needs our help up in the deck. I'm not really sure with what." He inhaled deeply. "So? How about you?"

"How about me what?"

"Where are you headed?"

"Oh. I'm going over to Captain's Armeen's quarters."

"His quarters?" He could literally see the color draining from the skin on his hands.

"Yes. We spent last night trying to find a path through the mountain pass. If we can locate it we'll be able to cut three, maybe even four days off our travel."

"He's the captain of a ship," said Falcon, unable to keep the irritation out of his voice. "I'm sure he knows every passage there is in the seas already."

"That's not true. He's very young. The youngest pirate captain, actually." She spoke with admiration, which infuriated Falcon even more. "There are many routes and secret passages he knows nothing about. Besides, the pass we're trying to find isn't one that is well known. It's not even on any maps. It's merely mentioned in certain early transcripts from ancient prophets. Serilda made mention of it, as did Atto the Grim."

"So you're looking for a pass that probably doesn't exist? Sounds like an excuse to spend time with him."

She blinked, looking at him with protruding eyes. "What if I am? I don't see how that's any of your concern."

"You're right. I just wish you were straightforward about it and not pretending to be looking for some pass that doesn't

170

exist."

"Straightforward?" she hissed. "You mean like you?"

"Me?" He pointed at himself, surprised by the accusatory tone in Aya's voice. "What do I have to do with this?"

"Faith."

Falcon shuffled his feet uncomfortably.

"What do you feel for her?"

"Well. Um…" He cleared his throat, which had suddenly become very scratchy.

"Don't even think about telling me you don't have feelings for her, because I know you do. I saw you talking to her once, at K'ran's home. You were on the roof. That was our thing, remember? But you still went and did it with her." There was a layer of pain and anger mixed in her voice. "Yet, I didn't interrogate you the way you're doing to me now."

"Well, um—"

"How about me?"

"How about what?" Falcon was really regretting saying anything. His muscles stiffened as he clenched his jaw.

"What exactly do you feel for me?"

He wiped the sweat that seemed to be pouring down his face now, despite the cool weather.

"I thought so." She locked eyes with him. "Don't lecture me about being straightforward." She moved past him, leaving her strawberry scent lingering in the air. He turned, wanting to say something, but found himself unable to form words. Her dark hair bounced after her as she climbed the stairs and disappeared above.

The silence that filled the hallway was haunting. He knew Aya was angry, but he hadn't realized she was that angry. But then again, there was merit to what she'd said. He hadn't exactly been open about what he felt. Whether he liked it or not, he would have to simply grit his teeth and let her do as she pleased.

"Is Nakatomi gone?" Sheridan slowly opened the old door. A rat, the size of a full-grown foot scampered out and into a hole on the wall. "Sheesh, Hyatt. She told you. I've never seen Nakatomi that angry."

"You heard that?" Falcon felt himself turn a deeper shade of red.

"It was hard not to. Nakatomi was yelling, and I was right next door." He leaned in closer, his face eager. "But never mind that. Give me the details. I only heard half of the conversation. What happened with you and Hemstath that made Nakatomi so angry? Did you finally kiss those little holy wielding lips?"

Falcon ignored him. "C'mon. Armeen wants to see us both. Something about helping around the ship."

~~~

Aya came up on the deck. The sun's rays rained down on her eyes. Heaving loudly, she put her head down and

172

walked toward the back of the ship. Her heart was still pounding from the confrontation she'd had with Falcon. She couldn't believe he had the audacity to question her. Even harder to believe were the words that had come out of her own mouth. Aya didn't even know she had felt half of the things she'd said. But now that they were out in the open, she realized that she had always felt them. They had been there, bubbling within her, threatening to explode or engulf her.

"Good morning, Aya." Faith leaned closer and waved, a smile on her face. Hiromy was beside her, spinning in place and humming a melody.

Aya peered at Faith. "Good morning." She felt a slight discomfort about being so close to the person who had been the subject of her rant mere seconds ago. There was no reason behind it, but part of her felt like a bad friend.

"Would you like to join us? We're about to do some meditating."

"Not right now. Perhaps another time, yes?"

"Sure."

Aya set off in a rapid walk toward the captain's quarters. She knocked on the door. Besides the metal skull insignia hanging at the center, it was as time worn as the rest of the doors in the ship. From her time reading, she knew that adorning ships with metal skulls was an ancient tradition practiced by captains of times long past. She found herself enjoying the small ancient details spread across the Gold

Chaser. The moldy smell was welcome too. It made her feel as if she were part of history. Nothing but a speck of dust in the tale of the cosmos. Somehow, this seemed to lessen her troubles a bit.

The door opened.

"Nice to see you," said Armeen, gesturing for her to come in.

Aya walked in, taking in the scent of burning wax. Light from an open window at the side of the room let in rays of light, where dust particles danced wildly. Two lit candles stood over the husky table at the back. Over the table, countless maps were scattered. Books were also lying about. Some were open, while others rose in uneven stacks.

"What woes trouble you, young lassie?"

"Nothing of importance," said Aya. She took a seat and picked up the book she had been examining the day before and continued where she'd left off.

Armeen marched over to the small cabinet he had full of books against the walls. He picked two out and tossed them on the desk.

"I think those two might have some information on trade routes used by Missea during the era of the Emperor Tanul. Around page eight, if I'm not mistaken."

Aya looked up from her book. "Why don't you get the information and write it down with the notes I've taken?" She gestured over to the piece of parchment that she had written on the previous day.

Armeen's expression went from shocked to delighted. He smiled, exposing perfect aligned white teeth. "How about I just serve us some wine to get us through the day?" Against the left side of the wall was a scalloped wine rack nailed down. It held twelve wine bottles, mostly dark, though a few white bottles were also laid down vertically. He reached for a bottle and held it up to Aya. "Strawberry wine is your favorite, right?"

Aya set her book down. The previous day Armeen had done the same thing. He had lain back and downed glass after glass of wine, without doing much work. Aya herself had drunk one too many wine glasses. On her way back to the cabin, she had almost taken a nasty spill on the floor more than once. She was not about to make the same mistake again.

"What do you think you're doing?" she asked.

He poured the light pink red liquid into a clear glass and slid it toward Aya. "Simply giving us something to get us through the day."

"We don't need wine. What we need is to get through these trade logs and see if we can find anything useful. This may not be important to you, but we need to get to Missea. Peoples' lives are at stake."

"Yes. Of course." He gave her a mock salute. "I will get to work right away."

Without saying another word, Aya returned her attention to the trade routes.

But despite Armeen's assurance that he was going to help, he didn't. Instead, he spent most of the day describing his many exploits on the seas. Many were the stories of the times he cheated death. He also had countless tales of stealing gold and provisions from the wealthy to provide for the poor. Even though Aya was only half listening, she couldn't deny that he found his tall tales entertaining. Armeen spoke with a contagious confidence that inspired loyalty. It was easy to see how he had become a captain at such a young age. She also found herself chuckling from time to time, something that she would have thought impossible mere days ago.

"So how did you end up escaping?" asked Aya, after Armeen had described a particular situation where he'd been tied to a stake by a group of savage natives determined to sacrifice him to a flame god.

"I used the very fire they lit under me to burn the ropes they had tied me with. I then threw myself down a three-hundred-foot cliff, landing safely in the raging river below."

"That sounds very…hard to believe."

"Most of my many exploits are difficult to grasp," said the captain, seemingly unfazed by Aya's doubts.

Their eyes met. A strange sensation rushed from her toes to her neck. Rattled, she looked down and buried her eyes on her books, not wanting to show the captain her flustered expression.

~~~

Gertie gave both wielders a small brush and had them wipe the floor of the deck. As they worked, Sheridan continued to pester him about what had transpired between Aya and him. Falcon found it extremely annoying. So much so that by the middle of the day he had pretended to throw up on five different occasions just to get away from him, which ended up not mattering much. Sheridan followed him to the side of the ship as Falcon feigned to vomit overboard.

Finally, after almost an entire day of questions, Falcon had to tell him to stop talking about him and Aya, which Sheridan took as a sign to go on a rant about Hiromy and just how beautiful her hair was. He talked about the way it flowed. The way it looked as the sun hit it. The way it smelled when she washed it.

By the time the moon peeked over the distant rain cloud, Falcon's head was pounding.

"For Va'siel's sake. Stop yammering!" yelled Falcon, putting down his cleaning brush. "Nobody cares just how much Hiromy's eyes glisten from afar, or how cute it is when she slurps her noodles, or just how her voice drips like honey when she sings."

Sheridan, who had been on all fours cleaning, stood, looking down with a menacing look. For a second Falcon thought he was going to space wield a meteor at him. But instead, he clenched his fists. "Be careful how you speak about Hiromy. I won't tolerate anyone disrespecting her."

Falcon looked up at him with indifference. "Whatever."

"You've been warned." Sheridan grabbed his bucket of water and stormed toward the front of the ship.

A group of pirates stared at them with amused looks on their faces. Apparently, they had gathered to watch the exchange. Falcon shrugged. He could care less what those thieves thought about him.

But as he returned to cleaning, he noticed two people who he did care about gazing at him: Faith and Hiromy. Surprise registered in their faces. Hiromy especially seemed hurt. She looked as if she were on the verge of tears.

"You don't like me. I'm annoying," she said, her voice anguished.

"No, no, no." Falcon brought up his hands. "You're not annoying. I like you."

"Liar!" she screamed. She ran to the back of the ship and huddled in a ball. Faith followed after her, trying to comfort her. Through all this, the pirates watched with great interest. Some looked over at Falcon, as if they were plotting to throw him overboard. Ignoring them, Falcon moved toward Hiromy. But Faith gave him a leave her alone for a while look so he backed off. Feeling like a fool, he returned to scrubbing the deck, wondering how he had managed to anger all his friends in the span of a day.

Chapter 14

The dark blue, sunlit water sparkled splendidly under the morning sun. At least it did until Falcon threw up over the side of the ship for the second time in just one morning. Many of the pirates, who seemed to not sleep at all, snickered to themselves.

"If you continue to vomit every few minutes, you're never going to finish scrubbing the decks," said Armeen in a matter-of-fact tone. He had just come out of his cabin, where he and Aya had spent the majority of their time for the past six days. With the pompous stride that Falcon hated, the captain walked across the deck and took hold of the wheel. He wore a ridiculously large hat with a dark feather towering from it.

Falcon held up the small brush that wasn't even as long as one of his fingers. "Maybe, if you gave us something better to work with." He tossed the brush in the bucket of dirty water. "And while we're on the subject, why are you making us clean? I know that we're on your ship and I volunteered to help with something, but surely there is something more worthwhile we can do. We are Rohad warriors after all. Sheridan there..." He motioned toward Sheridan, who was scrubbing the mast without complaint. Even when Falcon mentioned his name, he did not bother to look up. No doubt he was still angry. "Is a space wielder. Do you have any idea just how rare space wielders are? You have one on your ship, and you have him cleaning decks."

"Oh." Armeen looked slightly amused. "And what exactly would you have me do with a space wielder on a ship? Should I ask him to wield a hail of comets upon us?"

Falcon hesitated then offered an answer. "Maybe Sheridan wouldn't be much help here, but surely I would." He brought up his hand. His gray emblem sparkled radiantly. "See this? I'm a void wielder. This means that I can wield water and wind wield. Need favorable winds? I can wield some in no time."

For the first time, Armeen looked alarmed. "No, no, no. I won't have any of that artificial garbage touching my ship."

"Artificial?"

"Yes. As in not real."

"It's real."

"You misunderstand." Armeen spoke as if he were lecturing a child, which only further angered Falcon. "I have no need for wielders who have no real control over the elements. You see those?" The captain pointed at the sails above. "Those are antiques, made from a fiber that is long gone. They serve a very specific purpose. They catch the winds and move the ship unlike any other sails in Va'siel. Can you guarantee me that you won't wind wield in excess and rip my sails apart?"

Falcon recalled the many times he had lost control.

While it was true that he had gotten much better at controlling certain elements, he wasn't exactly a master of energy regulation.

"I take that silence as a no," continued Armeen. "And I have a feeling that your space wielder friend won't be much better. Space is an advanced element. It requires much more focus to control. How long do you think your friend could space wield before he became completely drained?"

Again, Falcon remained quiet.

"Now, if I had a capable wielder who knew what they were doing like the Golden Wielder or the Ghost Knight-"

"You know of the Ghost Knight?" asked Falcon, surprised by the fact that the captain would know the powerful wielder.

"Of course I know the Ghost Knight."

"That's strange. A minute ago you were declaring your mistrust of wielders. But it sounds like you admire him."

"I admire wielders who know what they're doing. He saved my life once. I would entrust him to pull my entire ship into one of those space rifts if he wanted to. And unlike your friend over there, I'm sure the Ghost Knight wouldn't even put a scratch on it. Come to think of it. I doubt that Sheridan fellow and you put together could wield a space rift big enough to teleport this ship."

"How did you know—?"

"That you could space wield?" finished Armeen. "Aya

told me."

Unease crept through Falcon's body. How could Aya have trusted this man she barely met with Falcon's ability to wield all the elements?

"So in a way," continued Armeen. "You're to blame for all the scrubbing you have to do. Your lack of control is making this trip much longer than it has to be."

Falcon's eyes narrowed as he balled his fists. He'd heard enough sermons from everyone around him to last him a lifetime. He certainly didn't need this from someone he had just met.

Before he could retaliate, a soft hand slipped into his. "There you are, Falcon." Faith's touch, like always, instantly brought his anger levels down to the point of being non-existent. "Come with me. I want to show you something."

"I found it!" cried Aya, coming out of Armeen's quarters. She had a red, leather-bound book in her hands. Her eyes widened as her eyes settled on Faith's hand nestled in Falcon's, but she quickly looked away. "Come see this, Armeen."

The captain wasted no time in hurrying into his quarters and slamming his door shut.

"I'd wager the captain will show her a real good time in there," said Gertie, winking.

"I'm sure he is," added a stubby man whose entire face was hidden behind a bush of hair. "No wonder she never wants to leave his quarters."

The pirates laughed and jeered, piling on more comments about Aya's long times spent with Armeen.

"Hey!" Falcon's voice was exasperated.

Oblivious to Falcon's discomfort, the pirates continued with their laughter.

"Ignore them." Faith pulled Falcon to the back of the ship. She sat cross-legged and looked up at him. "Sit, please."

He mimicked her style and sat. Faith locked eyes with him, forcing Falcon to look away in discomfort.

"Don't look away," she said. "Keep on looking at me."

"Why are we—?"

"Just do it."

He looked back up at the green emeralds in her eyes and gulped. Despite his racing heart, he retained his gaze with hers. They remained there, for what seemed an eternity. Once in a while, he would try to talk, but every time Faith would nod her head, signaling for him to remain quiet.

His nervous thoughts drifted from the softness of her skin to her peachy scent, even to the small curve of her lips. The thought of touching them unwillingly sprang into his head. He blinked it away. It wasn't an unpleasant thought, but he knew it was out of place. They had bigger things to worry about.

"What did you think about?"

"Errr..."

"Exactly."

"Ummm... exactly what?"

"You didn't even experience the motion sickness, did you?"

"No, actually." He had been so busy being angry at Armeen and then being nervous around Faith that the nausea he got from the ship's movements had become a faded memory.

"I've been thinking a lot about what Shal-Demetrius told us."

Falcon felt a twinge of pain at the mention of the old man. He'd only known him for a few days, but in that short time, he'd grown very fond of him. The fact that Demetrius had been a chaos wielder like himself and had retained a good heart gave him hope that perhaps he could do the same.

"What have you been thinking about?"

"You recall how he wanted you to use special memories to help you keep control, right?"

"Yes. I remember. The Ghost Knight told me something very similar as well."

"Yes. You managed to use love to chaos wield when we fought Lakirk."

Just thinking of Lakirk, the demented fool who had allowed himself to be seduced by the power of chaos, made Falcon cringe. The man had changed not only mentally but physically as well, becoming a monstrous, scorpion-like

184

creature. Only by chaos wielding did Falcon manage to teleport inside Lakirk and cut him from the inside out. But it was only the thought of saving Faith that had allowed him to wield the chaos properly. It had also been the only time he had managed to do so. Every other time he tried to wield chaos, he had become an uncontrollable monster. Literally.

Faith smiled warmly at him, her eyes full of a serene happiness. "You don't have to go into details and tell me what you thought about."

That's good, mused Falcon. He had no desire to recount his feelings. The last time he'd tried it, things hadn't gone well for anyone involved.

"Before, the only way you had been able to keep chaos in check was with my help. When you chaos wielded against Lakirk, however, I felt the emotion of love emanating from you. It was love that allowed the holy energy to spill out of you and keep the chaos in check." Her face lit up. "It was the first time you managed to wield chaos, but I prefer to concentrate on the biggest accomplishment you managed that day."

"What is that?" he asked, baffled. Chaos had always been the element that had given him the most trouble. He would have thought that the fact that he managed to control it, albeit for a short time, was the biggest accomplishment.

"You held command over holy," she said happily. "Don't you see? Holy is the key to everything, not chaos. Remember what Demetrius told us about his wife?"

Falcon recalled Demetrius mentioning that it was only through his wife, the holy wielder Lunet, that he had managed to hold the corruption of chaos at bay. "I remember. But what exactly is the point? Do we have to… you know?"

She blushed, turning a deep shade of red. "Oh, sorry. I didn't mean to make it sound as if you needed to marry me." She fidgeted with her fingers. "What I meant to say is that I believe you may have the ability to control holy yourself. Unlike Demetrius, you don't need someone to keep it in check for you. You showed that during the battle. So if you did it once for a short while, you can do it again… indefinitely. And once you do that, not only will you be able to hold sway over chaos but all the elements, even the ones you're not particularly gifted at like poison, darkness, and mind. The balance that holy provides will allow this."

Falcon definitely liked the sound of that. While he had the ability to wield poison and darkness he had never shown much skill in it. "How?"

"The motion sickness you felt is a good step, I think."

"I don't follow."

"When you were angry and embarrassed I noticed you didn't experience motion sickness. It was a subconscious move your body made, guided by its rush of emotions at the time."

He nodded. He hadn't really thought about it, but now that he did, it was around the time he began to speak to

Armeen that his sickness went away.

"Using love to suppress something like a stomach pain would not work," she said. "It would be overkill. So I want you to focus on things that you like. This will be a good gateway into having you fully control your holy. Once you have mastered this, you can move on to larger emotions and eventually holy." She lowered her head. "Master Demetrius wanted you to have full control of your elements, not just control over them when it randomly came to you in times of need. I want to aid you both by fulfilling that wish."

"Land ho!" came a cry from above.

Falcon and Faith looked up. Gertie was standing in the crow's nest, a big grin on his face as he pointed up ahead. "We're home, boys."

Falcon stood and ran to the front of the ship. Off in the distance he noticed a small speck of brown and green. It looked like a dot in the middle of a canvass of deep blue. The closer they moved, the larger the dot became.

"We're going to hit some incoming waves," called Gertie. "Brace yourselves!"

The small ship rocked from side to side.

"Arghhhh…" Sheridan screamed as he tumbled into a pirate, sending both of them falling to the floor.

An influx of sickness rushed to his stomach. He felt his body goosebump as it threatened to get rid of the morning's breakfast.

No! Think of something I enjoy. Food rushed into his mind, particularly Yinjue nuggets. His favorite snack. He took in the crunchiness of every bite and the warm feeling he felt the rare times he had one.

Suddenly, his stomach didn't feel as if it was waging war with itself anymore. On the contrary, it felt quite serene. Gone too was the urge to vomit.

He turned to Faith, feeling good, physically and emotionally, for the first time since he'd stepped foot on the Gold Chaser. "I did it. I sensed some of the warmness of holy within me. I'll be wielding holy in no time."

"One step at a time," she said, giving him one of her usual smiles.

Feeling satisfied at his progress, he stood happily next to Faith and stared at the small island coming into view.

Chapter 15

Much as he had done in Makeda, Armeen navigated the ship through a river that cut directly into the island. A green jungle surrounded them from both sides. The sounds of wild birds and chimps filled the air. On his right side, Falcon noticed a family of monkeys jumping from tree to tree, as if following the ship. Above him, all manner of lush-colored birds he had never seen before took to the air.

A moment later, they arrived at a large lake where the pirates docked the ship. They all disembarked and walked on foot through the lush jungle. Trekking the vine-and root-infested environment brought back memories of the Rohad exam he had taken back at Ladria. Those events had transpired mere months ago, but with everything that had occurred, it seemed more like a lifetime ago.

"What are we doing here?" asked Sheridan. He held his sword in hand, ready to cut any vines that impeded their way, which was proving quite useless. The pirates apparently knew a passage through the jungle free of natural obstructions. The winding path cut through the trees in a line of zigzags. "I thought we needed to get to Missea as soon as possible."

"Don't fret," said Armeen. He walked ahead of everyone. "You will get there in due course. However, at this time, it is imperative that I bring supplies to my people. They are in dire need of it."

Falcon took a glimpse behind him. Now he understood why some of the pirates had tied ropes around their waists and were dragging crates behind them. Still, it didn't make sense to him that Armeen had spoken about his people. What people could a pirate who lived on the seas stealing and raiding possibly have?

The long walk would have been a silent one had it not been for the Captain. He and Aya walked ahead of everyone. He kept on pointing out the different kinds of plants and flowers along the way. At one point he even plucked up a red flower from a bush they passed and handed it to Aya. Falcon winced. The entire display was sickening.

No doubt sensing his discomfort, Faith stood beside him and asked him if he would like her to describe the variety of different plants along the way. Usually, he would have refused. Faith was the lover of plants and flowers. He was not. He had no interest in learning about plant life cycles or why a flower is a certain color. But at this moment, anything was preferable to hearing Armeen speak about the 'charming lotus dew' the red flower provided for his morning teas.

"And that's a blue cohosh," said Faith, pointing at a series of white and blue tinted roots that were protruding from the ground. "They need a lot of shade to grow, which is why they only grow in jungles."

"Oh," said Falcon, absent-mindedly. With his eyes, he

was drilling a hole in Armeen's back.

"What else?" asked Hiromy, standing a little behind Faith. Unlike Falcon, she was hanging on Faith's every word. She listened intently as the holy wielder went on a long-winded description of the trees and the reason for their extreme height.

"Home!" cried Gertie, taking off at a sudden sprint. His legs were so chubby and short that watching the man run was almost comical. He bobbed from side to side, every step threatening to send him tumbling to the floor. Somehow, however, he didn't fall as he took off toward the blur in the distance. Slowly, the blur turned to a collection of oval-shaped straw huts. Beside it stood a series of squared pieces of land that were being used to grow rice, squash, and corn. Bales of wheat were stacked high at the side of the farmlands. Seeing them reminded Falcon of the time he had spent farming alongside his master, K'ran.

The village itself didn't seem all that spectacular. It looked run-down and sloppily made. Many of the huts had large openings in the roofs and walls, where the pieces of wooden sticks didn't fit well over each other. There were a few holes in the ground with slabs of wood covering them. Did someone actually live down there?

What Falcon saw above, however, left him speechless. It was as if someone had built a small city in the trees. Wood panels connected from one tree to another, providing crossing bridges. There were even railings on the side to prevent people from falling. Long, thick ropes were tied to small, wheel-less carriages. Falcon counted four of them. Two were waiting above, while the other two rested at the bottom.

"Fwooooot!"

Gertie's whistle echoed across the air. Suddenly, the village that had been so quiet mere seconds ago became a hub of commotion. The slabs of wood on the ground were tossed aside, revealing people huddled beneath them. Someone does live down there! The sloppy hut doors opened, and out poured groups of men and women, hollering and cheering at the top of their lungs. They were all grimy, and their simple clothing was caked in dirt. Falcon presumed that they had been working on the small farmlands.

From above, dozens of beady eyes appeared, looking down at them.

"Armeen!" shouted three small voices at once. They belonged to a trio of children whose heads had just appeared over the railing above. "You're back!"

"Don't come down," Armeen shouted. He held up his hand. "I'll be up there in a short while."

If Falcon thought that the children had been glad, he hadn't seen anything yet. The villagers all ran to Armeen as if welcoming a conquering hero. They smiled and surrounded him, bombarding him with a multitude of questions. Men patted his back, women handed him flowers, and a few children tugged at his coat, vying for his attention.

"Calm yourselves!" ordered a woman. She had snow-white hair and deep wrinkles marring her long face. She walked slowly. Her luxurious jade cane seemed to be the only thing keeping her standing.

The small crowd parted, allowing the woman to approach.

"It is good to see you safe and sound," she said. "You bring this old heart much joy."

"It is good to see you too, Mother." Armeen embraced the woman in a long hug. "Were there any problems while I was gone?" He motioned over to the clumsy-looking huts. "Besides the obvious one. It looks as if Jonas had a hard time with the homes."

A tall, lanky man that Falcon assumed was Jonas spoke up. "I tried to build the huts just as you instructed me, Armeen. But the sticks wouldn't stick together. I even tried letting the mud rest as you said. But no matter what I tried, nothing worked."

"Don't fret about it, Jonas. We will go over it first thing tomorrow morning before my departure."

There was a wave of disappointment from the crowd of people.

"You're leaving so soon?" asked the elder woman. Her voice trembled as she spoke. "But you barely returned to us. Won't you stay at least until the next harvest?"

"My apologies, Mother. But I have given my word that I am to aid these Rohads. I am obliged to honor it."

"Of course, my son. I understand."

Falcon watched this exchange with great interest, still at a loss for what exactly was going on. He had gathered that the woman was Armeen's mother, but he hadn't figured much beyond that. The fact that Armeen was so young and was commanding people twice his elder was even more mind-boggling.

The young captain motioned to the crates that had been dragged behind him. "We relieved the governor of Terasa of the meats and rice he was hoarding for himself. Jonas, gather some men and carry the food to the kitchens. Have the women prepare it. We're feasting tonight!"

A loud cheer from the people rang out. A second later, the crowd dispersed as they resumed their business. Many went to their farming; others headed back into the underground holes. Falcon could only assume that that was where the kitchen was located.

"So who are these fine people?" asked the elder lady. "I judge from the dragon insignias that they are Rohads." She looked quizzically at her son. "That is strange. I have never before known you to side with Rohads, or anyone else for that matter. What brought this change?"

"They paid their dues," said Armeen. "And one of them knows the seas quite well. Together we located the pass between Missea and the Coral Sea."

She nodded. "That's good to hear."

Armeen introduced every single one of them by name. Afterward, the old lady headed underground.

"Is there anything I can do to help?" asked Falcon. He looked over at the small plots of land. A long evening working the lands seemed like a great way of spending some time. It would help ease his mind and give him time to concentrate on his holy wielding.

The captain called Gertie over. "Have him join you in making the rounds."

Rounds? Falcon didn't like the sound of that. Usually when someone had to make rounds it was because there was someone about to attack. But considering that Armeen was a wanted criminal, it wasn't all that surprising.

"Do you really think your enemies can find you deep in here?" asked Aya doubtfully.

Gertie answered. "The cap'n is just taking precautions. We're so well hidden that it's unlikely that we'll ever be found by anyone. One can never be too careful, though. Especially now that Ferenzie has moved into the neighboring island."

"Ferenzie?" asked Sheridan, voicing what Falcon was thinking.

"He's a man who has been hunting the cap'n for some years now. He must have gotten information that we're in the nearby area because he set up a temporary base on Chia

Island, which is a little southwest of here."

"He is of no importance," said Armeen. He did not look worried in the slightest. "He's a fool that knows nothing of the jungles or of tracking. He will give up his search and be gone in no time."

Gertie scratched his head, not looking entirely convinced. "I don't know, cap'n. When you stole the last batch from him he looked mighty furious. I don't think he'll be giving up his chase until he has hounded you to the ends of Va'siel. Especially since you were once part of his—"

"Your concern has been noted," said Armeen, arching his eyebrows at the man. "Now do as instructed, Mr. Gertie, and make the rounds."

Gertie seemed to understand that he had over spoken. Silenced, he stared at the captain for a split second and then looked away. It was only for a fleeting moment, but Falcon saw it. There was something they were both hiding. A secret, perhaps.

"Let's go," said Gertie, tugging at Falcon's jacket.

"I'm going too," said Sheridan.

Hiromy's eyes lit up. "If you're going, than so am I. I want to see more of those flowers."

"This is no sightseeing tour, young lassie," said Armeen. "It may be best if you stay here where it's safe. I'm sure Miss Faith is eager to do some more of that media...er... mudata."

"Meditation," finished Faith.

Sheridan stepped in front of Hiromy defensively. "She can take care of herself."

"So be it. Do not complain to me if the young lassie gets hurt."

Feeling quite content that he wasn't alone in his dislike for Captain Armeen, Falcon took off after Gertie. Faith headed into the underground tunnels and disappeared below.

He waited until they moved deeper into the trees. The air was thick with the aroma of fresh dirt, and in no time, the usual wild of the jungle returned. He sighed, wishing he had stayed back at the small camp. Trekking a forsaken, humid jungle wasn't his first choice when it came to filling his empty schedule.

The silent walk was made even more uncomfortable by the fact that Sheridan was still not speaking to him. For someone so carefree, he could really hold a grudge.

"Quiet!" called Gertie, after yet another one of Hiromy's high-pitched lullabies. She would break out in a song from time to time, which didn't seem to be sitting to well with the short pirate.

"So?" asked Falcon. "What exactly is Armeen's past with this Ferenzie fellow?"

A number of branches snapped in half as the pirate stepped over them. His mouth remained unmoving.

"So?" continued Falcon. "It sounds like your boss was

once was in league with this Ferenzie. Did that gutless Armeen betray him and steal his gold or something? That is what he does, isn't it?"

"Shut it," said Gertie. "The cap'n is a great man. Something the likes of you wouldn't understand."

Falcon winced. It was clear that Gertie was loyal to Captain Armeen. If he was going to find out what they were hiding, he would have to do it another way.

"Can I hear your heartbeat?" asked a chirpy voice behind him. Falcon raised an eyebrow as Hiromy moved close to him. She put her ear on his chest and listened intently. "Wow. Such a beautiful heartbeat."

"Shhhh..." hissed Gertie.

Falcon used this as his chance to take a step back.

The young princess frowned as she watched his retreat, but she quickly forgot all about him and returned to her humming.

"See that?" Gertie pointed to a small island obscured by a veil of misty fog.

Falcon nodded, crouched behind the green bushes as Gertie was doing. He was quiet for a long while as he examined the small fort. From this distance, he barely made out a large wooden fence that appeared to have been made out of freshly cut logs. He leaned forward, hoping to get a better view. It did not help much. He thought he saw movement, but he wasn't entirely sure.

"What is that?" asked Sheridan.

"It's Ferenzie's temporary camp. He's been launching search parties for the cap'n from there."

"Seems awfully close," said Sheridan. Falcon was thinking the exact thing.

"No. We're safe here." Gertie sounded uncertain. "He doesn't know where to begin his search. As long as we don't draw any attention to ourselves, we're in no danger."

Gertie had just finished spewing his last word when the water rose into a wave fifteen feet high.

"Oh no!" Sheridan ran after Hiromy, who now stood enveloped knee-deep in the water. She waved her hands, and the water whirled and rose even higher.

Sheridan reached her just before she increased the height.

"What's wrong?" asked Hiromy, oblivious to what she'd done. "I just wanted to make the water dance. It was so sad and alone."

"Get out of the water, you fools!" hissed Gertie.

Falcon watched from behind the bushes with sinking spirits. Sheridan had pulled Hiromy out of the water and back behind cover, but Falcon doubted that was enough. There was no way that the men from the fort had not seen the water tower. Not only had it been unnaturally high, the splash it had created had sent loud ripples emanating through the water.

"You were supposed to be watching her!" Gertie was

visibly furious. "It would be a miracle if they didn't see her wielding!"

"I'm sorry," said Hiromy. Her lips trembled, and she began to cry into Sheridan's shirt.

"Let's get back. I must report this to the cap'n!"

The walk back to the camp was much quieter than before. Besides Hiromy's regretful sobs, nothing was audible. Falcon doubted she even knew what exactly she'd done wrong. She was simply crying because she understood enough to know that she had messed up yet again.

Sheridan, who had done a superb job at ignoring Falcon before, finally broke his icy silence.

"I just looked away for a split second," he said regretfully. The way he spoke, it sounded as if he wanted Falcon to reassure him that everything would be fine. He couldn't do that. The truth was, Falcon didn't know if things would go well or not. All he knew was that they had more than enough troubles as it was. They didn't need to add to it by having one of Armeen's enemies coming after them. Though he had no lost love for Armeen, he knew that their fates were, whether he liked it or not, momentarily intertwined. If the pirate captain became entangled in a battle with this Ferenzie, it would take days or even weeks to defeat Armeen's foe. That was time they didn't have. With every passing moment, the Suteckh threat increased. He could feel it with every fiber of his being.

~~~

Aya and Armeen stepped into a large carriage that had had its roof completely torn off. At the top, a metal hook that held a triple-braided rope had been attached to it. The fancy curved lines outside the white carriage told her that it had belonged to someone of wealth: royalty, or perhaps a noble.

He whistled once, and the carriage began to ascend.

"Don't worry," assured Armeen. "We use the sturdiest carriages. We're completely safe."

Aya smiled, trying not to show her discomfort. She wasn't the slightest afraid of the carriage breaking under their weight. What did scare her were heights. It was a fear she had always carried with her, despite her best efforts to overcome it.

Fortunately, in seconds the carriage stopped moving and she stepped off onto wooden planks. Nervously, she held onto the oak wood railings, making it a point not to look down.

The children, who had earlier called out at Armeen, embraced him. Like the adults, they shouted thousands of questions at him.

Their words became a distant echo in the back of Aya's head as she took in the sight with awe. From the bottom it had been hard to see, but now, from up here, she had a firsthand look at the wondrous village. Dozens of sturdy bridges connected countless trees to make an intricate system of paths and intersections. Some of the bridges led up to even higher sections of the trees. Some of the trunks had been cut open and doors had been attached to them, essentially making them small homes. At other spots, entire wooden huts, much better looking than the ones on the ground, had been built. Many of them had windows where people could be seen going about their business.

What amazed Aya the most was the fine detail of the work. Like a complex puzzle that had been completed, everything looked completely safe and in place. There wasn't a single board, nail, or plank out of place. Whoever had constructed this village was obviously an exceptionally experienced craftsman. And even though she was used to living in a large city, she found herself enjoying the rustic feeling of the place.

"Who built this?" she asked once the children had scattered away.

"I did," said Armeen matter-of-factly.

"You?" She was certain he was jesting. Armeen was much too young to have created something this grand. Where would he have found the time and the skills? No, this was surely the work of a patient, age-experienced master, something Armeen could not possibly be. "I'm serious. Who did this?"

"I'm also being serious. I did."

"Fine. Don't tell me, then."

Armeen shrugged indifferently and motioned for her to

follow him. They walked past dozens of people. Many of the men were carrying planks up a sloped bridge. She took this as a sign that they were expanding, making their home in the trees larger. A number of women cooked outside their homes over an open fire. Many of the kids ran around, playing with a number of balls. Despite the extremely wide walkways, she couldn't help but feel a bit scared for them.

"They're perfectly safe," said Armeen, noticing her discomfort. "The railings I built for them will hold."

She nodded and continued to follow in silence until they arrived at a cabin that looked unlike any other she'd seen thus far. This one had no windows and, like a layer of bark, completely surrounded a thick tree. It had no roof.

Armeen pushed the door and held it open, which Aya took as a sign to go in.

The place was simple enough. In fact, it reminded her of Armeen's Gold Chaser quarters in more ways than one. There was a small bed against the wall that looked as if it had never been slept on. A desk, much smaller than the one on the ship, rested beside it. She walked around the circumference of the tree. Large holes had been cut into it, making room for hundreds of neatly arranged books. They were arranged according to color. There was an entire line of red-leather bound books, followed by green ones, black ones, and so on.

Armeen took out a yellow-stained parchment and

handed it to Aya. "I think this is it."

She examined the map with great interest. Indeed this was the map written by Linius, the famous Master Record Keeper from Missea. Once, she'd read that the man had collected maps from around Va'siel and had himself mapped his hometown and surrounding areas. She knew exactly what to look for.

While she searched, Armeen drank from his many bottles of wine. After about twenty minutes, he slumped against the wall. His cheeks were slightly rosy and his feet wobbly.

"There!" She pointed at the straight golden-colored line on the map that stretched from Missea to the Coral Sea. That had to be the hidden pass that Linius had found, it just had to be.

"I wonder why he never revealed the location," slurred Armeen. "A shortcut like that could shave days, even weeks off travel. If you hadn't discovered his method of mapmaking, the pass would have gone undiscovered for who knows how many more years."

"You're amazing," said Armeen. He stared directly into Aya's eyes, and, for a fraction of a second, she saw sadness in them. It wasn't the first time she had noticed it. She sensed it before when they were alone in his quarters. It was faint, and to anyone else it might have gone unnoticed but not to her. Then, quite suddenly, Armeen grabbed her by her shoulders and leaned in, going for her lips.

Her heart beat faster as she moved her head to the side. The captain's kiss missed, landing on her cheek and leaving behind a lingering scent of alcohol.

He breathed in heavily and, still clutching her arms, took a step back. "My apologies. It's that Rohad Falcon, right?" He didn't wait for her to answer. "What am I saying? Of course you have feelings for him. It's as clear as day."

"That's not it." Aya excelled at garnering tidbits of information and discerning a bigger picture. The more she stared at Armeen, the clearer his story unfolded before her.

"What was her name?" she said.

"Whose name?" asked Armeen, taking a seat on the rocking chair. He looked up at the leaves above.

"What was the name of the girl I remind you of? When you see me, I sense you searching for her. Was she also a slave?"

His eyes grew wide. "How did you know?"

"Back in the Gold Chaser you found every excuse imaginable not to read, even though you have dozens of books." She motioned to the books inside the tree. "Usually people categorize their books alphabetically, but you categorized yours by color." She met his eyes. "You don't know how to read, do you?"

"Very few slaves are taught in the ways of literature." He breathed in heavily. "Is that all it took to give it away?"

"No. You also have beds, but never use them. The one here hasn't even been slept on because you're used to sleeping on the floor."

Aya stopped talking. She could continue on with more odd intricacies, but what good would that do? She'd proven her point. Besides, he had yet to mention the girl that she reminded him of.

It took a long time, but finally he spoke. He recounted his story as she listened silently. He told her how he was born into slavery. He would work from sunup to sundown. It was there that he was taught carpentry. Even as a child, he was expected to keep up with the grown men, so he worked hard and learned quickly.

Suddenly, Aya realized Armeen had been telling the truth. He had indeed built most of the village himself. His training as a slave had ensured that.

"She was a slave in Ferenzie's slave camp as well," continued Armeen. "Seeing you reminds me so much of her. She was strong. You should have seen that lassie. The way she stood up for everyone was inspiring. And despite being blind, she could fight with the best of them."

Aya found her interest suddenly peaked. A blind girl who could fight? There couldn't be too many of those.

"What was her name?" she asked.

Armeen looked up at her with wary eyes. "Keira."

Chapter 16

"What did you say?" asked Aya.

"Keira. That was her name."

She couldn't believe it. She had met Keira on her previous mission to Sugiko. She did recall Nanake saying that Keira had been lost for a few years and that she never spoke of her time away, but Aya had assumed that Keira had been hiding in the woods. Even stranger, Armeen didn't seem to know that Keira was a princess. Well, empress now. Aya herself had aided her in reclaiming her rightful place as Empress of Sugiko.

"How did you escape?" Aya asked, opting not to tell him that there was a strong chance she knew the person he was speaking about. Getting his hopes up falsely would only be cruel.

But Armeen didn't answer. Obviously exhausted, he crumpled to the floor and fell in a deep sleep, his snores echoing loudly off the walls.

Aya undid the sheet from the bed and carefully set it over the captain.

"Dream well. I'm sure you'll find who you're looking for soon enough," she whispered as she closed the door and walked outside.

~~~

The next few hours passed in a blur. The first chance she had, Aya got on the carriage and headed back down to the jungle floor. Sitting beside a hut, she went over the navigation book she had borrowed from Armeen, trying to figure out the weather patterns along the sea. Surely with a little studying, she could chart out the best course of travel. However, she found it impossible to concentrate. Before, the task of finding the shortcut and getting to Missea had kept her mind from focusing on her family. But now? She found that she did not have anything to keep those thoughts from invading her mind.

The images of her father flashed in her mind, reminding her that she was not a Ladrian, but a Suteckh like her sister, the Blood Empress.

She had spent so much time thinking her sister was dead, and now part of her wished she were. Selene had been twisted from that innocent sweet girl she knew as a child to a ruler of destruction. How was she supposed to get past countless years of brainwashing?

Sensing the hopelessness of the situation caused her eyes to burn as slow tears fell from her eyes. Selene? What have they done to you? What have they done?

~~~

Falcon was surprised to find Aya sitting alone by a hut when they walked back into the camp. Her eyes were red, almost as if she had just finished crying.

"What happened?" she asked, wiping her eyes. She looked from Sheridan to Falcon.

Gertie shoved his finger at Hiromy's direction. "She alerted Ferenzie of our location!"

"We don't know that yet," countered Sheridan as Hiromy stared down at the ground.

Gertie simply groaned and headed up to the trees, no doubt to report to Armeen what had occurred.

When the captain came back, he did not look nearly as angry as Falcon thought he was going to be. If anything, he looked rather jubilant and well rested.

"If what Gertie said is true," the captain declared, "then we must make haste across the sea at once. If we leave tomorrow morning, we may yet make it to the pass on time."

That was certainly good news for Falcon. He yearned to get to Missea as soon as possible.

"What about Ferenzie?" asked Aya.

"Don't fret about him. Even if he saw the water tower, it would take him quite some time to locate us. Remember that I said his tracking skills are sub-par. Besides, we know not if he even saw the water tower. We'll leave at first light tomorrow. That will give me more than enough time to return and see to my people."

The news that Ferenzie might have spotted them did not hinder the spirits in the camp. The main reason for this was the newfound supply of food that Armeen had brought.

Faith, along with the women from the kitchen, brought out plate after plate of food. Children ran around the camp and up into the trees, carrying food to the people above.

"They certainly don't seem worried," said Falcon. He sat beside his group of friends on the ground. Hiromy and Sheridan were sharing a plate of drumsticks and peanuts together. Aya had a full plate of food, but she barely picked at it. Faith carried a deep bowl with a variety of herbs.

"That's because they have complete faith in their captain," said Faith.

Falcon sighed silently. Not Faith too. It was bad enough Aya saw stars every time she was with Armeen.

"I think he's hiding something," he said, taking a bite out of the buttery pichion drumstick. "I heard Gertie saying something about him being with Ferenzie once. I think that perhaps they were once partners, until Armeen stole from him, that is."

"He stole himself," said Faith.

"What?" Falcon looked at Faith in confusion.

"I spoke to his mother when we were preparing the food. She was a slave when she gave birth to Armeen, which meant that he too was a slave."

Aya nodded knowingly, and Falcon flinched back, taking a deep breath. Apparently I'm the only one who doesn't know what's going on.

Faith took a small bite from a piece of crunchy lettuce

before continuing. "He escaped soon after, but he didn't stop there. He came back and freed hundreds of slaves, including his mother. Since then he's been going around freeing slaves from all over Va'siel and bringing them here, where they can live in peace."

"That's bad news for you, Hyatt," said Sheridan with a smirk.

"Me?"

"Yes. You've been looking for a reason to hate him, but it's hard to hate a pirate who steals people to give them their freedom."

"I don't want to hate him," lied Falcon. The truth was that Sheridan was right. He had hoped that the secret Armeen was something less… well, noble. But as luck would have it, he seemed to be a bona fide hero.

The thought that his sense of judgment was so terrible brought a smile to Falcon's face. He didn't mean to, it just spread across his face unwillingly, fueled by the years and years of times he'd been wrong about so many people: Professor Kraimaster, Braiden, Lao, and now Captain Armeen. What's wrong with me? The more he thought about it, the more comical it became, and he found himself chuckling under his breath.

"That's a first," said Sheridan, looking down at Falcon's emblem with eyes wide. "It looks like Hemstath's rubbing off on you."

He looked down at his emblem and saw that indeed his emblem had taken a slight white color of holy. A warm feeling spread through him as he and Faith's gazes met, and once again he chuckled, no longer sure what exactly he was so happy about.

Everyone in the group, including Aya, looked at him in confusion for a while, then they too broke out in contagious laughter.

There, under the stars, the five friends rejoiced and told stories, making the night pass in a blur of strange bliss.

~~~

The next morning they trekked through the jungle and boarded the Gold Chaser before the suns had even reached the top of the mountain. More jubilant than he'd felt in a long time, Falcon was still feeling the effects of the small control of holy wielding he had experienced the night before.

The fact that Aya was no longer locked up in Armeen's cabin helped raise his spirits.

Faith, Aya, and Hiromy had spent most of the walk behind everyone else, lost in conversation. And now, aboard the ship, they were doing the same. The trio stood at the front of the deck, snickering quietly among themselves. For a while, at least, things seemed to be relatively back to normal. Except for the fact that he and Aya hadn't really spoken much other than that morning when she had yelled at him.

"We're making good progress," called Armeen. The

captain walked across the deck, his footsteps echoing loudly on the old wood. "I knew that we would be there." He stood at the front of the ship and spread his hands, letting the fresh breeze flow around his body.

"Hey, Hyatt," called Sheridan. Like Falcon, he was bent over cleaning the wood panels with a small brush. "Can you believe that guy? He might be some great liberator, but he's still a pest. He could have us do anything, but instead he has us help with the lowest of the jobs here." He pointed to the dragon insignia on his chest. "We're Rohads, not some peons."

"He's not too bad," said Falcon.

Sheridan stopped scrubbing and looked at him suspiciously.

Without saying a word, Falcon looked down and continued to work. I can't believe I just said that. What was he thinking? Armeen was the same man who had been robbing him of the time he could have spent with Aya, the same man who had made him clean decks. He couldn't defend him now. But despite searching for something negative to say about him, nothing came to mind. Apparently the holy wielding had worked a bit too well.

He supposed that was good news. That could only mean that he was getting a step closer to controlling the chaos. Nonetheless, he remained quiet as he continued to work. Who knew what this holy energy would make him do next. Why, next time he might actually go on an Armeen-complimenting rant.

It was many hours later and dusk had begun to settle in when Gertie finally called out that land had come into view.

Falcon looked out at the horizon, struggling to see the land that Gertie was referring to. He searched aimlessly, but all he made out was dark waves clashing and rising. Falling against each other.

"It's right in there." Armeen handed Falcon the long spyglass he carried around his waist.

With it, Falcon managed to spot a small speck of gray and white in the vast sea.

"That's the pass?" asked Falcon, doubtfully. The piece of land, if it could even be called that, looked barely big enough to hold a dozen people. He failed to see how that constituted a shortcut to Missea.

"Yes, at least that is what the young lassie, Aya, believes." He looked over at Aya and gave her a long stare that Falcon did not like.

The Gold Chaser moved closer, and the small piece of land took a form. As Falcon had suspected, it wasn't much to look at. It had a few white, sharp-edged rocks, some specks of sand, but nothing much beside that.

The Rohads, Armeen, and Faith got off and moved around the small island. Everyone else remained on board.

Aya got on her knees and began to brush away the

sand.

"What does she search for? Treasure?" asked one of the pirates, his eyes twinkling with hungry anticipation.

No one answered, opting to watch Aya as she continued to brush away the sand.

There's nothing there. As the thought crossed his mind, a piece of metal revealed itself, embedded under the sand. A few wipes later and the squared rusted hatch came into view.

Everyone held their breath when their eyes fell on the insignia that had been burnt into the very metal. It rose from the hatch as if someone had fire wielded it with blue fire.

Even Sheridan, who was always ready with a comment, had fallen silent.

Falcon took in the oval shape with a cross in the middle with awe and fear. Even he recognized the insignia of the Onaga clansmen, a race of diabolical creatures that had been thought to have gone instinct over a century ago.

~~~

Melousa, Queen of the Orian warriors, took a large bite of the chunk of meat in her hands. She savored each salted bite. In her other hand she carried the entire leg of a lamb. In no time, all that was left was bare bone. She enjoyed eating, but consuming food was more of a necessity than pleasure. She stood over fourteen feet tall, with powerful legs that were long and easily six feet by themselves. A muscular figure like hers required an immense amount of energy.

She tossed the bones over to her two chileras, which flanked her at her throne, a piece of rock with another piece of rock behind it to lean on. The giant cat-like animals tore at the bones with a ravenous hunger. Usually, she would have fed them meat as well, but events had not been going well in her jungle-kingdom for some time now. Food was scarce, and more and more land was being lost every year.

"Damn imperials," she cursed under her breath. The capital cities from across the ocean had been constantly poaching her land, looking for rare spices and animal fur. It didn't matter how many she killed. The city fools kept on coming like a locust plague, intent on taking all her domain.

Melousa glared around her. There was a large collection of palm-leaved huts sloppily spread about. No one was inside any of the huts, however, for now was the time of the gauntlet. Every single one of her female warriors was expected to be outside, at the center of the village, to either watch or participate in the battles.

There had been no wars in many years, and this had become the only way to appease the savage nature of her warriors.

"Clete," she called. A bronze-skinned warrior stood and walked to the battleground, which was nothing more than an oval clearing surrounded by long spikes. Many were the warriors who had met their end on those spikes, and Melousa was certain many more would follow. Whenever one of them died, she would not mourn them or give them a proper burial. To die in battle was to be weak and weakness was something the Orian warriors did not tolerate.

"Scyleia!" This time, a woman, almost as tall as the queen herself, stood and entered the arena.

Both women grabbed a spear and faced each other.

"Show no mercy to yer fellow sister!" Melousa ordered to both women. "Kill!"

The woman moved against each other, but just as their weapons were about to clash, something strange happened.

The earth shook.

"Find the wielder!" yelled Melousa, her rage instantly intensifying. She recognized the power of earth wielders immediately, and if there was anything she hated more than capital city people, it was earth wielders. "Bring me their bloodied corpse so I be breaking every bone from their body myself."

"No need for such violence," called a calm voice. The earth moved forward in waves, holding above it a man who looked to be made of Earth itself. He had deep brown skin that looked to be cracked in pieces. Every cut of his body was etched in a deep crimson. "I'm Kaidoz, General of the Suteckh Empire. I have a proposition for you, great queen."

~~~

Kaidoz's eyes met those of the wild queen that sat on a dreary piece of rock. Hundreds of skulls and bones surrounded her "throne." Indeed, the stories he'd heard had been true. Melousa was the tallest woman he had ever seen. Like many of her kind, all of her skin was a deep purple. She wore a dark brown rag that covered her breast, and another old rag hung under her waistline. A long bone ran horizontally through her nose and circled on both sides, coming together above her thick lips. Her untamed, dark hair was long, reaching to her lower back. Another explosion of spiked hair spurt atop her head, pointing to the skies. Dozens of bracelets dangled on her arms and legs. A long necklace of bones fell from her neck.

"I be wanting no proposition from yer!" roared Melousa. Spears in hand, her warriors took an offensive stance. "For yer insolence I be having yer killed."

Kaidoz held his hand up. "I have information on your children!"

"Cidralic and Dokua!" She stomped her foot, her fangs bare as they spit out drool. "I could be caring less of those two. Cidralic left his own kin to be a lowly commander to those Suteckh. Can yer imagine the shame? A son of mine, serving capital city vermin!" She rolled her massive fist. "Dokua was no better. She left seeking revenge for a brother that be not worth it. And to be making everything worse, those two died in battle!"

Kaidoz nodded. He was well aware of the Orians' beliefs. For them, dying in battle was a sign of weakness. A public mark of humiliation that branded one unworthy. It was the dream of every Orian warrior to die of old age. This was the only way of proving one's superiority over one's foes.

"Great Queen—"

"No more words. Yer be bringing me unpleasant news. Yer shall die a painful death at my hands!"

The queen stood. Despite his hint of apprehension, Kaidoz remained still. It was imperative that he remain calm. Besides, the queen was blessed with skin of the ancients. This meant that she could take a lot of attacks, even elemental ones, without going down. This might account for why she was over one hundred years old but showed no sign of her age.

"I thought you wanted revenge on Empress Latiha of Missea," he said. As he'd expected, the queen stopped dead in her tracks. Her face registered a sense of confusion. Kaidoz could tell she was having an inner struggle. Part of her wished nothing more than to kill the earth wielder before her, but the other, more vengeful side, wanted to know what news he brought of her ancient rival.

"It not be mattering what I want with that squaw," she said, her curiosity winning out. "The Golden Wielder put a protection shell over her. Even I be not strong enough to defy his earth power." Her gaze turned to Kaidoz, and she stomped her foot, causing the skulls to rattle as they tumbled crashed into each other. "I be hating earth wielders! Yer die!"

"Truly you are grossly misinformed, great queen. The

Golden Wielder, Aadi, is no more. It's been years since he left this world. Whatever protection shell he cast went with him."

Immediately, Kaidoz saw that he had gotten the reaction he had wanted. The queen's lips twisted into a cruel smile.

"So yer be saying that the squaw no longer has the protection!" It was more of a statement than a question. "That be meaning that I will finally be getting my revenge on her for taking my sister all those years ago." She turned to the women beside her and raised her arm. "Orian warriors, ready yerselves! We be going to war!"

Kaidoz smiled, glad at how easy it had been to manipulate the queen. Now all he needed was to enact the next phase of his plan.

Missea was to be his next stop.

Chapter 17

Hiromy, apparently oblivious to what the sign meant, bent down and caressed the lumpy insignia. "How beautiful." Her voice was dreamy.

"Perhaps you should reconsider your trek through this pass, lassie."

"No," Aya answered without much thought. "We need to get to Missea as soon as possible and, like it or not, this is the fastest way there."

"Then I shall pray for you, lassie." The captain took Aya's hand and gave her a gentle kiss. "I hope that you quickly rid yourselves of the woes that loom over you."

"Thank you for everything." Aya planted a kiss on Armeen's cheek. "I hope to see you soon." Then without looking back, she moved the slab of metal aside and jumped into the hole.

Hope to see you soon? What did she mean by that? Had they agreed on something that he was unaware of?

"Are you four coming or what?" asked Aya from down below.

Falcon nodded a quick goodbye to the pirates and hopped into the hole. As he did, he noticed a face of dread across every single one of the men. Armeen, in particular, appeared exceptionally distraught. His eyebrows were drawn together, and his posture was stooped. It was as if he knew that the Rohads were entering their underground grave. He couldn't say he wasn't thinking the same thing. Onaga clansmen were terrible beings who tried to exert their dominance over Va'siel many years ago. Had it not been for the interference of the Golden Wielder, they probably would have succeeded in attaining their goal. It wasn't only their ruthless behavior that made them dangerous. The Onaga's were said to have different abilities. Some could absorb wielding attacks, others withstand them. Many other abilities remained lost to time. To this day, it remained a mystery as to how exactly the Golden Wielder had singlehandedly managed to defeat the entire court of Onaga royalty. It was hard to defeat one, but to take out all seven of them, especially when they all possessed such diverse abilities, was nearly inconceivable.

Sheridan landed beside him with a loud thump. He took a quick glance around and shrugged, unimpressed. "I still don't see why this place has everyone so spooked. So it has the Onaga insignia. What of it? They were all defeated."

"There lies the problem," said Aya, her voice strained. "The history books don't have too much information on what exactly happened with the Onagas. We know more about the scorch that plagued Va'siel than the Onagas. However, many of the books reference the fact the Golden Wielder did defeat them but not kill them."

"What does that mean?" asked Faith. Her voice was as low as a mouse's.

"The books suggest that the Golden Wielder locked them up somewhere in Va'siel. It might very well be that this is the hidden sanctuary. That would explain the sign at the entrance."

"Phewww!" Sheridan said incredulously. Falcon could tell that he wasn't believing anything that he was hearing. "Why would the Golden Wielder lock them up? Why not just kill them and be rid of them?"

Aya threw up her hands. "I don't know, Sheridan. I don't have all the answers. I'm simply saying what I know. Besides, this would also explain why this pass has been taken off most maps. Look around. It used to serve as some kind of merchant pass. But it looks like it hasn't been used in a long time."

Falcon quietly took in the scenery. The air was thick. Grimy stone walls that seemed to be feet thick flanked them from both sides. Torches blazed on the walls, providing an ominous red and orange glow. Normally, he would have wondered how a torch could have lasted a century without its fire extinguishing, but at the moment that was the least of his worries. Through the darkness, he managed to make out a number of broken down stalls leaning against the walls. When he closed his eyes, he could almost see the room buzzing with activity as vendors sold to passing customers. Now, however, old beat-down memories were all that remained of that time long past.

"Lithan." said Faith. Instantly, a ball of light materialized before her. It bobbed up and down, its translucent white body moving with every step its caster took.

"I don't get why some of you guys do that?" said Sheridan.

"Do what?" asked Faith.

"Announce the ability you're casting. Seems like a sure-fire way to tell your enemy what you're about to do."

"It has some drawbacks," said Faith, much more patiently than Falcon would have answered. "But announcing what one is about to do is a way to enhance one's abilities."

"Many martial artists like me yell before an attack to focus our power," added Aya. "It's the same as you. I've seen you yell before you lunge in for a sword attack. You do it because it's a way to focus and drive your energy. Isn't that the same as announcing to your enemy you're going in for an attack?"

Sheridan shuffled in his feet. ""Well, I suppose so."

"Why are we talking about this?" asked Hiromy.

Falcon nodded in agreement, and he couldn't believe that it was Hiromy of all people who had to call them out on it. Here they were, in the middle of a possible Onaga sanctuary, and they were trying to explain basic attacks strategies to Sheridan that he, for all intents and purposes, should have been already aware of. It was first-year stuff, after all.

They moved in silence for a few minutes. The deeper they traversed, the darker and colder the narrow room became. Had it not been for Faith's light, they would have been completely blind.

Falcon held up his hand. A snake-like wave of fire surrounded his arm. He waved it around, trying to spread the light and warmth his flames provided. He smiled inside as he noticed Aya getting a bit closer to him. He wasn't sure whether it was just a coincidence or she was trying to be closer to the heat, but either way, he enjoyed it.

A moment later they arrived at an end. They now stood at the top of a set of descending stairs. Falcon followed the stone path with his eyes until the steps disappeared in pitch darkness.

Faith had the best source of light, so she led the way down. Falcon and Aya followed closely behind. Hiromy and Sheridan up back the rear. They had their hands wrapped in each other's and walked so close together that Falcon was sure they were having no problem staying warm. Something that, despite his flames, he couldn't say for himself.

The path down became extremely narrow. So narrow that Falcon's elbows were constantly grinding against the hard walls. The stairs appeared to go down forever. They walked hour after hour, with no apparent end in sight. Once in a while they would sit to rest their aching legs, but every rest was only a few minutes long, and every stretch of walking was at least two hours.

Finally, when Falcon thought he was going to drop in exhaustion they came to the end.

"About time!" called out Sheridan.

"Wow," Hiromy spun in place. She looked to be the only one that wasn't tired. "It only gets more beautiful by the second!"

Falcon grimaced. Obviously he and Hiromy had vastly different opinions on what constituted beauty. The massive room had hundreds of thick stone pillars that stretched up until they disappeared in the distance. No doubt, somewhere, miles above them, there was a ceiling. The room had an air of abandonment hanging around it. Hundreds of skulls were spread across the floor. The room was so large, though, that even with the countless skulls, it was easy enough to walk across without stepping on one. Like the small entrance, this grand hall was also filled with long torches blazing on the walls and pillars.

"Beacoup-Lithan." The ball of light that Faith had created before was now joined by four other ones, so that now five white lights were floating above her. She spread out her arms, and the lights stretched out farther away from her. This allowed them to have a much wider view of the area around them, which revealed more skulls, but no clear path in which to follow.

Faith looked at Falcon with concern. "Now what?"

Falcon tried to look confident, even though he had no real idea what he was doing. He couldn't show that, though. Everyone looked up to him to lead them. It was his job to lead them through this with all of them intact.

"Let's keep moving forward. I'm certain the way up will be up ahead."

Everyone followed his word, and they moved. The place was so large that their footsteps would echo loudly across the room. At first, Falcon thought the repetitive ghostly footsteps annoying. Nonetheless, after a while the noises blended into his subconscious and became the norm.

A wave of apprehension washed over him as they passed yet another pillar. His stomach felt heavy. Where am I leading them to?

At that exact moment, when he was about to suggest that perhaps they were lost, he felt a strange sensation spurt within him. It began on his head and spread down to his eyes. It was strange and warm, and suddenly, he saw a golden aura stretch before him. The aura spread in a single line. It moved forward and then folded around a pillar and disappeared around the corner.

"Do you guys see that?" he asked.

Aya stared at him and then ahead to where Falcon was looking. "See what?"

"The light. That glowing path there." He pointed at it, as if willing them to see it.

His four companions looked at each other, confusion etched in their expression.

"Falcon," Faith said. Her green eyes bore into his. "There is nothing there."

"How can you not see it, Faith? It's right the—"

He stopped speaking. It was obvious that he was the only one who was privy to the golden glow. Every fiber of his being told him to follow the light. It called on him, and something inside compelled him to obey.

He took off in a fast sprint. He could hear the footsteps of his companions close behind.

"Wait up!" yelled Aya.

"This air has driven Hyatt mad!"

"It's nice to not be the one who everyone is screaming at," said Hiromy in a sleepy, yet excited, voice.

He ignored their comments and continued to run as he followed the golden glow. The coldness of the room was now long forgotten, replaced by an eager hunger to discover who or what was calling to him. He reached an opening on the wall with an arched top. In his haste, he paid no mind to the fact that same Onaga insignia from before had been painted beside the entrance in black paint.

The long corridor that he followed afterward weaved and rose up and down in an uneven path. When it came to an end, Falcon stood in a long, rectangular room. Ahead of him were sets of stone steps that led up to a podium. On it were seven human-sized crystals standing against the wall. They looked strangely similar to the same crystals that he had seen back in K'vitch a few weeks prior. One of the crystals had been used as a self-imposed prison by Shal-Demetrius; the other ones had been used to suck the energy from the kidnapped children. Is there someone in those too?

"Careful, Hyatt. I don't like the feeling of this," Sheridan said.

Falcon paid him no mind. The golden trail led him to this spot. He was meant to be here; he could feel it. But why?

Faith walked up to one of the crystals and put her hand on it. There were visible cracks on it.

"These look a lot like the one back in K'vitch," she said, echoing Falcon's own thoughts. Carefully, she swiped away the layers of dust that covered the crystal. She staggered back, seeing what appeared to be a person's face inside it. He had some type of strange black hat that ran down its sides and covered his chin. Or was it a she? The thick crystal layers distorted the person's features, making it difficult to tell the sex. Their skin was a deep green. They had a wide nose that seemed to cover most of its face. A thin, wicked smile was spread across their lips, almost as if they were glad when they were trapped.

There was a plaque above it that read Vaenadia the Defiler.

Aya wiped away the dust of the second coffin-like

crystal. This one revealed a wrinkled dark face. Their skin was the darkest shade of black Falcon had ever seen. It almost looked as if they had been burnt by black fire, or as it was most commonly known, scorching death. The thought of that fire ability caused a heavy weight to befall on his chest. It had been that very same fire that had reportedly ended his brother's life all those years ago. The plaque above this black figure was too scratched to be fully read. Falcon made out the letters Xe, but anything beyond that had become a dark blur.

"I don't believe it," said Aya. She wiped away the dust of yet another crystal. This one was much larger than the other ones, about five times the size. In it rested a stubby man with easily the largest belly Falcon had ever seen. Besides the beady black eyes and gargantuan stomach, it was difficult to see much. The plaque above it read: Hapaphon the Devourer.

"Pheeewwwww!" said Sheridan. "This guy puts the Emperor's gut to shame."

"Hey!" said Hiromy, sounding slightly offended. "That's my dad you're talking about."

Sheridan put his hands up. "Sorry."

For a while Falcon was afraid Hiromy was about to go on one of her crazed rants, but she just pouted and went back to investigating the crystals.

"Are they dead?" asked Faith.

"I don't think so," said Falcon. "They're in a deep sleep."

"How would you know that?" asked Aya. Her voice

dripped with doubt.

"I can sense it."

Everyone exchanged worried looks.

The air grew thick with quiet tension. Falcon knew what they were thinking. They been underground for a long time, and they'd been without much food or water. They believed he was going mad down here. That perhaps all the stress and confined spaces had gotten to him and were driving him to say and see things that weren't really there.

Finally, Aya spoke.

"Falcon. How could you possibly sense this place?"

"I didn't. I told you I saw the golden light, and I followed it."

"You just said that you sensed their energies." Faith motioned over to the beings inside the crystals.

"Not at first." He could hear the frustration increase in his voice. The doubtful look in their eyes also became more apparent with each passing second. Even Hiromy, of all people, was looking at him with fear on her face. "I saw the golden light and followed it. Once I got here I sensed their vague energies." He looked around at all of them. They all remained quiet. "You guys have to believe me. I'm not crazy!"

"Calm down, Falcon." Faith put her hand on his shoulder. "We're just trying to help you. A lot of wielders went mad when they came close to the power of the Onagas. You know that. We're just trying to make sure you're well."

He took a step back. "I'm fine!"

Indeed he recalled the stories that many men had gone berserk under the ancient power of the Onaga's. The vague tales that had been recorded told of people who had murdered their own families, turned cannibalistic, or much worse. In many ways, these powers reminded him of those of a mind wielder, and he certainly didn't feel he was under the control of any mind wielder.

His friends closed in.

"Let us help you, Hyatt."

Falcon's insides turned icy as he took in the bizarre turn of events. Are they going to attack me? Maybe they're the ones who are going mad!

Then, all of a sudden, the ground shook. It only lasted a second, and as quickly as it had begun, it stopped. Pebbles and dust that smelled of wet dirt fell from the ceiling. Falcon and Faith sneezed as dust made it into their nostrils.

"My apologies for this confusion," a firm voice echoed through the room.

Falcon forgot all about his itchy nose and scanned the surroundings, searching for the source of the voice. A bright glare burst from within the center of the room. The outline of a large, husky figure could be seen in the middle of the light.

Ghost Knight? No. His armor is much slimmer.

The light dimmed, revealing a golden-colored knight. A large, red cape fell from his shoulders.

Falcon looked at his friends, wondering whether they too were seeing this or he was once again imagining things. The shock in their faces made it clear that they were witnessing the same thing he was.

The newcomer's armor clanked against itself as he faced Falcon and then raised his hand in greeting. "Salutations, savior of Va'siel. I've been waiting a long time to meet you."

Falcon's jaw dropped. "Who? Whaaaa?"

"It appears that I'm still causing nothing but confusion." The knight crossed his arms, and his armor dissolved away in a swirl of golden dust. A brown-skinned man with kind eyes stared back at him. "I'm Aadi, or as history has come to know me, the Golden Wielder."

Chapter 18

Falcon's head was reeling in doubt. The Golden Wielder? How could that be possible? He had lived over a century ago. Even if the man before him was indeed the Golden Wielder, he would have to be an old man by now, but the man before him looked to be in his early thirties. He wore a simple light brown shirt and pants. His hair was also a dark brown, and there was an earthy scent emitting from him. It reminded Falcon of the aroma of dirt after it had rained.

"You're the Golden Wielder?" asked Sheridan. There was apprehension in his voice. "That's impossible. Isn't it er… sir?"

"I am a memory of the Golden Wielder," said the man. "A recollection he left here many decades ago to be found by the savior of Va'siel."

Sheridan looked more confused than before. He extended his hand and ran it through the Golden Wielder. The image of the man became distorted like a wave of smoke. Seconds later it recollected, and the man returned to normal. "So you're not really here. I get that much. I still don't understand why you left a memory of yourself. You did say you left this memory for the savior of Va'siel, and you're the savior."

"Please," said the man, his soft eyes softening into a

smile. "Call me Aadi. I always hated all those sir, Golden Wielder, and savior labels people put on me."

"But you are a savior," said Falcon. All doubt was now gone. He felt a familiar connection with the man before him, and somehow he knew that he was indeed the wielder of legend. "Everyone knows the story of how you defeated the alien creature that was taking the energy from the planet. Va'siel wouldn't be here if it weren't for you."

"That's only one occasion," added Aya. Apparently she too had made up her mind that this man was Aadi. Or perhaps she was playing along. Falcon wasn't sure. "There were many other times you helped people in need." She pointed at the crystals before her. "Like the time you defeated the seven Onaga clansmen."

Aadi shrugged off the compliments. "No. I failed. Shal-Volcseck was the menace I never managed to locate. Even with my energy reading abilities, he eluded me for many years."

"Volcseck!" The mere thought of him made Falcon's heart fill with anger.

"I see that the power of chaos is within you, Falcon Hyatt," said Aadi. "You are indeed the savior of Va'siel."

The young wielders looked at each other in confusion.

"In my time a great calamity befell Va'siel, as you well know. The energies of the planet were being stolen. I found the creature that was responsible and put an end to him."

"Yes, we know." Falcon was well aware of the story that Aadi was relaying; he'd heard it more than enough times to know all the details.

"What you don't know was that the energy the creature had taken couldn't be returned to Va'siel at once because the sudden surge of energy would have destroyed the planet. The power needed to be put in a native of the land. This way, throughout their life they would release the power to the planet gradually, rather than all at once. Zoen and I placed it on a crystal where it lay dormant until someone who could control the power would be born. At that point the power would transfer to such person. It was highly unlikely that a being that could control all the elements would ever be born. Many, like my good friend, Zoen, thought it to be impossible. I, however, never had any doubt." The Golden Wielder stared into Falcon's eyes. "And here you are."

Aya, who always looked to be on top of everything, seemed lost for once. "So all the power from the crystal went to Falcon when he was born. Is that why he can wield all the elements?"

The Golden Wielder nodded. "Yes, that's correct. Good thing too. The crystal had only about three decades to go before it was unable to control the combination of energies. At the time it would have released all the power of the elements at once, and Va'siel would have ceased to exist."

If Falcon's world was spinning before, now it was

somersaulting right before his eyes. He grabbed one of the crystals to keep his legs steady. His hands slipped on the polished texture, and he almost stumbled to the ground. At the last minute, Sheridan gripped him by the arm and pulled him up.

"It can be a lot to take in," said Aadi.

No kidding! Falcon took a breath and tried to think of things he liked. But not even the thoughts of his favorite foods and scents could change his uneasiness. "H...how can you just come out and tell me all this like it's no big deal? Va'siel was on the brink of extinction."

"Simple. I never doubted that someone who could control all the powers would be born."

Falcon nodded his head unbelievingly. Aadi obviously was hugely optimistic. The total opposite of himself.

Aadi's smirk turned into a frown. "However, even with you born, Va'siel faces certain doom."

This time Sheridan spoke before Falcon could. "Volcseck!"

"Yes." Aadi nodded his head. "I searched for him, but he did a superb job of concealing his powers. Many times I came close to getting him, but every time, something or someone got in the way." He looked down at the crystal coffins.

"Zoen told me something similar," said Falcon. He tried to keep his voice steady as his heart thumped against his ribs.

238

He didn't want to reveal to everyone what he felt. He was confused, angry, but most of all he was excited. Here he was, speaking with the legendary Golden Wielder. Perhaps he would provide a key or tactic as to how to defeat Volcseck once and for all.

"Once I realized I wasn't going to find him," Aadi pressed on, "I settled with leaving a memory here for you to find. Luckily for me, Zoen was gifted enough to help me with that little task."

"How?" asked Falcon. "We found this place by accident. Had we not been searching for a shortcut, I would have never found you."

"No. You were destined to come here. You might not have known it, but ever since you were born, you were destined to walk this hall. Everything happens for a reason, and this is no exception."

"Say, I believe you," said Falcon, opting to forego the idea that he did not believe in destiny. He liked to think that he made his own choices, and that they weren't part of some large, elaborate scheme of the cosmos. "You're nothing but a memory, a long lost echo of a man who lived long ago. How could you possibly help me now?"

"You'd be surprised at the power that a simple memory can possess." For the first time, Aadi looked away from Falcon and turned to Faith. "You are the holy wielder that Volcseck searches for."

"Yes, sir," said Faith. "I am Faith Hemstath. It's an honor to meet you."

"No." The Golden Wielder gave Faith a slight bow. "The honor is all mine. In many ways, you're the key to Falcon's success. It is your kind heart that must guide him when the darkness threatens to envelop him."

"I'll try my best," said Faith, bowing slightly to Aadi as well. "May I ask a question, sir?"

"Certainly."

"The stories mention that you could wield without an emblem? That is supposed to be impossible. How did you do it?"

Falcon looked at Faith curiously. Indeed there was no emblem on either of his hands. But he did not see the point to asking such a question at a time like this. What did it matter if the Golden Wielder could wield with or without an emblem?

Aadi eyed Faith from top to bottom, as if he had no trouble knowing why Faith would pose such a question. "Most wielders control the power of their element with the physical element they carry with them. I, however, carry mine within." He brought his hands to his chest. "It lives inside of me. To tell you the truth, I don't know much beyond that. I only know it was the energy given to me from my father when I was but an infant. I heard legends of other wielders who have managed to wield the same way, but I could not tell you how it's done."

Faith smiled warmly, seemingly content with the answer

that only seeded more questions in Falcon's head. "Thank you for the information, sir."

The room suddenly shook, more viciously than the first time. A section of the wall broke into a web of cracks. Crystals moved from side to side but amazingly remained in place.

"I'm afraid there isn't much time left," said Aadi.

"Time for what?" asked Hiromy. She gazed around the room worriedly. "Is something coming?"

"The power of a memory comes at a price, and I'm afraid that it is one you'll have to deal with."

"Deal with?" Falcon didn't like the sound of that.

Aadi grinned. "Don't you worry. I'm certain that with the friends you have, you'll have no problem disposing of it when the time comes." He extended his hand toward Falcon. "Volcseck might have thought he had eluded me, but I have other ways to get to him." A golden swirl of dust emitted from his hands and surrounded Falcon. It remained in constant motion around him for a moment.

"It's so beautiful," said Hiromy. She reached for the dust, but Sheridan pulled her back before she could touch it.

Once again, she pouted, but remained calm.

The swirl of golden mist flowed into Falcon, passing through his clothes and settling within him. He felt a strong, vibrant feeling infuse his very core. The energy of a thousand earth wielders raged within his chest. Strangely, it did not bother him in the slightest. An earthy taste of mana settled in his mouth.

When the last of the dust had disappeared into Falcon, Aadi brought his hands down. "To you, Falcon Hyatt, I give the power to sense energies. This will allow you track people and beings for miles, and in time, perhaps even continents away. My own personal earth shield now coats your body as well. It will provide some protection from any attacks, regardless of the element. However, Earth attacks are a different story. You are now impervious to all earth attacks, no matter the magnitude of the power."

"Thank you," said Falcon, unable to control his emotion. He was practically trembling with excitement. He had expected something great from the Golden Wielder, and he had not been disappointed. Now he was one step closer to matching Volcseck's power. Even more, with his energy reading abilities, he would be able to track down his brother. He would finally be able to prove to everyone that Albert was still alive!

"Now," said Aadi. "The power to read energies isn't absolute. It can be used against you if you're not careful. You will have to hone it as I did. If you do not, I'm afraid that you may not survive the incoming battle."

"I will stop Volcseck!" Falcon assured Aadi. "That's a promise."

Aadi looked over at the crystals, his gaze settling on the cracks that were now becoming more apparent. "My hold on these prisons is weakening. Trust me when I say, Volcseck isn't the only menace that can befall Va'siel." Falcon noticed that Aadi was now looking at the crystal at the very end. It was the darkest of them all, making it impossible to see who or what was inside. "There are some beings that are even more ruthless than Volcseck."

More ruthless than Volcseck? What was the Golden Wielder talking about?

"I wish I could explain further," said Aadi. "However, it appears that our time together is about to come to an end."

The image of Aadi had become ghostly white. While before it had appeared solid, it was now translucent. Clearly, most of the memory's power had gone to Falcon.

"For the sake of Va'siel, I wish you the best of luck. I must return now to my beloved. Best fortunes to you."

"Return to your beloved?" said Aya. She had been so quiet during the entire exchange that Falcon had almost forgotten she was there. "Surely she died long ago along with you."

"Dead? I may not be as dead as some would believe me to be." Aadi smiled at Aya. "You have a strong spirit, much like Ishani. She no doubt would have loved to have met you."

Before anyone could say anything more, Aadi waved goodbye, and his image dissolved, leaving behind him a dozen unanswered questions.

As soon as Aadi disappeared, the ground trembled

once more. This time, unlike the other time, however, there was a loud growl that accompanied the shake. It appeared to be coming from the grand, pillared hall where they had been traversing before Falcon started chasing the golden glow.

"The Golden Wielder—" began Sheridan, before Hiromy interrupted him.

"Aadi!" she said.

"What?" asked Sheridan.

"He said he wanted to be called Aadi, not Golden Wielder."

"Anyhow," said Aya. "Aadi…" She made it a point to look at her fellow water wielder when she said this. "…mentioned that there was a price to be paid for leaving a memory. Perhaps this is it."

The wielders rushed out of the room and into the large hall. There was nothing that looked out of the ordinary, though Falcon could sense a strange sensation closing in. It was unlike anything he'd ever felt. There was a futuristic, alien aura hanging around it.

"Over there!" said Faith, pointing at a pitch-dark space between two pillars.

"I don't see anyth—" He stopped speaking once he saw the two yellow eyes appear. They were large and glowed brightly, illuminating the path before them. Metal scratched against stone as a long body snaked out of the shadows. But this was no snake. No, this creature was definitely not a native of Va'siel. It was large and had a squid-like body, with eight long tentacles spreading from in front of it. Its entire body appeared to be made out of metal, with some type of strange cables running through holes in its tentacles. It had two circular cogs under its eyes, much like the ones Falcon had seen used in butter churns. With every move it took, it released a mass of steam from a pipe that came out from the top of its head.

"What in Va'siel is that?" asked Sheridan, taking Hirmoy's hand and backing away, all the while keeping his eyes locked on the creature.

"It looks alien," said Aya. "Retreat slowly. There is no way of knowing how it's going to react."

The five wielders took a few tentative steps back. The all-seeing eyes of the creature followed them. It slid forward, matching their pace.

Suddenly, the squid opened its mouth and released a blood-curdling shriek. It was high-pitched, forcing Falcon to cover his ears to drown out some of the noise. A misty smog poured out of its mouth. It reeked of burnt oil.

"That's it!" said Sheridan. "This thing is going down." He twisted his hand up and then drove his hand forward. "Space forc—"

"Stop!" cried Aya, slapping his hand down. "You can't wield in here. You'll bring the ceiling down on us!"

Falcon could see that Aya was right. The creature's

simple shriek had caused the large pillars to tremble, raining down debris on their heads. He could only imagine that wielding would prove disastrous.

The squid did not seem to share in their fears. Falcon watched anxiously as it brought up all eight of its tentacles and swung them at them. It tore straight through a pillar, causing a thunderous echo to rock though the hall.

"Run!" yelled Falcon, realizing that the whole building could come down on top of them at any moment.

Sheridan didn't have to be told twice, even before he had yelled; he'd taken Hiromy by the hand and dashed away without bothering to turn back. The three remaining wielders took off after them.

They dashed the opposite way they had entered from, passing pillar after pillar with no end in sight. Falcon wasn't entirely sure if they were headed the right way. He simply ran and hoped for the best.

Then, as if to make matters worse, a few feet ahead of them the hall came to an abrupt end. An intricate series of paths and bridges criss-crossing and floating over a dark abyss awaited them.

"Which one do we take?" yelled Sheridan.

"Just pick one!" said Falcon, eyeing the countless different paths.

Sheridan and Hiromy ran across a stone path that led them straightforward. Falcon followed, hoping it didn't lead them to a dead end, or worse.

A resounding crash and the sound of rock breaking filled his ears.

Behind them, the squid had followed them. The stone splintered and collapsed under the weight of the five wielders and the creature.

Before he lost his footing, Falcon jumped to his left, landing clumsily on a much wider stone path. Beside him, Faith hopped as well. She miscalculated the distance and barely managed to grip the edge of the stone with one hand. Screaming, she reached out with her other hand and took hold. But Falcon could see that her grip was slipping, burdened by the fact that she was sustaining her entire dangling weight.

"I got you!" He reached out for her. Her hand slipped, but before she could disappear into the dark abyss below, he took hold of her hand, holding on to her with grim determination. With monumental effort, he pulled her up to safety.

Exhaling with a strange combination of relief and tension, he looked around. Sheridan and Hiromy had already made the jump to a different, narrow path. Aya, who had always been scared of heights, stood stiff, her eyes shaky.

"Aya!" called Falcon.

She provided no answer.

"Aya!"

This time she turned her head toward him. The footing under her crumpled.

Falcon tried to wield the rocks under her, but as he did, the squid jumped, landing directly in front of him, shaking the fragile stone holding them up. He tumbled to the ground, expecting the worst.

Somehow, though, Aya managed to hop on the falling stones one by one, as if climbing a set of stairs. With a high front flip, Aya landed gracefully beside Sheridan and Hiromy.

The creature's calculating gaze darted from Falcon to Aya. Clearly it was trying to figure out which group it was going to pursue. Silently, Falcon wished it was his.

To his dismay, the scalp of the squid opened and two steel, bird-like creatures emerged. They spread their wings, which easily covered over five feet in length. A long, bronze beak protruded from their eyeless head, and a large hooked talon emerged from their webbed feet. They screeched in unison and dove toward Hiromy.

Aya shot a burst of water at them, but the strange birds flew past it without even flinching.

"Run!" shouted Aya. She turned and took off. Falcon realized she was right. Getting in a wielding battle with three metal creatures while hanging over an unforgiving drop was foolish. At any moment the creatures, or one of them was going to break yet another bridge, sending them plummeting to their death. He could always try his space wielding, but in such a fragile place, he wasn't sure he could pull it off without causing more harm than good.

An excruciating heat caressed his body, accompanied by a light. He turned to see the squid shoot a gust of fire from its mouth. Before it could reach them, Faith threw a rainbow-colored shield before them. The flames slammed against the shield and, with nowhere to go, shot out to the side, destroying other uninhabited stone bridges.

Faith's hand landed on his shoulder. "We have to move before this thing destroys everything!"

Falcon stood, and together he and Faith sprinted down the bridge. He looked and noticed that Aya's, Hiromy's, and Sheridan's path was taking them upward, while Falcon and Faith were descending even lower.

There was no time to stop now. He could only hope that they would find their way to each other.

The sound of breaking glass erupted behind them, and Falcon knew that the squid had ripped through the shield.

His chest heaved as he continued to sprint, not bothering to look behind him. An unexpected scent of oil returned. The scent was so strong that he could practically taste it in his mouth.

The dark liquid flew past him, creating a curtain of oil before them.

It's trying to get us soaked in so it can burn us easier. Despite this information, he knew he had no choice but to run through the sudden dark waterfall spread before them. There was no stopping now.

Inches from touching it, a light flew from Faith's emblem. It created a perfect oval path through the oil. Faith and Falcon hopped through. Even in his haste, he couldn't help but admire her focus.

The squid emitted an angry gurgling shriek. It was obviously growing frustrated at its inability to trap its prey.

A faint light appeared on the horizon. There were nearing the end of the path.

Falcon dug deep and put his all into the final stretch. He could feel Faith's heavy breaths beside him.

The light grew in size, until it revealed itself to be a small opening into yet another room. The stone path trembled with increased tenacity. Falcon and Faith had to crouch just to make it into the entrance.

The squid had no such reservations. It threw its massive body through the air like dead weight. It crashed into the wall, destroying what was once a small opening and turning it into a massive circular hole on the wall.

A lightning display burst from the creature's eyes and tentacles, and for a second, Falcon expected it to simply fall into a heap of rubble. Instead, however, the squid whipped the tentacles at them, almost taking Falcon's head clean off.

Another tentacle flew toward him. This time he hopped over it and, in mid-air, called on the power of lighting. Surely this beast wouldn't be able to handle that.

Yellow ripples shot viciously at the creature. It brought all its tentacles together, essentially creating a shield. The suction cups under its tentacles lit up, as if sucking in the attack.

He felt the energy inside the creature increase. Great! I just brought it back to life!

The squid moved its tentacles aside and opened its mouth, shooting a ray of strange energy from it. Falcon wind wielded the air under his feet, shooting himself up and clear out of the deadly attack. Simultaneously, he summoned raw energy from the tremendous pool of power he had to call from. A gust of wind, so large that even he was surprised by the size, shot from his hands. It slammed into the squid, sending the creature crashing loudly into the wall.

The wall splintered in a thousand places. Water crept inside every hole and crevice.

Oh no! He could water wield, but Faith could not.

He turned to her, but in his haste he did not notice the sharp sound of the wall erupting, sending a chunk of rock flying toward his head.

An unexpected spasm of pain assaulted his forehead. His world turned into a blur. He made out the smell of salty seawater. He thought he saw a blurry person coming toward him, but his head was reeling so much that he couldn't be certain.

A freezing cold came over him as he was engulfed in a wave of water. Have to water wield. Have to—

With that thought, the water rushed into his mouth, as everything turned dark.

Chapter 19

A warm burst of air blew into his mouth, raising his chest an inch. Falcon heard the muffled shouts of Aya calling to him. Then another puff of air blew life into his lungs. His eyes snapped open, and he found himself staring up at the worried faces of his four friends.

With the exception of Faith, everyone else was standing. She brought her soft lips down on his and blew, sending the now familiar gust of wind racing into his lungs.

What is she doing? He had no opportunity to voice his questions. A sickening sensation of liquid traveling up his esophagus made it impossible to speak. He clutched his chest, heaved loudly, and sat up, just in time for an eruption of water to surge form his mouth.

Faith let out a low scream. She brought up her hands and put up a small bubble. The water bounced from the shield and back into Falcon's face, soaking him entirely.

"Sorry," she mumbled, looking down apologetically. "My muscle reflex sometimes gets the better of me. Are you alright?"

"I'm fine," said Falcon, in a quavering voice. His chest ached, and his head felt as if it had gone into a duel with a dozen hammers, but the thought of Faith's tender lips on his drowned out any thought of the pain.

They stared at one another, nervous and silent.

"Sorry," he said. "I shouldn't have passed out like that."

"No, I'm sorry," she said almost instantly. "It took me so long to get you out. You almost drowned."

"I think Hyatt would gladly risk drowning more often as long as he gets you to nurse him back to life every time," said Sheridan, smirking widely at Falcon. "Am I right?"

Aya pressed her lips together.

"Why would he want to risk drowning?" asked Hiromy, looking at Sheridan in confusion. "He could..." She gasped in an overly dramatic fashion. "...die!"

"What I meant to say was that—"

Falcon jumped into a standing position. "It's fine, Sheridan. No need to go into details." His face flushed. "I think we all know what you meant."

"Hiromy didn't get it. I think I should explain better."

"Better yet, explain how we got here," demanded Falcon, eager for a change of subject.

"The wall crumbled, letting in the seawater," said Faith. "You were hit by stray piece of rock and passed out. I tried to get to you before you swallowed too much water, but that squid kept coming after us, and it swam much faster than me."

"Where is it?" he asked, his eyes darting about nervously. For the first time, he got a good look at the area around him. They looked to be washed up in the shore of a beach. There was a cliff to the right of them. A large plot of sand spread outward over three hundred meters, and then was replaced by lush pasture. There were no trees in sight. Instead, blades of grass the size of a child and long-stemmed yellow sunflowers covered the land.

"It was crushed by the same tumbling rocks that hit you. It's stuck at the bottom of the sea. At least it was the last time I saw it. If we're lucky, it was destroyed." Doubt filled Faith's voice. "After that I put up a bubble and tried to swim to the surface. I managed to cover a few miles, but it was too hard. I had to put a bubble around us, but the currents and pressure made it impossible to move." She looked down, her expression saddened.

"Don't beat yourself up," said Aya, patting Faith's shoulder reassuringly. "You got him halfway up."

"So how did we make it out?" asked Falcon.

Aya pointed at a cliff that rose beside them. There was a large hole a few feet up which, judging by the amount of sharp edges and steepness, was next to impossible to reach. "We followed the path we had found up and came out through there. My guess is that there was once an opening here that led to the pass, but the Golden Wielder sealed it when he trapped the Onagas. Sheridan had to blow open that small hole there. After that, I focused my mind and pinpointed yours and Faith's faint energies under the ocean."

"You found us way down there?" Falcon asked, genuinely shocked. They were but a small speck in a vast body of water filled with the living energies of thousands of sea creatures. He couldn't imagine ever coming close to pinpointing an energy reading with such precision.

"It wasn't too hard," said Aya. "You both have very unique auras." Falcon was certain she was referring to Faith's holy and his chaos. "I then simply water wielded you to the surface."

Aya spoke with an air of normalcy that made it seem as if her energy detection was a thing of everyday occurrence. He realized that even with the gift of the Golden Wielder, he would never be able to pinpoint energy levels remotely close to her level.

"I can't believe you got knocked out by a piece of rock." Sheridan chuckled. "And it happened only minutes after getting a shield that protects from all earth attacks." He burst out in another fit of laughter.

Despite his near-death experience, Falcon cracked a smile. "I guess it only works for wielder attacks."

Once Aya had pulled out the water from their clothes, they all headed down the prairie. Along the way Sheridan told him the story of how Aya and Hiromy had each dispatched the metal birds by bringing down pillars of water over them. For some reason, in his story, Hiromy came out as the more heroic of the two girls. While Aya had simply thrown a lot of water mindlessly at the bird, Hiromy, in Sheridan's words, had expertly judged the amount of liquid she needed to render the creature helpless. With graceful ease she danced a deadly dance as glittering drops of aqua surrounded her, converging into precise sharp spears that demolished the bird in a single hit. He moved up and down, flailing his hands and screaming as he dramatized the events that had occurred.

Hiromy seemed to enjoy Sheridan's exaggerated tales.

"Do it again. Do it again!" she ordered. As they walked down the winding path that cut through the prairie, Sheridan obliged, repeating the entire dramatization over and over again. Every time he told the story, Hiromy's feats became more and more unbelievable.

Falcon did enjoy seeing his friend Hiromy happy, but he would be lying if he said he wasn't finding the story a bit unbearable after he heard it for the twelfth time.

Sheridan finally stopped talking when they came upon an old man struggling to push his wagon. The wheel had gotten stuck in a puddle of mud.

"Go, I say," ordered the leathery-skinned man in a frail voice. The two dark horses made a half-hearted attempt to pull as the man pushed from behind. After the failed attempt at getting the wheel loose, the man threw down his straw hat in frustration. "Garn darn good for notin' colts, should have never spent any coin on you two, but of course I just had to listen to that old hag back at home. 'We need a good pair of horses,' she said. 'They will make the—'" The man noticed the wielders approaching. He grunted defiantly. "I have no money, you young good-for-notins'. Robbing me will get you notin'. You hear that? Notin'!"

"We had no intention of robbing you, sir," said Faith.

The man eyed Faith for a second. He stood in silence, as if struggling to decide whether he believed her or not.

Finally he said, "If you're not thieves, just what are you doing so far from the city, anyhow?"

Judging from the sweet-smelling bread that emitted from under the covered sheet over the wagon, Falcon could only assume the man was a merchant. A baker. His raggedy white shirt and trousers only further confirmed this.

"We're Rohads," said Falcon, pointing at the dragon insignia on his chest. "See?"

The man smiled widely at the sight of Falcon's gray emblem, which only increased his wrinkles so that his face looked like a crumpled sack of potatoes. "I see you're a void wielder. No doubt you could work a little bit of your earth magic and get my wagon unstuck?"

Falcon sighed. "It's not magic!" If there was one thing he hated, it was when some misinformed person would erroneously refer to the natural ability of wielders as magic. He wasn't some type of magical wizard. He was about to go on a long rant debunking the baker's flawed views, but the man did not seem the slightest bit interested in what he had to say.

"Yeah, yeah, whatever." The man pointed at the wheel. "So. Can you do some of your mag— er... wielding?"

"Since you asked so nicely. How could I refuse?" Falcon hardened the mud. Usually it would have taken him a few seconds to get the dirt to solidify fully, but this time he did it in the mere blink of an eye. The power Aadi had passed to him was obviously having some profound effects.

His newfound speed did not go unnoticed. Sheridan and Aya both looked at him with an impressed gleam in their eyes, and Falcon couldn't help but relish the small amount of attention he had gotten, especially from Aya. Especially after all the days of drifting by invisibly.

Even the baker looked dazzled. "That was amazing! The void Rohads back at Missea aren't nearly as fast."

"What void wielders?" inquired Aya.

"I haven't seen them much, but the century queen hired a few Rohads as protection. Three to be exact, two void wielders and one earth wielder. They came from the Rohad academy of Ladria. Three other ones were sent from the Rohad academy of Belwebb. A fire and lightning wielder, if I recall. Can't be too sure."

Falcon took this as good news. If the empress of Missea had hired extra security, then perhaps she was already aware of the threat the Suteckh posed. Having her join against the Suteckh might be easier than he'd initially thought.

On the way to the city, they traveled alongside the baker, who provided them all with a loaf of soft bread. They devoured it eagerly as the man proudly spoke of the century queen who, according to him, had been ruling over Missea for over one hundred years. It sounded far-fetched, and Falcon found it hard to believe that he had never heard of this one-hundred-year queen before, but then again, he never really paid much attention in class. The fact that Aya wasn't questioning the man led him to believe that he was indeed speaking the truth.

"She must have been very young when she took over as ruler," said Sheridan. He took another bite of his piece of bread, and then, noticing that Hiromy had finished her piece, offered his remaining loaf to her. She took it happily.

The baker nodded. "Oh, yes. Emperor Tanul died when she was seventeen years of age. She led Missea through the scorch that nearly wiped out all of Va'siel, and was a personal friend of the Golden Wielder." There was pride in his voice. "With her, Missea has enjoyed the most prosperous era in its history."

As if planned, as soon as the baker stopped speaking, the massive golden gates came into view. They were twice the size of those from Missea's sister earth capital, Sandoria, and much more luxurious. Falcon judged the gates to be over seventy meters in height.

"Shiny gold!" cried Hiromy.

"Oh no, little missy," the baker corrected. "It's not real gold. It simply looks that way. The Golden Wielder knew that having real gold walls would only bring out the worst in people.

Can you imagine? Sections of the walls would go missing every night. But you won't find stronger walls anywhere else in Va'siel."

Falcon could see how Hiromy could have mistaken the walls for real gold. The yellow from it glistened, nearly blinding him. There were wavy patterns running along the bottom of the wall, and at the top there were wide crenels that were no doubt used to launch arrows or wielding attacks in case the city needed to be defended. Silently, he hoped it wouldn't come to that. The small dirt path they were taking converged with dozens of other paths that led to a wide stone road. The road led them directly through the gate into the city. Unlike every other capital city Falcon had seen, Missea did not have two double doors at the center. Instead, it had a massive archway, with no sign of the thick wooden doors that he had come to associate with the cities. As they neared the entrance, he continued to look for them with no luck.

"There are no doors," said Aya, noticing his confusion. "When the city needs to be closed, the earth wielders will raise the rock barrier from the ground." She pointed at the area directly under the gate and, sure enough, there was a twenty-foot section of the ground that was a deep black, a sharp contrast to the mostly yellow stone path. "Earth wielders wield the wall in position from below."

Falcon nodded in silent admiration. It seemed like such an ingenious idea that he wondered why other cities hadn't adopted a similar form of defense.

After a short inspection by the city guards, they made their way into the city, which was buzzing with hectic activity. There was so much going on that, to Falcon at least, the entire scene seemed to blend into a sea of people, horses, mules, vendor stands, dust, and wooden cabins.

"Sure smells earthy!" said Sheridan, taking in a deep whiff of the air.

Falcon thought it smelled more like horse dung than earth.

"What now?" asked Faith. "I don't think we can simply go up and seek an audience with empress."

"We can if she goes with us." Aya motioned at Hiromy, who was walking hand in hand with Sheridan. "She's a princess, after all. Royalty should have no problem gaining an audience." Aya frowned as she glanced at the princess' clothing, which was ripped in many places and stained with dust, grass, and oil. She then took a look at her own beaten-down wardrobe. "I think we should get a change of clothing first, though."

"Falcon and I will check us into an inn," Sheridan suggested. "You ladies can go on ahead and find something nice to wear."

"Sounds good," said Aya. She turned to Faith. "Are you coming?"

Faith looked genuinely surprised. She pointed to

herself, as if she couldn't believe she would be invited to go shopping. Coming from a farming village, Faith wasn't used to navigating the wardrobe shops that large cities offered. "Me? Um… Yes. Of course I would like to go."

She waved goodbye, looking absolutely giddy as she joined Aya and Hiromy and disappeared into the crowd of people.

~~~

Faith had ventured to Sandoria a few times with her dad. As mayor of a small village, her father had made frequent visits to attend yearly meetings to discuss farmlands, agriculture, sales prices, and a lot of other topics that she found boorish. On those trips, she had passed the many clothing shops, seeing from afar, but never actually stepped foot in one.

"There is no need for such things," her father had once told her when in her five-year-old naivety she had asked for a pristine blue dress hanging in a window. She imagined herself as a princess playing with her hay dolls, ordering them around as they attended to her every need. "You have enough shirts and pants back at home."

In many ways, the dreams of that small girl were still alive and well, though this time she knew better than to think she could ever be a princess. Ironically, she was now in the company of a real princess.

"Maybe I shouldn't have left Sheridan," said Hiromy

shyly. She looked at the mass of people around her uncomfortably. "I need him around."

"Don't worry." Faith patted her back, reassuring her that everything would be fine. The princess had grown fond of Sheridan, and, thanks to him, her mental health had improved drastically since the first time she treated her. However, Faith wanted Hiromy to also be able to fend for herself. She would never be the same, and she would probably need someone to watch over her the rest of her life, but she at least needed to get back some degree of independence.

"Y...yes, of course," Hiromy stammered.

"This place seems like a good shop," Aya walked into a small wooden hut. The sign that dangled on the outside read Katrina's Imports. The inside of the shop was small and cozy. It smelled strongly of potpourri, which Faith enjoyed since it reminded her of flowers. There were different tables with paper labels dangling above them. The names of different capital cities were written over them. Faith assumed that the labels corresponded to the city the clothing had been imported from.

"May I help you ladies find some wares?" asked a stubby, older lady wearing a luxurious pink dress.

"I already know what I'm getting, thanks," said Aya. Determined, she headed to table that had a paper that read Zhangshao. She picked up a blue blouse that resembled a kimono and a blue skirt. The skirt had white flowers dotted throughout.

Hiromy, apparently, had kept her same tastes, because she trudged to the Ladria section and chose a tight-fitting one-piece suit, though this one was black instead of her usual blue.

Seeing that two of her customers had already made up their mind, the shopkeeper turned her attention to Faith. "How about you, young lady? Is there anything that interests you?"

"I always wanted a dress..."

"Are you going to a dance?"

"No. I just never had a chance to wear one for too long."

The woman looked at her curiously. She took out a measuring tape and circled Faith, mumbling numbers under her breath. "I have the perfect thing that will go with your skin tone."

The woman disappeared behind a hung curtain that led her to a hidden room. She emerged a few seconds later with a white dress with a pink outline around it. At the bottom it was surrounded by two pink lines with butterflies above it.

Faith's eyes grew wide. "It's beautiful."

"It just got it from Lastria this morning. I'm certain it would look stunning on you."

"It's so pretty," said Hiromy. She circled the dress as if admiring a once-in-a-lifetime anomaly. "You have to get it."

Faith pondered on it. She couldn't really trust Hiromy.

Lately the princess had found almost everything beautiful or stunning in some way or another.

"If that's what you want, you should get it," offered Aya.

That was the last little push she needed.

"I'll take it." Breathing hard, she took the dress in her hands. She would wear it while they were in the city and then go back to her usual jumpsuit once they resumed their travels. He owed her younger self that much. Silently, she wondered if Falcon would like it.

~~~

General Kaidoz's insides smiled at the news, though he kept his outer appearance as stoic as usual. Draknorr was dead! The Blood Empress herself had just confirmed it. Now he would have command over the entire army, answering only to the Blood Empress.

It wasn't power that he was after. That could be taken. But constantly having to communicate and plan with Draknorr had become tedious. Now he could lead the Suteckh in the battlefield to the glory they so richly deserved.

Kaidoz silent thoughts were interrupted by the woman's low, almost hiss-like voice. His gaze shifted back up to the image of the Blood Empress. Through the cloud of dark mist, only her mask was visible. He much rather preferred to conduct these meetings in person, but speaking through dark wielding mist was far quicker than traveling all the way to Tenma. Not to mention far more convenient.

"Be wary, General!" she warned. "We are weaving a fine thread. Our original plan of capturing the emperors and empresses of Va'siel and forcing them to sign their lands to us may have been hampered, but we will still come out of this the victors."

Kaidoz' stomach hardened. He knew all too well about their original plan. It had been his idea, after all. Draknorr had wanted to simply take over the capital cities by force, but Kaidoz had recognized that that wasn't a feasible task. He suggested capturing the leaders and coercing the signatures to take over their land. Then, their rule would be undisputed. Everything went wrong almost immediately back in the attack on Sandoria. Draknorr, in his stupidity, had assigned the capture of the Sandorian emperor to a simple captain who had recently joined their cause. Not surprisingly, the captain failed in securing the emperor. Mere weeks ago, Dokua had been unsuccessful in her quest to capture the emperor of Ladria when she had been killed by the princess. These inexcusable failures had forced them to change their strategy and become more aggressive.

Kaidoz knew that the key to victory was a mix of both strategies. Aggressiveness was needed with a combination of maneuvers in the dark.

"Keep an eye on the group of Rohads," continued the Empress. "They could make our plans troublesome."

"Indeed." He bowed his head. "I won't fail. I have

already enlisted the Orian warriors to do our bidding."

"Kill them, along with their leader as soon as they are of no use to us. There can only be one ruler in Va'siel. Me."

The image dissolved, leaving him alone in the jungle with his thoughts. When the young girl had been kidnapped years ago with plans to be made into a vessel for the Suteckh, he had thought the idea to be folly. No one could be forced to be ruthless; either you were born with it or you weren't. However, the young empress had quickly proved him wrong. She was tenacious, aggressive, and cunning. All the things he admired in a leader. She excelled in the program she was thrust into, beating out all the other powerful wielders she was pitted against. Not only had all her adversaries suffered mysterious and gruesome deaths, but she had managed to unite all the warring tribes of the Suteckh under one banner. Something never done before. Now, they were on the doorstep of eternal Suteckh glory, and he wasn't about to let some mindless group of young mercenaries stand in his way.

He would soon get his audience with Empress Latiha, and put his plan into action. The gears had already been set. Nothing could stop it now.

~~~

Falcon's line of sight skipped over Hiromy. He looked speechlessly at Faith and Aya as they walked into the room of the inn. Both girls looked stunning in their new wardrobes. As he had himself, they had stopped to bathe in the bath springs.

Their clean skin, wet hair, and scented aroma made that clear.

He wanted to say something to them, but found himself speechless.

Sheridan had no problems telling Hiromy how he felt. He ran up to her and picked her up by the waist, spinning her around as she giggled and cheered her heart out.

"You look so beautiful!" He shouted so loud that Falcon was certain everyone in the inn had heard him. He slowly brought her down so that he was still holding her up, but they were now face to face. Then, quite suddenly, they began to kiss with a passion Falcon had never seen anyone display before. He ran his hands through her hair, and she wrapped her legs around his thighs. The audience before them did not seem to bother them one bit.

Falcon and the girls looked away, waiting for the loud kissing session to stop. It took a good minute, which seemed to last hours, before they finally broke apart from each other.

Sheridan was breathing heavily, but was all smiles.

Falcon felt a twinge of envy. He wouldn't mind having someone feel for him the way Hiromy felt about Sheridan.

"Now that that's over," said Aya, "perhaps I could have a word with you, Falcon. Alone."

"Sure," he said, scarcely daring to breathe. The last time he had been alone with Aya, things hadn't gone too well. He had no reason to believe that this time things would be any different. They both quietly walked out of the room, down the steps to the lobby, and into the outdoors. It was night out, but the city was still very much alive. Most of the shopkeepers had retired to their homes long ago, but food vendors in stalls, artists, and street performers were still scattered about.

It was strange to him how things had changed. There was a time, not too long ago, that being alone with Aya would have been welcome. Now, however, there were times she seemed so angry with him that even that had changed. He couldn't blame her, though. Her world had changed, for the worse, in a very short span of time.

Rays of lights and snippets of private conversation filtered through the many homes they passed in silence. "Do you want to talk about your family?" asked Falcon.

"No, not really." She ran her hand through her hair, spreading the scent of fresh strawberries.

Falcon dropped the subject of her sister and moved on. "So, what do you want to talk to me about?"

Aya looked down at the ground then back up at him, meeting his gaze. "It's about the way I've been acting lately." He stood frozen for a second, unsure if he heard what he thought he just heard. Her voice was pained, which was a far cry from what he had been expecting. "I shouldn't have snapped at you when we were on the ship. You don't owe me or anyone else an explanation of…" A lump travelled down her throat. "Who you have feelings for. That is your business, and I shouldn't have meddled. I'm sorry. I don't like how we've been around each other lately."

For a moment, the wielders stood shoulder-to-shoulder.

"I'm sorry for questioning you, too," said Falcon. "I would also like to stop fighting. I miss you."

She smiled and took a step closer to him as they turned the corner, coming out at the long canal that seemed to run directly at the center of the city.

"Would you like a tour of the city through the beautiful canals?" asked a voice.

Falcon looked sideways and found himself facing a man with a long mustache that curled into a circle at both ends. He was sitting in a canoe holding onto two paddles. Falcon was about to say no when Aya jumped into the canoe and motioned for him to follow her. Left with little choice, he hopped on too.

The man paddled them down, following the soft current. Unexpectedly, Aya pressed closer to him and rested her head on his shoulder. Besides the splashing of the water and Aya's soft breaths, they moved down the river in complete silence.

"It is tradition for the couples to kiss when we pass under a bridge," said the man as they passed under an overpass that held the clattering of horse hooves above.

"Ohhh, we're not a coup—" began Falcon, but before he could finish, Aya pressed her lips against his cheeks and planted a soft kiss. At that moment, as his heart pumped wildly, he wished he could have made the moment last forever. Her warm breath, the moon rippling in the water, even his shaky body, everything came together in a symphony of rushed emotions. Only in his dreams had he dared to hold Aya this close, and now that it was happening in real life, he didn't want to let her go.

The ride ended, and Falcon reluctantly stepped out of the boat and paid the man.

As they walked down the moonlit road, a fresh breeze blew by, and Aya's skin goose bumped. Falcon quickly took off his jacket and threw it over her shoulders. Again, she leaned close and slipped her hands into his as they moved wordlessly. At this moment, there was no war, no chaos wielders to find, no broken family ties, just the two of them.

Much sooner than he'd expected, they arrived at the inn's entrance. Besides the song of hidden crickets, the city slept in a deep slumber. The night had been full of surprises, but as Aya turned to face him he was certain the biggest one was about to come. She looked into his eyes, and he gulped loudly, hoping that the sweat that had formed in his face wasn't too visible.

She simply stood there, staring into his eyes, and he had the sense that she was waiting for him to make some kind of move. All of a sudden, Aya's black hair turned a golden brown, and then he found himself staring at Faith. A blink later, the green-eyed girl had disappeared, replaced by Aya's almond eyes.

The peace that had bubbled within him seconds ago had now washed away and had now been replaced by agitation and guilt. He cared for Aya, of that he had no doubt, but he also cared for Faith. The words of Father Lucien, the man he'd met in K'vitch, came back to him. Sooner or later, we must all choose what we really want in our life. Or who we want. The heart cannot wholly belong to more than one.

How could he possibly choose?

The door to the inn flew open. Sheridan stared at both of them with wild eyes. "About time you two got back. We have trouble. Kaidoz is here in Missea!"

Chapter 20

Falcon, Aya, and Faith traversed the street, deep in thought. The imposing front of the majestic castle rose behind hundreds of cabins, shops, and stalls that paled before it. The closer they walked, the larger it seemed to get. When they reached the golden picket fence, the guards stood aside and let them in without bothering to question them.

They passed the garden in silence and Falcon made a mental note of the cactuses that were spread about the garden. He wasn't sure why such a trivial fact would implant itself in his mind; it must have been the nerves.

According to Sheridan, he and Hiromy had gone to see the Empress late last night. But they were not the only ones there; the general of the Suteckh was there as well. Seeing that he was sent by the ruler of the Suteckh, he had been granted an audience first thing in the morning. Hiromy, being a royal, was also given priority.

He had never met the man, but he did know that it was he who had brought Dokua to attack Aya back in Ladria. That alone insured that he hated him and everything he stood for.

Two guards that stoically stood outside the ornate door pushed it open, showing them in. The trio walked through a grand hallway and down toward two more doors that were open, leading into a grand room. At any other time, Falcon would have been admiring every detail. From the golden vases spread feet apart, to the pristinely clear arched windows. It was in this castle, after all, where Aadi had lived after escaping the hellish prison, Kilead Keep. He could imagine the secrets and stories these walls held. If they could speak, what would they tell him of the Golden Wielder?

Thoughts of his hero had to be set aside as he entered the grand hall. Their footsteps echoed loudly on the marble floor. The entire room was surrounded by soldiers that wore the usual golden armor, helmet, and faulds. Golden-hilted swords hung on all their waists. A few of them carried pole arms and spears as well. A grand throne rested at the center of the oval hall. Within it, an older woman who wore a long yellow robe stood, her eyes missing nothing. A golden tiara rested on her head, and as Falcon moved, she followed him. At each side of the empress, there were four more guards. Falcon eyes widened as he realized that he recognized some of them. Lenka, a skinny, bony-cheeked girl, and Relis, two void wielders who he'd known from Rohad academy stood at the Empress' left side. To her right, stood Laars, the boy who had made his life miserable at school. He didn't recognize the other wielders that stood at attention, but judging from the tiger insignia on their chests, he was sure they were the Rohads sent from Belwebb.

Lenka smiled at him and gave him a quick greeting in the form of a wave. Falcon wasn't sure whether he should wave back or not. Was that proper in the presence of an empress? The girl had always been friendly toward him, so he returned the gesture.

The empress looked down at them with a gleam in her eye. Despite her age, an aura of authority and grace clung around her. "Greetings Rohads and friend." At the mention of friend she turned to Faith. "I am Empress Latiha. I've been informed that you come to me with dire news."

"That is correct." Falcon introduced himself and eagerly told her everything in great detail. From the initial attacks on the village of Asturia for its food source, to the uncalled attack on Sandoria, to the sacking of Ladria.

"These are all lies!" boomed a voice from behind. A man with deep brown skin and red scars walked into the hall. He wore a loose tunic and baggy dark pants. "This Rohad's claims are preposterous. If the Suteckh were indeed carrying out such attacks, surely your grace would have heard of it by now." He stood a few feet beside Falcon and gave the queen a slight, respectful bow. "Are we to believe that the Suteckh are carrying out mass attacks and"—he chuckled to no one in particular—"sacking capital cities without the knowledge of the people of Va'siel? How? This Rohad insults your intelligence with such claims!"

Falcon's insides burned. He had witnessed his fellow

villagers die in an ambush back at Ciompi, had seen firsthand the cruelty toward the children at Ladria, had smelled the stench as hundreds of civilians burned in Sandoria. And now this man was going to stand here and actually claim that it was nothing but lies? "He lies! I was there. I was there when—"

"More myth," said Kaidoz. Even though his voice was loud, he did not scream. Instead, it echoed with confidence. "Can we really believe a simple Roha—?"

Latiha looked down from her throne calmly and held up her hand, signaling for a stop to their bickering. "Careful with your words, General. The grandmaster of the Ladria branch of Rohad is a good friend of mine."

"Of course." Kaidoz bowed again. "Grandmaster Zoen is a respected wielder, but these..." He rolled his eyes as he cast a sidelong glance over at Falcon's group. "These children do not represent him. They no doubt claim they do, but they are here on their own accord with no knowledge of the grandmaster."

Empress Latiha acknowledged Kaidoz's information with a slight blink of the eyes. "I don't know how you do things over in Suteckh, and honestly do not care to know. In my throne room, however, you wait until I call on you."

Despite his calm demeanor, Falcon noticed the slight tremor on Kaidoz' cruel lips. Obviously he wasn't much too pleased with Latiha's choice of words. Nonetheless, he remained silent as the empress spoke.

She turned to Falcon. "I have a deep respect and admiration for Rohads, as you can see." She motioned to the Rohads besides her, protecting her. "However, I cannot overlook the points that the general has brought up. You come to me seeking my aid, Falcon Hyatt, but I'm afraid you have no proof to your claims."

Falcon countered. "Send a messenger to Ladria or Sandoria. I'm certain that they will verify what I've told you."

"We have tried that already. Every messenger we've sent has failed to return."

"No doubt you're behind it!" said Falcon, pointing an accusing finger at Kaidoz. "You didn't have your fill attacking innocent villages, huh? You have to go for messengers as well?"

Kaidoz flashed a confident grin. "Your highness, unlike these children, I have a witness that can corroborate what I have already told you. I present to you…" There was a long pause. "Councilman Nakatomi, the leader of the Ladrian council."

Quiet footsteps reverberated through the grand hall. Falcon did not have to turn around to see who it was. Aya's sudden heavy breaths and trembling frame were enough to tell him that indeed, her father had entered the room.

He stood beside the general. "Your most serene highness. I come from afar to end these blasphemous lies. These people would have you take military action against the

Suteckh, but the truth of the matter is that Ladria is as safe as ever. There has been no attack."

"Why would you, a councilman, travel all the way here to tell me this?" asked Latiha. "A man of your status surely has dozens of messengers at your disposal."

"That is true. However, being that my own daughter is involved in these blasphemies, I felt that I had to personally shed light in this situation. I cannot stand idly by as my own family disrupts the honor of my name."

Now it was Aya's turn to shout. "Honor! How dare you speak about honor?"

Latiha held her hand up at Aya, and she stopped screaming.

The councilman continued. "I have served as a leader of Ladria for many years. Trust me when I say that life in my city flows with the same normalcy it has grown accustomed to after many years of peace and prosperity."

In his anger, Falcon would have made some type of reply, but Aya had already done so for him.

"He lies!" she snapped. She took a step forward, and Latiha's guards, including Laars and Relis, grew rigid. "Empress, I know you don't know me, but I speak the truth. This man is a Suteckh spy. He was planted there many years ago to gain the confidence of the Ladrian people. His daughter is the Blood Empress." She staggered for a second as her voice threatened to crack. "If he sold out his own daughter, imagine what he will do to the people of Missea once the Suteckh invade?"

Kaidoz chuckled, which only made Falcon want to tackle him to the ground and beat him until that sick smirk came off his face. "Spies? Abductions? These are the product of a troubled teenage mind. Are we to believe her claims that the Blood Empress is her sister?"

"Don't speak of my sister!" Falcon didn't think he had ever seen Aya so enraged. Her cheeks huffed loudly. Her chest rose and fell at an accelerated rate. She faced Kaidoz as her voice drowned to a hush whisper. "I killed one Suteckh general, trust me. I have no problem killing you too."

For the first time, Kaidoz' eyes gave away the slightest hint of fear.

"Stop this at once!"

At Latiha's command, Aya stepped back, trying to collect her breath.

Faith reached out and took her hand. "Calm down, Aya. This won't help our cause." Her words seemed to take effect. Aya's rapid breaths slowed, and her eyes returned to her regular sharp blue.

"That is quite a story," said Empress Latiha in a monotone voice that didn't betray her feelings. "I will need some time to ponder on what I heard here today. Come to me tomorrow. I will have an answer."

Without saying another word, the Empress waved her

hand, and the guards escorted her visitors out.

~~~

"What be the meaning of this?" demanded Melousa. The tall woman stood, the top of her head almost slamming into the roof of the cave. "Yer assured me that yer would get Latiha's confidence. Did yer not? Yer were supposed to draw her out of the castle so I be killing her!"

Kaidoz glanced around. He and Councilman Nakatomi stood inside a cold cave on the outskirts of the Missea prairie lands, surrounded by enraged Orian warriors. The councilman played with his fingers, fear etched in his trembling face.

"Why should I not be killing yer here where yer stand for yer failure?"

"Great queen," said Kaidoz as the warriors continued hissing and mumbling threats. "There is no need to fret. The empress requires a day to make her choice. Believe me, she will side with us. And once she does, I will draw her out, and you shall have the revenge you've been seeking."

"Yer best be right. If yer not I will find yer and cut yer down." She stomped her foot before the councilman, raising a mushroom of dust and sending him to the ground. "And my warriors shall tear this city dweller limb by limb."

"Get up!" ordered Kaidoz to the flinching man on the ground. He was a Suteckh citizen. How dare he cower before a wild creature?

Kaidoz waited until they had left the cave and were

clear across the prairie before he spoke. "You should really develop more of a backbone, councilman. If you possessed half the nerve your daughters carry, you wouldn't allow yourself to be intimidated by such trivial threats."

"Do not speak to me that way, Kaidoz!" With the peace of mind that Kaidoz would not harm him, the councilman had apparently found his courage. "I was a decorated fighter many years ago. You would do well to remember that I outrank you in every way. You answer to me, and I demand to know what you're doing with those women."

"In times of war I outrank you. As for the Orian warriors, it was the Blood Empress who thought of enlisting them. Are you suggesting I follow your orders instead of hers?"

The councilman said nothing, which Kaidoz took as an opening to continue questioning him. "Is there a reason you didn't tell me your other daughter was as strong as she claims to be? She killed Draknorr. A wielder of her caliber can cause a lot of problems for us."

"I told you she was strong did—"

"What is the meaning of this?" The loud hiss silenced even the nearby birds.

The pit in Kaidoz' stomach settled as he took notice of the cloud of smoke that had formed beside them. He hated when the Blood Empress appeared to him unannounced.

"Tell me what happened," demanded the empress.

Kaidoz relayed the information. Behind her mask, he

found it impossible to gauge how his superior was taking the news.

"Keep me updated on tomorrow's hearing," said the Blood Empress once the General had informed her how the meeting went. "I'd much rather have Missea unprepared when we launch an attack, but if they do not fall for our ploy, so be it. They shall still fall. As for this water wielder…" She stopped, waiting for someone to forfeit a name.

"Aya Nakatomi, your grace," said the councilman.

The Empresses' head jerked from side to side, and for a moment Kaidoz thought she was having a seizure.

"Empress?" called the General, unsure of how to react to the strange reaction.

"I…I…" She clutched her head. A soft moan echoed from behind her mask. "I shall kill this Aya myself!" The dark smoke dissolved, taking away the image of the empress.

Kaidoz waved away the burning stench that had been left behind as he cast a questioning glance at the councilman. "Is it possible that she remembers?"

"No," answered Nakatomi, too quick for Kaidoz' liking. His answer sounded fake, as if it had been rehearsed a thousand times. "I was there when she was brainwashed. There is nothing left of Selene."

"For all our sakes, I hope you're right, councilman."

~~~

Falcon entered the room of the inn with the bag of

vegetables in hand. He handed them to Faith, who quickly cut them into pieces and added them to the steaming pot that boiled on the iron stove.

"I'm making your favorite, Falcon," she said, stirring the broth.

The aroma of the pichion drumsticks drifted out of the pot and into Falcon's nostrils. He knew what she was doing. Making his favorite meal was a way for her to make him feel better, to make him forget about what had transpired in the Empress' court. But despite the promise of a good meal, he could not get the morning's events out of his head.

"I still can't believe that Empress Latiha actually listened to what the Suteckh had to say." Sheridan threw himself on one of the four beds spread along the long room, causing the mattress to creak under his weight. "I thought she was supposed to be some kind of wise ruler. Doesn't she know what's been going on for the past few months?"

"Apparently not," said Aya. She sat quietly, looking out the third story window. She seemed to be lost in her own world, and Falcon was certain she was thinking of her father, sister, and her role as a Suteckh. Part of Falcon wanted to console her and tell her that everything would be fine, but how could he when he himself did not know how this would turn out?

"I'm going out," said Falcon.

"Where are you going?" asked Faith.

"Out."

"Where?"

"Just for a walk."

"Don't you want to eat?"

"I'll be back in time for dinner."

She looked at him with her sad emerald eyes, and he had to force himself out the door before he changed his mind. He did not wish to hurt her, but he needed to get away for a while and clear his head. The room, despite its large size, was suffocating him.

He walked across the moonlit city. Unlike the night before, it did not seem magical in the slightest. The brown walls seemed boorish. The people, with their rambunctious conversations, bothered him. Even the river, with the loud seagulls flying overhead, proved an annoyance.

When he finally got back to the room, his friends were all deep in sleep. On the small table in the corner rested a small bowl of pichion soup. He took sip after sip of the cold broth until all the contents were gone. Then, without thinking much, he threw himself on the floor and fell asleep.

~~~

The next morning, when they walked into the throne room, the Empress was already sitting on her throne, waiting for them. Her usual guards were already there. Again Lenka, who this time wore a dark grey suit, waved at him. Falcon returned the greeting. He was so glad he hadn't been assigned to a job like hers. Standing stiff all day would drive him nuts.

Falcon noticed that the councilman was nowhere to be seen. Instead, Kaidoz was being accompanied by two male guards wearing simple dark robes. The insignia of the Suteckh raven was stitched on their chests.

The general spoke. "I'm certain that with the time you had, you no doubt found that the Suteckh are indeed innocent of the crimes raised against them."

Latiha looked down as a slight smirk formed in her lips. "I have been empress for many years, general. Do you think I would have lasted as ruler if I couldn't see through lies?"

"Of course not, your highness." He regarded her quizzically. "Are you insinuating I'm a liar, Empress?"

"Not insinuating. I know you are. I can read it all over you. It is in the tone of your voice. In your malicious eyes. In your pathetic attempts to flatter me."

Now it was Kaidoz' turn to smirk. "Am I to believe that I bring forth a witness to corroborate my story, while these children do not, and you would still take their word over mine?"

"Unlike you, general, the Rohads, do not have the eyes of one who has been tainted with malicious intent."

"If you were so sure of my guilt, why wait to tell me today? I was here yesterday, was I not? Why not arrest me then and there?"

"My senses are just one thing I use. I also rely on good

people to aid me. I was fortunate enough to have two very good eyewitnesses confirm the stories the young Rohads told me. Since many of my messengers had gone missing, no doubt by your hands, I had to find out by other means."

Falcon found himself taking an immediate liking to the empress. He had been so sure that the cold empress was going to side with Kaidoz that this sudden outburst by her had caught him by pleasant surprise. Now he understood why the empress had been so stone-faced the day before. It had been her way of not giving away any sign of what she felt.

Kaidoz shrugged. "Whoever these witnesses that you have are, can they possibly be a more reliable witness than the respected councilman I provided?"

"Will an Empress suffice as a reliable witness?"

There was an immediate murmur throughout the hall. No, not murmurs. More like exhales of fear and admiration.

Falcon turned behind him to see what the buzz was about. His jaw practically dropped. A man, who stood even higher than Cidralic had stood, entered the room. His face was painted with red streaks, and he had bulging muscles coming out of his tunic. His neck alone had to be over twenty-five inches and his arms over twenty-six. He wore a leather skirt. Amazingly, the man was not what Falcon or most people in the hall were looking at. Instead they looked past that, their eyes settling on the two massive bears that had just entered. One was black, the other brown. A young girl with snowy white

287

eyes stood between the animals. At her heels followed a much smaller white bear.

"Hello," said the blonde-haired girl. "I'm Keira. Empress of Sugiko."

Chapter 21

Keira did not look in the slightest the way Falcon expected an empress to look like. Her hair was tied in a ponytail and braided with countless pigtails. Her brown tunic ended a little under her chest, exposing her slim waist. Unlike every other empress he had ever seen who wore robes, Keira donned brown leather pants.

The bears stopped moving, and the young empress came behind them and patted them both. "Draiven, Aykori, stay here." Falcon half-expected the savage animals to turn on Keira at any moment, but amazingly, both bears stood still as they had been instructed.

"She uses the bears to see," said Aya, noticing his confused look. "Don't think too hard on it. It will just make your head hurt."

Aya? How does she know about this Empress? His curiosity was now piqued.

"Empress Keira," said Latiha politely. She stood and, as if greeting an old friend, embraced the younger empress in a hug. "I welcome you to my city. I'm greatly honored that you would make the journey to Missea in person."

Keira look flustered, in an I can't believe I talking to my childhood idol kind of way. "The honor is all mine, great empress."

By the time Empress Latiha had returned to her throne room, Keira seemed to have recovered.

"I made a promise to a friend that my people would rise against the tyranny of the Suteckh if they had to." She looked over at Aya. A knowing glance passed between them, leaving no doubt in Falcon's mind that the girls knew each other. "When I heard of the Suteckh's claims, I just had to come here myself and shed light on their lies. The truth is that my people have confirmed the attacks on both Ladria and Sandoria."

Kaidoz, who usually had a retort to any claim against the Suteckh, had gone unusually quiet. His eyes suddenly widened. "Get her!" He yelled as he pounced at Latiha. The Rohads beside her immediately formed a protective barrier around the ruler of Missea.

Kaidoz reached them before anyone else had a chance to get there. Five of the wielders, including Relis, Laars, Lenka, and two other Rohads Falcon didn't know, stood before Kaidoz, trying their best to deflect the earth attacks he had been firing. Even outnumbered five to one, Falcon could see that the Rohads would soon be outmatched.

The two Suteckh guards who had accompanied the general battled the remaining Rohads. One of them, the taller one, flipped under the young guards and moved toward Latiha, dagger in hand.

Falcon wielded a protective layer of wind, but even with the enhanced speed, he knew it wouldn't get there in time.

He quickly realized that his wielding was moot. The empress apparently was no damsel in distress. Still sitting, she blocked the incoming attack with ease. She twisted her attacker's arm, and the blade clattered to the floor. Before the would-be assassin could recover, the empress kneed him in the face. His body crumpled down, where he remained unmoving.

The other Suteckh guard was winning his battle. He was so busy, however, that he did not notice as the gargantuan man came behind him. Massive arms wrapped around the short man. He kicked and flailed, but he might as well have been kicking a stone wall. The giant man picked up the man high in the air and, without any sign of emotion, brought him down onto his knee. There was a bone-crunching sound as the guard's body seemed to bend almost in half. His eyes rolled back, and like his counterpart, he dropped to the ground, where he remained still.

By now, General Kaidoz had floored all of his opponents. Having done so, he turned his attention to Latiha. He ran full-speed with a deadly sharp earth spear in his hand.

A fire whip latched on to his foot, and in his haste, the general tripped to the ground. Kaidoz flipped and was up on his feet in a second. Laars wrapped another fire whip around Kaidoz. In the moment it had taken him to break free, the two bears had closed their distance on him. With hungry fangs, the two beasts pounced on the wielder.

Kaidoz fired two earth fists at them. Before they made contact with the animals, Falcon fired a gust of wind that diverted the earth attacks. Aya and Faith clapped their hands, each shooting out defensive walls. One was a serene blue barrier, the other a rainbow-colored bubble.

The general's wild eyes travelled from Latiha to the dozens of enemies now converging on him.

"Terra Bastille!" he shouted. Instantly, a wave of brown sand surrounded him in a coffin. Falcon stood frozen for a split moment. To wield at such speed was near inhuman. Now he knew why Zoen had said Kaidoz was the strongest earth practitioner since the Golden Wielder.

Then, as if to further prove his strength, Kaidoz' body dissolved into sand. The grains of dust swirled around the earth coffin. A moment later the chunk of earth, with the empress still inside, flew out of the window, and out of reach.

~~~

Faith couldn't believe it. They had Kaidoz severely outnumbered, and the man had still managed to kidnap the empress right under their noses. She wasn't about to let this man simply walk, or fly in this case, away.

"Read his energy," she told Falcon, a little bit more forcefully than she intended to. Shal-Demetrius had instructed her to be firm with Falcon, but even after all this time, she still found it difficult to be too demanding.

Falcon's face paled. "How? I just got this power. How

am I now supposed to track his energy?"

"This is the perfect chance for practice." As she finished speaking, she felt the power of Kaidoz growing dimmer. He moved fast, that was for sure. But the speed of earth was no match for that of light. Perhaps there was a way of pushing Falcon in his training, as Demetrius had instructed, without being forceful verbally. She was going to be forceful by action. "I'm going after him."

"What?" Falcon exclaimed.

"Find me." She closed her eyes and called on her power. Blaze of light!

~~~

Falcon reached out for her, but in a brilliant flash of light, Faith had disappeared, leaving behind a golden trail of mist that originated where she had last stood and moved out the window.

"You have to go help her!" said Aya, looking worried. "You're the only one who can teleport to her and find her in time."

"I...I..." He knew he had no more excuses. He needed to get to Faith as soon as possible. But how? First, he needed to use a power that he had next to no experience with. Then he needed to call on the power of teleportation to reach Faith. Space was too slow, and with no image of where to go on his mind, he couldn't rely on it. No. He would have to call on the power he hated the most—chaos.

~~~

She moved in a blur of light, tracking the earth energy. It didn't take long for Faith to catch up to it and intercept it.

"Well, well," said Kaidoz, landing with a loud thump in the open field. "I hadn't expected you of all people to get to me. It looks like there is much more to you than meets the eye." As he spoke, he brought the terra coffin down beside him with care.

Faith racked her brain. Why was he being so careful with Latiha? Why not just kill her? Could it be that he was planning to take her to someone? That doesn't matter, Faith. Concentrate on the here and now. She seemed to be back in the prairies of Missea. This place was a bit different, though. The short grass was yellow, with many patches of sand that were devoid of plant life. There were many small hills that rose and fell, making it impossible to see too far ahead in the distance.

"Am I interrupting something?" asked General Kaidoz. He looked absolutely amused at Faith's concentrated expression.

"Return the empress and I won't hurt you." She tried to make her voice sound as threatening as possible, though she was sure she wasn't having much success with that.

"You would like that, I'm certain, but I cannot oblige. Why would I do that? You may be a holy wielder, but you're untrained. You have no experience and no proper teacher."

He smirked. "No. I think I'll simply make quick work of you and be on my way."

With a cry, Kaidoz moved in. His speed was staggering, and only a last second summoning of her staff saved her from the incoming attack.

She twirled her staff into her opponent's hands and brought them down with trained force. She moved in, hoping to butt the end of the staff into Kaidoz' forehead, but moved back when he brought his hand up in a jab. It happened in an instant, and Faith had only the barest of milliseconds to glimpse at the sharp daggers that were now poking out of the general's chest. He can make his body into a weapon?

Faith reeled her head back, avoiding a right punch. A left jab came under her. She blocked the deadly blitz with her staff. This time she infused her weapon and ran it up the length of Kaidoz' arm, using his own body as leverage.

The staff rocketed into the man's face. His lips curled in agony, and he grunted under his breath. She twisted her staff and brought the other end over his head. This time the general dissolved in a mist of dust, only to reappear behind her.

Had it not been for the invisible holy field she had put around her, Kaidoz's attack would have surely ended her. But instead, she turned to parry the attack. She drove forward, pressing her advantage and pushing her opponent back. In her haste, however, she misjudged her advantage. Kaidoz dropped under her and drove his sharpened knee into her gut, simultaneously extending it. Ignoring the pain, Faith jumped back to avoid the sharp dagger that almost impaled her through the stomach. Kaidoz had brought an earth wall up behind her, and she slammed her back hard against it. She fell to one knee.

Infused with her healing abilities, Faith was quickly back on her feet. She dropped into a defensive position, breathing hard.

"Looks like you're tiring," mocked Kaidoz. "This dance is all but done." Again he disappeared in a puff of smoke, leaving behind the earthy smell.

Faith looked around her, trying to pinpoint where he would come out from. She was alone. The gray skies, dead grass, and silence were her only companions.

He suddenly appeared again behind her. Faith drove in with her staff, only to have him disappear again in a fit of laughter.

"You can try all day, but you'll never get me."

He re-appeared at her side. She took a good, hard look at him, allowing her eyes to settle on his chest. Every time he teleported his chest would materialize first, followed by his head, arms, and legs. It happened so fast, though, that it seemed as if the materialization was instantaneous.

An attack came down on her. She bopped her head out of the way, but a kick managed to graze her cheek, cutting an even line across her face and drawing blood.

She didn't bother healing. Her energy was better suited elsewhere. This time, when Kaidoz reappeared she would be ready.

I'm here with you. The voice of the previous holy wielder, Lunet, had first come to her when she was a child, and though she learned most of her wielding on her own, Lunet had been with her many times during her training. She had accompanied her during her battle with Cidralic, when she lost her mother, and the many times in life when she needed counseling. It wasn't the real Lunet, of course. She had died thousands of years ago. But she shared a bond with her deceased holy sister, a bond that allowed her to see through her eyes and gather her experience. For many years she had not even known her sister's name, but when she met Demetrius, she discovered the name and through it developed a richer connection with Lunet. Now it was time to put it to work.

Her voice changed, so that it sounded as though there were two women speaking instead of one. "Celestial lasso."

Kaidoz had been reappearing every ten seconds, which probably meant that was how much it took for him to charge his ability.

Six, seven, eight, nine, ten. Like clockwork, his chest was the first to appear. With the power of holy light, she materialized the chains at the side of the chest. When his hands and legs appeared, the chains locked around them and pulled back. The entire set-up was done and finished in the blink of an eye.

"Looks like I underestimated you, holy wielder." Kaidoz's face registered shock and fear. "I suppose this is where you finish me off."

"No. You will stand trial for your crimes. I'm no executioner. A jury will decide your fate."

"Unacceptable. Kill me and let me die as a warrior!" He was ranting now, his calm demeanor giving way to his bottled emotions. "I must die on my feet. Not hung by the noose like some simple thief!"

"You are in no condition to make demands, general. I took the life of a man once when I thought I was healing his sickness." Her stomach cringed at the thought of Cidralic's final moments alive. She had been so eager to stop Cidralic, sure that it was the poison that ran through his blood that had contaminated his mind, that she had killed him in her attempt to save him. That moment plagued her mind many restless nights, and even now it caused a tear to escape her eye.

"What is this?" said Kaidoz, seeing an opportunity to escape. "I see that—"

He didn't get to finish speaking, for a deep dark blur with shades of purple suddenly fell from the sky. The thick liquid oozed down, revealing a head, hands, and legs.

"Falcon?" asked Faith, recognizing her friend's clothing. His face, however, was far different than the kind one she had come to know. His skin was a deep brown, his eyes were hollowed purple lights, and deep lines traced his face. She had seen the chaos take hold of him before but never to this extreme. Even his hair had grown long, coming to an end at his lower back. I pushed him too far! What have I done?

~~~

Falcon mustered all his strength to hook onto the faint reading of holy energy. His heart pounded. He concentrated on the glistening trail left by Faith, but even with the visible cue, he could not single out her holy energy. It had moved so fast that he could not trace it long before it became a tangled mess. The air, wind, voices, bird chirps, everything muddled his concentration.

Left with little choice, he thought about the raging anger he held within. It wasn't hard to bring forth. It always rested on the brink of exploding, waiting to be released. His body convulsed as he tried to focus the untamed ferocity. With the extra power, he could make out the faint trail of energy left behind. But it wasn't clear. It zoomed in and out of focus.

"Are you okay?" Falcon thought he heard someone ask from behind him. It might have been an illusion.

He closed his eyes and allowed himself to be carried away.

When he opened his eyes the fearful voices from the palace were no more. Neither were the fine walls and fine gold statues. Instead he was now in a hilly prairie that was in obvious need of rainfall.

His name echoed in his head. Is someone calling for me?

"Falcon?" This time there had been no mistake, someone was definitely calling him. He craned his neck and noticed Faith. Her eyes were glowing a radiant white, and her entire body was emitting a glow so bright that he had to cower back a few feet. She circled her hands, and the glow disappeared, returning her eyes to their usual emerald green.

"Faith? Is that you?" He blinked. His head shook. The girl before him had suddenly become a stranger. An anger deep within him beckoned him to attack her. To tear her limb from limb. He was the embodiment of chaos, and she was holy. Holy was the enemy of all beings that romanced in the shadows. "I must eradicate her!"

He pounced toward her. Suddenly something slammed inside his head, and he crumpled to his knees. "Calm down," whispered a voice. "Listen to me. Do not let the chaos take hold of your mind."

"Get out!" With tremendous force, he shoved the voice out of his head. He turned, seeking the culprit. Behind him stood three men. At the center was an elderly man, rubbing his head. He had a pained look, and a large hunch rose from his back. At his left stood a short man wearing a blue uniform and a deep frown. At his right stood another man. This one was much taller and wore a deep red uniform. He held a large sword between both hands.

"Are you well, grandmaster?" asked the crimson knight as he turned to the hunched man.

"Yes..." said the grandmaster. "I'm afraid, however, that the chaos may have claimed too much of him. I've never seen him go this far."

"Fortunate that we were nearby," said the short man. "We can stop him before he goes on a rampage."

Falcon hissed. "No one interferes with my prey!"

The attack Falcon was so intent on providing, however, was foiled once again. He sensed a powerful energy converging on them, an energy far more insidious than his own. In his trance he did not notice as Faith came in behind him. She planted her hands on his shoulders and released an extreme level of holy energy.

No you don't! He tried to reach behind him and make her pay for her insolence. She responded by increasing her power twofold. Rays of light shot out from between their bodies as Faith continued to pour her power into him.

Falcon heard a loud wail filled with rage from deep within him. It was the power of chaos, attempting to fight back. It clawed and bellowed in a futile attempt to stay in control. The light enveloped the dark pit within him, hushing the growl into a muted silence.

The stench of blood filled his nostrils, and he looked down at his hands to find them covered in blood. He staggered back, and the gray sky blurred as he fell, ramrod straight. A last-minute interference by Faith saved him from slamming into the hard ground. Still on the floor, she held him in her arms.

"Falcon! Talk to me, Falcon!" Her screams were filled with pain.

"F...Faith?"

She looked down at him, allowing his head to rest on her legs. "You scared me half to death."

Out of thin air the black-robed menace that had haunted his dreams since he was a child appeared. The usual red cracks were spread across the robe and cloak that obscured his face.

"Very kind of you to make your presence so easily known to me, holy wielder." Shal-Volcseck laughed sharply. "I was having difficulty locating you, but with the amount of energy you've used, I could have been clear across Va'siel and found you."

Kaidoz, who had remained quiet until now, had used this opportunity to break out of his imprisonment. He brought his hands together. Besides the loud clap, nothing happened.

"You're not going anywhere, general." Slowly, Volcseck faced Kaidoz. "You and your empress have interfered with my affairs far too many times. Now you almost cost me my ultimate prize." He stared down at Faith. "Such insolence cannot go unpunished."

"What do you want with the holy wielder anyway?" asked Kaidoz. "What do you plan to accomplish by having an emblem of each element?"

"Just like a mountain does not answer to an ant, I do not answer to you."

Three figures suddenly stood beside Kaidoz, and Falcon recognized that a silent alliance had been forged out of necessity. Wait. I know them! One of them was Grandmaster Zoen. To his sides stood Professor Dunn and Professor Rykas, who wore his familiar crimson armor.

He tried to stand, but his exhausted body dragged him back down. Strangely, besides his drained spirits, he felt no real pain. So where was the blood coming from? He looked down at his hands then back up Faith, whose eyes had begun to flicker open and closed.

His world froze as he realized that the blood wasn't his—it was Faith's.

Chapter 22

There was a gash on Faith's left arm. A second cut traced her hand, where blood poured out freely. The injuries did not seem life threatening, but Falcon knew that if she continued to lose blood, he would lose her.

"Stay with me!" he ordered. His chest heaved as she closed her eyes. A second later she opened them, groggily looking down at him. He took off his jacket and wrapped it around Faith's hand. He then switched spots, putting Faith on his lap. He put pressure on the cut she had on her arm. Beside him, he heard the telltale sounds of the battle that had ensued. Professor Dunn's loud Kya screams, Ryka's clanking armor, Kaidoz' earth attacks, and Zoen's almost silent mind attacks hung in the air. Falcon paid them no mind. Faith was his only concern.

"Lost too much blood," mumbled Faith, mimicking his exact thought.

"Heal yourself."

"Not enough energy."

"Use mine."

Faith's eyes closed and opened again. She looked as if she was about to drift away into a coma.

"Use my energy, Faith. I have more than enough."

Her head bobbed. "Y... yes. I w...will."

He guided her hand to his face, shivering slightly as she rested it on his cheek. Immediately he felt his energy being sucked out of his body and traveling into hers. As he watched her twitching lips, the cuts, and the blood on her dress, he couldn't help but feel guilt wash over him. How could he have done this to her? How many times had people around him provided helpful words and tips on how to control the chaos? And yet, besides some small progress, he was no closer now to having control than the first time the chaos power took over him back at the Rohad trials.

His breathing settled as the cuts began to close. The healing process was much slower than her usual, but at least she was getting better. That was all he could ask for.

Now that Faith seemed to be out of mortal danger, he looked up. The battle was not going as he had expected. He knew Volcseck was strong, but he would have thought that the power of the four warriors would have been enough to bring him down. The scene before him shook him back to reality.

Professor Rykas, the elegant swordsman, lay sprawled, face-down, on the ground. The yellow grass under him was sprayed in crimson red. His own sword had been run through his neck, coming out the top of his skull.

Zoen stood still. Around him were thousands of whooshing whips that remained in constant rotation. With his eyes closed, he pushed both hands forward. The purple whips wrapped around Volcseck, holding him tightly in place. Kaidoz, surprised to see his opponent locked down, bombarded Volcseck with a flurry of earth spears and cubes. Zoen's and Kaidoz's creations converged in a loud explosion of dust and rubble.

"Die!" yelled Dunn. His stubby body dashed across the grass and he threw himself through the air. "Piercing flames!"

A shrill scream reverberated from the mass of attacks, sending Dunn flying, head first into a tree trunk. He crumpled down. Like Rykas, he remained unmoving.

The earth and mind masses of energy dissipated, leaving behind a bored-faced Volcseck.

There is no way! How could he have walked away unscathed?

"The quality of wielders has gone done considerably throughout the years." Volcseck's monotone voice only served to further anger Falcon. How he yearned to hurt him and wipe away his calm demeanor. Despite his vengeful thoughts, the reality that Faith needed his energy forced him to remain in place. "You two are recognized as some of the more esteemed wielders of this era, and like many others, I must declare myself..." He took a long breath, letting silence dangle in the air. "Disappointed." The chaos wielder turned to the general. "You there. Those earth teleportations you're so fond off are nothing but a cheap imitation of chaos."

Kaidoz did not seem amused by Volcseck's claims. "Don't flatter yourself. This skill is something I took from space wielders and made it my own."

"Who do you think space wielders took it from?"

"Enough talk." Kaidoz clapped his hands. "You may have impeded my movements last time, but with the focus the grandmaster is providing, you won't be able to stop me this time." Just as Kaidoz had said, he clapped his hands and dissolved in a mist of dust. The dust swirled toward Volcseck. It closed in around Volcseck and hardened around his arms.

Despite being rendered immobile, the chaos wielder did not seem the slightest bit worried. His lips, the only things that could be seen under his cloak, remained closed, with no sign of struggle or pain.

A moment later, Falcon saw why. Volcseck snapped his fingers. A ripple of power burst from the man. The earth around him crumpled to the floor, taking form of the general. Kaidoz lay on the floor. A gurgling sound filled his mouth as blood gushed out. "Hhhhow diiiiid yo…u?"

"The power of chaos isn't one for the likes of you to comprehend." With that, Volcseck brought his boot down on Kaidoz's neck. The sound of bones snapping and a man whimpering his last breath followed. Volcseck turned his attention to the elder man. "I had the privilege of dueling and killing your apprentice, General K'ran. It will bring me great pleasure to end your life as well."

The mere mention of K'ran, his adoptive father and master, being mentioned by that monster made Falcon's insides boil. How he wished to join in the fray. One look at Faith, however, and he saw that leaving her was not an option. Despite her closed wounds, her body was in an inner struggle, her cells desperately trying to make up for the blood loss. His energy was the only thing keeping her in this world.

Zoen did not say a word. He was wheezing. His posture was more hunched than usual. With a determined look, he stood a little straighter. His eyes closed and he mumbled under his breath.

"Those chants don't work on me, Grandmaster. I ascended over such paltry powers long ago."

Bursts of ripples that seemed to bend the air shot from the Grandmaster's forehead, and despite Volcseck's confident words, he found himself staggering back after they both passed through him. Falcon followed the ripples through the air as they turned around and came back toward their target.

Volcseck teleported out of view. Whooshing loudly, both ripples spun in circles, awaiting the emergence of their target.

When Volcseck once again reappeared beside the earth coffin that held Latiha, the attacks rained down at them. The chaos wielder opened a dark circle in front of him. The attacks turned tightly to avoid it, but it was too late. The circle sucked in both attacks and closed before they could escape.

Zoen blinked away his obvious shock. "You sent the mind arrows to another dimension? That goes against the very rules of nature, chaos wielder. There is no saying where they may end up."

"I suppose you better be more careful what you throw at me, then. Wouldn't want one of your powers hurting an innocent bystander, would we?"

Falcon could see that Zoen was running on fumes. Everything from his ragged breaths to his sweaty forehead pointed to the extreme energy consumption he was using in order to keep up with Volcseck.

No! Falcon screamed from within as the man he hated the most closed in on the grandmaster, a dark sword with red cracks spread throughout had materialized in his hand. His heart went icy as Zoen fended against a multitude of sword attacks. Volcseck appeared and disappeared from every angle, cutting deeply everywhere on Zoen's body. His face, legs, arms, chest. Everything was fair game.

Two long, white hands erupted from Zoen's back, reaching for the man who was inflicting damage on their master. They were too slow, and all they managed to grasp was air as Volcseck danced around them, always a step ahead of them.

The hands stretched. Volcseck duck under them and ran his sword up. The weapon arched upward and into Zoen's stomach and chest.

With a low "Oh," Zoen tumbled to the floor, his face staring at the sky.

Volcseck brought his dark boot down on his vanquished foe's bleeding chest. "Any last words, grandmaster?"

"Leave him alone!" screamed Falcon. His eyes burned with the threat of oncoming tears. How much more could Volcseck take from him?

"You may have run from Aadi while he was in Va'siel." With a resolved look, Zoen turned to Falcon. "But the legacy that the Golden Wielder left behind will catch up to you before this is over."

Even though Zoen did not say his name, Falcon knew he was speaking about him.

"Misplaced faith won't save you, grandmaster." Volcseck brought his sword up and ran it through Zoen's neck. The old man seemed to smile as the light went out of his eyes. There was no scream, no shout of pain. Only a haunting silence.

Falcon stared at his master's face, frozen in shock.

"Stand aside, young wielder. It is time for me to claim my prize."

"You'll have to get through me if you want to get to her." Falcon knew that despite the finality in his voice, Volcseck would not be fazed by his claim. But he also knew he had to try everything and anything to save his friend.

"That will be no problem."

"Leave…Falcon," stuttered Faith in a faint voice. "There is nothing you can do." Her eyes snapped open. "Leave me."

310

"No!"

"This is all so very touching." Volcseck's boots crunched over the sand as he took a few more steps toward them, bringing with him the scent of death. "Leave it to a holy wielder to throw away her life for nothing."

His words seemed to have woken up Faith, because her eyes suddenly opened and she stared directly at Volcseck. "Did you forget that it was through holy that you live today?"

"What nonsense are you spewing? I owe nothing to holy. I'm the master of chaos, the one true element that all others cower before."

"Yet, you would have died from the injuries you sustained ten thousand years ago at the hands of Demetrius. It was Lunet's interference that kept you alive. You owe everything to holy, whether you like it or not, and by extension you are a product of the love from that holy wielding."

"Love," Volcseck answered, and he took a moment to submit the rest of his thought. "That is an emotion I know nothing about nor do I care to comprehend."

"Liar!" Falcon was surprised to hear Faith speak with such force, despite her obvious weakness. "Lunet loved you! That is why she kept you alive. She believed in you. She knew you were meant to be a force of good, not evil."

"Look around you, holy wielder." Volcseck pointed at the deceased men that lay on the ground. "Is this the love you

311

speak so fondly of? You are highly misguided if you actually think that I have love inside of me. I love no one, not even myself. All I feel, all I know is a lust to end this miserable world and all the wicked who inhabit it. I'm tired of the suffering that plagues mankind. I am the savior that will put an end to it. And you, holy wielder, are the key to it."

Falcon's mouth opened at the sheer impudence spewing out of Volcseck's lips. "You speak of wicked people as if you were so righteous. It is you that has caused more suffering through Va'siel than anyone else in history. You killed my parents."

"That's of no importance. Your parents were in the way of the ultimate salvation. They had to be cleansed."

"You killed my parents so that you could rule Va'siel?" Falcon's heart thumped with nervousness, but strangely, he felt no anger toward Volcseck. He should want to hate him and rip him apart limb by limb. Faith's holy energy that leaked into him made it impossible, though. Her power relaxed him, giving him focus despite the precarious situation. He knew what he needed to do. He had to keep talking, dragging the conversation enough so that Faith could heal and he could space wield them away to safety.

Volcseck met his gaze. "Rule Va'siel? Haven't you been listening? I have no desire to rule anything. I am Va'siel's savior, not its ruler."

"What do you mean?" As he asked the question Falcon

knew he was out of time. The chaos wielder moved in with a fierce determination. The man had obviously caught on to his ploy. "Please don't kill her. She's suffered enough. She doesn't need any more."

"She will no longer feel any pain where she's going."

Falcon watched in horror, and time itself seemed to slow down as Volcseck lifted his sword and ran it toward Faith's heart.

Chapter 23

It took Falcon a moment to realize that time slowing down wasn't in his mind. Time really had slowed down! Volcseck's sword moved in slow motion, and Faith was opening her eyes at a snail's pace.

He recognized it as space force, the ability to put unnatural levels of gravity around a person or a group of persons, making it nearly impossible to move. Who is causing this? Sheridan was the first person who came to mind. The thought quickly left him though. His Rohad friend was a gifted wielder, of that there was no doubt, but there was no way he could space force someone of Volcseck's ability.

He only knew of one more space wielder.

Volcseck seemed to recognize the culprit as well. He took a step back as his speed returned to normal. "Why do you hide yourself, Ghost Knight?"

A loud boom echoed through the air as a ripple formed before them. Out of it emerged the wielder clad in white and gold slim armor. The same imposing white cape he had worn the last time Falcon had seen him was draped behind him. The knight's head jerked from Zoen's corpse to Faith and then to Falcon. From behind the visor Falcon scarcely made out a determined gaze.

"I have no words for you, knight. So I will make this quick." Volcseck's sword swooshed through the air. A long spear that appeared in the Ghost Knight's hand met the attack. The spear shot down, bringing the sword down with it. The knight used the opening to sweep in with his leg. Volcseck dodged it and countered with an elbow to the face.

The visor shattered as the knight staggered back. Still in motion he shot a volley of small meteors from his hand, only to have them easily swiped away by his opponent.

There was a burst of a red glow beside Volcseck. It moved toward the Ghost Knight.

The space wielder opened a portal before him, and the attacks moved straight in. Another portal opened behind Volcseck. Too late did the chaos wielder realize his mistake. He turned with barely enough time to react as his own attacks rammed him from behind. His body took on a U form as the red glow dug into his lower back. His hands flailed and with a loud grunt he fell face-first to the floor.

Falcon felt a surge of excitement. He'd never heard of anyone even come close to landing a hit on Volcseck, yet here he was, flat on his face eating grass. Better yet, Faith's strength had returned. She was no longer relying on his energy, which meant he could join the fight against Volcseck.

Volcseck stood. "No more games." Despite the blow that he'd been dealt, he retained his usual calm tone, and Falcon was left wondering if he had celebrated a little too soon.

"Agreed," said the Ghost Knight, matching Volcseck's placid tone.

Falcon stood behind the knight, ready to join the fray.

The Ghost Knight did not seem to want his assistance, though. He held out his hand. "Step back, Falcon. They need you more than I do. Get them far from here."

"But—"

"Don't argue. You did enough of that when you were younger. You're no longer that child. Stop talking and listen to me."

What is he talking about?

"As for you," said the Ghost Knight. He turned his attention back to Volcseck. "When you attacked my village and murdered my parents I had not yet awoken my space wielding. I tried to fight you back then, but you tossed me aside and killed my father, Anson, before my eyes."

Falcon staggered back. Anson? Anson is my father.

The Ghost Knight pressed on. "So today your opponent will not be the Ghost Knight, the space wielder. No. Today you duel Albert, the wind wielder." With a blinding flash the white and golden armor disappeared, replaced by a simple green tunic and trousers. The white cape had altered to a green cape held fast by brown trimmings. He donned dark boots and gloves. What surprised Falcon most was his face. He had seen the Ghost Knight unmask himself once. In that moment he had come face to face with a square face, light gray eyes, and raven-black hair swept back behind his head in a series of waves. The face that he looked at now was totally different. It was the face of his brother, albeit a bit older. He had the same slender nose, same light tan skin, same curled eyelashes, and the same wavy brown hair he recalled from all those years ago.

"Since you fight me with no mask..." Volcseck reached for his hood. "I shall do the same."

Falcon stood in awe at the sight. He had expected an elderly, wrinkled man with saggy skin. Volcseck was none of this, however. He looked as young as he had in the image he had seen with Demetrius. His raven-black hair fell back evenly. His handsome features were those of a man who had lived no more than twenty-five seasons, not ten thousand.

"You're not well," said Faith behind Falcon. She caught him as he fell back. His head was reeling with too much information. The day had started like any other, and now here he was face-to-face with Volcseck and Albert, the two people he had spent half a lifetime searching for. What could he do? What could he say? It was all too much for him to take in.

He was still lost in his shocked mind when Volcseck made a dash at Faith. Albert met Volcseck's sword with his spear. Their weapons clashed with a thunderous crack, as the energies of both wielders converged in a single spot.

"I told you to get them out of here!" ordered Albert, this

time more forceful than before.

Falcon snapped back to reality. Albert was doing his part. Now he had to do his. He opened a rift in space and jumped in, taking Faith and the fallen warriors with him. They emerged atop a high cliff. The lifeless bodies of Zoen, Rykas, and Dunn came out first, followed by Faith and Falcon. The unconscious Queen Latiha was the last to be pulled through. With Kaidoz gone, she was out of her prison, but she had yet to wake.

"She'll be fine," said Faith, examining the empress.

Falcon nodded, embarrassed to say that the empress's safety was the last thing on his mind. From up above, he witnessed the tremendous duel taking place in the valley below.

The two wielders met time and time again, their speed so fast that it was near impossible to follow, especially at such a long distance.

A scream drowned in Falcon's throat when Volcseck managed to take hold of Albert's spear and snap it in half. He was certain that that would spell the end of his brother. Albert, however, grabbed the incoming sword with his hand and, infusing his elbow with wind, broke the chaos wielder's weapon in pieces as well.

Falcon took a breath. His gaze dropped down to the grandmaster. He had lost so much today. Was he going to lose his brother too now that he had just gotten him back?

"Don't worry," said Faith, hugging him tightly. "He can do this."

Despite her words of assurance, doubt dripped from her voice. They both knew that Albert was locked in a duel to the death against a man who had never known defeat.

Falcon held his breath as his brother kicked the air. Visible arched green gusts of wind shot from his feet.

Volcseck threw his arms up above his head. A red wall that had to be over twenty feet high rose into the air. The wind arched around the wall and continued on to its target.

This time Volcseck fired purple energy arches of his own. The green and purple attacks met in a frightful display of flames and fireworks. Is he mimicking his attacks?

Falcon's eyes narrowed, and he noticed a slight green glow emit from above his brother's head. A clear liquid fell over his head, almost as if were a waterfall of wind energy. Then he took off in a sprint, throwing himself into the air and flying straight, head on, at the wall.

The way he glided, suspended through the air, reminded Falcon of an arrow that had been fired to fly straight and true. Except, no arrow moved at this speed. His brother was shooting so fast that the ground behind him shattered in his wake, lifting up rock and deep-rooted plants alike. He blew past the wall with ease.

Volcseck teleported. Albert seemed to have predicted this, because he rounded in a tight turn and blew back from where he had come. No sooner had Volcseck reemerged when Albert slammed into his chest. The tip of the waterfall above his head hit as if it were the end of an arrow. The chaos wielder grunted as he rolled across the ground until his flailing body crashed into a tree. The trunk splintered in a dozen places with the force.

Amazingly, Volcseck got to his feet in an instant. His skin turned a deep dark brown, and his skin wrinkled. His eyes were dark pits now. Even from afar Falcon made out the glow of crimson intensity.

Chaos state! No. No. Run, Albert! His insides screamed, but he knew there was no use. Even if Albert could hear him, he doubted he would listen.

It was Volcseck's turn to attack. He moved at a staggering speed, closing the distance between himself and his foe in a blink of an eye. They became locked in a series of parries, blocks, and attacks.

Falcon licked his lips nervously. He knew that it was only a matter of time before his brother was cut down. Volcseck was the faster of the two.

Then, like a cruel nightmare, Volcseck's fist made it past Albert's defense. Albert flew through the air, crashed into a large rock, and dangled over it, blood gushing from his nose and mouth.

Not one to let his advantage pass him by, Volcseck swooped in to his fallen enemy.

Stung by the realization that his brother was about to die, Falcon tried to space wield to him, only to have Faith hold him back.

"You can't help him in your condition," she said into his ear. "You'll only die too."

What happened next was quite unexpected. A long spear that seemed to be made out of flesh, complete with pumping veins and arteries materialized in Volcseck's right hand. As he brought the weapon down, he was shot back by a blur of green power.

Albert front flipped back to his feet.

Falcon's insides surged with relief.

His brother dug his hands into the dirt, much like an earth wielder. A thunderous snap followed as thousands of rays of wind burst from the ground. The earth crumpled into a thousand pieces as howling winds shot out in straight lines of raw power.

Falcon covered his eyes, trying to keep the dust that had risen in a mushroom cloud out of his eyes.

Volcseck tried to escape by teleporting up into the air and firing circular rays of red energy from his hands. Each shot shattered the countless shards of rocks that now littered the battle space.

Albert's body was now glowing with a bright green aura, and Falcon knew it was his raw wind power leaking out of him.

Both wielders met within the vociferous showdown.

They flew through the air and crashed into each other. Each time they met, shockwaves of energy would ripple from their bodies, causing the ground to tremble.

Water sprang from the many ruptures that had been cut through the prairie, sending geysers of liquid high into the clouds.

"That's unreal," remarked a scratchy voice behind him. Falcon spun to find Dunn standing behind him. "I've never thought such power was possible. They're rearranging the entire landscape!"

"I thought you were dead," said Falcon.

Dunn frowned. "Don't sound too disappointed. I was merely unconscious. It takes more than a chaos wielder to kill me." He had just finished speaking when he noticed the corpses of Zoen and Rykas. The professor's hands trembled, and he beat at his chest. "No!" Desperate, he threw himself at Zoen, checking for a pulse.

Falcon heard what sounded like a low hum at his side. It quickly grew louder as Volcseck teleported beside them. He made one more attempt to grab Faith, only to have Albert ram into him and shove him back.

The two warriors stood face to face.

The chaos wielder breathed quick, raspy breaths. Albert did the same. Both of their clothing had been ripped to shreds in numerous places, exposing their muscular physiques.

"This is not over," hissed Volcseck. "This battle has given me more than enough information on your abilities. Pray we never bout again, Albert Hyatt, for if we do…" He let his silence drift for a second. "I will end you."

A teleport later and the chaos wielder was gone, but Falcon was certain that they had not seen the last of him, not by a long shot.

Chapter 24

According to Dunn, Ladria was free. Zoen had led the attack that reclaimed the city. With the absence of Draknorr, it had proved an easy task to overrun the Suteckh forces. After their victory, Zoen had decided to take a small escort to Missea to assist the young Rohads. It was on this trek that they ran into the skirmish against Volcseck. With the extreme energy levels they'd been emitting, it had proven childishly easy to find them.

The freedom of Ladria should have been welcome news. Falcon could not find himself to smile, though. Not with the nightmare unfolding before his eyes.

The two coffins rested, lids open at the center of the grand hall. The usual yellow tapestries had been brought down and replaced with dark ones. In the three days since the grandmaster's death, hundreds of nobles and royals had poured from all around to pay their respects to Zoen. They all stood now, heads down as they crowded the hall.

Two men and a tall woman, all wearing black robes, stood over the oak wood coffin and laid a dark rose within it. Falcon recognized them as the grandmasters from the other Rohad academies. He wondered how they could have reached Missea so quickly, when he and his friends had struggled so much to do the same. Indeed, being a grandmaster sure made life easier sometimes.

The trio of grandmasters then moved to the second, red marbled coffin and laid a flower within it as well.

Once done, they took a seat atop the wooden platform that had been erected at the end of the hall. A somber-faced Empress Latiha made her way to the center of it. She faced the crowd, gathering her breath for a moment.

Her head rose. "Zoen was a wonderful being and an even greater friend. When I met him a century ago, he was no more than a child, but even then he displayed the qualities that would lead him to become a great man. Qualities like strength, duty, honor, respect, and above all else...compassion..."

The empress continued her speech. She spoke of Zoen's time with Aadi. She then went on to tell the story of how a simple beggar boy had risen through the ranks to become the longest serving Rohad Grandmaster. For the next hour she unfolded the story of the man that Zoen had been. How he had amassed a following at Rohad academy, reinvented the rules that catered to the nobles, and formed the strategy that ended the Ladrian war. Falcon zoned out some time into the speech. It wasn't that he didn't care. At any other time, he would have given anything to hear these long-forgotten stories of his mentor. With the amount of loss he had experienced, however, he was in no mood for stories of how wise and benevolent Zoen had been. The grandmaster was gone. No amount of kind words was going to change that.

Despite his lack of enthusiasm for the somber words, they continued on. For the next few hours, one person after another took their time speaking of their experience with Zoen.

Falcon heard Hiromy clear her throat beside him. She had buried her head in Sheridan's shirt and was crying quietly. At her side, Faith also let out tears. Aya was the only one who wasn't crying, though her red eyes told him that she had been crying some time ago. In private, perhaps. Falcon noticed that the blind girl, Empress Keira, stood beside Aya. She rested a comforting hand on Aya's shoulder. The two massive bears flanked her from each side. The animals bowed their heads as well, making Falcon wondered how the empress had earned such obedience from the savage creatures.

Why am I thinking about that at a time like this? He shook his head. All the stress was getting to him. Standing idly by was only making things worse, and the more he did it, the more suffocating it became. He felt the walls closing in on him. The people seemed to be moving closer, violating his space.

Unable to take any more, he darted out of the room, down the palace halls, through the garden, and out into the city.

Things didn't get any better. Nature itself seemed to be grieving the fallen grandmaster. The skies were a dark gray. The air was thick and moist, signaling an oncoming thunderstorm. The sobbing people that stood outside the palace made it next to impossible to move.

"Excuse me!" cried a woman who Falcon had just bumped into.

"Quit running into people, young man," complained another woman Falcon had crashed into as well. "Have some respect. Don't you know that a son of Missea has died?" She looked at him with judgmental eyes. It was the same look he had gotten time and time again as he grew up in Ladria. That same you're worthless to the world kind of look.

In silence, he darted away from the crowd and into an empty alleyway. Where was he going? He himself didn't know.

Moments later, in the solemn silence of the outskirts of Missea, Falcon found himself staring through the small open window of a pub. The pub itself didn't grab his attention. Why should it? It was a plain muddy structure of hay, rocks, and sticks. Even the name of the place, Lowly Scrap Heap, which had been etched into a rock, quite sloppily, screamed of depression and abandonment.

What did attract Falcon was the man that he saw through the window. Sitting alone at the end of the small room was Albert, sipping slowly from a mug. Every time he drank from it he would gaze at the mug as if it held some deep secret, and then he would set it down and unblinkingly stare at it.

He opened the door, taking in the scent of moldy seaweed and stale ale.

Albert looked up, and with a swing of his hand, motioned Falcon to join him.

The irony of the situation was not lost to Falcon. He had spent many sleepless nights, thinking of the time he would come face to face with his long lost brother. The one everyone was convinced had died in that cave attack. Now here he was. Except, the grand celebration he expected at the time of their meeting was absent. There were no joyful hugs and cheers. Instead, only a few sleeping drunkards and a frail old bartender, who sat behind a counter, would bear witness to this event.

The first words out of Albert's mouth only further cemented the anti-climactic aura surrounding this much anticipated event in Falcon's life.

"Care for a drink?" he asked.

"I don't drink," said Falcon. "But maybe I can make an exception today."

"Hey, Nolan!" called Albert. "A drink for my little brother."

Nolan, the old bartender, lifted his head, leaving a web of drool that spread from his mouth to the counter where he had been laying. "H... help yoooorseelf... f." He pointed to the bottles of rum, wine, and ale behind him. He then lifted his head and took a hard look at Albert. "You have a brother. You never told—" His head suddenly crashed back down as he returned to his rambunctious snores.

Albert took another slow sip of his drink. "He's a bit eccentric, but he's a good man."

Falcon searched for the cleanest mug he could find, which wasn't easy. They all were all dusty with streaks of grime. He finally settled on a small one that seemed to be the cleanest of the bunch. He gave it a swipe with his shirt and helped himself to a brown bottle with the words The Ugly Wielder on the sooty label. The dark liquid rose to the top, fizzing and bubbling as it poured out of the bottle.

Nolan lifted his head at this. "Watch yourself, boy. I'm trying to run a respectable establishment here. No dirty business." He scratched his behind as his head dropped to the counter once more. His muffled, slurred speech could still be heard. "You are family of Albert, so I will see it fit to let this pass. He's a good man. Very good man. Got me and my family out of a tough problem many times. Good man…good man…"

"He knows you more than I do," said Falcon, much more accusingly than he had intended. He took a seat and gripped the cold steel of the handle. Quickly, he took a sip. The bitter taste assaulted his taste buds, causing him to gag and spit some of the ale. Not wanting to look a fool, he took another long gulp of the drink, trying his best to retain a straight face.

"It's an acquired taste," said Albert from behind his mug. "Take it slow. There's no rush."

"Is this the part where you impart wise words? I could have used those over the last few years when I was alone, abandoned by my own brother." He was well aware of the poison in his voice, but he didn't care. Who was Albert to tell him what to do now, especially after being gone for so long? In another sign of defiance, he took a long swig, downing the remaining ale.

If Albert was angry, sad, glad, or a combination of these sentiments, Falcon did not know. His features remained passive and unreadable.

"I really like this place," his brother said. "It's quiet, and only a certain kind of people come here."

"Yes. I can see that. The owner seems very selective of the people he allows in here." Falcon took another glance around, his eyes settling on the few hiccupping drunkards.

"You can jest all you want, but this is a simple place. These are good folk, unlike like so many other you'll encounter throughout your life. Zoen would have liked this place."

"Is that why you're here and not at his funeral?" As he asked the question, it occurred to Falcon that Albert could not possibly know what Zoen would or would not want. How could he? He'd never even met the man.

"You're wondering how I could know what Zoen would want." said Albert as if reading his mind. It was more of a statement than a question, and Falcon cursed himself for being so easy to read. "I knew Zoen well. After all, it was he who kept me updated on your progress in Ladria."

"You checked up on me?"

"Of course I did. I'm your big brother, am I not? Was I simply supposed to abandon you?"

His insides fumed. "You did abandon me!" Nolan shot a disapproving glance, causing Falcon to lower his voice. "What was it that you told me that night? 'Don't worry. I won't leave you alone for long.' Except you never came back. You left me to die in the forest."

"Did I now?"

"Yes."

"Didn't you ever think it strange that K'ran just happened to find you? Didn't you find it odd that he would just be roaming the woods in the middle of a thunderstorm?"

Falcon's silence was all the answer Albert needed, and his brother pressed on. "It was I who told him where to find you. And once you went to Rohad, I kept close communication with Zoen and K'ran. That way I could make sure that you were fine. I must say, I was quite proud of how you handled the situation back at Sandoria."

"Zoen and K'ran knew? They knew all along and didn't tell me?" Betrayal rose in his voice.

"They didn't inform you of my whereabouts to protect you. They knew you had bigger problems on your mind. Like controlling your powers, for one."

That wasn't a good enough excuse for Falcon. He had

trusted both K'ran and Zoen. How could they have withheld this from him? He felt a cold, precise anger toward the man before him. He wanted to hurt him, to make him pay for everything he'd been through.

"I get that you're angry at us, and frankly you have the right to be. In time, I'm sure you will see that we were correct to withhold this from you. It would have only caused more problems being associated with a wanted criminal. You didn't need that."

"Why didn't you just take me with you?"

"And do what? Live your life running and hiding? No. I was cursed with that life, but that didn't mean you had to be."

"It is true, then?" asked Falcon. In his mind he replayed that morning, when the guards had told him that his brother had murdered the Ladrian council. He recalled the smell of wet dirt as the bloodied corpses were carried away. "You did kill them?"

"Yes." He took a gulp and sighed. "I did."

"Why?"

"I see no use in reliving a past that is long dead."

"I do. I stayed up many nights wondering why you did it."

Albert studied him for a long time before finally speaking. "The members of the Ladrian council were planning a revolt. They had control over a large branch of the army, but they needed a commander."

"You?" asked Falcon. He finally understood why the council had asked for his brother all those night ago.

"Yes. They wanted me to lead a coup and take over the city. That was something I could never do."

"Why kill them, though? You could have just said no."

"If I had declined their offer, they would have simply found another commander. Once that happened Ladria would have been thrust into a civil war that would have claimed thousands of lives." He took a long breath. "There was an unflinching desire in them to rule. I saw it in their eyes. Their souls had been corrupted by the promise of power. For them, the death of their citizens was a small price to pay. I couldn't allow that. So I did what I had to...I eradicated the corruption at its core."

"Except you didn't," countered Falcon. He told him of Councilman Nakatomi's claim that it had been he who had caused the demise of the council.

Surprisingly, Albert took this news in stride. Did he already know?

Albert brought his hand to his chin, rubbing it for some time before speaking. "That would make sense. I had my suspicions that someone else was orchestrating the plot from the shadows but never had any strong leads as to who it could have been."

"There is still something I still don't understand," said Falcon. "You took off your mask for me once, remember? You looked different than you do now." He pointed at the space emblem. "How long have you been a space wielder?"

Wordlessly, Albert stood and served himself from one of the bottles behind the counter. When he returned, he said, "Grandmaster Zoen put a mind charm around me, so when people saw me they would see someone else. It wasn't always on, however, which is why it was important that I stay masked most of the time. Also, there was always the possibility that another mind wielder could detect the charm and figure out who I was. Which is why I stayed away as much as I could. When Zoen died, well, I suppose his charm wore off." He caressed the deep blue emblem with shooting stars coursing through it. "As for this. I would have thought it was fairly obvious. I'm a dual wielder. It was something I didn't discover until long after I had left."

Falcon shook his head. He wasn't quite sure what he was feeling, but of one thing he was sure. He didn't want to be anywhere near his brother at the moment. He had gotten answers, which was all he'd wanted.

"Little brother," said Albert, taking his hand. Falcon pulled away. "Don't go through life thinking you were the only who suffered. Everyone in this world has their own tribulations to face."

Falcon began to walk away.

"Do you think it was easy for me to desert you and live a life of solitude?"

There was no answer from Falcon.

"Something I learned from the Golden Wielder is that the bad times make the good times that much better," said Albert. "And they open the doors to new opportunities. If I had stayed, what are the chances that you would have met your friends, Aya and Faith?"

"I had never thought about that," muttered Falcon, feeling the air leave him. He couldn't imagine a life without his friends.

"My departure allowed you to form bonds that would have otherwise eluded you."

Falcon knew that Albert was right, but that didn't make him feel any better. He had been lied to by the three men he admired the most. But then again, he now had his brother back. Should he simply overlook the bad and concentrate on the good? Could he? Especially when there was so much bad still left.

"How about we talk about something else?" asked Albert.

"I think I'd rather be alone. There is nothing more I want to talk about." He headed to the door.

"Not even Dad and Mom?"

Falcon stopped cold, feeling his insides churn.

"Sit down," Albert suggested.

Unable to resist, Falcon took a seat.

For the next few hours Albert shed light on those

childhood years long past. A childhood that he knew very little about but that Albert obviously still had a sharp memory of. He recounted story after story, ranging from the day their parents met, their wedding day, and even Falcon's birth.

Falcon absorbed every ounce of information, eager to drink from the pool of information that Albert provided.

He saw the scenes in his head, reliving them as if he were walking through them in real life.

He wasn't sure when it happened, but sometime during the tales, he forgot all about his problems and found himself laughing alongside the man before him. He was no longer the freak of Rohad, and Albert was no longer the traitor of Ladria. Right now, at this time, they were just two simple brothers reminiscing on old times over drinks.

Chapter 25

The chirping crickets, the howling wind, and the sound of footsteps were the only sounds outside the old hut. From within, Faith made out the loud cackles of a group of men. One of them sounded strangely familiar.

"Another round of drinks!" yelled the voice.

"Was that Falcon?" asked Aya.

"I think it was."

Faith couldn't believe it. She and Aya had scoured Missea high and low, searching for Falcon. They had gotten a few scattered reports from people around the city who had claimed to have seen a young Rohad with a leather jacket headed this way. But of all places, she'd never thought they would find him inside a pub. Especially one that looked in such a miserable state. Why, there wasn't a single flower in sight.

The surprises were far from over.

When she opened the door, she was met with the sight of Falcon banging a mug on the table and laughing harder than he had ever seen him. It was strange, seeing him so red-cheeked and happy all of a sudden.

He stood and spun, pretending to be holding someone in his arms. "Like this, Albert. This is how Mom would dance."

Albert looked a lot more in control of his senses, though

he looked a bit droopy as well. He grinned and offered his brother a smile, and Faith couldn't help but admire just how alike they both looked.

"I think he's drunk!" said Aya, her voice somewhere between shock and amusement. "I never thought I'd see the day."

Their presence had not gone unnoticed. Albert, who had seen them come in, waved them over.

"I think he had a bit too much to drink," he said. "Perhaps you ladies could take him back to his room."

Faith and Aya both took hold of Falcon, each supporting him under an arm.

"Tell him I'll meet him here tomorrow morning if he wishes to speak to me some more," said Albert.

Faith nodded as she and Aya struggled to keep Falcon upright. As she had predicted, Falcon was proving uncooperative on the walk back to the inn. He stumbled over the girls' feet and loosened his weight, making it impossible for them to move at a decent pace.

More than once he would stop to lean over a barrel. His face would turn a deep green, as if he was going to barf, but nothing came out.

"I love you both soooooo much," he said. He extended his hands as wide as possible as he wobbled from side to side.

"Okay, lover boy," said Aya. She grunted under his

weight. "How about you just concentrate and keep walking. We're almost there."

"I'm serious. You two alwaaayyss..." he slurred as he almost fell to one side again. With supreme effort, Faith pulled him back upright. "Always there for me." With his little speech complete, he buried his face in Aya's hair. "You smell so good." He leaned in and puckered his lips, causing Aya to jerk her head back.

"What?" Falcon giggled and hiccupped all at once. "No kiss? That's fine." He bopped his head toward Faith. "You smell really good, too. I love you so much. You'll kiss me, right?"

Faith looked away, her cheeks turning red. How many times had she dreamed of Falcon saying those words to her? In her mind, however, he was sober, not dead drunk. He didn't smell of bile and ale, and they were in a flower garden, instead of the middle of a strange city.

"No kiss from you either?" Falcon seemed thoroughly disappointed. It didn't last. A few seconds later he was singing at the top of his lungs. "Oh wielder boy, wielder boy, wi...what were the words again?" He didn't wait for an answer. "It doesn't matter. The Golden Wielder sang this song so I'm going to sing it too."

Faith caught a couple of late night walkers giving them disdainful looks.

"Nothing to see here," said Aya, not appreciating the

stares. "Keep it moving."

"See why I'm glad we don't have a Rohad academy in Missea?" said a passerby, loud enough for them to hear. "My sister back in Belwebb says they are always causing scenes like this."

Another woman, who held her nose high in the air, had harsher words. "Back in my day you would have gotten a flogging for public intoxication. Oh, how I wish that law had not been banned."

When they finally reached the inn and laid Falcon down on his bed, Faith was beyond worn out. Her calves and arms were killing her. She had a headache from all the alcohol fumes Falcon had blown in her face. Nonetheless, as she laid herself down in the bed beside Falcon and saw his chest rise and fall, she felt happy for him. Ever since they were kids, she had loved the tender sound of his laughter. Hearing it today had brought back so many of those fond memories.

"I love you, Falcon," she said under her breath. "Sweet dreams."

~~~

Aya could see that Faith was exhausted. Sure enough, a little after lying down, she fell in a deep sleep.

She leaned in and did something she'd been wanting to do for a long time: plant a soft kiss on Falcon's cheek. He twitched at the touch of her lips, but as she had suspected, he didn't wake up. Feeling a bit lighter on her feet, she quietly made her way out the room and down into the street, where Keira was waiting. She was accompanied by the white cub.

"I only brought Maru with me," said Keira, patting her animal on the head. "People around here run away and scream when they see Draiven and Aykori."

"Having two massive bears following you along isn't exactly normal."

Keira giggled. "No. I suppose not." Her features focused. "So, what is it that you wanted to speak about?"

"First of all, thank you for coming. It means a lot to me."

"Think nothing of it. We're bond sisters, remember? I'll always be here for you."

Aya still couldn't get used to hearing Keira say that. A few weeks ago the empress would have never thought of speaking to a Rohad, and coming to the aid of one would have been out of the question. But after Aya helped her and showed her kindness, Keira had become much friendlier toward Rohads.

"Do you know a man called Armeen?" asked Aya.

Keira drew a sharp breath. It was the answer Aya needed. In a quick, rapid voice she told her about the encounter she'd had with Captain Armeen, where he lived, his goal of finding his family, and the fact that he had not forgotten her.

"I've been dead to him for so long," said Keira. "I don't think it's my place to simply come back into his life out of nowhere. He would never accept me."

"Maybe you should let him make that choice."

Keira met her gaze. "Thanks for telling me this. I will think about it."

"I was hoping for a favor."

"Name it."

"You have messengers and scouts everywhere, right?"

"Almost everywhere. Why?"

"Have you heard anything about the Suteckh? Their generals might be dead, but I doubt they will simply run back to Tenma and declare peace."

"Only tidbits of troublesome information."

"Troublesome?"

Keira hesitated for a moment. "It's the Blood Empress. She is marching out of Tenma with her army. Some of my scouts have even reported seeing the Northern barbarians, the Omega warriors, and the hollow clansmen of the lost sea marching alongside with her."

"That can't be." Aya looked at Keira, her eyebrow rising with doubt. "Those clans all hate each other. They would never reunite under the same banner."

"That's not all."

"There's more?"

"It looks like the Neikan Demons of old and Scaiths might be with them as well. You know what that means. No wielding."

Indeed, Aya recalled the Scaiths ability to nullify wielding in the area surrounding them. She, herself, had managed to find a way around it, but she doubted most wielders at Missea could do the same.

"Things are going to get very bad," said Keira.

Aya stared at the star-filled sky. Somewhere out there, under the same moon, her sister was moving toward her. Selene. Where are you? she thought desperately.

~~~

Melousa knew she shouldn't have trusted a filthy earth wielder. He had promised her so much, and now the idiot had gotten himself killed. Which meant that pompous Empress Latiha would get to live another day.

She screamed into the air, her shout piercing everything around her.

"You brought us here for nothing!" cried Scyleia. "We won't even get to see wielder blood run free."

Some of the Orian warriors nodded in agreement.

Melousa rose from the rock she'd been sitting on. Her long strides covered the ground as she walked clear across the roaring fire. Sparks of red and yellow sprayed into the air. "Yer challenge my authority!"

Scyleia's eyes gleamed with rebellion for a split second. She hunched back, bowing her head. Through gritted teeth, she spoke. "No. Of course not, my queen."

At the moment, Melousa realized that she was close to

losing control of her warriors. They had come here expecting to kill wielders, not sit idly by in the middle of this prairie. She needed to do something to satisfy their bloodlust. Perhaps attack a farming village on the way home would be the answer.

"I would have killed any subordinate of mine who spoke to me in such a manner," hissed a low voice.

Melousa eyes narrowed at the dark figure that now stood in the middle of the warriors. It was clad in dark garments and wore a white mask that had streaks of dried blood coming out of its hollow eyes.

"Who are you to come into our clan, uninvited?" roared Scyleia.

The strange newcomer's head jerked unnaturally toward Scyleia. "I'm the Blood Empress. I have a better question for you. Who are you to speak on behalf of your leader? Last I checked, the queen of the Orian warriors was Melousa."

Recklessly, Scyleia leapt from where she stood. "Die, wielder!"

Suddenly, she stopped moving. She aimed her wild punches at creatures that existed only on her mind.

"Get away! Get away!" She fell to the floor. She slammed her head into a nearby rock. Blood spurt from the deep cuts she was inflicting on herself. "My head. They're here. Get out."

None of the warriors moved. They all watched in horror as one of their best fighters finished herself off.

Melousa took a step back, fearful that the insanity Scyleia was experiencing would pass on to her.

Moments later it was all over. The blue-skinned warrior lay on the ground, her face was ripped apart beyond recognition. One of her eyes had been torn out of its socket; the other one halfway crushed.

"Do yer think yer can simply come into my camp and be killing my warriors?" demanded Melousa, getting over her initial shock. "I be ending yer for this."

"Then you shall never get your revenge," said the Blood Empress gently. "And your warriors will not get to kill capital city wielders."

"That be not mattering anymore. Latiha be knowing of yer attack. The entire surprise plan be ruined!"

"I don't need surprise. I have more than enough power to take down Missea, and after that, every other capital city in Va'siel shall fall to the Suteckh."

Out of the shadows they emerged. A dozen large, humped black creatures that stood on two stubby, arched legs. Tusks dangled out of the corners of their mouths.

Neikan Demons, thought Melousa. She had heard of the creatures, of course, but had never actually seen one.

The surprises were far from over, though. Beings that stood like men but were completely translucent blue emerged from behind the Neikan Demons. Hollow Clansmen. At their side emerged steel-helmeted men. Melousa knew them as the Northern Barbarians. Large fur coats hung from their shoulders.

Countless other figures emerged, but Melousa was no longer paying attention to their appearance.

"Yer think this be frightening me? My warriors be fighting to the end."

"Frightening you? My dear queen, why would I do that? These are your allies."

Melousa felt the words like typhoons of elation. Now she understood what the empress meant when she said she had power on her side. "What role will I be playing in this?"

There was a slight pause as the empress nodded her head. "You have one of the most important roles of all. It will be up to you to rid us of Missea's leader. Empress Latiha."

The savage queen grinned in silent approval.

Chapter 26

The awareness that Missea was firmly on their side put an extra spring in Falcon's step when he woke in the morning. The bed he had slept on had been the most comfortable he had experienced in years, and he took solace in the fact that his brother was no longer a long-lost ghost. He was alive, and with the newly discovered corruptions committed by Mr. Nakatomi, it might even be possible that the charges against Albert could be dropped. Now he just wished he knew how he'd gotten to the Inn. He recalled taking a few drinks as Albert spoke to him about their father.

But beyond that, everything was a blank.

The scent of chicken broth fell upon him as he passed the small chicken noodle stand outside the inn. As he had expected, Sheridan was there. There were three empty deep bowls at the table where he sat. He was halfway through his fourth bowl. Hiromy sat beside him, working on a small roll of sushi.

"Hyatt." Sheridan waved as he slurped a long noodle strand into his mouth. "Over here."

"He eats so funny," said Hiromy, before returning her attention to her own food.

"Have you two seen Aya and Faith?" asked Falcon. "They weren't at the inn when I got up."

"Some time to wake up, Hyatt. It's nearly midday."

Falcon looked up. Indeed the first sun was close to the center of the sky. "I had a busy night."

"So I heard." Sheridan smirked.

"What is that supposed to mean?"

"Nothing."

Hiromy looked up, her eyes blissfully wide. "You have a gorgeous singing voice, by the way."

Singing voice? What was she rambling about?

"Good, you're all here." Falcon turned to see his two missing friends walking through the door. Aya took a seat. Faith did as well. "We just got back from seeing Empress Latiha."

"For what?" asked Falcon.

"We needed to inform her of the Suteckh's movements. Well, it's all speculation as of now. Nonetheless, Keira wanted to keep Latiha as well-informed as possible."

"How come I wasn't told?" complained Falcon.

"You were asleep," said Faith.

Aya nodded. "You were out so late last night. I know that you've been through a lot. Your brother is back, and we lost Zoen, but seriously, Falcon. I don't think this is the time to be getting intoxicated."

"I got drunk?" Falcon couldn't believe it. That would explain why he didn't recall most of the night's events. He felt an overwhelming sense of shame come over him. "I'm sorry. I didn't mean to cause any trouble."

"I wouldn't say you caused much trouble." Faith smiled. "You're more of a nice drunk, not those angry ones that get all violent and stuff."

Aya and Faith shared a knowing look and he had the feeling they were withholding something from him. Whatever it was, he wasn't sure he wanted to know. He was certain it had something to do making himself look the fool.

"I hate angry drunks," said Hiromy quite suddenly. "We had this crazy man Father and I always visited. He was some type of diplomat, and he would started screaming and breaking things when things went bad—" The quiet evening turned rowdy really fast. Hiromy, who had been chirpy and smiling, clutched her head, complaining of a headache.

Sheridan leaned beside her, trying to comfort her, but she swatted him away, and her hands began to tremble. Everything was happening so fast that Falcon barely had time to register the blood coming out of her nose, squeezing through her fingertips, and pouring onto the table.

Faith jumped to action, resting her hand on Hiromy's head. It took a moment, but the blood stopped flowing.

Falcon's heart drummed in his chest as he noticed the blood was not the usual red. Instead, it was a dark shade of crimson mixed with green. Faith's worried look told him everything he needed to know. Poison.

~~~

"So what happens now?" asked Falcon. He was sitting in the middle of the room with legs crossed.

Faith, who was sitting in front of him, opened her eyes. "Falcon. Meditation usually works with one sitting in absolute silence. It doesn't do much if you keep on talking throughout it."

"I know. It's just that I can't concentrate when I keep thinking about Hiromy." After the incident at the food place, Faith had discovered that some of the poison that Hiromy had absorbed during her battle with Dokua was still affecting her. It had lain dormant inside her brain but had now begun to leak out, threatening to claim the princess's life. Faith had managed to locate it, but Hiromy had not fully woken. Instead she lay in a dormant state. She would drift in and out of consciousness.

"Hiromy is doing her part, fighting through this. We have to do our best for her. Now close your eyes and concentrate."

He did as he was told.

"Now," began Faith. "I'm going to show you something. It's about Shal-Volcseck."

"Good." Falcon liked where Faith was headed. Perhaps she had discovered a weakness in their last encounter.

"I wanted to show you a scene of his past."

A scene of his past? That seemed like a complete waste of time to Falcon. Why would he want to waste his time with something like that?

She must have noticed his apprehension because she quickly said, "In order to defeat him, it is important that you get to know him."

"I'd really rather just kill him."

"Knowledge can be a powerful weapon. Much stronger than a wielding stone, at times."

"We already saw some of his past. Remember when Demetrius showed us Volcseck's transformation into a criminal? And that knowledge didn't do much to help us when we ran into him."

"This is different. This scene is from some time before all that. I think you will find it invaluable."

Falcon didn't necessarily agree, but he bowed to Faith's knowledge on the subject of meditation. "Go on."

She took his hands, and his skin goose bumped as her soft touch caressed him. "Now. Holy wielders can't show other people past memories like chaos and mind wielders can. However, I can pull knowledge and scenes from previous holy wielders. In this case I will tap into some scenes from my predecessor, Lunet."

"You mean Demetrius' wife?"

"Yes. After meeting with Demetrius I was able to form a much stronger bond with her."

Now Falcon understood why they were holding hands. Faith would bring up the memory with their holy wielding, but she would need to tap into Falcon's mind wielding to show the events of the past.

"I'm ready," he said. And just like that, he seemed to be freefalling through the air. Black blotches whizzed past him at mesmerizing speeds. A while later, those formless masses of dark condensed into different-shaped creations. Some took the long forms of trees. Others became a soft white snow. Before he knew it, he was standing in the middle of a forest. The ground and pine trees were covered in sheets of snow. A thick misty fog rolled across the land, making it difficult to see beyond a few feet ahead.

"What am I supposed to be seeing?" asked Falcon.

She brought her finger to her lips. "Just watch."

It wasn't long until a pale, short woman who wore a ragged dress and a large straw hat came trudging around a family of trees and headed straight for him. Falcon didn't notice at first, but after a few seconds he noticed the young boy that was struggling behind her. The boy wore ragged clothing as well except, unlike the woman, he donned a heavy coat that had to be at least five sizes too big.

"Follow them," said Faith. "Don't worry, they can't see us."

Falcon didn't need this information. He had seen these types of visions before, and he knew that they were mere unseen ghosts to the people around them.

"I don't trust him, Mother," said the boy to the woman.

"Voly," said the woman.

Voly? Of course. He'd seen Volcseck as a child before in a vision Demetrius had showed him. On that occasion, however, Volcseck had been much skinnier, almost as if he had not eaten in days. In this place in time his cheeks were fuller, and he had a healthy pink to his skin. He couldn't say the same for his mother, whose sharp cheekbones and hollowed sockets could be seen from a great distance away. No doubt she had been feeding most of their small portions of food to her son.

The woman continued. "We need to aid those less fortunate than ourselves. Compassion is the only way this world will become a better place."

"Yes, Mother," said Volcseck. He sounded apprehensive, but it was obvious he took her words seriously because he turned around and ran back, following his own footsteps. "Not much longer, sir. The cabin is a little up ahead."

"That sounds just great." A man Falcon hadn't seen before turned the corner around the trees. He shook violently as he hugged himself in a futile attempt to fend off the cold.

"Take my coat," said Volcseck, taking the thick robe off and handing it over.

The man held his hand up. "I couldn't possibly."

"Don't you worry, sir. Mother and I have lived here our entire lives. We're used to the cold of the high mountains."

The heavily-bearded man took the coat and threw it over his shoulders. "Thanks."

Despite his brave front, Falcon could tell that Volcseck was cold. The bumps on his skin and slight tremble in his voice made that clear. It was strange seeing the lord of chaos portray such kindness. He'd always been known only bad stories about him. But if Faith thought this small scene was going to change his mind about him, she was sorely mistaken. Volcseck might have been a sweet kid, but that didn't excuse the atrocities he'd committed when he grew into a man.

The trio of man, woman, and child walked a few more steps up the cold mountain. Like Volcseck had said, in a short while they arrived at a small cabin. Seeing the miserable termite-hole building in the middle of practically nowhere brought back memories of his own time with K'ran in Wingdor Forest.

They went into the simple one-room cabin. The dark stove, small bed, and slab of rock made it slightly more welcoming than the outdoors. There was however, a tiny fireplace at the corner of the room that held the promise of warmth.

"This place will do just fine," said the grinning man. "It's not much, but it will get me through the winter." Falcon noticed that the man's voice had grown far more forceful, and much less timid.

The woman turned to the man. "You're welcome for a

few days to collect your spirits, but I'm afraid there is simply not enough room for you to stay the entire season. I can guide you to a nice family that owns a farm. They're always in need of a helping hand. I'm sure they will take you in."

"Shut your trap, you old bat. You and your son will get out now and leave or I will gut you both!"

The woman shuffled back a bit, the distress in her voice rising. "Sir, there is a storm coming. Surely you wouldn't seriously throw me out of my own home."

"I said out! There is hardly enough heat for one person." The man produced a large knife he'd been hiding under his robe. "I'm serious. I will gut you both. I've done it before, and I'll do it again. Starting with him."

The woman stood in front of her young child. "Not my Voly."

"Out with the both of you." Falcon could see that the man was on his last nerve. A thick vein was clearly visible, running down the length of his neck, and his stained teeth were bared like a wild animal's.

This time, the rightful owners of the cabin did not argue. They quickly made their way out the door. The woman tried to reach for a nearby blanket, but an evil look from the man made her abandon her plan and leave empty-handed.

"I told you I didn't trust him, Mom," said Volcseck once they were outside, exposed to the elements. "But don't you worry, Mom. I'll take care of him."

The boy reached for his pocket. When he brought it back out he held a shiny emblem with red cracks running through it.

The woman looked as if she'd seen a ghost. "Put that away! I told you to never bring that out in the open."

"But, Mom–"

"No buts. You know full well what happened last time you tried to use it."

"That was an accident. I can control it better now."

"Put that dreaded thing away." She reached for it but then seemed to think better of it. She retracted her hand, as if the simple act of touching it would contaminate her. "If it wasn't that you needed that emblem to keep you alive, I would have destroyed it long ago."

Volcseck would not give up. "Why do we have to suffer out in the cold? I can easily kill him. We don't have to live like this. I have more than enough power—"

"Shhhh… I will not have my child turn into a murderous criminal." Falcon couldn't get over the irony of the statement. If she only knew that sweet boy would grow to become the most wanted criminal in history.

Dropping his shoulders, Volcseck finally said. "So what do we do now, Mom?"

"If we hurry, I think we can make it to the city before sundown." But they did not make it in time. No sooner had they descended a mile down the mountain than the blizzard hit.

The woman huddled beside the paltry shelter a bush of leaves provided. She held Volcseck under her, as she took the brunt of the storm.

Falcon cringed as he noticed that the woman's clothes shred across her back. The thin skin over her bony spine grew bluer by the second, until it looked to be the same color as the very sky. As the storm raged, she whispered to her son. Falcon did not make out all of the words over the storm, but he did make out a few fragments of broken sentences. Things like, "Love you, Voly. Everything will be fine..." and toward the end, "Don't change."

When the storm finally subsided, the young Volcseck crawled out from under his mother. He tapped her shoulder. She tipped over and fell ramrod straight, facing towards the clouds.

"Mom!" cried Volcseck. Falcon felt his insides twist with agony. He himself had lost his mother around the age of the boy before him. Despite the knowledge that this boy was going to grow up to murder his own mother thousands of years later, he couldn't help but feel grief for the pained boy begging his mother to speak to him. "Mom... Mom...?" With trembling hands, the boy reached for his stone. He clutched his emblem tightly in his hands. Tears ran down his cheeks, and he cursed out loud. Suddenly, the boy disappeared.

Falcon recognized the movement as chaos

teleportation. Faith and Falcon moved with the boy. They now stood inside the old cabin, where a startled- looking man cowered by the wall.

"I didn't know you were a wielder. I had no idea." The man spoke in a rushed, distressed voice. He fell to the floor and held his hands before his head. "Show mercy. Give me a chance!"

"Did you show my mother mercy?" Volcseck's skin grew a deep brown, and his voice became inhumanly deep. "Did she get a chance?"

Before the cowering man had a chance to answer, Volcseck shot a purple mass of energy from his hand. The line of power dug into the man's forehead. It slowly dug into his body like a worm. Falcon saw the man's skin rise and fall as the energy moved over his cheek, down his neck, and into his chest.

Volcseck smirked. "The power will eat your insides, nice and slow. You will die a most painful death, just like she did."

The scene dissolved with a bright flash, and Falcon found himself sitting in the room with Faith. The serene aura surrounding him was a sharp contrast to the havoc he had just experienced.

"That was his first murder," said Faith, in a low voice. She reached out and turned off the waning candle with her fingers. The vanilla scent gave way to a burning incense.

"What was the use of seeing that?" asked Falcon. "To show me that Volcseck and I are one and the same?"

"That's not true."

"How so? He killed his mother's murderer, and I want to do the same."

"You have a kind heart." She rested her palm over his chest. "He doesn't. He wishes to destroy, while you want to end him in order to protect the ones you love. Back at the prairie you showed it. You could have left me and gone after Volcseck. But you chose to stay with me. You chose your friends over revenge."

"Of course. I wasn't going to let you die. Besides, when we touch it's always easier to control my rage. Your holy wielding makes that possible."

"Yes, I know." Falcon thought Faith sounded a bit sad, but he decided to not press the issue. They'd had enough grief for one day. "I want to show you a few more things, if that's fine with you."

"Yes, of course." In reality Falcon did not see any use wasting more time seeing Volcseck's past. But if Faith wanted to do so, then he wasn't going to deny her. "But I think we've had enough dread for one day." She looked at him curiously. "Want to join Albert and I? He's supposed to tell me more stories about my mom and dad."

"I don't know." Faith looked apprehensive as she bit her lip. "I wouldn't want to intrude."

He stood and pulled her up with him. "C'mon. I bet he even has some stories of your mom."

Faith's eyes lit up. "Really? You think so?"

"I'm sure of it."

Falcon was glad to see his friend in such an upbeat mood, even if it was for only a moment.

Chapter 27

Falcon spent the next few nights with Albert in the Lowly Scrap Heap. Most nights he would go alone, but Faith would accompany him from time to time. Her emerald eyes would light up as Albert told stories of her mother. It could have been the most mundane of tales. A story of a simple day by the lake, or an afternoon out farming the crops, or perhaps a simple dinner at Falcon's home. No matter what it was, Faith ate it up.

Falcon found that he was more or less the same. He awaited stories of his own mother with anticipation.

"Oh, look at the time," said Faith hurriedly during one particular night when they kept on talking past midnight. "We had a meditation session and we missed it."

Falcon thought he had gotten away with one of the boring sessions, but the next day Faith made up for it by extending their meditation twofold. By the time they were done, Falcon thought he was going to pass out. Sitting on his behind was not his idea of training.

It was for this reason that he found himself enjoying his training with Aya a lot more. Unlike the boring candle-lit rooms Faith trained in, Aya chose to exercise in the Missean training fields. Some days they would train in the forested grounds. Others they would work across the plains of the desert grounds.

His exercises with Aya did not last, however. She was convinced that the training wasn't doing Falcon any good. He was inclined to agree. Aya could focus her energy enough that even the devourers, who had the ability to nullify wielding, could not stop her from using her water. She tried to teach Falcon, but it quickly became apparent that he was no good at it.

Fortunately, Albert found a solution to this.

"The other way to defy the nullifying powers of a devourer," said his brother over a drink, "is to unload so much energy that the creature won't be able to suppress it."

"Is that what you do?" asked Falcon.

"I can go either way" was his brother's answer. "I fortunately have enough power to muscle through the barriers the devourers put up, and enough focus to simply deliver the energy in precise points around their nullifying walls."

"Of course," said Falcon, not really surprised.

With the permission of Empress Latiha, Aya examined the Missean wielders and found the ones that showed the most command over their energy. She them took them and chose the best to train in ways to work around the devourers barriers.

Falcon didn't know how she had gotten hold of them, but Empress Keira had stones that once had belonged to the Scaiths (the official name for devourers). As Aya trained the soldiers, she would walk around, randomly placing the stones beside an unsuspecting wielder. The closer the stone was to a person, the harder it would be to wield. The poor chosen soldier would then have to locate the stone, using only his energy that was being suppressed.

The few that passed the test were chosen to be part of the Elite Focus guard. These soldiers' job would be to take out the Scaiths quickly in the case they showed up on the battlefield.

Falcon gazed in admiration as Aya stood before the three dozen wielders who had passed her rigorous testing. Falcon had always been the one that Zoen had chosen to lead missions, but seeing Aya in action left little doubt that she too was a natural-born leader.

"In many ways," she said, "you will be the most important line of defense on the battlefield. If Scaiths are summoned, it will be impossible for our armies to wield. You can bet the Suteckh will have stones that will allow their wielders to be able to use their abilities."

"How come we don't use a similar stone?" asked a soldier from the crowd.

Keira, who stood beside Aya with her bears, answered. "Each Scaith produces said stone. I'm in possession of some stones that will allow us to wield, regardless whether Scaiths are nearby or not." She opened her hands, revealing circular black orbs. There was a small sigh of relief from the soldiers. It was quickly squashed by what Keira said next. "The Scaiths that I got these stones from aren't the same ones that the Suteckh are bound to bring into battle. Therefore they are useless to us. We need the unique stone that each of the Scaith's produce, and you can wager your life that we won't be able to get a hold of 'em. There's no telling where the Suteckh could be hiding 'em."

"Most likely they will be in possession of the Blood Empress," said Aya. "And if we know anything from previous battles, it's that she'll be at the rear, far from reach. It will be up to us to take down the Scaiths quickly. If we don't, our wielders will be dealt a crushing blow. We will not allow that to happen, will we?"

The three dozen wielders who stood in three lines of twelve raised their right hands and shouted. "No, ma'am."

Seeing Aya work so hard inspired Falcon. He asked for his own group of soldiers to train and was granted one. He had experience fighting the Suteckh, which was something Latiha valued greatly.

When he showed up to the desert training field, the scene before him was not what he'd expected.

Laars, with his usual wide nose and shaggy hair, was standing before a group of men and women. The skinny girl, Lenka, was there as well.

"Hello," said Lenka. She waved her gangly arm in the air, as if Falcon could not see her standing a mere three feet away from him.

"What are you two doing here?" asked Falcon. He had no problem with Lenka. She was a bit loud at times, but she was nice. And she was a Void wielder, like himself, which meant they had spent countless training hours together. Laars, however, was a different matter altogether. Laars had taken a dislike to Falcon ever since he first stepped foot at Rohad Academy. The pompous earth wielder never wasted an opportunity to remind Falcon that his brother was a traitor. Their rivalry had lasted throughout their childhood and carried on into their young adult lives.

For the longest time after Falcon had posed the question, Laars simply stood there, scratching his long brown pants. There was something different about him. He didn't have his usual condescending look, or his smug smirk. He finally broke the silence when he extended his hand and said, "Empress Latiha send us to assist you. She has entrusted you with three hundred soldiers."

"I think you're supposed to shake his hand," said Lenka.

Falcon snapped out of his shock and noticed that, indeed, Laars was still holding his hand out.

"What is this all about?" asked Falcon with suspicion. Something was not right. Laars had always thought himself superior to Falcon. And now Falcon was supposed to believe that Laars took a spot as his subordinate without the slightest form of rancor? Surely Laars had something up his sleeve.

"Nothing," his rival answered. "When I met Faith, she opened my eyes to what I had bloodied become, and..." He looked down at the ground. "I didn't like what I bloody saw."

Falcon took Laars' hand, though years of being berated by him kept him on his toes. "Yes, she can do that."

As they settled down and commenced the training, Falcon kept expecting Laars to challenge his authority, but to his surprise, it never happened. In fact, Laars followed Falcon's orders by the letter. If Falcon asked him to take a group of men and go over running or wielding drills with them, he would comply without the slightest sign of defiance. If he was asked to go fetch weapons, he would do so in an instant.

As the days passed, Laars only became more helpful. One day, when Falcon had stayed up too late with his brother the night before, he showed up to the training three hours late. When he got to the desert fields, he was surprised to see that Laars, with the help of Lenka, had carried on the training with no hiccups. A number of soldiers were running over the long hills, others were working on target practice, and many more were locked in duels.

As soon, as Falcon arrived, his hair a messy heap, Laars reverted command back to Falcon and settled in as his aide.

With Laars' cooperation, Falcon was able to focus more on overall strategy. Aya was focusing on a small select group of enemies—the Scaiths. Falcon, however, wanted his soldiers to be ready for anything. The Suteckh had many fearsome enemies they might bring into the battle. He needed them to be able to adjust on the fly to whatever was thrown their way.

So, after a week of basics, he moved over to training against a certain creature Falcon had experience against.

"They shapeshift?" asked a young female soldier disbelievingly when Falcon explained the dark creatures' affinity to change their tar-like bodies into any shape imaginable.

"Yes," said Falcon. "They're conjured by dark wielders. Each one can take out over a hundred regular soldiers. Physical weapons are useless against them." Falcon recalled how back in Sandoria the dark creatures had sucked up the swords, quivers, javelins, and spikes that landed on their bodies.

"We'll just earth wield, then," said the timid soldier.

"Most wielding won't work either," said Falcon. He noticed most of the soldiers' expressions drop in disappointment.

"There is a way to defeat them," he said before they lost all hope. "Do I have any fire wielders here who can wield blue fire?" Falcon counted about thirty soldiers raising their hands. It was not surprising, considering blue fire was a very advanced technique. He didn't even bother asking if anyone could wield black fire. He was certain no one had reached that level. "It will be up to you, blue fire wielders, to take out the dark creatures before they cause too much harm. Extreme levels of blue fire should be enough to boil their tar bodies to oblivion."

"You learned this in the battle of Sandoria, sir?" asked an ashen-faced soldier. He had a lumpy body and even thicker arms and legs. "Is it true that you met Shal-Volcseck?"

For a moment, Falcon refrained from answering. Volcseck was not what he wanted to speak about, especially to the soldiers. Nonetheless, he decided to be honest with them. "We have had a few skirmishes from time to time."

He might as well have told them he defeated Volcseck with one hand tied behind his back. The soldiers looked at him with sudden admiration as if he were some type of legendary hero form their childhood books. They spoke in awed whispers. Falcon felt his face grow hot. He was no one to look up to, and he definitely wasn't a hero.

"Listen," he said, attempting to diffuse the admiring looks he was getting. "We need to forget about Volcseck and concentrate on the Suteckh. They're the ones who may attack the city, after all."

"What kind of other creatures should we prepare for?" asked the chubby soldier.

Falcon was about to answer, but he found himself unable to form words. It was then that he realized that he didn't particularly have much knowledge in other creatures, soldiers, or weapons the Suteckh might be utilizing.

If he wanted to get more answers, he was going to do something he had long ago promised himself never to do again. He shuddered at the thought. He was going to have to step foot inside a library.

CHAPTER 28

Falcon, Aya, and Faith walked down the busy city streets. The usual loud banter of vendors flowed through the air, and dozens of messenger boys scurried through the streets. It seemed to Falcon as though he couldn't go a second without someone almost knocking him over.

"I'm so glad you decided to come with me to the library," said Faith. "It's so big in there and full of history."

Falcon threw up a little inside. Books signified everything he despised about school. Was there anything more boring than a bunch of letters crumpled together into hundreds, sometimes thousands of pages? Why would anyone ever want to sit reading countless scribbles of ink when they could experience anything they wanted first hand in the field?

"You'll get nowhere with this one," said Aya. She had decided to accompany them as well, which in itself wasn't surprising. Aya was one who enjoyed getting things done in a hands-on manner, but she could also get lost for hours within the pages of her books. "He doesn't understand the pool of knowledge a book or scroll can provide. I don't think he's ever read a book in his life."

"I have, too," countered Falcon. "I tried reading that poison wielding book last year, remember?"

Aya looked at him with a sly smile. "That book was meant for children, Falcon. It had more pictures in it than a coloring scroll."

"It didn't have that many pictures," lied Falcon.

"There it is," said Faith, as they turned the corner and came face to face with the large building that was the library. It was surrounded by a black gate. Countless flowers ran alongside the outer walls of the library.

"I planted those yesterday," said Faith proudly. "The Master Record Keeper of the library gave me his permission." She opened the gate and ushered them in, leading them to a set of blue roses. "Aren't they lovely?"

"Yes," said Falcon, welcoming the change in subject.

The door to the library opened. A chubby man stood at the door. He looked as old as Zoen had been. But despite his age, he appeared alert. His wide eyes darted from wielder to wielder. "I thought that was you I heard out here, Faith."

The holy wielder embraced the elder man. "Yes. I couldn't stay away for too long."

"I see that you brought more lovers of literature."

Faith faced the man. "This is Linius. The Master Record Keeper of Missea." She then motioned to her companions. "And my friends are Falcon Hyatt and Aya Nakatomi. They're both Rohads from Ladria."

Linius stroked his hairless chin. "Hmmmm… Indeed I've heard about you two from Zoen. In particular you, young

Falcon."

"Me?"

"Oh, yes. Zoen and I were good friends for many, many years. He was my predecessor."

"Zoen was a Master Record Keeper?" asked Aya, clearly as surprised as Falcon.

"Yes. It was he who helped bring books and knowledge to the forefront of education in Missea. Before him it was mostly swords and wielding."

Sounds like my type of place, thought Falcon.

With his cane, Linius ushered them indoors. The inside smelled of old pages and fresh oil. There were high towers littered with books of different colors and sizes. Clear draperies covered the long windows. Every table was polished to perfection, without a single visible speck of dust.

"What a very nice library," said Aya. "You've done a great job."

Linius acknowledged the compliment with a nod of the head. "I have Empress Latiha to thank for this. She's a lover of knowledge. It is through her that I've been able to keep the library in pristine condition, and it is through her funding that I've been able to gather many ancient texts." Linius trudged behind a desk that rested at the center of the library and laced his fingers around a long scroll. It was ripped and crumpled in a few places. A faded blue outline ran along the outer edges. "Speaking of ancient scrolls, I managed to secure the parchment you've been seeking, Faith. The library at Belwebb had the last copy. Let me tell you, it wasn't easy getting them to let me borrow it."

"Thank you so much," said Faith. She gently took hold of the scroll.

"You still haven't told me why you're so interested in this scroll," said Linius, still holding on to the parchment. "The power to have an emblem within you died alongside the Golden Wielder, and he himself didn't even know exactly how it worked."

Falcon recalled that Faith had expressed interest in Aadi's ability to wield without a physical emblem back when they had met the Golden Wielder. Like Linius, Falcon found himself wondering why Faith was so intent on learning about this strange power.

The questioning glances did not go unnoticed by Faith.

"I'm simply curious," she said, smiling warmly. Before anyone could say anything else, she took the scroll and sat alone at a far-off desk. She unrolled it and began to scan its contents.

Linius rubbed his generous-sized belly. "I have much work to do, but you two are welcome to look at any book in here."

Aya left to find information on Scaiths, while Falcon went to the second floor in search of books that would shed more light on the warrior they could end up facing: Neikan

Demons or Northern Barbarians.

Unfortunately, he had no luck finding anything on the Neikan Demons. It was almost as if they didn't exist. He did, however, manage to locate a book on the Northern Barbarians. It proved of little use. It spoke of their homeland over the northern mountains. They were a rugged people who etched a living in the wild and often unpredictable frozen lands of Lasteria. Their main source of food was meat, meat, and then for good measure, more meat. Falcon thought that may be the reason they were all so large. They were obsessed with animal fur, almost to the point of worshiping it as a gift from the gods.

Besides the long passages on culture, Falcon didn't learn anything useful for battle. Though the absurd idea of using fox pelts to bribe the barbarians to their side did cross his mind.

~~~

It was when Falcon closed the door to the inn that he heard Hiromy's voice and his insides rejoiced.

Faith and Aya heard it too. Together, they dashed up the stairs and into the room. Sure enough, Hiromy was sitting up in her bed. Her face was a shade of mild green and yellow, and she appeared to be groggy. Her eyes flickered as she took in her surroundings.

Sheridan, who had not left her side for a minute, looked up excitedly. "She was mumbling for a while, and then she just got up!"

Faith rushed over to check on her while everyone stood back awaiting her verdict. After a few minutes, she looked up somberly, and Falcon knew the incoming news wouldn't be good.

"We should step outside," she said.

Hiromy grabbed Faith's arm. "It's all right. Whatever you have to say you can say in front of me. I know I'm damaged and will never be the same, but I'm not stupid."

"I don't think—" began Faith.

"Tell me, please," begged Hiromy. "You are my friend. Don't hide—" She stopped and clutched her head. "I can handle whatever you have to say."

Falcon steeled himself as he toyed with his fingers. The scent of the dirty, muddy water in the vase only enhanced the sense of hopelessness that hung in the air.

Sheridan bit his nails, looking even more nervous than Hiromy.

"The poison is still spreading through your brain." Faith's tone was neutral, but Falcon could hear the sadness in her voice. "I can't stop it. I'm so sorry."

"How long?" asked Hiromy.

Faith took a deep breath. "You have a few days at most."

Chapter 29

From what Falcon could see, Hiromy was taking the news better than anyone else. He wondered whether she truly understood was going on or not. There were times that she seemed like her old self. At other times, however, she would rant about the most trivial of things. Like the colors of the wall, the number of heartbeats in a minute, or the amount of time it would take to walk from one capital city to another.

Sheridan was trying to keep a brave face, but Falcon could see his facade crumbling with each passing day. The first after the news he seemed to be in denial. The second and third days he passed with Hiromy, tending to her every wish. At nights, Falcon would hear him deep breath into his pillow. Despite Falcon's deepest urges to console him, he just couldn't. There was nothing more to say or do.

Aya and Falcon spent their days busy in training. It was the only thing they could do to keep their mind off the fact that at any moment they were about to lose one of their own.

The late-night dinners with his brother were now nonexistent. Albert had been granted the position of Temporary Grand General of Missea, a position not held by anyone since the Golden Wielder. The entire army of Missea was now under his command, which meant that his brother spent his days supervising men, attending military meetings, and passing in and out of the palace.

Faith, on the other hand, would divide her time between the library and healing sessions with Hiromy. She couldn't do anything to save her, but she was trying her absolute best to keep her alive as long as possible while she searched for some type of miracle. A miracle everyone knew wasn't going to come.

The only good in an otherwise bleak time was that he not been subjected to those boring concentration sessions Faith was so fond of. That all changed the afternoon of the third day.

"We need to go over one more scene," said Faith, as she came back from the library with a dozen scrolls under her arm, and Falcon was again forced to question what in Va'siel Faith was researching.

"Do we have to?" he said. He had just come back from a long training session. His legs ached, his head was pounding from within, and his entire body was begging for a long, warm shower. To top it all off, he was beyond hungry. Laars and Lenka had brought a few nuts and slices of dried salami, but that had barely been enough to sate his ravenous hunger.

"Yes," she said, setting her scrolls down on her bed. "I have one more scene to show you."

Falcon swallowed. "Fine. Let's get this over with."

He followed her to the outskirts of the city, beyond the

golden walls and past the road. They found a large rock and settled themselves on top of it. There, under the orange-reddish glow of the setting suns, they held hands and closed their eyes.

Then he was falling down a dark pit. Black fog surrounded him, compressing into masses. It didn't take long for the black mist to take the form of a home, surrounded by trees. The grass was covered in snow, though the severe storm from their first vision was absent. The weather was much cozier this time, perfect for a family outing.

He looked over at the cabin door, which had now flown open. A boy and a woman Falcon recognized as Volcseck and Lunet made their way out. The beautiful red-haired woman handed the young boy a mug of what appeared to be steaming warm milk.

Faith patted Falcon's shoulder. "Do you remember that Lunet took Volcseck in and nursed him back to health?"

"Yes," said Falcon. He indeed did recall the time when Demetrius had showed them a vision of his first meeting with Volcseck. Demetrius had wanted to turn Volcseck away, but Lunet, being the caring person that she was, invited Volcseck into their home and treated him like a son.

"Hurry up!" said Volcseck excitedly. He still looked a bit skinny, but the dark circles around his eyes had mostly disappeared. Falcon presumed this meant that he had been under Lunet's care for some time now. "The market will close

378

soon."

"He looks much better," said Falcon.

"Yes," said Faith. "Now pay close attention, because what happens next will shape Volcseck's life in ways I don't think even he imagined."

Falcon expected some grand revelation to happen. Perhaps a holy cleansing. But nothing quite that grandiose occurred. Instead they walked down the mountain deep in conversation. Quite some time later they arrived at a small village nestled around a body of water. It had no gates, so it was easy to see the few grass and mud huts that had been erected. Children played with rocks and sticks, chasing each other and pretending to be wielders. Two scraggly dogs followed them where they went, barking after them.

Before they even stepped foot in the village, Volcseck's expression turned sour. "I'll wait for you here," he said, motioning at a dead tree stump.

"Nonsense," said Lunet. "With Demetrius out hunting, I need a strong young man to help me carry the bags."

"But I—"

"Besides, this will give you a chance to make some friends. Go play with the boys while I get the food."

"If I can't wait here, then I'd rather stay with you." Volcseck's voice was timid, and Falcon wondered what it was that had put him in such a state alertness.

Lunet studied him for a second. "Fine, then. But next

time I expect you to play with the boys. I want you to make some friends. All those hours you spend alone in your room can't be healthy."

He nodded, though he did not seem the least enthusiastic about her proposal. They moved past the children and into the village, their footsteps smacking softly in the muddy ground.

"Why is he so scared?" asked Falcon.

"Watch," was Faith's only response.

Falcon noticed that Volcseck was doing a superb job of keeping out of sight. He kept close to Lunet with his head down. Whenever someone would walk past them, he would do something to cover his face. Sometimes he would scratch his cheek, rub his eyes, or run his hand through his hair.

"Good morning, Lunet," said a woman with a mustache that could rival any man's. She was covered in what appeared to be a potato sack, tied at the hip with a rope. Her arms and legs were the hairiest Falcon had ever seen. "Come for more cheese?"

Lunet nodded. "Yes, Mrs. Helfa. I was hoping to make some blue cheese broth for my two special men."

Volcseck blushed.

"Two?" This was obviously news to Mrs. Helfa, for her lips twisted in confusion. "I was unaware that you and Demetrius had a son. Where have you been hiding him for all these years?"

Lunet giggled softly. "I haven't been hiding him. He's my adoptive boy."

There was a low oh by Mrs. Helfa. Her eyes zeroed in on the small boy. "What's your name?"

Volcseck hid behind the holy wielder.

"Go on, Volcseck," urged Lunet. "Introduce yourself."

"Volcseck!" Mrs. Helfa's eyes grew wide. "Lunet, get away from that monster!"

"Monster?" Lunet seemed at a loss for words.

The few villagers nearby rallied behind Mrs. Helfa.

"Get back, creature!" cried a short man who held a knife in his hand. He had a bloody apron that identified him as the butcher.

Volcseck took a few steps back, gritting his teeth, and Falcon couldn't help feeling a bit sorry for him. He, himself, had faced the prejudices of people back in Ladria, and it wasn't something he wished on anyone else.

Lunet put herself between the villagers and the boy. "Step back, Mr. Loomis. You too, Mrs. Helfa. My little Volcseck is no monster."

As if itching to prove her wrong, Volcseck's skin turned deep brown with shades of black. Lunet gasped and her eyes widened, but a second later her features returned to normal.

"See?" said the butcher. "He is the son of the witch who lives on the mountain pass. The last time he was here he nearly killed my youngest one with his unholy power. He needs to die!"

The following events all happened in a matter of a few breaths. Mr. Loomis moved in with his long knife, determined to end the boy. In his rush, he tripped over his own legs and staggered to the ground. A low scream escaped his mouth, followed by a grunt. He turned around, revealing that the knife had dug into his ribs.

"Serves you right," said Volcseck. "Now to finish you off."

Lunet moved quickly. First she set her hand on Volcseck's head. The boy's normal features returned to him. Then, she turned her attention to Mr. Loomis. She pulled out the knife, which sent a wave of screams trough the scared villagers. Lunet then applied pressure to the wound. Her holy emblem glowed and a moment later the wound had closed.

The butcher's breaths returned to normal.

"See?" said Mrs. Helfa, spitting at the ground beside Volcseck. "That boy brings with him nothing but misfortune." The villagers nodded in obvious approval. "I think I speak for all of us when I say that you're welcome here any time you want, Lunet. That creature of yours, however, isn't."

Lunet's eyes flitted past the angry woman and to the people behind her. She looked sad but determined. "I'm sorry you all feel that way. If my boy is not welcome here, then neither am I."

There were a few protests from some of the women,

begging for Lunet to reconsider, but their words landed on deaf ears. She took Volcseck's hand and led him out of the village and back into the mountain.

Night had enveloped the land when Volcseck dared to speak.

"Why did you protect me? I'm a monster, you saw it yourself." Despite Volcseck's tough exterior, Falcon noticed he was breaking down inside. He could see it in his shaky hands, the long breaths he took, and in his watery gaze. Obviously he had not expected anyone to stand by him after he'd revealed who he really was.

"You're my boy now," she said, holding him in a close hug. "And even if you weren't, you have a special gift that should be shared with the world."

Volcseck's tears flowed freely as he returned the hug. He was sobbing into her dress, leaving deep wet marks on the cloth.

The scene dissipated, and Falcon found himself sitting atop the rock, staring at Faith.

"He found a mother that day," she said. "The same way you found a father the night K'ran took you in."

Falcon was at a loss. "What was the use of this? To show me that I'm destined to become a heartless criminal just like him?"

"No." Faith met his gaze. "This is to show you that Volcseck isn't as heartless as you may believe him to be. He was touched by the spirit of a holy wielder once."

"Yes," countered Falcon, feeling angry. Why was she defending the man who murdered both of their mothers? "A holy wielder that he killed, or did you already forget that?"

"He killed her physically, yes. I don't think he killed the spirit she gave him, though."

"Now I'm just lost. I don't know what you expect me to do when I meet him. Holy wield him? We both know that I'm no good at that."

"I don't expect you to do anything. You will make your own choices, as you have always done. I do hope, however..." Her voice cracked. "That when you meet him, you remember that killing isn't the only solution."

Really? Does she know who she's talking to? "You may be able to forgive and see the good in everyone, but that's not me. It's my lifetime goal to make Volcseck pay for what he did. I'm not going to let anyone take that away from me."

"Hyatt, Hemstath!" came the shout. It was Sheridan. He was running toward them waving his hands in the air.

Falcon readied himself. It seemed that every time Sheridan looked for him, it was to deliver bad news.

Sure enough, Sheridan did not break the norm. "The Suteckh are here!"

Chapter 30

Melousa strode down the palace hall, her footsteps echoing softly on the marble floor. When the Blood Empress had told her that she wanted her to simply walk into the palace through the front gates, Melousa had thought the empress to be mad. No one, especially somebody her size, could possibly walk into the palace undetected. Nonetheless, here she was, moving within the walls of her greatest enemy's' home. The cloak the Blood Empress had put over her was working much better than she had first anticipated, and Melousa found herself wondering how the dark wielder could manage to hold such an ability from such a long distance.

Melousa frowned, pushing her massive body against the wall as three Missean soldiers, clad in brown armor, dashed past her. They were so close that she could smell the human stench that reeked from them. It took all her will power not to reach out and snap their necks.

There was no use in giving away her position just yet. Surprise was an advantage she was not ready to surrender.

She stepped through the grand hall, savoring the kill that now seemed so close. She stayed close to the walls and waited for a moment, making sure to not run into the soldiers who were sprinting up and down. They were no doubt about to take positions around the castle in an attempt to protect the empress during the attack. She smirked at the futility of their plan.

Once the hall had been cleared, she moved toward the throne room, where her enemy would no doubt be.

She climbed the stairs. Her eyes settled on the wide open doors, beckoning her in. Within moments, she crossed the carpet and stood outside the grand hall. It was a large room with green and red plants aligned against the walls. The room itself was nearly empty, save for a number of cushioned chairs that were set up at the center. There was a large balcony that led to the outside. In it stood the woman who had ruined her life all those years ago. The years had definitely been kind to Empress Latiha, which only served to infuriate Melousa even more. Despite being over a century old, she looked to be in her late sixties. The empress stood on her balcony, overlooking the city. She wore a long white robe. Golden earrings hung from her ears. At her side stood two guards. From the pins on their chest, Melousa knew they were Rohads.

The Orian queen reached for the double doors and slammed them shut. Empress Latiha, along with the two Rohads, stared toward the explosion of sound, utterly bewildered.

"I see the Golden Wielder's protection spell had benefits to yer aging. Too bad he not be here no longer!"

"Melousa," said Latiha quickly, recognizing the deep

voice. "Why do you hide like a thief in the night?"

Thief? Melousa's blood boiled. She tapped her arm twice as the Blood Empress had instructed her to do. A second later she was fully visible. "The Queen of the Orians does not be a thief. It was yer who stole from me!"

Latiha took a step forward, her footsteps echoing loudly. "For the last time, Queen Melousa, I did not steal from you. Your sister chose to leave your clan by her own accord."

"Yer be quiet! Yer stole her from me. Now I will steal yer life as repayment!"

At the sign of the threat, the Rohads took a defensive position before the empress.

The male Rohad turned to his female counterpart. "I'll go in close range, Lenka. You back me up with your wielding."

The skinny girl with the void emblem nodded. "Y-yes, Relis."

The queen felt rejuvenated by the fear in the eyes of the Rohads. She knew that fearful prey was the easiest to squash. This was going to be easier than she had initially thought.

Relis moved in with his sword. From afar, Lenka closed her eyes, concentrating her attacks into blue orbs of water.

The queen recognized the strategy well. It was one that worked well in two against one attacks. One attacker would keep her busy with weapon attacks, while the other attacker would land element attacks from afar. It was a sound strategy but one that was useless against her. Her ancient skin would make sure of that.

Relis brought his curved sword down in an arch. Melousa grabbed the weapon, ignoring the flames that engulfed the weapon.

"Got her!" cheered Lenka. Her celebration died out when the paltry water orb splashed against her muscular ribs without even causing a dent. "What the?"

"Now be my turn!" The Orian warrior moved with a speed honed by years of intense training. Her fist drove into the unsuspecting Relis. Winded, he staggered back a few paces, only to have Melousa snatch the weapon from his hand. With a scream, she ran his own sword through his neck, almost severing his body in two.

Having dispatched one adversary, she turned her attention to the other two.

For a moment, Lenka stood still, body shaking. She took a deep breath, seemingly collecting herself. Her hands smacked together. She then opened her arms. From between her elbows emerged a sword of mud. It left a trail of muck on the floor as Lenka sent it flying forward, tip pointed at her enemy.

It didn't matter. Melousa took the hit to her chest in stride. Having closed the distance, she drove her knee into the skinny girl's torso. The sound of cracking ribs was audible as Lenka fell. She rolled on the ground heaving and spitting out blood.

"Weak void wielder be dead!" She brought her fists together and drove down, eager to deliver the finishing blow.

Her moment of triumph was taken by a well-placed blow to her ribs by the empress. Melousa rubbed the place where the attack had landed, surprised the old woman could hit so hard.

"Yer be strong, Latiha." She beat her chest. "But not as strong as yer used to be!" A hand clutched her around the leg. She looked down at the pathetic sight of Lenka trying to hold her back.

Seeing an opportunity, Latiha threw herself at Melousa with a flurry of punches. They were placed well enough but were slow. The Orian queen dodged the attacks easily. She counterattacked with a single punch that landed on Latiha's cranium. The empress fell down to one knee.

Tired of wasting time, Melousa wrapped her hand around Lenka's neck. She applied force, snapping the neck like a twig.

She savored the taste of victory as she thundered toward the downed Empress. "In our last bout yer had that wench, Ishani to save yer. Too bad she not be here anymore!" Melousa kneed Latiha in the face. The empress fell to the floor. Blood poured from her broken nose, soiling her white robe.

Latiha tried to say something, but Melousa brought her

elbow down on the empress's face. The sharp sound of bones breaking and Latiha's whimper of pain sent shivers of adrenaline surging through Melousa's veins. She mounted the empress, and with her giant hand, she covered most of Latiha's face.

"That be right," hissed Melousa as the empress kicked and flailed her arms in a futile attempt to break free. The Orian queen brought her muscular knees down on Latiha's arms, effectively pinning her to the floor. Her enemy's blood gushed between Melousa's fingertips and her body shivered. The thrill of seeing her mortal enemy so submissive was exhilarating.

She had come close to killing Latiha many years ago. She had held her down in this exact position, except that time, when victory was so close, the Golden Wielder's woman, Ishani, had come to her friend's aid. In her many years, Melousa had only tasted defeat that one time. Now, however, the savage queen reveled in the fact that there was no Ishani to hinder her plans.

"Where be yer precious friend now!" Melousa pressed down once more. Latiha moaned one more pained whimper, and then her body went still.

Elated, Melousa removed her hands, staring down at the bloody figure that was once the elegant empress. It was time to make an example of the Missean leader. She laced her fingers around her fallen adversary's leg, pulling her toward the balcony. There she would hang Latiha for her subjects to see. With their beloved empress dead, the Missean people would surely lose their will to fight.

"Come say hello to yer people," she said, making sure to break Latiha's knees as she pulled her. Latiha could feel no more pain, but the sound of snapping bones sounded so good that she did the same to every finger, toe, and arm of her adversary.

Cackling to herself, she tied the rope around Latiha's neck. It was time to make the Missean army crumble.

Chapter 31

"Let me in," said Keira. Maru, her polar bear cub, ran beside her, providing the vision she needed to move so quickly. The loud footsteps of her aide, Raji, thundered a step behind her.

The guards who stood on the palace gates apparently recognized her, because they moved aside, letting her dash through the yard, into the palace, up the stairs, and down the hallway.

As a young girl, Keira had thought that being blind was a handicap. After all, many were the playing sessions she couldn't attend because of her lack of vision. The palace plays put on by the jesters provided no entertainment. How could they when she had no idea what was going on? However, now she knew that having been born blind was actually a blessing. It had allowed her to create a bond with her bears that before would have been unheard of. And having lost the gift of sight had other unforeseen, but beneficial consequences. Her other four senses, taste, sound, touch, and smell, had been enhanced to the point where she had inhuman intuition, an intuition that led her here.

Moments ago, she had been on the frontlines with Aya, ready for the attack, when she sensed a slight disturbance moving beside her. She had looked over at the collection of large rocks that rose and fell unevenly. The feeling that something or someone was moving over them came again. Aya had told her that there was nothing there, and indeed, using the vision provided by her bears, she herself did not see any movement.

"I must be going crazy," she had told Aya, returning her attention to the Suteckh army that had amassed before the city walls.

However, three minutes ago the feeling had come again. This time it was inside the palace. The cloak seemed to have fallen, revealing a dreadful vengeful spirit.

"I have to go," Keira had said. "The empress is in danger."

Aya, who had learned to trust her unconditionally, nodded and said, "Go then."

Her black and brown bears, Draiven and Aykori, had wanted to come with her. Keira had ordered them to stay behind, though. They would be needed in the upcoming battle. Besides, she only needed one bear for visibility. It wasn't as good, but it was better than nothing.

Keira breathed heavily as she ran up the stairs. She had the feeling that she was too late. Her sense of dread intensified when she saw that the doors to the royal palace were closed shut.

"Knock it down, Raji," ordered Keira, glad she had brought the massive warrior with her.

The ever loyal Raji ducked and drove forward, elbow first. His frame slammed into the thick door, sending it swinging open.

For a long moment Keira stood motionless as she took in the sight before her. She blinked time and time again, trying to make the scene disappear. It didn't.

A massive woman, matched only in height by Raji, was standing on the balcony. Her legs alone had to be the height of Keira's entire frame. The woman was holding the mangled corpse of Latiha. Her face had been beaten beyond recognition. Keira only knew it was the empress because the corpse wore a white gown that had been painted in blood. As if she hadn't caused enough damage, the empress's killer was now tying a rope around Latiha's neck, as if to further defile her.

The sight stirred a hate inside Keira she had reserved for her deceased uncle. She clenched her trembling fists. "Let her go!"

Seeing that his master was in obvious pain, Raji moved in to retrieve the corpse.

The woman dropped the body and brought up her hands. Both massive warriors clashed time and time again. Neither tried to dodge or feign an attack. They stood toe to toe, swinging and punching each other into oblivion. Each attack seemed to send shockwaves, and Keira wondered how either warrior was able to take such raw punishment. Both fighters stepped back, breathing heavily.

Keira noticed the corpses of two Rohads lying on the floor, and her anger rose. It was in this adrenaline-filled state that she sensed the same feeling from before. Oh, no.

Someone else, using the same cloak as before, was leading a small army under the tunnels of Missea. Before she'd met Aya, she would have never been able to make a reading from so far away, but her friend had pushed her to new limits. She was sure there was no mistake.

"Stand down, Raji!" ordered Keira. "I need you to leave and deliver a message for me."

Raji, who had hardly spoken and had never questioned her orders looked back at her, confused. "Leave? I cannot abandon my empress in such a dire situation."

"There is no time to argue. I need you to deliver a message to Aya. Tell her that the enemy moves through the underground tunnels. If you don't, she and the Misseans will surely die."

The warrior who had not once in his life failed to follow an order found himself struggling to form a bow. "Yes, Empress Keira." Somber faced, he ran out the door, not once looking back.

The purple-skinned woman smiled, a large grin that only made Keira want to beat her even more. "Yer be an empress. That be good. Today be the day I be cementing my legacy as Melousa, Queen of Orians, and murderer of empresses!"

Melousa rushed forward, grinning widely.

Keira took one last look at Latiha, the woman she had admired her entire life. She hunched in a defensive position. "Come forth!" she screamed fearlessly. "I will teach you what happens to a queen that thinks herself an equal to an empress!"

~~~

Falcon stood beside Aya, Faith, and Albert. He sensed the surge of power once more coming from below. He tried to ignore it, concentrating instead on the army that had seemingly appeared out of nowhere. They had formed in long set of lines. From this distance, they looked like an indistinguishable mass of black and white.

"What is it?" said Aya, noticing his distracted look.

"Nothing. I thought I sensed movement coming from under us, but it's probably just my imagination."

Aya and Albert shared a concerned look.

"Aadi gave you strong energy readings," said Faith. "If you're sensing something, it's worth looking into." Falcon was about to dismiss Faith's suggestion, but that changed when Raji showed up and spoke of Keira's warning.

"This is too much to be a mere coincidence," said Albert. "Someone has to check it out."

"I will," said Aya. "If they're using cloaks, there's a chance Selene is with them. I have to see her."

"I'm coming with you," said Falcon.

"Me too," said Faith.

Albert nodded. "Fortune be with you. I will stay here and lead the Missean army."

"You're leaving?" asked Laars as Falcon took off after his friends. "The men need their bloody leader."

"They have a leader," answered Falcon, not breaking his stride. "The unit is under your command now."

Laars features stiffened in determination. "I won't let you down!"

Falcon followed Aya, not really sure where they were headed. There was a part of him that felt guilty for leaving the army behind when they needed him the most. The other half knew that this was something he had to do.

"This way," said Aya, turning the corner into an empty path. The streets were devoid of people. The men were out in the battlefield. The women and children hid in their homes.

They passed countless eerily quiet homes. The usual glowing lights flowing from their windows were absent. The soft tip taps of children's footsteps as they raced over the creaky wooden panels were gone, replaced by a muffled silence.

"Where are we headed?" he asked, hungry for some sound besides their clattering footsteps over the rocky road.

"The Golden Wielder had a sandworm, remember?" Aya didn't wait for an answer. "Well, the worm, along with its family, made the land under Missea its home for some time. Many of the tunnels they created are still there. There must be many entrances and exits spread throughout the city, but the books only spoke of one."

As she finished speaking, the trio exited through the southwestern gate. They ran down a dirt path that circled a pristine blue lake. A pair of ducks floated above, oblivious to the battle that was about to ensue.

Beside the lake was a small green mound, and in its side was a hole. Wordlessly, Aya pointed inside.

A shadow flickered over their heads.

"You!" Falcon spoke with fury, eyeing the chaos wielder who had landed directly before them.

"Who were you expecting?" asked Volcseck. He wore the same dark cloak he always wore, except this time he hadn't bothered to cover his face. "It is I who is destined to take the holy emblem, and this time there is no one who will get in my way."

"Falcon," whispered Aya, "we don't have time for this. The Suteckh could come out anywhere in the city. If they flank the Misseans in the middle of the fight, they'll be done for." Falcon knew what she was going to say before she said it. "I have to go on ahead on my own." She reached out for his hand and gave it a hard squeeze. "I know you want to come with me, but you're needed here."

"But—"

"No buts. You have your duty." She looked over at the circular entrance. "And I have mine."

Before Falcon could object, Aya took off in a sprint. As Falcon had suspected, Volcseck made no attempt to stop her. She wasn't his target, after all.

Falcon's heart sank as Aya entered the cave. It didn't take long for her frame to turn into a dark silhouette. An instant later, she had been engulfed by darkness. Heart pounding, Falcon turned to Volcseck. This man had been responsible for so many deaths, and now he was standing between him and Aya. It was time for him to die. The familiar anger rose from within. He closed his eyes and thought of the two people who he cared for the most: Aya and Faith. He didn't try to choose between them; doing so would only have caused his mind to dwell deeper in uncertainty. Instead he saw them both as two separate entities, each guiding him in different paths of his life. Aya: courage, determination, and loyalty. Faith: compassion, friendship, and kindness. Together, they personified everything he strived to be.

He opened his eyes. Despite the small feeling of holy, the chaos was still bubbling within him. He clutched his chest as both energies struggled for supremacy over him. Gritting his teeth, he fell to one knee.

Volcseck's laugh was audible over his inner struggle. "Why do you fight the power that is chaos? You have been granted a gift. Instead of accepting it you reject it as if it were a disease. Pathetic."

"He has been granted a gift," said Faith. She took a few steps toward Volcseck. "It is the same gift you were granted once, but were too weak to accept."

"Me? Weak?" Volcseck smiled slyly. "Chaos has made me all-powerful."

Faith looked sadly over at Volcseck. "You've spent so many years wasted. Searching for something you always had. I pity you, chaos wielder." She brought up her arm, showing off the holy emblem on her hand. "This is what you always wanted, right? Come take it. I hope it finally gives you the peace you've been looking for."

The only thing that ran through Falcon's mind as he stared at her was Faith. What are you doing?

There was the slightest flicker in Volcseck's arm, and Falcon knew he was about to teleport.

"Watch out, Faith!" He took off after her. A moment later, he bounced back, falling on his back. Too late did Falcon realize that she'd put up a holy bubble around him. From behind the multicolored specter, he watched in horror as Volcseck appeared in front of Faith. Falcon's face pinched with fear as he noticed the long organic sword in Volcseck's hands. The sword's loud beats were only drowned out by Falcon's own pounding heart.

Faith stood still. Her eyes were closed. Her hands rested by her side. A faint smile spread on her lips.

Volcseck drew his hand back, and with a firm thrust he ran his weapon clear through Faith's chest.

Chapter 32

The bubble that had surrounded Falcon burst in a silent pop. In fact, everything around him had grown silent. The only things he could hear were Faith's soft moan and his own pounding heart that seemed to be beating in his ear.

Volcseck, who looked extremely pleased with himself, took Faith's emblem and clutched it in his hands. A teleportation later he was gone, taking with him the artifact that had eluded him for an eternity.

Clutching at the spot where the sword had penetrated, Faith fell to her knees.

"No!" yelled Falcon, feeling his entire world crumble. He flung himself across the floor. His arms wrapped around Faith, catching her before she hit the green pasture. He knew from the distinctive shallow breaths she was taking that he was losing her. He also knew that Faith couldn't heal herself, not without her emblem.

"I'll heal you." He tried to move her hands away from her injury, but as soon as he moved her hands, blood poured out. It ran down her white dress, turning the pink flowers on the cloth into a deep crimson.

"W-what do I d-do?" he stuttered, swallowing hard. Think, Falcon. You have holy. You need to use it.

"Shhhh…" said the sweet honeyed voice he had gotten

so used to hearing. She looked up at him with glassy eyes. "There's nothing to do anymore. This is the way it has to be."

"No, n… no, no!"

Weakly, she brought her hands to his lips. "You did a great job at getting rid of much of your anger." She coughed a few times and closed her eyes.

"Faith. Faith!"

Her eyes snapped open, and for a second she looked lost. A few blinks later she seemed to have returned to normalcy. "Y…y—" A loud swallow later she said, "You were given an unfair amount of chaos energy, much more than any human was ever meant to have. You alone cannot control it. It is time I do my part in this."

Falcon felt as if someone had just delivered a wielding blow to his chest. The air in his body escaped him as he realized what it was that Faith had been doing at the library all those days. At last, he understood why she had been so intent on knowing everything there was to know about Aadi's unique ability to hold earth energy without an emblem.

"You figured out how to hold energy within yourself?" said Falcon. As he spoke he barely registered the dripping streaks of rain that had begun to drum on his back. "But the ability to do so costs your life, doesn't it?"

Faith's warm smile was all the answer he needed.

Falcon's looked down at his trembling hand that was settled over Faith's wound. "I can't. I'm not ready."

"With both our holy energies, you will be able to do things before thought impossible. Please tell Aya and Hiromy they have my thanks for being my friends."

"You can tell them." Falcon kept on hoping for a miracle, something to wake him from this nightmare.

"We both know that can't be." A tear dripped down Faith's cheek. The color drained from her once pink face. "I'm glad I met you." Every word she voiced was a struggle as the last of her energy left her. Slowly she caressed his face and ran her hand through his hair. "I love you, Falcon."

She pulled him in.

Shaky breaths of pain, regret, and denial coursed through him. Even the simple act of talking was painful. His eyes burned as tears welled up. "I love you too, Faith. You're the person I've always strived to be." Their lips met. The scent of peaches and wet dirt coursed through the air.

As they kissed, a surge of warm light travelled from Faith into Falcon. He felt it move through his body and settle in the pit of his chest.

When their lips parted, her emerald eyes, which had been full of life hours ago, were cold and lifeless.

"Faith?" He shook her. His voice cracked with a pain he had never felt before. "Faith." Tears and raindrops traced down his cheeks. "Wake up, Faith. I need you. Please wake up."

But the holy wielder did not wake. And as Falcon

closed her eyes and held her tightly in his trembling arms, he knew that he was never going to hear her beautiful laughter again, never experience her warm touch, and never take her out dancing as he had planned to.

Faith, his better half, was gone forever.

Chapter 33

Hiromy and Sheridan raced down the empty streets. The serene silence the homes provided was a welcome change from the usual voices booming in her head. Ever since she had found out she was going to die, the voices had grown unusually silent. She only wished that her mind was clearer. Her thoughts remained mostly obscured by a muffled cloud, a constant reminder of her duel with Dokua.

"We're almost there!" cried Sheridan. He had at first been apprehensive about letting her go into the battle. She convinced him, however, that she would rather die on her feet, fighting alongside her friends, than cowering in a room.

She closed her eyes and staggered as a wave of pain suddenly assaulted her cranium.

"Are you okay?" Sheridan leaned down, looking concerned.

She stood up slowly. "Y…yes. I'm fine."

"I need to get you back to the inn. You'll only get hurt out there."

"I said no." She stood. "Aya and Faith need me."

Sheridan gave her the same defeated look he had given her back at the inn when she had announced that she was headed into the battle.

"Let's move, then."

Move they did. They ran at a determined pace. The silence that had been the norm minutes ago gave way to the sound of clattering weapons and screams. Once in a while there would be a thunderous clash, and she knew that someone had just used a wielding attack.

"About time you two got here!" called a familiar voice when they reached the first Missean lines. Before them spread a wide open field where a climactic battle was taking place. Behind the Suteckh lines, which looked like a mass of black, spread the ocean as far as the eye could see. The Suteckh ships, which all had black and silver sails, were exchanging cannon fire with hundreds of pirate ships. Leading the charge were the ships Hiromy recognized as those belonging to Captain Armeen and Redclaw.

"Professor Dunn," said Sheridan. "What is going on over there?"

"What do you think, you worthless fool? The pirates have come to our aid. Without them we would have been overrun. They are holding back the Hollow clansmen of the sea. Pirates hold allegiance to no one. I don't know why they are doing this!"

Hiromy smiled, thinking of Faith.

"What can we do?" asked Sheridan.

"You can help by not asking stupid questions and getting into the fight." The short man turned to Hiromy, and his voice took on a much softer tone. He bowed slightly.

"Princess. Always a pleasure to see you."

"Leotris!" called a man Hiromy had never seen before. He had the same handsome features as Falcon. He wore a wind emblem on one hand and a space emblem in the other. Hiromy got a sudden urge to jump on the man and listen to his heartbeat. She was sure it had to be the strongest she had ever heard. She took a breath and drowned out her emotions. Her training with Faith had served some purpose after all.

"Yes, Albert!" said Dunn.

"I need you to reinforce the Master's battalion."

Hiromy looked over to where Albert had pointed. In the middle of the skirmish was Laars. He was wielding earth pillars, trying to keep himself and a group of men safe from a giant creature coming down on them.

"At once!" Dunn took off into the battlefield, screaming atop his lungs.

"Oh, no," said Sheridan. "What in the world is that?"

Apparently the Suteckh were done messing around. To the right end of the battlefield, a Neikan Demon had emerged from a dark portal. This one was not the usual green. It was a deep crimson. It had to be three times the size of its counterparts. Its tusks at the end of its mouth snarled as it swung the chained mace it carried, bringing it down on a group of screaming Missean soldiers. Behind it, three dark creatures had emerged from a similar dark hole. A group of wielders, each flicking water and ice at them, rushed to meet them. The attacks bounced off the tar-like bodies as if they were simple specks of rain.

The largest of the dark creatures morphed one of its hands into something that resembled an oozing black sword. Its yellow eyes flickered to life as it swung its makeshift weapon in a circular arc. A few water wielders managed to crouch under the attack. Three of them weren't so lucky. They were severed in half in one fell swoop.

"I was hoping to stay back as much as possible to oversee the battle," said Albert. He looked over at the red Neikan Demon. "This threat is too much to overlook."

"What about the dark creatures?" asked Sheridan.

"Trust me," said Sheridan. "Those monsters of darkness are mere playthings compared to the destroyer of worlds."

As he spoke the Neikan Demon roared. It was a tremendous growl that sent ripples of power coursing through the air. Friend and foe alike were thrown back, their mangled bodies falling in a pile of corpses. It turned its attention to the city. It beat its chest and took off in a slow and determined run. Every step sent a tremor through the ground.

Albert spoke. Hiromy drowned out his voice. A fear swelled within her unlike any she had ever experienced. The city was doomed. There was no way anyone could stand up to the terrifying presence looming toward them.

"Hiromy!" called Sheridan. He gripped her by the

elbows. "Are you ready?"

"Y… yes. Yes." She blinked, trying to regain control of herself. "Ready for what?"

"To take out the dark creatures. Albert ordered us to aid the water wielders. Don't you remember?"

"Yes, I remember," she lied. The last thing she needed was for him to think she wasn't ready, which in all reality she wasn't. Her head was pounding. Her legs were trembling, and the voices were beginning to talk to her again.

"Let's go, Phantom." At her side, Albert had just mounted a dark horse that had appeared out of a black hole. It had red lines sketched across its muscular body. The steed stood on its hind legs, and with a mighty whinny, it took off after the Neikan Demon.

She took Sheridan's hand and gave him a quick kiss. His mere presence drowned out the voices enough for her to regain some control. Still holding his hand, she rushed onto the battlefield, sure that this was the last time she would ever feel his touch.

~~~

Thick droplets of water echoed around Aya as she moved deeper into the cave. She had initially thought that it was going to be pitch dark down here, but the walls had thousands of crystal minerals embedded in them, which shined brightly, illuminating the path with a translucent blue glow.

She had been walking for some time now, expecting to run into some type of Suteckh scouts or battalion. Instead, however, she had walked in relative silence, with only her thoughts and footsteps to keep her company.

She turned another corner and headed down a steep path. The soft gravel under her crunched softly.

The path led out into a domed room. It was large, and unlike the rest of the cave (which carried the aroma of water), this section had the unmistakable scent of earth. Once again, the lights provided a clear view of the room in its entirety. There were boulders scattered throughout. Two dried husks of shed skin rested against the walls. There were a number of small holes in the walls.

This had to be place the worms used to nurse. She did recall the books mentioning that Dharati, the Golden Wielder's pet worm, had a two offspring.

Suddenly, the pleasant aura in the worm nursery turned vile, as if all the good in Va'siel had just been extinguished. Aya stood at the ready, certain that she knew what was behind this shift in the environment.

Her suspicions were confirmed when, directly before her, a woman with dried blood running down from the eyes of her mask emerged. She did not wear the dark cloak she had been wearing the last time they'd met. Instead she had a black, sleeveless tunic, exposing her slim figure. Her pants were of the same color, as was the hilt of the sword that hung at her waist. She had silver and black tattoos on her arms. Most appeared to be of wild animals, but a few were insignias Aya did not recognize.

Selene! She had been cloaked, which would explain why she appeared out of thin air. Strangely, the soldiers she had expected to be accompanying her did not emerge at her side.

"Did you think that the Blood Empress needed guards escorting her as if she were not a master of darkness?" asked Selene, apparently reading Aya's questing features.

Aya felt a sudden burst of pain. She was standing toe to toe with the little sister she had loved so much. Even after years apart, that love had never ceased. The rush of emotions coursed through her body, threatening to overtake her.

"Selene," she said in a strained voice. "I'm Aya, your older sister."

"There is no Selene," said the Suteckh Empress. There was no anger in her voice, nor any sign of any other emotion for that matter. "There is only the Blood Empress, ruler of Suteckh, and soon to be ruler of Va'siel."

"No," pleaded Aya. "Father and Mother had you brainwashed. You're no Blood Empress. You're Selene."

"Shut up!"

Aya barely had time to react as her sister dashed at her, sword in hand. She reached at her waist and took out her katana. Usually, Aya preferred to bring her batons, but those had been given to her by her traitorous father. So instead she now relied on a katana and wakizashi, a smaller sword.

The swords clanked against each other as they met with ferocity. Time after time the weapons clashed. Their sword skills were near identical, with neither one having a clear advantage over the other. Aya noticed that Selene was slightly faster, but she was stronger by a hair. At this rate, the battle was going to take an eternity to finish.

Selene's sword whooshed past Aya. Instead of blocking, she took a step back and reached for her wakizashi. Two weapons would be the tipping point of this sword battle, she was sure of it.

Before she could put her new plan into action, Selene also stepped back.

Aya was certain her sister was about to wield. Aya readied for the elemental attack that never came. Instead, Selene threw the sword forward. Two sharp ends split up from the sword, turning the weapon into a triple edged menace. A long chain emerged from the hilt.

That was too close, thought Aya, barely dodging the trio of blades that wheezed over her crouching head. She took a step forward, but Selene pulled the iron chain back. This time Aya hopped over the attack.

She feigned a move left, but at the last moment dashed to the right. Selene took the bait, but as soon as she saw Aya switch postures, she pulled on the chain, arching the weapon back to cut across Aya's path.

Water surrounded both the katana and wakizashi as Aya parried every attack that came her way. She was at an impasse. She couldn't get closer to her sister. Selene was a master with the iron chain, using it to defend, attack, and cut off her advance as she cut through the air in graceful sweeps.

The iron chain swept over her and down, threatening to cleave her head. Aya's katana met the attack. She felt the hit register on her blade, which shook violently. With her left hand she ran the wakizashi directly into the hole in one of the chains. She twisted the small sword. The sound of the chain breaking in half did not come. Instead Selene pulled her iron chain weapon back, forcing the wakizashi out of her hands.

Selene grinned with satisfaction as she took Aya's wakizashi in her hand. "You should really be more careful how you handle your weapons. Giving them to your opponent is a poor strategy." Then she was upon her. Up until now Selene had remained very stationary. Now she ran and took to the air. Suspended in mid-flight she front flipped countless times. Her weapon spun with her, creating a loud whizzing sphere.

The long chain came down hard.

Aya, knowing full well that there was no way her katana could take such a blow, moved to the side.

The trio of swords clanked on the ground, splintering the earth and raising a cloud of dust.

Squares of ice blew from Aya's hands, only to have

Selene shatter them in mid-flight with her weapon. Before the ice fell, Aya softened it into water and pushed it at her enemy.

Selene weaved masterfully between attacks. The water hit the ground and dispersed out of view.

"My turn." Selene flipped and spun in a series of acrobatic maneuvers. Her iron chain danced around her, like an extension of her body.

If it wasn't for the fact that she was fighting for her life, Aya might have stopped to admire the display of swordsmanship.

The iron chain whizzed across the ground. Aya jumped to avoid the attack. Selene kicked the air. A burst of dark energy emerged before her feet. It was too late for Aya to dodge, and the attack connected directly on her torso. She fell to the ground but quickly grounded her hands and pushed up, back flipping back onto her feet. It was becoming apparent that she needed to get the weapon away from Selene. But how? Every move she made was countered immediately. Keeping her head focused on the weapon, she fired a volley of water spurts. As she had expected, Selene moved her weapon to intercept the attacks.

Aya followed behind her water, coming in high over Selene.

Her sister grunted as Aya drove her fist into her belly. She didn't go down. Instead, Selene grabbed Aya's arm and twisted it.

Hot, searing pain ran down Aya's elbow as it twisted forward in an unnatural arc. With her right hand, she brought her katana forward, forcing Selene to let go.

She's trained as a grappler. The revelation didn't exactly surprise her. Nonetheless, it did mean she would have to be more careful whenever she landed a physical hit. Any part that connected could be used against her.

Selene danced from side to side, her weapon still firmly clutched between her hands.

The water wielder decided it was time to try a different strategy. She called on her usual water gloves. An aqua lion formed on her right hand. On her left hand a screeching hawk made of see-through blue liquid had taken form. The water animals were some of her favorite weapons to use. They were light as a feather, but as soon as she made contact with her target, they would harden. It was this mix of soft and hard that made them her go-to ability.

The iron chain came down again. Aya brought both hands up, and the animals crashed into it. She skidded back a few feet, not expecting the power behind the attack. The trio of swords lifted and came down once more. This time Aya didn't challenge the attack. Instead, she moved her hand and put her fist over the end blades. With all her might she pushed down, giving the attack more power. The blades dug into the hard earth.

The empress grunted as she struggled to get her

weapon free. Aya pressed her advantage, closing the distance between them. Selene let go to meet the incoming attack, but it was much too late.

Aya rocked punch after punch into the mask. The mask pulsed with adrenaline as she took out its frustration on it. The mask represented everything she hated about the Suteckh. It had to be destroyed.

The white mask fractured through the middle. A punch later it shattered into a dozen pieces and fell to the ground. Selene rubbed her head, struggling to remain on her feet.

Aya brought down her fist one more time, sure this would be the final attack.

Rage in her eyes, Selene surrounded her own hands with a dark aura. The black mass intercepted the animals. Aya watched in horror as a black mist leaked into the water, turning the water into dark energy. Aya dissolved the aqua animals a second before they were fully overtaken by the dark mist.

That was close, she thought. Had she allowed the darkness to take over, it would no doubt have corrupted her energy.

Now that the battle had slowed down, Aya finally got a glimpse of her sister without the mask. The same features from when she was a little girl remained. The years, however, had given her a rough edge that had been absent when she was a child. She had long almond eyes, and a scar running down her right cheek. It looked to be the work of a sword. Her lips and her eyes were rimmed in a jet-black line.

Seeing her sister's face after so many years caused something inside her to stir. She wanted to hold her close and protect her from the evils of the world. To protect her from the monster they had made her into.

"Please," Aya pleaded. "Our family may have betrayed us. The Suteckh may have brainwashed you, but you're not alone. You have me. I love you, Selene." She extended her hand. "Let me help you."

"I...I..." Her sister clutched at her head.

I'm getting through to her. Aya continued to talk. . "The sister I knew would have never hurt anyone. She loved Va'siel an every living thing in it."

"Why is the bird on the ground?" asked three-year-old Selene. "It should be up the air flying with all the other birdies."

Aya examined the strange way the white bird hopped from side to side. It flapped its wings, hoping to lift from the ground, but every time it was rewarded by crashing back down after lifting a few inches into the air. The culprit seemed to be a small cut under its right wing.

"It's hurt," said five-year-old Aya. The sisters were out playing on the prairies of Ladria. Their game of hide and seek had been interrupted by the discovery of the dove hopping along one of the many rocky paths that cut through the grass.

The younger sister said softly, "We have to help it."

"We can't take the bird home. You know father will not let us bring it into the house."

"He doesn't have to know. I won't tell him. Neither will you."

Aya's lips twisted as she thought about it. The truth was that she didn't want to leave the bird out where a predator could snatch it.

"Preetttty pleeease," begged Selene.

"Fine," said Aya, giving in, "but not a word about this to father. You know how he gets about this kind of things. Deal?"

The youngest Nakatomi took the bird in her hands, caressing its feathers gently. "Deal."

Aya took one step closer to her sister, drowning out the vision of long ago. "Take my hand."

Selene whimpered and mumbled under her breath. A moment later she became eerily silent. When she looked up, all the doubt was gone from her face. Only a hateful gaze remained.

"I am the Blood Empress! You cannot trick me with your mind games."

"Mind games? I'm a water wielder, Selene. I know nothing of mind wielding."

"No... no. You must be a dual wielder." The Empress's voice was frantic as she ranted in an uncontrolled, breathless gibberish of connected words. "Yes, that's it. You're a dual wielder. You're planting images in my head that aren't really there."

"No." Aya lowered her voice. She needed to get through to her sister. "Being close to me is obviously waking up something inside you. Don't fight it."

"Aya," said Selene. Her voice was pleading. She screamed once more and clutched her temples. "It hurts, Aya. They opened me up. They... they..."

"Don't listen to her, Great Blood Empress," came a sudden voice Aya had not expected to hear. Standing behind her sister was the man she had once called father. He put his hands on Selene. "She's an enemy who wishes to rob you of what is rightfully yours. You mustn't allow it, your highness. Finish her off."

Aya ground her teeth as she moved toward the councilman. "Don't you dare touch her!" A sudden whip of dark energy forced her back.

Mr. Nakatomi's cruel lips twisted into a smile. "I'm glad I followed the Blood Empress. I was certain you would find a way to interfere, Aya."

The introduction of her father had reawakened the trance Selene had fallen under. Her hands were covered with a black mass. She moved toward Aya, focused on finishing her.

"So be it," said Aya, realizing that in order to help Selene, she was going to have to defeat her alter ego first. It was time to finish off the Blood Empress once and for all.

"It's flying," said the young Selene. "We did it. We really did it!"

Aya looked up at the bird, who had now taken off and joined a nearby flock. It had been three weeks since they first found the bird and, against all odds, they had managed to nurse it back to health, or at least that was what the younger sister thought.

"Do you think it will be fine, Aya?" Selene looked up at her with begging eyes.

Aya felt an ounce of guilt as she spoke. So she looked away, hoping that not seeing those sweet, tender blue marbles would make lying easier. It didn't. "Yes. It will join his bird friends, and they will fly through Va'siel. She will live a life of fun and adventure." She did not have the heart to tell her that the bird they had found died a week ago and that she had snuck to the market to buy another one to replace it. As Selene hugged her, though, some of the guilt drifted away. Selene was her baby sister. She would do whatever it took to protect her.

"Die!" screamed Selene. Spit of rage dripped from her lips.

"Kiya!" thundered Aya. Water sprang up around her.

The dual screams rang off the thick earth walls as the sisters took after each other, each determined to end the other at all costs.

Chapter 34

Falcon sat motionless, holding Faith in a tender embrace. He faintly made out the sound of footsteps beside him, followed by heavy breathing. The person moved closer. Falcon remained motionless. He knew who it was but didn't care. All he wanted was to remain close to her.

"What is the meaning of this?" sneered Shal-Volcseck.

The young Rohad did not bother to turn. He was certain that the chaos lord had discovered that the emblem he took from Faith held no more holy energy.

"You killed her," he said. "She was my friend and you took her from me."

"It is the way of the world," said Volcseck matter-of-factly. "People kill for land, love, lust, power, greed, or any combination of those reasons. It is a vicious cycle that I set out to stop long ago."

"Stop!" For the first time, Falcon forced his gaze away from Faith and to the murderer. The faint light of the moon distorted his hard-to-see features, making him appear more monstrous than Falcon had envisioned. "You who have murdered thousands of people throughout your life have no right to speak of how you tried to stop it from happening."

"But I have. All those murders were only done for the greater cause. I needed to get hold of an element of every emblem. I did what I had to do to attain them, and I would do it again." Falcon and Volcseck's eyes met, and for the first time he saw what had always been there. A lack of humanity long lost by centuries of killings. An impossible desire to save the world from something it could not be saved from. It was this idealistic view that made him such a menace. For in Volcseck's eyes, everything he'd done up until now had been for the greater good. His next words further confirmed that. "If I could only get ahold of each element, I could bring forth an ability that would destroy all of Va'siel in a single day."

Falcon did not say a word. Instead, he wiped the tears from his face and set Faith down. He moved her hand over her without much thought. A see-through rainbow-colored blanket of holy covered the girl.

"I see" said Volcseck. He hummed under his breath. "She passed on her power to you. Then perhaps there is still an opportunity to wash away the sins of this world. I will kill you and take the holy energy."

Hardly paying attention, Falcon opened a space rift, and lifting Faith's body with wind, pushed her in. He gulped as her corpse lay silently on the snowy mountain. The blanket he had put over her would ensure that she was safe and no wild animal could get to her.

He turned his attention back to the man who had taken so much from him. He wanted to hate him, to loathe every fiber of his being. The compassion that Faith had left within

423

him made that impossible. Every time he felt the chaos rise, it was quickly put in check by the holy dwelling within. The chaos power wasn't quenched, or snuffed completely out. It remained raging in his chest, but unlike before, the chaos and holy seemed to be working together, feeding off each other and growing stronger from the newfound harmony they shared.

The next series of attacks by Volcseck were sudden and precise. Falcon dug his hand into the ground and pulled the energy from it. His entire arm was now encased in a thick skin of earth. With it he blocked the attacks from the lance Volcseck had produced.

Seeing the bloodied weapon that had been used to murder Faith awoke a fire that stemmed from his chest and filled his body with untold power. The lance drove, tip first, at his chest. With the earth-encrusted hand, he took hold of it. Still gripping it, he released the earth and changed it into poison. The green ooze dripped over the flesh, and Falcon felt it vibrate and wheeze as it dissolved into nothingness.

Volcseck's eyes grew wide as he released his lance. The small part of it that was still intact fell to the ground, emitting the sickening stench of rotting flesh. The veins and arteries running through it beat a few more times, and like a dying heart, its falls and rises dwindled. A moment later it's thumping ceased.

You'll be able to hold sway of chaos, but all the

elements, even the ones you're not particularly gifted with, like poison, darkness, and mind. The balance that holy provides will allow this. Faith's words rang inside him. She had been right. The elements that had once proved a struggle now were second nature. As easy to control as moving his hand. He didn't think about it, he simply did it.

A gush of water rose from the ground, keeping him high in the air. Two tornados, one of earth, the other of fire, raged around him. The power of wind kept their ferocity constant.

Volcseck did not seem fazed by his opponent's mastery of the elements. He came at Falcon with fierce determination.

Falcon readied himself; this was to be the ultimate challenge. This time, he was ready to face it head-on.

~~~

Senses still reeling, Keira weaved between the massive legs that continued to come her way. She had blocked the attacks time and time again, and her aching arms were beginning to complain. The truth was that she simply couldn't continue to intercept the blows. Each one sent her stumbling ten feet back.

"The end be near!" cheered Melousa. She brought her fists together. Her veined muscular arms came down.

Keira did a triple backflip, landing clear out of the queen's grasp. The opponent she was facing was a master of raw power. There was no strategy, no tactics. She did not need them. Her thick skin and inhuman strength made such things completely unnecessary.

Other warriors might have cowered before such a fearsome foe but not Empress Keira. She saw Melousa's strength as her greatest weakness. She relied too heavily in it. It was this overreliance that Keira was hoping would lead to Melousa's downfall.

With the sight her cub provided, Keira made out the faint blur of the large woman studying her. The empress and the queen moved in for an exchange.

Keira barely grazed Melousa's hand and moved aside, letting the woman fly forward with her own momentum. While the queen staggered, Keira brought two fingers onto her opponent's neck. Before they could make contact, Melousa regained her footing and blocked the attack, forcing Keira to move back yet again.

If only she had been blessed with Melousa's freakish strength, she could have ended this duel long ago.

Melousa pressed once more. Punch after punch was deflected to the side by the empress. Keira kept waiting for a sign that her foe was tiring. A loss in power, heavy breaths, or an obvious slowing in the movement. The queen, fueled by anger, seemed to be getting stronger by the second. Each attack forced Keira to use up more and more of her waning stamina.

A swinging kick moved toward Keira's head. She dodged to the side. Sticking to her strategy, she redirected the leg to her right. As she did, Melousa jumped in the air, throwing her other leg up. The empress did not have time to react. The hard sole rammed her chest.

All the air in her body left her at once as she was thrown clear across the hall. She crashed into the wall, webbing the marble tile into countless fissures.

Had it not been for the years of training she had undergone, the hit would have surely knocked her out cold. But Keira was a warrior, and this was not the first time she had been dealt such a crippling blow. She slowed her breath and ignored the pain bubbling up within her.

The quick footsteps of the queen, who seemed to be certain of her victory, thundered toward her.

"Yer be dead!"

The kick came in so close that Keira's hair stood on end. She ducked under the leg and brought up both her fingers, digging them into the back of the queen's knee. The big woman screamed as her leg gave out. Keira rolled her hand into a fist, careful to leave the middle knuckle a few centimeters ahead of the rest. With all her might, she pressed the knuckle directly into the end of the purple bicep.

Melousa staggered to her feet, keeping a wary distance from Keira. She stretched her arms and legs, trying to regain a sense of composure. It was obvious she hadn't expected the counterattack from a foe she had thought to be defeated.

The young empress used this time to steady her

breath. Her chest ached, her arms were beyond fatigued, and her vision connection with Maru was growing increasingly blurrier. If only Draiven or Aykori were here. Her connection with them was so strong that seeing through them was like not being blind at all. Maru was just a cub, though, and her connection with her was still a work in progress. Despite the handicaps, Keira grinned. She had hurt the queen. There was something even all those mountains of muscles couldn't protect. Pressure points.

Melousa seemed to have regained her usual confidence, because she stood straight and said, "It be over for yer, Little Empress."

If Keira thought the Orian warrior had been lethal before, she had not seen anything yet. With a gut-wrenching shriek, she came down on her like a force of nature. It was unlike anything she had ever faced before.

She parried the first attack, only to have a leg swept out from under her. She front flipped. A muscled elbow brought her back down to the ground. Quickly, she summersaulted back to her feet. The elbow came again. She retreated. The knee flew at her face. Keira retreated once more.

Keira swallowed hard as she realized that there was nowhere else to run. She had been herded into the corner of the hall, like a hog led to the slaughter.

The queen came down on Keira, continuing the hard-to-read attacks. A fist made it past her guard, forcing itself into her gut. Keira slumped forward. She would have crumpled to the floor had Melousa not gripped her thick fingers around the blind girl's neck.

"Time to die!" Melousa tightened her hold and lifted her victim so that they were face to face.

The gunk of Melousa's stench filled Keira's nostrils. She felt her neck bones moments away from caving in. She tried to breathe, but her windpipe had been completely closed. Shoving her panic to the back of her mind, she ran her fists into the side of Melousa's neck.

The grip loosened, and Keira inhaled the breath her body had been searching for.

Despite the searing pain she felt, the empress scrambled to her feet and took off after her stumbling opponent. The queen was gripping her neck and closing and opening her eyes quickly, no doubt trying to regain the focus of her vision. Keira had no intention of letting that happen. She attacked the other side of the woman's neck.

It was the blinded Melousa's turn to panic. She swung wildly, searching for an opponent she couldn't see. If she had only stopped and listened, she would have heard that Keira had just crouched under her flailing arms. The princess rained down a volley of hits, each connecting on a pressure point. Soleus, Achilles tendon, hamstring, inner thighs. Every part of Melousa was fair game.

The queen retaliated, swiping her hand down. Keira, however, remained on the move. If Melousa attacked from the right, she came from the left. If the hit came from above, Keira sidestepped.

"Arghhhhh!" screamed the queen, after Keira had delivered a precise hit to her knee.

Fuming with anger, Melousa tumbled to the ground. Keira wasted no time in throwing herself over the Orian's arm and gripping it. It might have been freakishly muscular, but Keira knew that providing pressure at the right spot would...

Snap!

There was another pained yelp from the queen.

Wasting no time, the empress pounced on the left arm. She gave it the same treatment as the right.

Crack!

Keira stepped back, looking down at the heaving queen.

Melousa spit with rage. "Yer be nothing. I will kill yer. Kill yer!" Sweat ran down her face and chest.

The empress kept her tone calm. "So you like to break necks, do you?" She took one glance at the void wielding Rohad sprawled across the floor. Her neck was twisted in an unnatural arc. Latiha's body, too, was beyond mangled. Every part of her body seemed to be pointing in a different direction.

"Let's see how you like being given the same treatment."

Melousa's eyes widened. "I only be doing as I was told. I cannot be at fault!"

"You came looking for a fight with an empress, and you got it." She kept her voice conversational as she moved behind the queen.

Melousa tried to stand on wobbly legs.

Knowing full well that any advantage given to her foe could prove deadly, Keira pounced on the woman's back. Her arms wrapped around the queen's neck. Melousa fell on her back, crushing the air out of Keira. Nonetheless, the empress tightened her grip. The large woman's gurgling sounds rang in Keira's ears. It almost sounded as if she wanted to speak.

"I have heard enough of you." Keira made one last monumental contraction. Melousa's legs shot up as she kicked in one last, futile struggle to break free. A minute later it was all over. The thick gargles had given way to a sullen silence.

Grunting, the young empress pushed the dead weight off her.

Maru rushed over to her. Keira took the cub in her hands and held the furry creature close to her throbbing chest. As she sobbed quietly, a bittersweet feeling settled in. She may have vanquished her foe, but it had come too late. Latiha was dead. No amount of victories would ever bring her back.

Chapter 35

The two Nakatomi girls sat inside one of many finely-decorated halls of the mansion. The fire blazed in the chimney, filling the room with a woodsy scent.

"I told you to stop climbing the house, didn't I?" Five-year-old Aya looked down at Selene, who had a nasty cut on her left palm. Even at her young age, Aya had become something of a mother figure to her younger sister. It came naturally, especially since both their parents were almost always away from home in council meetings.

"I just wanted to see the baby birdies," said Selene. She pouted her lips. "You're not telling Mom, are you?"

Aya's heart softened. She could never quite say no to that face. "Fine. But don't do it again. This time you got off easy. If you fall again, there's no telling how hurt you could get."

"I promise I won't."

"You better not, my little sparrow. I would go crazy if anything happened to you." Aya ran her hands through Selene's strands of hair. She pulled her in and held her close. Minutes later the young Nakatomi was sound asleep. Her soft snores mixed with the crackling wood in the fireplace to create a symphony of harmonious music.

She wiped away the line of drool that had begun to

make its way down Selene's mouth. Leaning in close, she planted a soft kiss on her forehead. Selene mumbled at the intrusion in her sleep. Aya moved back, warmth filling her as she took in her sister's peaceful features.

Selene's hateful eyes bore down on Aya as she came at her from above.

The water wielder moved to the side, sending the dark wielder hurtling past her and into the cave wall. The dark energy she had condensed around her hands bore into the earth.

"You cannot take this from me. I will rule all. All. All. All!" cried Selene. She was ranting now. Long forgotten was that calculating empress. The one who examined every angle of a situation with the coldest and most cunning of minds. Being close to her sister had awoken something within her, a part of her humanity that was supposed to have been extinguished long ago.

"You must kill the water wielder!" said their father. His voice was high and demanding and reminded Aya of the many times he had punished them as children for breaking one of his overly strict rules. It could have been something as trivial as forgetting to close the door, or failing to fully understand an elder manuscript. The punishment was always the same. Three hours on their knees while they recited the broken rule nonstop.

Heat flushed through Aya's body as she wielded a slab

of ice on her father's mouth. He mumbled and pulled at the obstruction as he shot her a hateful glare.

Aya turned her attention to the only Nakatomi she cared for. "Selene. Don't listen to that man. I'm—"

"It's Blood Empress!" shrieked her sister. Her hands dangled uselessly by her side. She twirled them, creating two dark whirls around her. "It's time for you to experience the power of a true dark wielder." Out of the vortex they emerged. Two small children, a male and a female, with sickening features glared back at her. Upon closer inspection, Aya realized that they weren't children at all. More than anything, they appeared to be puppets, though there were no strings attached to them. They walked in unnatural, jerking movements. Moist skin hung from their drooling fangs. They were both small, about three feet tall, but that didn't make them any less intimidating. The boy had a crooked nose. The girl had long, red ponytails that seemed to have been dipped in a glass of oil. Her blue dress had blotches of grime and blood on it.

The male pounced at her. Aya fired a water burst at him. Before it could connect, something wrapped itself around her arms. She looked down to the sight of spider webs. What the—?

The girl opened her mouth, spewing another gush of spider webs. This time, the sticky substance covered her entire face. She tried to break free, but the hold was too strong.

Something whizzed at her side. Aya listened for its trajectory. A millisecond later she hopped over the attack. The male puppet's kick missed by a hair, which was lucky. With the little visibility Aya now possessed, she noticed that blades were attached to the male's hands and feet. One wrong move could very well mean the end. But then again, one right move could liberate her.

Aya purposely stumbled to the ground, feigning a loud scream of pain. As she had expected, the boy wasted no time in pressing what he thought was his advantage.

The blade of his right arm came toward her head. Aya jerked to the side and brought her arm up. The end of the blade cut clean through the web encasing her hands.

Now free, Aya pulled off the webs on her face. She expected it to come off easily, but she only managed to get enough off to regain her vision.

Selene grunted in frustration. She moved her arms and flickered her fingers.

She's controlling them! mused Aya, shocked. She had never heard of such an ability.

She didn't have much time to register the strange power, because the girl once again opened her mouth, shooting a stream of thick webs.

Cursing under her breath, Aya flipped to the side.

It only took a quick observation of the patterns of their

attacks for Aya to realize that the puppets were trying to back her into a wall. She had no intention of letting that happen. She condensed her power. Blades of ice shot from her hands. Like ninja stars, they impaled the boy.

Amazingly, the ice seemed to have no effect. He came at her, cackling, with blades atop his small head.

Of course. I have to get the caster. Weaving between web shots and blade attacks, she rolled across the ground and sent a zigzagging flurry of water coursing through the ground. Earth shattered as the water broke though it and slammed into the young girl.

Selene's body flew through the air. The second she made contact with the wall, her puppet creations disappeared in puffs of smoke. Webs and a scent of death were the only things that remained of their short time in the world of the living.

Aya barely had time to celebrate her small victory. With a hammering heart, she crossed the distance of the room.

She skidded to a halt as Selene recovered, surrounding the entire area around her in a blob of darkness.

She's calling on those dark creatures. I have to stop it. Aya formed a mass of clear water before her. Both girls grunted and huffed as they stood face to face. The only thing that prevented their hands from touching was the raw energy they were putting on display.

There was a thunderous crash as the two energies

clashed, fighting for supremacy.

The water wielder skidded back a few steps as the dark power bore down, threatening to engulf her. The intensity left in her erupted. She breathed deeply and released more of her energy. The water turned a deeper shade of blue.

"Aaarghhhh!" groaned Selene as she struggled to keep the immense power from engulfing her.

Just one more push. Sweat dripped down Aya's face. Her head, hands, torso, legs, and knees trembled as she called on one final surge of water to finish the fight. Across from her, Selene was doing the same.

Aya kept on waiting for her sister to buckle under the pressure, but instead she rose up to the challenge, matching her determination.

Cloudiness slithered to the rims of the water wielder's vision. Her muscles felt as if they were about to be torn apart. Strength draining, she remained on her feet by sheer will.

The ruler of the Suteckh was not faring any better. Her eyes were droopy and her body quaked.

The fight was coming to an explosive end. Only one sister would remain standing.

It was not one of the girls who caved in first, however. The walls had been enduring the power within them as well. It had proven too much. The earth fractured at a thousand places. There was a sharp blast as the roof collapsed.

The sisters let go of the energy they'd been holding

onto. They both stumbled back. Aya remained on her feet, but Selene tumbled to the ground. It took Aya a second to realize that a rock had fallen on Selene, causing her to fall.

The older sister in Aya came alive. Ignoring her possibility to run and escape, she threw herself toward her young sister. She landed on her knees. In one sweep, she created a thick block of ice above them. The ice extended, providing a path out of the cave-in and into the next room.

It was a path to safety that she could not take. Aya's hands were the only thing holding up the thick block of ice. As soon as she let go of the energy, it would come crashing down, killing her.

Selene opened and her eyes. She looked up at her older sister, who was accomplishing the impossible by holding the entire weight of the rocks at bay.

Chest searing, Aya shouted. "Run. Can't hold it much longer!"

Selene's face clouded with insecurity. "Why would you save me? I'm your enemy."

There was no more energy to shout. Darkness crept to claim Aya as she whimpered her final words. "Can't leave you. You're my b... b-baby sister."

"I... I..." Selene looked over at the way out and then back at her struggling sister. Her features softened and then became rigid with determination. "I won't let you die." She put her hand on the ice, releasing a dark mist into it. The ice that had been cracking seconds ago became silent. Selene grabbed Aya's hand and put it over her shoulder. "C'mon. It won't last long!"

Sure enough, cuts splintered through the ice as the wielders dashed out of the deathtrap.

They had barely thrown themselves out of harm's way, landing in a cloud of dust, when the ice crumpled behind them. The sound of the falling debris died into silence, leaving only the weary breaths of the sisters behind.

Aya held Selene's hand and turned to face her. The dark wielder was caked in grime, sweat, and dirt. Her hair was a tangled mess, and her eyebrows were covered in dust. Nonetheless, Aya had never before seen her be more beautiful than at this moment. The Blood Empress was no more. There was only Selene.

Chapter 36

Falcon and Shal-Volcseck had been fighting for what seemed an eternity. The ground had been broken in pieces, and trees had been uprooted and flung around as if they were mere sticks.

The chaos wielder moved back a few steps after yet another failed attempt to break through the elemental tornadoes that raged around Falcon.

"No more hiding!" A red glow surrounded Volcseck's feet. The crimson emitted a jet of light, sending Volcseck swaying through the air.

He can fly! Falcon barely had time to register this new event when he had to return his concentration to the circumstance at hand.

Volcseck moved through the air, coming straight at him.

Good, mused Falcon, certain that even with his immense speed, there was no way that the chaos wielder could get through the tornadoes. Why, back in his duel against Lao, he had even stopped the mythical Onyx Phoenix without breaking a sweat.

Volcseck suddenly lurched upward. He came down from above Falcon, muscling through the wind shield and completely ignoring the tornadoes.

Falcon dissipated the tornadoes and brought his hand up for a block. A thin coating of earth managed to shield him before Volcseck rammed into it. His arms trembled painfully as he fell. He quickly bounced back up, only to have Volcseck fly into his stomach. The chaos wielder wrapped his arms around Falcon's torso. The void wielder was caught in his opponent's forward thrust.

A sharp pain burst from Falcon's lower back as he was forced into a large stone.

Volcseck's boots landed on the ground. Before he could attack, Falcon blew out a low breath that sounded more like a hum. From his mouth poured a thick green gas.

"Poison!" Volcseck dashed away from the gas.

Crackling lightning burst from Falcon's left hand. He guided it, forcing the blur that Volcseck had become back into the poison.

The chaos wielder was inches away from falling for the trap, when he disappeared.

Teleportation. Of course. Falcon blew out again. This time a black gas surrounded him from every angle. If his foe wanted to get him, he was going to make it past the deadly trap.

"Do you think this is the time I've dueled a poison wielder?" asked a deep voice. It sounded calm, too calm for Falcon's liking. "I have crossed paths with the Onaga of poison. Your gas is a mere shadow of what he could do."

Volcseck appeared directly in front of Falcon. He breathed in the mist, but the ragged breaths Falcon had expected did not come. Instead the chaos wielder looked down at him with a face of serene casualness. Then he said, "I learned a lot from my duel with the Onaga. As you can see."

Falcon threw a punch. Volcseck's punch was faster. It hit Falcon square on the jaw and sent him reeling out of the ball of gas and beside the lake. He took in the salty scent of the water before feeling a dreadful energy coming down on his back.

The earth around him rose, surrounding him in a ball of brown.

A hit later and the sphere of earth had been shattered.

Falcon twirled through the air. As he did, he sent rings of wind gushing out from his arms, feet, torso, and head.

The lord of chaos took the first two hits without flinching, but the ones that followed had been infused with the purple power of mind. The rings hit Volcseck and sent him sprawling through the ground. As Falcon had expected, he stood instantly. His robe was torn, revealing a muscular physique.

"Very good, boy." Volcseck's voice was edged with iron. He reached around his robe and threw it to the side. He was now wearing nothing but boots and baggy black pants. There was a series of red inked images etched across his chest. They seemed to continue onto his back. "Very few wielders have lasted this long against me. The time for games, however, is over." His skin turned a dark brown. His chaos state. His eyes were now a fiery red. Fangs had replaced his teeth. After a deep breath, he shot out the essence of chaos from his fingertips.

Falcon arched his head back. A line of crimson energy whizzed so close to his ear that it cut into the skin beside it. He fell to one knee as he inspected the cut. There was no blood. His nostrils, however, had been filled with the scent of burnt skin.

Before his foe could close the distance, Falcon punched, firing a pillar of flames from his right fist, all the while blasting dark wielding cubes from his left fist. Volcseck dodged the fire but landed on the black tar Falcon had set up on the ground.

The Rohad smirked. Nowhere to go! The thought had just left his mind when Volcseck teleported out of the trap. Darn. He can even teleport out of dark wielding energy. How am I supposed to defeat him?

As if reading his mind, Volcseck said, "All your powers are futile. There is nothing you can do that I haven't seen."

Falcon called now on his two ultimate powers: holy and chaos. His skin turned a light brown. The Rohad had expected the shade to be much darker like from before, but it was obvious the holy was only allowing enough chaos to seep into him as was required to boost his power without losing control.

The warriors locked in a fierce battle of speed, energy, defense, and offense.

Two blurs moved across the land, hopping atop rocks and flying through the air.

Each time they clashed, there was a thunderous explosion of energy that emanated from their very core. Despite the extreme vitality being used, neither wielder seemed ready to give in to the other.

Embracing his destiny, Falcon called on Faith's power: holy.

He was not only battling for the future of Va'siel. He was fighting so that this sadistic creature of chaos would never again rob another family of a loved one. He was dueling for every person who had lived in Va'siel in years long ago past, for every person who currently lived, unaware of the end that now loomed so close, and for every soul that had yet to be born.

Today he fought for life.

Thoughts of Faith coursed through him, giving him the focus he needed to continue on. He came down on Volcseck. The holy wielder was firmly in mind with every swipe of energy and every attack he made.

There was a display of intense light as Falcon gathered his power once more. Volcseck swiped the attack away, only to have a ray of translucent light beat him back.

The young Rohad sensed Volcseck weakening. He saw

it in his opponent's increasingly clumsy blocks. He sensed it in the energy that was now barely strong enough to read.

Then, something happened that Falcon had before thought impossible. The lord of chaos, who had been undefeatable for ten thousand years, staggered back after taking a ray of holy energy to the chest. He blinked rapidly then crumpled to the floor.

Not wasting anytime, Falcon surrounded his stumbling enemy with a chain of light. The golden-colored string encircled around the chaos wielder, preventing him from making a move.

"You may have defeated me, boy." Volcseck spoke with the voice of someone who had no fear. "But you will never kill me. Unlike you, I have fully embraced chaos, which makes me invincible."

Falcon fell down to one knee, the sudden realization of everything that had occurred hitting him all at once like a force of nature. He'd won. His lifelong dream had been fulfilled. However, it felt hollow without Faith. Warm tears full of sorrow fell on the green pasture. He wiped his eyes and looked up at the tied man glaring down at him. In those hollow marbles, Falcon saw the young boy once called Voly. The same boy who hoped to fix all the wrongs from the world. "You had everything and threw it all away."

"I had nothing."

"You had love!" Falcon shot back. "You loved Lunet,

and she loved you. She was your mother."

"Adoptive mother."

"Her blood didn't run through your veins, but she was your mother nonetheless. Or was it not her who offered you a home when you were left alone in the world? Was it not her who healed you when as a boy you fell ill with the yellow plague? Was it not Lunet who stood by your bedside?

Volcseck's voice lowered an octave. "Love would not have brought Va'siel peace."

"Don't you see?" said Falcon. His voice became small. His breath was shallow, and his insides felt empty. "The world will never fully be at peace. There will always be someone who will rise up and instigate havoc. All we can do is rise up with it and do our best to protect those we love. If I kill you now, the world may be at peace for some time, but eventually someone else will come and threaten that peace." As he spoke, he felt Faith within him. She was speaking through him. "We can only hope that someone is there who is strong enough to stop the evil."

"There's no evil, boy. There are only different points of view. Telling yourself that you're some kind of righteous person doesn't make you good."

"I've never claimed to be good. I'm just a simple man trying his best to get through life."

Volcseck looked away. "I have no more words for a blind fool who cannot see the truth. Kill me now. If you can."

There was a hint of challenge in his voice.

"No. I will not stoop to your level. Besides, you said it yourself, you cannot be killed." Falcon opened a rift in space. He stared at a volcanic world surrounded by magma and oceans of lava. A single speck of land drifted over the crimson liquid. He pushed Volcseck through. There was a loud pop. A second later the chaos wielder landed on the small crust of earth.

"With the power the Golden Wielder gave me, I will always be able to sense your every move. Trust me when I say, you won't be able to sneeze without me knowing about it. In a way, you never escaped Aadi. I'm the legacy he left behind to stop you." Falcon took one last glance at the man who had caused so much misery. He felt sadness overcome him at what could have been. "You were a powerful wielder, Volcseck. With your gift, you could have been a blessing to Va'siel. You could have brought forth an era of peace and prosperity. Instead you became a herald of evil."

Volcseck attempted one more half-hearted tug at his chains.

"I've chosen your prison well," said Falcon. "I'm the only way in or out of this place."

The face of Volcseck was contemplative as he gazed into Falcon's eyes. The lava cast an orange glow on half of his face; the other remained obscured in darkness.

The heir of the elements closed the portal, forever

leaving behind the lord of chaos in his fiery confinement.

Chapter 37

Falcon gritted his teeth, trying to prevent more tears from escaping. It did not work. At his side, Hiromy embraced Sheridan, sobbing into his shirt. Aya took his hand, trying to comfort him. She was crying as much as he was, and she only made him feel worse. For all intents and purposes, they should be glad. They had won the battle. The Suteckh had been defeated. Albert had even managed to vanquish the crimson Neikan Demon.

The victory had come at a heavy price, though.

Two funeral pyres had been set up in the grassy field. Around the pyres were countless rings of people, paying their respects. Most were people Falcon did not recognize, but he did see Laars, Professor Dunn, Keira and her bears, Captain Redclaw and Captain Armeen staring at the ground somberly.

Moonlight drenched over the attendants, and a low wind coursed through the air as the flames claimed the bodies of the two women, Faith Hemstath and Empress Latiha.

Faith lay peacefully in her white dress. Her hands were crossed over her chest. She looked as if she were sleeping. A part of Falcon was still expecting her to open her eyes. To have her run to him and tell him that she was fine. That it was all a horrible nightmare.

The other, saner, part knew that his childhood friend

was not going to wake, regardless of how much he wished it so.

"I love you, Faith," said Falcon under his breath as his chest tightened. The flames reached her dress and began to consume her. He stared into the stars and, for a flicker of a second, thought he saw Faith smiling back at him in the sky. "Thank you for coming into my life."

Falcon closed his eyes, drowning himself in the many memories he had of her, as the soft sound of drums rolled in the background.

Chapter 38

"Just let me die," said Selene. With somber eyes, she stared at Aya from behind the prison cell. It had been six days since the battle had come to an end and, somehow, she was still alive. She should be dead, just like the thousands of people who died at the hands of her bloody attacks on Va'siel.

"No," said Aya

"I deserve it." She sat on the rocky floor. It had a few strands of hay scattered about. There was a miserable bed posted to the wall, but Selene never slept on it. She slept on the ground, like the animal that she was. No sane person would have ever orchestrated the mass extinction of lives that she had.

"Quit blaming yourself for what happened. You were brainwashed. You had no control over your actions. It was father's fault. Not yours."

Selene looked up, afraid to peer into her sister's eyes. In those webs of red, she saw a girl who had not slept in days. A girl who was trying to keep a ruthless leader alive, despite the fact that the entire city of Missea wanted her dead. She saw the pain she'd caused. It was too much, and she looked back down, her eyes settling on a slab of gray stone.

"I may have been brainwashed," murmured Selene,

blinking, "but that does not excuse me from the atrocities I committed. I must be punished, and I will be soon enough. I heard the guards talking. It's only a matter of time before I'm justly executed. Hopefully they burn me at the stake. A slow and painful death is exactly what I deserve."

"Don't speak that way," insisted Aya, pain on her voice. "Father might have disappeared after our battle and left you, but I haven't given up on you, and I won't allow you to give up on yourself."

Selene laid her pounding head on the stone. She closed her eyes. She heard the tormented wails of women and children crying as they were cut down by her soldiers. She saw a woman clutching a baby to her breast. The ragged woman held up her dead child. "Why did you murder my baby?" she demanded. "Why?" Suddenly, the woman was joined by countless other corpses. All limping forward, eagerly reaching for the girl responsible for their misery. A wave of blood flashed in her mind. Her eyes snapped open. She heaved loudly, knowing full well that no matter how much she wished it, that sea of red would never be washed away. The reality of all the pain she'd caused settled over her, falling upon her heart like a hammer.

"Selene!" cried Aya. "Selene, are you okay?"

"Just leave me alone."

"Selene."

"I said leave me alone!" Her sister did not say another

word. A minute later the sound of footsteps filled her ears, followed by the creaking metal door opening. The footsteps became dull thuds before completely fading away.

Sadly, the dark wielder realized Aya was not going to give up. She would continue to fight to keep her alive. The thought that her sister might actually succeed terrified her.

~~~

With both our holy energies, you will be able to do things before thought impossible. For the next few days, Falcon mused on those words that Faith had told him in her final moments. It didn't take him long to figure out what she'd meant. With his newfound holy abilities, he was able to reverse some of the damage done to Hiromy's brain. Not much but enough so that she would not die from it.

After Falcon healed Hiromy, she, Sheridan, and Dunn headed back to Ladria. Not only did they have to begin rebuilding Ladria in the wake of the Suteckh's attack, but Hiromy was taking Faith's death very badly. Like Falcon, she would wake in the middle of the night, drowning in sweat as she cried out her name. It became obvious that being in Missea was only further aggravating her condition. And even though Falcon enjoyed Sheridan and Hiromy's company, he found himself enjoying the solace the day at the inn provided in their absence. It gave him time to dwell in thoughts. Maybe it wasn't the best way to deal with his loss, but it helped him cope.

"You have to get out and get some air," said Aya after she walked into the inn. She appeared more tired today then she had in the past few days. Falcon was certain she'd just come back from seeing her sister.

"I'd rather stay here," said Falcon, burying his head in the pillow. The room was almost pitch dark, with only a single candle providing a speck of light.

"Falcon. Please. I miss her too, but she would have not wanted you to drown like this. She would have wanted you to be happy and move on. Please promise me you're going to stop this and go out a bit tomorrow."

The pleading in her voice compelled Falcon to nod, even though he didn't actually have any plans of going anywhere.

She looked at him doubtfully. Falcon knew that he hadn't fooled her. Without saying a word, she took his hand. "C'mon."

"Where are we going?"

"Shhh… just follow."

Falcon did not have the energy to argue. In drone-like movements, he allowed Aya to lead him out of the window, up the stairs and onto the roof. She sat down. Falcon took a seat next to her. Something inside him came alive. Maybe it was the companionship, or maybe it was the fresh air, but he felt a sense of life breathe into him. They stared at the stars without saying a word for over an hour.

"Thank you," said Falcon, finally breaking the silence. "I know you've been going through a lot with your sister. You don't have to go through the trouble of looking over me."

"Don't say that. I would do anything for you."

She spoke with such sincerity that Falcon couldn't help feeling guilty for not taking an interest in her as of late.

"How is Empress Keira?" he asked, trying to quell some of his guilt.

"She's gone back to Sugiko. Captain Armeen is taking her home himself." She managed a small smile. "I think they have a lot to talk about."

"And your sister? The Bloo–err... I mean...Selene?"

Aya's facial features stiffened. "Not that well. She doesn't want my help, and..." She gulped. "Things aren't going so well with the Missean council. I think...I think..." Her voice became raggedy, cracking and breaking between words. "I think they mean to kill her."

Falcon settled his vision on the flower constellation at the center of the sky. He couldn't care less what happened to that monster. He did, however, care too much for Aya to see her suffer like this. He closed his eyes, not believing the next words that came out of his mouth. "I could speak to the council on her behalf." Ever since Falcon defeated Volcseck, the people of Missea had come to see him as the hero that Aadi once was. They had come to the inn offering everything from food, to a position as the general of the Missean army, to his own castle. He was certain that a word from him would go far in sparing the Blood Empress's life.

"You would do that for her?"

"I would do that for you."

There was a moment of silence. "Thank you. Thank you so much."

"Don't mention it," said Falcon, apprehensively, not sure he'd made the right choice.

When they finally went back into the inn, the candle had burnt out into a moldy pile of wax. Falcon did not bother to fire wield. He'd spent so much time in the dark room that he knew exactly where the beds were. He threw himself on the unkempt bed at the far end of the room. Aya did the same on her own bed.

As he had done for the past few days, he tossed and turned in his sleep. The few times his eyes managed to close; they were snapped open with visions of Faith. To his left, he heard Aya rolling in her bed as well, unable to rest. It had been like this for them for the last few nights. Both unable to sleep longer than an hour, yet pretending that they were fine for each other's sake.

This time the bluff came to an end. Unlike every other night, he heard Aya stand from her bed in the middle of the night. She stumbled over to him, crashing into the other bedposts in the process. His exhales intensified when she sat at the edge of the cushion.

"May I join you?" she breathed softly.

Falcon's heart raced. "Y... yes."

The bed groaned under the new weight.

Aya lay down. Both wielders faced each other. Even through the darkness, Falcon made out her blue eyes. A sudden realization came to him. A realization of how fortunate he was to still have Aya with him, guiding him. Before he knew it, he was caressing her. He began with her hair, but then slid his hand down over her cheek and arms. She took his hands into hers. They breathed the same warm air.

She planted a kiss on his forehead and laid her head by his chest, allowing Falcon to hold her close. His heart drummed, but he found himself not caring if she heard it. They'd gone through so much that his nervousness seemed trivial in comparison.

He took in the scent of her strawberry hair. For the first time in a long time, he felt at peace. He didn't even know when it happened, but before he could register it, he'd fallen into a deep sleep.

~~~

The morning came, but they remained clutched in each other's embrace long after they had awoken. When they finally got up, Falcon was knew what he had to do. The night with Aya had provided the clarity he had been waiting for.

"You're leaving, aren't you?" said Aya. Her voice was

free of any form of accusation. Instead it had a tone of understanding. This was something that she knew he had to do.

"Yes. There are places I need to see. People I need to visit." Mayor Seth (Faith's father) and Iris came to mind. "Don't worry, I will stop by the council and have a word with them. Your sister's life will be spared. I promise."

"Thank you." Her chest rose and fell steadily as she fixed her hair into a quick bun. She straightened her skirt. "I will be waiting for you here when you return," she murmured. "As long as it takes. I'll be here."

Without saying another word, Falcon turned and walked away, unsure of when, if ever, he would see her again. All he knew was that if he stared into those sea blue eyes a second longer, he might never leave.

~~~

Like he'd promised Aya, Falcon stopped by the council to speak on the Blood Empress's behalf. After that unpleasant talk, he visited the pub and shared a drink with his brother. He stuck to water this time.

"I think going on a pilgrimage will be a good thing for you," said Albert after Falcon had told him of his plans to travel Va'siel. "I recommend that you stop by the swamps of despair."

"Swamps of despair?" repeated Falcon, without much

enthusiasm.

Albert smirked. "It's not as bad as it sounds. I spent two years there with the monks. They live a simple life, away from the temptations of the city. It's a plain place."

"Plain may be exactly what I need."

"It will hopefully help you find some peace, like it did for me."

It was at this time that Falcon realized just how little he knew of Albert. Most of the time at the pub he had spent speaking about their young lives back at Asturia. No time had been devoted to Albert's years after the massacre of the Ladrian council. Where had he gone? How had he discovered his ability to space wield? How did he not go crazy out there all by himself all those years?

"You have a lot of questions," said Albert, as if reading his mind. "Stories for another time, perhaps."

The young Rohad nodded. "Yes. Another time." They shook hands and after a quick pat on the back, Falcon made his way out of the bar, through the city streets, and out of Missea.

Not until he reached the top of a grassy field did he finally stop and look back at the grand city.

Years ago, he had left the city of Ladria in similar fashion. So much had happened since that day that it seemed to have occurred eons ago. He was no longer that kid who had left on their maiden mission, erroneously thinking that killing Volcseck and finding his brother would be the solution to all his problems. He knew now that life wasn't all that simple. Nonetheless, he looked back at those times with a fondness and yearning to retrieve what had been lost.

He clutched at his chest, looking out into the blue sky. Birds flew overhead. A warm breeze brushed his skin. In the pleasant current, he felt Faith's touch. He caught the scent of peaches and smiled. The green-eyed girl would always be a part of him. He knew that now. Her holy energy would dwell in his chest. Her memories in his heart.

"Thank you, Faith," he said. The darkness that had threatened to consume him so many times was now non-existent. "You were the light my life had always been searching for."

He didn't look back as he began his long trek. He wasn't entirely sure where his first destination would be. Somehow, it no longer mattered. With Faith's spirit guiding him, he was certain he would never be lost again.

Epilogue

His boots rattled loudly as he walked down the path. A small cloud of dust rose in his wake. He scratched the short stubble on his strong chin before stopping atop the same hill he had left that fateful day.

The young Rohad stared down at the city of Missea. He had not set sight on those golden walls for many years. Now, on his twenty-third birthday, he treaded slowly toward the city, not entirely sure he wanted to go inside, for within those golden barriers lay his entire future.

She had told him that she would wait for him. It had been a long time since she muttered those words, though. Much could change in five years. Did she still remember her promise? Had she moved on? She was a beautiful girl. He was certain that many men had attempted to court her.

Steadying his breath, he walked into the city. The entire scene became a sea of colors as people scurried about.

"Read all about the harrowing exploits of the great Falcon Hyatt!" screamed a young boy. He had yellow-stained teeth and a crooked smile. He stood atop a wooden box that barely seemed strong enough to sustain him, while holding a parchment over his head. A bag filled with countless other scrolls rested against his shoeless feet. "Travel with him as he vanquishes foe after foe on his wild adventure." The boy spotted the traveling wanderer. His eyebrow lifted. "You there, sir. Surely you would like to learn all about the great hero of Va'siel. It's so realistic that you'll feel as if you were actually him."

The young man decided to humor the kid. "How did you acquire such accurate descriptions of his life?"

"I know Falcon Hyatt, sir. He's a good friend of mine, and he recounts his stories exclusively to me."

"Does he now?"

"Oh, yes." He patted his chest. "You can trust Mokin to always tell the truth."

The Rohad reached into his pocket and pulled out a gold coin. He tossed it into Mokin's expecting hands. The boy's eyes glistened as he eyed the shiny trinket on his palm.

"Get yourself some shoes, boy," said the man.

"Of course, sir." Mokin blew kisses at the generous person before him. "A thousand blessing to you, sir."

The boy grabbed his bag. Before he could take off, the Rohad took hold of his collar. He met his gaze and said, "And quit with the lies, boy. It will only bring you misfortune in the long run."

Mokin gave a mischievous smile. "Of course, sir." He then dashed into the crowd, turned the corner and disappeared.

A splash of water fell from the skies. A look up revealed a leathery-skinned woman staring out a second-story window.

She carried a bucket in her hands.

"Watch where you're going, stranger," said the old woman. "I almost drenched you from head to toe, I did."

The Rohad gave her a half-hearted smile. "Many thanks for the tip."

As he made his way around the pool of water, he heard the woman muttering to herself. He only caught the words, "Darn foreigners."

The air smelled of salted meat, horse dung, and fresh water.

As he passed yet another stall of fruit he waved the flies away from his face. Despite the many small distractions the city had to offer, he found his anxiety growing. He could not say exactly why. Odds were the girl wouldn't even be here anymore. She had probably returned to her hometown of Ladria.

He turned another corner, passing the city council, which, if the marble sign outside the splendid jaded doors were to be believed, had apparently been renamed Aadi and Falcon Chambers.

That wasn't the only thing that had been renamed. The same inn that he had dwelled in all those years ago now had a sign that read The Hyatt Sanctuary.

Then he saw her, and his heart skipped a beat. She was coming out of the oak finished door. Five years had done little to lessen her beauty. Her dark hair had grown to her waist. She wore a black blouse and a black skirt.

She looked up, and their eyes met. Her neck rose in a gulp.

The Rohad knew that this was the crucial time he had both yearned for and feared.

If the girl had indeed waited for him, she would hug him; he was certain of that. But if she had moved on and found a man in her absence, then she would welcome him as a friend. She would speak to him, perhaps even shake his hand, but the girl had honor. He knew that if she were attached to another, she would maintain proper distance. She would not dishonor her beloved by embracing another man.

The crowd around them became invisible. Sounds drowned out as they slowly made their way to each other. Under the shade of a flower stand they met, standing face to face. Her lips moved, but the man heard nothing but the sound of his own beating heart.

He shook his head, forcing his mind to return to the present. The scent of honeyed flowers filled his nostrils.

"Falcon?" said the girl, as if not believing who was standing before him. "You… you came back."

Falcon's heart sank to his stomach. He couldn't help but notice that Aya was maintaining a well-mannered distance between them. Of course. What had he expected? That she would simply halt her life at his convenience? That he could just show up and she would welcome him with open arms?

Before he had an opportunity to dwell on those thoughts, she closed the distance between them. Her arms laced around his torso. Her warm breath caressed his neck, and the rigidness he had carried with him dissolved.

A soft kiss grazed his forehead.

He'd waited far too long and been haunted by her absence for far too long, to settle for a peck.

His skin tingled. Before he had a chance to think too much on it, he pulled her in. An explosion of emotions rushed through his body as their lips met. His fears faded, washed away by the taste of strawberry the girl with the soft lips left behind.

When they broke apart, her face was flushed in a deep shade of pink.

"You waited," he said in a shallow breath, seeing his future in those sea-blue eyes.

Her lips formed into a smile. "Always."

He pulled her in, tasting the sweet taste of strawberry all over again.

~~~

Councilman Nakatomi grunted and cursed as he trudged slowly into the damp cave, dragging the white sack behind him. In his wake, he left behind a trail of blood. There was a dark blotch of purplish red on the sack. It was the sixth sacrifice he'd killed.

He inspected the cuts on his arm. This one had been a

feisty one. He had lured her to his small cabin, with the farce that he was a simple farmer who needed help tending to the animals.

A smirk spread across his lips as he thought back at how eager she had been when she thought she finally had a job to feed her struggling family. Of course, he hadn't expected the peasant girl to put up a fight, even after he had landed a blow to the back of her head. No matter, she was dead now, and he was one step closer to fulfilling his goal.

The councilman walked into the room. The seven crystals were spread about. Fire torches clung on the grimy walls, providing much needed light. He tasted the thick, oily air and more than once he had to breathe through his nose to avoid the burning sensation that would travel down his throat with every inhale he took.

The old man moved to the first and smallest of them. The brown crystal had hundreds of cracks. Inside it he could barely make out the figure of a long, stretched-out woman. It was hazy from countless years of neglect.

With monumental effort, he took the corpse out of the sack and tossed it atop the crystal. He took the girl's cold hands and rested them at her side. He looked away as her cold blue eyes met his. They reminded him of that wretched she-devil whom he'd helped bring into the world, Aya. The simple thought of how she had stained his name with dishonor caused his teeth to grit with anger.

He pierced two deep cuts in the girl's ribs. He closed his eyes and imagined that he was cutting into his daughter instead. The thought made him find his smirk once more, and he let his anger flow away with the blood that was now dripping out of his victim.

The liquid traced the cracks of the crystal, adorning it in a web of red.

Suddenly, two crimson marbles lit up inside the crystal. The councilman's chest rose with excitement. It was working!

The light went out a second later, but what remained was the sweetest sound he'd ever heard.

It was the soft thump of a heartbeat. The wicked pounding of a creature who had rested for far too long. He would have to go out and find a few more sacrifices to fully awaken the hellion resting within. That would be easy enough. There were more than enough simple-minded girls around Va'siel he could lure to their deaths.

His skin shivered at the thought of the legacy he was so close to fulfilling. He would be known as the man who ushered in the end of the human age. The name Nakatomi would forever be linked with the destruction of Va'siel's way of life.

There was one who stood in the way of his legacy: Falcon Hyatt. He had become too powerful.

There was, however, also an answer. He licked his lips as his eyes fell on the black crystal at the end of the room. The being who lay dormant within was more than enough to handle the so-called heir of the elements.

A new era was coming. The era of the Onagas.

Acknowledgments:

As I write this acknowledgment, like many other times when I write, I find myself alone in my room. Nonetheless, this series wasn't brought forth by me alone.

I thank God, for giving me a chance to share my creativity (as minor as it may be) with the world.

Thanks to my son, Cesar Adrian Gonzalez. Thank you for listening to my stories and getting so invested in the world of Element Wielder. I love you more than you will ever know. I'm glad I get to pass everyday with you, buddy.

Thank you to Natali for allowing me to steal your computer on a daily basis to write (Sorry).

Then there's my cover artist, Dennis Frohlich. His amazing artistic ability and valuable input is always greatly appreciated. To my editor, Laura Hutfilz. Thanks for your keen eye as you fix my awful (and I do mean awful) grammar.

Last, but certainly not least, I thank all of you who bought, read, and recommended my book to your friends and family. I conceived the idea of Element Wielder when I was an 8th grader. I'm glad that dream I had all those years ago has reached so many of you out there.

Thank you for following the adventure of Falcon Hyatt, from a lowly orphan boy to the Heir of the Elements. His adventure isn't over, and I sincerely hope you all follow along with him as he begins a new chapter of his life.

Don't be a stranger. Feel free to e-mail me with your thoughts on the series, or stop by the website. I like hearing from you all.

***New space Action/Adventure series by Cesar Gonzalez,

STAR RISING, will be available for pre-order on 5/30/2015.***

Prologue to STAR RISING

Star Rising

PROLOGUE

Reave gazed out the window, taking in the sight of the blue sphere hanging in the darkness of space. He'd heard many stories of K'strala, a planet so far in the outer border of the galactic jurisdiction that some even claimed it didn't exist. Those who did believe its existence often regarded the jungle planet with dread borne of mysticism, claiming a race of half-lizard men had claimed it as their own.

Reave smiled inwardly at the gullibility of the simple planetary folk. Over the past twenty star cycles, he had scoured space in over a hundred missions. Never had he encountered anything that remotely resembled such a creature.

"Five minutes until touchdown!" yelled the pilot from the cockpit. The small ship shook violently. Empty tin cans and bullet shells tumbled noisily on the metal floor. A simple light dangled above his head, filling the room with a faint orange glow.

In the edges of his vision, Reave could make out Tory and Lester by his side. Both rookie Alioth warriors tumbled from side to side, their weapons almost falling from their hands.

"Keep those snipers under control," ordered Reave. Internally, he cursed. Why couldn't the Bastion have sent him alone? It was bad enough he was being sent on a useless mission to some long abandoned planet. Did he really need two green soldiers, barely out of Alioth academy, to babysit?

Tory, a long faced, tall girl who couldn't be a day over twenty struggled to her feet. "I'm sorry, sir. This old ship is shaking so much. I think it's going to crash."

Lester, who looked to be the same age, saw fit to add to the ridiculous claims. "I think Tory is right." His green eyes glanced around the ship nervously. "These old Stromcaller class ships crash all the time. Father always said they would be the death of me."

"Quiet, both of you," ordered Reave. "We're entering the planet's atmosphere. That is all."

Despite his assurance that everything would be fine, the rookies continued to cast nervous glances out the window. They took their seats on chairs that had long ago lost their soft padding.

"I didn't sign up for this," whimpered Lester under his breath. "This is too dangerous."

Reave gazed down at the boy, his stomach tightening in frustration. The lenses of his dark-rimmed glasses made his eyes look three times their normal size. "If you wanted to be safe, you should have taken a job as at a desk over at the Bastion."

"No, n…no…" Lester whined. "My grandpa and father were both Alioths. I need to follow in their footsteps."

Tory sighed. "I didn't think we would be sent so far out into the border of the galaxy. I thought we were going to be stationed at the Bastion. Patrolling traffic, maybe catching a few looters. A far-range expedition, though? This is too much."

"Don't worry," said Reave. "The reading that Bastion caught emanating from K'strala was probably nothing more than a ruptured underground pipe. K'strala used to be a mining planet. It's been abandoned for hundreds of years, but the lines underneath are probably still intact."

The rookies looked up at him with a look of apprehension. Reave couldn't blame them. He had to admit, the entire situation was strange to say the least. In the past century, those lazy bureaucrats of the Bastion had never approved a mission into any of the outskirt planets. Not officially, at least. What had changed that would lead those law-writing nobodies to suddenly order Alioths to investigate? The whole situation had a bad aura clanging around it.

"Five seconds until touchdown!" called the pilot from the front.

Reave tossed the glass of alcohol against the hull. It shattered on contact.

There was a loud click, followed by the creaking whine as the old hatch opened.

The three Alioths marched out. Reave stepped off the

rusted ramp and onto soggy mud. Heavy raindrops splashed his leather jacket, and he frowned. It had been a present from his sister. What would she say when she noticed he had ruined yet another one of her expensive gifts?

The scenery before him was much of what he had expected. Light fog hung around them like a curtain. The green plants were drenched in moonlight. The air smelled earthy, mixed with the scent of fresh water. They were surrounded by so many trees that the veteran Alioth found himself wondering as to how the pilot had located an open patch of dirt to land the ship on.

"What is that?" whimpered Lester.

Reave followed his line of sight, and his gaze landed at what Lester had been looking at. It was a small tower of mist protruding from a hole in the ground about twenty feet in front of them. It was red in color, and Reave's hand subconsciously turned into a fist.

Red smoke only meant one thing. Fire. And fire meant that a Cinder had been here.

The red mist did not go unnoticed by the rookies.

"Someone from the Black Sanction was here," mumbled Tory. Her lower lip quivered.

"Don't you worry about that," said Reave. "Our job is to locate the source of the energy spike, not let ourselves be scared by someone who may or may not have been here."

Lester played with his hands. His face had grown

ghostly pale. "The Black Sanction are no men. They're demons. Demons who long ago abandoned their humanity for the power of fire, lighting, psychokenisis, and—"

"I'm well aware of their abilities," said Reave irritably. He caressed the burn mark that covered part of his right cheek and a quarter of his head, where no hair had grown in years. Images of that night long ago filled his mind. He saw the dark silhouette of a man shoot fireballs into the cabin, the same cabin Reave had grown up in. He heard his sisters cry out to him, begging for his help. He felt the weight on his shoulders as he carried Miranda out of the scorching heat. He was the youngest of siblings, but somehow he'd managed to carry a girl who was twice his weight.

"Sir," called Tory, "are you okay?

Reave returned to the humid jungle. "Of course I'm okay!" He gazed down into the hole. It looked to be an opening to an underground building. "You two stay up here and guard the pilot. I'm going down to investigate."

There was no arguing from the rookies. Not that he had expected any. They were just glad to have their necks out of danger.

His boots thumped softly as Reave slipped into the hole and landed on the hard floor. He was standing in the center of a large hall. The walls were a depressing gray. A few flickering lights lined the ceiling, providing a dismal source of light. The sensor around his wrist signaled that the abnormal readings were a little up ahead.

He treaded forward, well aware that he was walking in a place that should not exist. This planet was supposed to have been abandoned long ago. Yet, here he was, moving down through a building that was obviously functional mere days ago. What would the Bastion say once he reported what he'd found? Something inside told him that they already knew.

He turned the corner and his eyes widened. He was standing in what appeared to be some sort of cafeteria. It was massive, with hundreds of wood fold and roll tables filling the crowded space. Trays with food still atop of them littered the tables. Some of it looked good enough to eat. A half bitten apple lay on the ground. Slabs of roasted ham glazed with a coating of honey. Even the beef strips emitted a salted aroma that told the Alioth this food was served less than a day ago. His stomach growled.

So where is everyone? he mused. Did they just pack up and evacuate? Impossible. This place is too large. The manpower alone would have taken days to evacuate. There is simply no way…unless…

Deep in thought, he brought his hand to his chin. Could it be that he was dealing with a binary member of the Black Sanction? Usually, their members could only use one ability, but a few of them had been known to use two. It still made no sense. Even if he were dealing with a practitioner of psychokenisis, there is no way they could have dissolved all the bodies. It would have taken an army to accomplish such a feat. Or an extremely powerful being? For a fraction of a second, he thought of him. That being who had terrorized space and almost wiped life from the galaxy, but he quickly abandoned the thought. That monster was gone. He would never return. He himself had made sure of that.

Slowly, he made his way through the cafeteria and into another hallway. He passed countless office-like rooms. Each was like the one before it: full of furniture and desks but devoid of any people.

He reached the end of the corridor and made his way into a large hall. What he saw there froze him to his very core.

Unlike most men, Reave was not a man who could be easily stunned. In the short twenty star cycles he'd been alive, he had seen more than most soldiers witnessed in a lifetime. When he was seven, he took his first life. He had marched into battle at the young age of twelve. With the exception of Junia, he had eradicated more Black Sanction members than any other Alioth currently active. He had single-handedly vanquished dozens of Deargs. There was no part of his body that had not been injured in some way or another. A decade ago, he had been directly responsible for the eradication of the monster that almost brought the universe to its knees. Yashvir.

He stood atop a grand staircase. At the bottom of the stairs lay the tiny corpses of hundreds of children. They lay atop of each other in mangled heaps.

His insides went icy as he took in the sight, not believing what his eyes were showing him. Who could have done this?

A soft wail echoed in the air.

The expression of the Alioth turned to that of hope. Not thinking much about it, he dashed down the stairs.

In silence, he waited for the cry to come again.

A minute passed.

Two minutes.

Three.

Four.

Five.

The trickle of hope was about to fade, when a sharp cry rekindled it.

He moved with the speed of a madman, following the cries like a hound dog. He stepped over countless bodies. He avoided looking at the eyes. Seeing the emptiness in them only brought back painful memories he had spent a lifetime running away from.

At the corner of the room, he located the source of the bawls. A baby boy who looked to be barely alive. His crying had been replaced by slow, shallow breaths. There was a deep, vertical scar on his chest, directly above the spot his heart should have been. He had a few strands of silver hair and deep blue eyes.

Without wasting another moment, Reave took the baby

in his arms. He heard his own voice speak to it. "There, there. It's going to be fine." He pounded the button on his wrist sensor. "Lester. Get the medipack ready. I'm headed up with a survivor."

Silence.

"Tory. Can you read me?"

Static buzzed through.

Reave cursed under his breath. Even rookie Alioths like the duo he had left up top knew better than to not answer their communicator. A sick sensation settled in the pit of his stomach. Something was wrong.

Clutching the baby, he dashed back to the ship. He ran up the stairs, down the corridor, through the cafeteria, and back through the hall.

He looked up out of the hole. A gray sky with lingering dark clouds loomed above. "Tory. Lester!"

Left with little choice, he took off his jacket and wrapped it around the baby. He tucked him under one arm. With his free hand, he gripped the rim of the hole. He grunted as he pulled his weight up with one hand. He reached up and set the baby at the top. Now with both hands free, he pulled himself up into the jungle.

It was quick, and any other person might have missed it. But Reave wasn't any other person. He heard the bow shoot from above. The speed he had honed over years of training came to him as he unsheathed his sword. He arched it upward, cutting the arrow in half. Two metal pieces fell to the ground by his side.

Reave stood straight, scanning the branches above for the attacker.

His search proved useless. The culprit landed with a loud splash a few feet before him.

"Bravo," said the attacker. He wore a loose shirt and pants. A metal arm fell out of his right sleeve. He had a long nose above a ridiculously longer face. "It was so easy killing your friends, I was beginning to think this job was not worth taking." He eyed the sword. "Such a crude tool. In this time of science, where the body's energy can be used as a weapon, why would someone waste their time with a sword?"

The Alioth ignored the remarks and dared a quick glance over at the ship. The pilot lay sprawled on the ground. An arrow stuck out of his temple. The two rookies were stacked over each other in an unrecognizable pile of burnt flesh.

"I'll be taking that baby now," said the attacker, grinning widely.

"What use do you have for a baby?" The rain was pouring harder now, and Reave's thoughts lingered on the small human wrapped in his leather jacket. Was he still alive?

"That's none of your concern. I was paid to deliver a specimen from the lab. And that's what I intend to do."

"Lab? Specimen?"

The stranger cackled. "You truly are lost, aren't you? Don't your Bastion leaders tell you anything before they send you out on a mission?" Another fit of laughter followed. "You're just a dog of the Bastion. Obeying any order blindly. Truly pathetic."

Reave did not respond to his accusations. "Tell me, bounty hunter. Who sent you? What use do you have for this baby?"

The man looked offended. "I'm not just any bounty hunter. I'm the most legendary of all bounty hunters: The Black Centipede."

"The Black Centipede?" Now it was Reave's turn to laugh. "Never heard of you. Which is surprising. With a stupid name like that, you should be the talk of every comedian in the galaxy." He added a hint of mockery to his next words. "Black Centipede. Phew."

It had the desired effect. The man gritted his teeth and balled his fist.

Good, thought Reave. People with no control of their emotions are always more likely to open their mouths.

The Black Centipede did not spew out the information Reave wanted. Instead, he eyed the leather jacket with hungry eyes.

Reave took two steps back, putting himself between the bounty hunter and the infant. "You're not taking this baby without getting through me."

"That can be arranged." The metal hand turned crimson red, and Reave knew that his opponent was readying the flames.

The two fighters squared up. There were no more words. This was a battle to the end. They both knew it.

Reave spared no time moving against his foe. His long sword cut swift arches before the bounty hunter.

The man bobbed his head between the attacks, his eyes clearly showing surprise at the ferocity of the attacks. Once in a while, he would throw a kick or punch.

They battled across the jungle planes, moving around the corpses and through the heavy vines that dangled from the tall trees. Reave did not commit to any lethal moves. Instead, he analyzed his opponent. Every poke, every feint and combination tested the reactions of the bounty hunter. Once he felt he had enough information, he pressed his attack.

The Centipede brought his metal hand up, barely blocking the blade that was inches away from digging into his chest. The sword dug into the metal, almost cleaving the makeshift arm in two.

The bounty hunter staggered back. "What the—"

With a sweep to his legs, the Alioth knocked his opponent to the ground.

The man was more agile than Reave had expected. He flipped back onto his feet. Swiftly, he threw the dangling piece of his arm to the floor. "That sword of yours is quite sharp to cut through metal like this. Acolyte steel I assume?" He pointed his arm forward, not waiting for an answer. "You're not the only one with special weapons, though. Even in this state, this little baby is fully functional."

A wild burst of flames burned the air.

The Alioth swallowed, taking in the warm air.

The fire moved in a straight line. A sidestep proved enough to dodge it. Another burst of flame burst from the man's weaponized arm. Once again, the Alioth sidestepped.

Reave grinned. The bounty hunter had more than enough fire power, of that there was no doubt. He had, however, no control over it. He couldn't arch it or guide it the way the experienced Cinder could. There was also no shape to the attacks. They came in predictable straight lines. This was already over, and his foe didn't even know it yet.

The next barrage of flames came in the same line, albeit a bit wider than the ones before it. Reave didn't dodge. He clicked the button on the hilt of his sword and the shield around the blade extended. With untamed ferocity, he rushed at his opponent. The hilt grew hotter by the second, sending flares of pain coursing through his hand. He ignored it. This was nothing compared to the pain he'd felt that fateful night.

The shield made contact, and the Centipede splashed into the mud. A click later and the shield retracted, leaving only the long blade. He brought it down on his opponent's neck.

The bounty hunter rolled out of the way, throwing a handful of mud into Reave's eyes. Through his blurred vision, Reave saw the Centipede produce a sword of his own.

"I forgot to say, I don't play fair!"

Reave closed his eyes, listening to the sound as the weapon whooshed through the heavy raindrops as it headed toward his chest. At the last second, he ducked under the attack. In a single move, he took hold of his opponent's sword, twisted it, and impaled it into the Centipede's torso.

The veteran soldier faced the sky, letting the rain wash away the mud. Beside him, the gurgles of pain were followed by the sound of the bounty hunter crumpling to the floor.

"W...who are...a...re you?" mumbled the bounty hunter. He gazed down at the sword protruding from his body. Blood gushed out of the cut, mixing with the clear splashes of water.

"Reave."

His face twisted in recognition. The face Reave saw staring back at him was the same one he'd witnessed his entire life. It was the face of admiration, mixed with compassion he had grown tired of seeing. How many times would he have to be reminded of those nights? "Reave? T...he hero of the wa...war? I ne...ver would have fought you...you, sir, if I had know. I didn—"

Pushing the thoughts to the back of his head, he

sprinted to the mound of leather on the ground. His skin goosebumped as he noticed that the leather jacket had been hit by a stray line of fire. It was now completely engulfed in flames.

"No!" cried Reave as he gazed, almost dreamily, at the orange and red flames. He dashed toward it, snuffing out the fire.

The scent of burnt leather filled his nostrils. Hoping against hope, he unwrapped the charred jacket. Time slowed as the Alioth locked eyes with the infant, not believing what he was seeing. Somehow, the boy was alive. Not just alive, but unlike minutes ago, when it was teetering between life and death, he now looked as healthy as any baby born in the Bastion. His skin was a healthy shade of pink. His giggles were the product of a hearty set of lungs.

Reave was so enthralled by the twist in circumstances, he almost didn't notice the light. Once he saw it, he wondered how he had missed it. There was a crimson glow under the scar, shining brightly. It was as if his very heart had absorbed the flames, using them to empower the boy with vigorous energy.

The words the bounty hunter had used to refer to the boy came back to him: Lab rat.

Any other person might have discarded the boy at this moment. Tossed him the ground and left him to the elements, or to become a meal for the animals who roamed the planet.

He was not another person, though.

The steel-hearted soldier felt something soften within him. Something he had not felt in a long time. It stirred his insides, tugging away the layers upon layers he'd placed over his emotions. A single tear traced down his cheek. Feeling a wave of embarrassment, he wiped it away. He had not cried in over ten star cycles. He was not going to start now.

Nonetheless, he couldn't deny that there was something special about the boy. Somehow, as unlikely as it sounded even to him, Reave felt a deeper bond with this infant than he had felt with anyone in the universe.

With the laughing baby clutched in his hands, they boarded the ancient ship. The roar of the engines was audible as they struggled to life.

Moments later, the ship took to the air, carrying with it two beings with a bond forged by fire.

~~~

From a cliff erupting out of the jungle, a lone hooded being watched the ship until it became but a speck in sky.

The boy had escaped him this time, but it did not matter. He would be his soon enough.

A cruel smile formed on the lips of the hooded figure. They thought they had vanquished him a decade ago. They had no idea how wrong they were.

Once he had the boy, he would bring the universe to its knees.

The boy was to key to everything.

~About The Author~

Cesar Gonzalez lives in Bakersfield, California, with his space-wielding son. To learn more about Cesar and see artwork from Element Wielder, visit his website at **http://cesarbak99.wix.com/element-wielder**

Become a full-fledged Rohad by joining Cesar Gonzalez' e-mail newsletter (visit website or follow link). **Members will receive 2 free books.**

http://wix.us9.list-manage2.com/subscribe?u=f4ec4abf3f25dccaad395c259&id=a3134c0c4b

He can also be found from time to time on his

Twitter and Facebook handles:

https://twitter.com/CesarAnthony84

https://www.facebook.com/cesarwriter

1. **Book 1- Dawn of the Lost (Prequel to THE LOST AND THE WICKED).**
2. **Book 2- The Lightning General.** (A short story following Falcon's master: K'ran Ryker.) Will be released to members of the newsletter soon).

Other Books By Cesar Gonzalez

Void Wielder Trilogy:

-Legacy of the Golden Wielder: Prequel to the Void Wielder Trilogy.

-Element Wielder: Book 1 of the Void Wielder Trilogy

-Legacy of Chaos: Book 2 of the Void Wielder Trilogy

-Heir of The Elements: Book 3 Of the Void Wielder Trilogy.

Star Rising Series:

- Star Rising: Heartless (Book One)

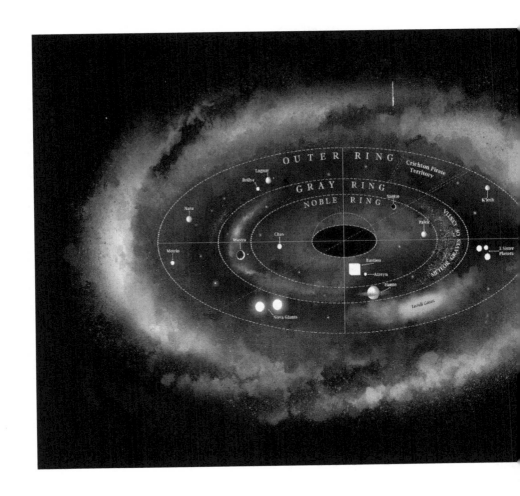

Map of Cestia Galaxy

54116567R00305

Made in the USA
San Bernardino, CA
08 October 2017